MINGO DRUM VERCINGETORIX, BIRDMAN

Illustrations, 3rd edition

Keith Hulse

Copyright © 1980 Keith Hulse

All rights reserved

The characters and events portrayed in this book are fictitious. Any similarity to real persons, living or dead, is coincidental and not intended by the author.

No part of this book may be reproduced, or stored in a retrieval system, or transmitted in any form or by any means, electronic, mechanical, photocopying, recording, or otherwise, without express written permission of the publisher.

ISBN-9798880241774
Cover design by: Art Painter
Library of Congress Control Number: 2018675309
Printed in the United States of America

*Dedicated to romance,
Science Fiction,
Heroes.*

CONTENTS

Title Page
Copyright
Dedication
Chapter 4 Vern Attack   24
Chapter 5 Peace Marriage (trumpet fanfares)   38
Chapter 6 Boudicca Strath   43
Chapter 7 The City of Monoliths   53
Chapter 8 Woman Trouble   67
Chapter 9 Spirit Flight   79
Chapter 10 Amenities   89
Chapter 11 I am Mingo Drum Vercingetorix   99
Chapter 12 Madrawts   109
Chapter 13 Hero   113
Chapter 14 The Dragon   122
Chapter 15 The Temple of Light   126
Chapter 16 Lonely   131
Chapter 17 Conchobhar   137
Chapter 18 Snake Season   143
Chapter 19 Clash of Cultures   155
Chapter 20 Counterattack   165
Chapter 21 Truths   178

At least someone had promoted him from the beast!	179
Chapter 22 Introducing	185
Chapter 23 Gododdin	199
Chapter 24 Swamp Dragon	205
Chapter 25 Hated Foes	213
Chapter 26 The River of Skulls	218
Chapter 27 Captured	231
Chapter 28 He kills.	242
Chapter 29 They wished each other dead and bloated	252
Chapter 30 The Great Fire	260
Well, done Mingo Drum Vercingetorix.	276
Chapter 32 2 New Imperial Laws	282
Chapter 33 I Visited	288
Chapter 34 Cartimandua	298
Chapter 35 A Year Ago	303
Chapter 36 Reunited	315
Chapter 37 Satan's Princedom	322
Chapter 38 The Old Man Again	328
Chapter 39 It is you	335
Chapter 40 Flee Diviciacus Flee?	341
Chapter 41 Who Would Expect Me?	347
Chapter 42 Home Sweet Home	353
Chapter 43 And HE came for HE was Mahbon Reborn	358
Chapter 44 He was too late	364
Chapter 45 Space Pirates	370
Chapter 46 A Christian, Muslim, and Jew Rolled in One	381
Chapter 47 The Call of the Beast	384
Chapter 48 He Thought of Tara 6 at Last!	391

Chapter 49 A New Ball Game	403
Chapter 50 The Hunt Begins	412
Chapter 51 The Greatest Gift	424
Chapter 52 Reeman Follows	433
Chapter 53 Flies	442
Chapter 54 Lies or Truths?	460

MINGO DRUM VERCINGETORIX
by
Keith Hulse

93579 words, 552 pages

3rd edition

Flesch	78.7
FleschKincaid	4.6
Coleman-Liau	7.1

It is easy to read. Plain English.

Aberdeen

lugbooks@gmail.com

www.interestingsite.com

[Chapter 1] — Mingo Drum The Birdman

For the Attention of the High King Arthur Verica,
Palace of Maponos, New Alexandrius, Tara 6.

"I have obeyed your command, written for your reading the early life of your father, Mingo Drum Vercingetorix, King of the Artebrate Bird Nation and High King and War Chief of all Bird Nations during the Wars of Survival, as known amongst the Bird folk and known as the Maponosian Wars amongst the human/alien settlers.

You wanted the truth about Mingo Drum's life. Legends exist.

I also note the political expediency of a popular book on his life to strengthen your throne and emphasize that you are his heir.

We inherit dangers and inter-tribal warfare.

Therefore, my version of the truth is my manuscript

Vercingetorix, Birdman,"

Vern Lukas, Imperial scribe, City of Torrs, Tarra 6, winter, 45185.

*

"Then the sky glinted purple, mauve, crimson, various shades of, the twin purple suns rising, and the Birdman soared high with the warming wind, his dark shadow soaring across the pink limestone slabs underneath.

Intelligent creatures ran from that shadow.

Below, a military staff hovercraft had come to a stop.

The Bird Man saw heat shimmering from the craft's yellow sides. There was also the painted red harpy with a rider and purple sun.

The markings of Warlord Tzu Strath, whom he was sitting in the enclosed weapon-proof bubble of the passenger compartment.

You never knew who was an assassin?

A hover lorry of escorts behind and two scout Zimmers ahead. The man knew his business at staying alive!

Now, two troopers in bronze-colored metallic body armor dragged a young woman out of the staff craft.

The Birdman saw it all.

Saw the War Lord throw something at her.

Was it bread? He thought as a bird.

Or a makeup kit to hide her tear-streaked face.

One man raised a laser pistol at the young woman's head. His shadow, the Birdman's, swept across those below.

Swift, it was, blocking out the purple suns like a sudden eclipse.

The gunman, pistol pressed to her head, shielded his eyes, looking upward. — at what?

A shadow prophesizing trouble.

War Lord Tzu Strath Looked seeing the large mass soaring overhead. The Birdman saw him smile, and the troopers drove away.

A Birdman's eyesight was good, enabling him to watch the driver of the staff car chew gum.

The young woman remained in a sitting position.

Our Birdman glided after the departing soldiers.

He gave his call, *a grunting cough*, the call of The Birdman.

Tzu Strath turned his head and looked, and he was no longer smiling; he was crying.

He had left his most precious possession behind.

Then, readers, why leave it, we ask?

And the Birdman followed for thirty miles. Then soared back to the woman.

Lo-and-behold found her gone, so the Birdman Mingo Drum Vercingetorix landed on the top of a huge red sandstone monolith.

Just as we find in Western films.

This was his domain.

He scoured the desolate landscape, searching for any sign of life.

Remember, smart life at the approach of his racing shadow sought shelter or might end up as

'steak on the wing.'

*

"The War Lord has kept his promise, general," Reeman Black Hair expert in a thousand disguises, say, looking at the woman.

"Order the army to advance," General Ce-Ra replies and strode forward to collect his prize.

Reeman Black Hair obeyed, then scurried after his Lord. His jeweled hands held his long and short laser swords at his sides. He was Lord Madrawt Ce-Ra's pet, and some said lover? *Just* to be nasty!

He was a repugnant Madrawt. Long, flowing, black hair complemented his small head.

Had large bulbous amphibian eyes, a large abdominal area, muscular legs to carry his weight, and a multicolored gigantic codpiece that bobbed with his walk.

But he loved himself. When he looked in the mirror, he saw a handsome Madrawt. The humans were ugly, not him.

I wonder if he asked his mirror if he was the most handsome frog in the land.

Also, the young woman sitting saw these aliens. She hoped they thought her tears resulted from the scorching sun shining in her eyes.

The general knew she was crying out of despair, for she still lived.

And she looked up into Reeman's tiny eyes that peered at

her beneath the gold slits of his helmet.

She looked him Ce-Ra up and down.

She saw that someone had made his bronze body armor a size smaller to act as a girdle.

Saw his gold leg armor that acted as a support for his massive weight.

His exposed groin. It smelled strongly of sweat and pee.

She saw the large, ornamented codpiece.

She looked at Reeman Black Hair from a safe distance out of his master's vision, rubbed his codpiece, opened his mouth, and gaped while a snake-like tongue flicked out of that mouth.

He was telling the woman her fate.

A villain in the tale reader.

Tzu Strath had not granted her the wish of death. The bargain was for her to live. For a second, she thought the tough War Lord was going to order the trooper to fire his laser.

Into her head.

Such an auburn head.

"Are you hot, dearest wife?" General Ce-Ra asked as he clicked a finger for Reeman to help drag her to her feet.

Reeman Black Hair enjoyed her struggle of protest, for it meant his fingers pawed

her smooth human flesh between the gaps of gold mosaic body armor.

Madrawt's skin was lumpy from glands that sweated moisture onto their velvety skin.

In the end, she slapped his face.

It also explained why his groin smelled offensive to a human, but to his species, lovely.

Anger glared in his eyes, and his right hand shook, and Reeman Black Hair clenched his nails into his palm tight to stop himself. This was his lord's property and not just some human woman.

"Another time," Reeman thought, "when my master got bored with you. Then like the dog I am, he will throw you from his table like a bone for me to gnaw and play with."

The young woman shuddered because she read his thoughts. "Why have you deserted me, Tzu Strath?" She asked herself and knew the answer.

They heard The Birdman's grunting call. They knew who made it.

This was his domain, his land.

He held sway here over life and death.

And they were trespassing.

So, the general gave orders for his escort to hurry.

Years of Stardust Galaxy combat instilled a fear of birdmen.

Especially one called The Birdman,

Mingo Drum Vercingetorix.

Each bird man's call sign was unique; the grunt he heard belonged to him, the enemy, whom the folk of this planet called

THE BIRDMAN.

Fear gripped General Ce-Ra.

Reeman Black Hair was afraid, too but would not admit it. He usually felt brave and powerful next to his Lord General Ce-

Ra.

The warm purple air crackled with another grunting cough.

Nervous tension made Black Hair's amphibian tongue dart out.

"My domain. I have seen a wrong. These rocks are my castles, the warm winds my roads, and my call is law to my people that hear.

You, Tzu Strath, violated the peace today.

Who invited you into my domain?" The powerfully built Birdman called as he looked out across the barren land and clumps of forest, his domain.

Then he walked to the edge of the red sandstone monolith, coughed again to his people, shutting his eyes until he felt the warm breeze on his eyelids. Only wind rustled about his purple toga where a short sword and laser pistol hung.

His mind reached out through the implanted chips and wires to his subjects.

The smart critters still waited in shelters till he cleared off.

Chips implanted there by the Stardust Genetic Corporation, courtesy of their Chairman Glen Zowanski, Atlantic City, Old Earth, West Compass Point, Empire of Alexander Caesar Vortigern.

Why, a small green lizard under the shade of a basalt slab opened its eyes as its chips received The Birdman's probing mind?

Chameleon's eyes rotate, and it sees General Ce-Ra and his party halted for a water break.

From Chameleon's viewpoint, the Well Urd was visible to The Birdman.

Courtesy of implanted chips readers.

His mind reeled at the sight of the Madrawts and knew Ce-Ra and Reeman Black Hair, and his alien kind had putrefied his domain.

The Birdman opened his eyes and coughed to the winds. Then he stepped straight off the ledge.

Remember, he is a bird, so spread his arms as the River of Dust that trickled a thousand feet below, rushed up to meet him.

I, or you readers, kept falling.

The membranes that stretched from his wrists to his ankles went taut as the warm wind current jerked him swiftly up and away.

UP, UP AND AWAY.

Behind his spade-like tail ruddered him towards the Well of Urd. And his people heard his call.

Five answered.

One had eight legs and a head like a lion's, and it ran to the call of its master Mingo Drum, The Birdman, at a steady speed of fifty miles per hour.

It was fit, so it did not wheeze or pant.

Another was house-sized, stuffing fruit into its mouth with two proboscises when it heard the cough.

It answered, a bellowing trumpet, thundering towards the Well of Urd.

Small critters wished the Birdman would stop coughing.

The third answering the cough looked like a monkey. It had flight membranes like the Birdman was stuffing a beetle into its mouth. Its prehensile tail, flattened at the end, had suckers.

The beetle was juicy and tasted like hot butter, and Little Drum decided she could fly faster than Mingo Drum, the birdman. She had plenty of time to get the beetle's mate from under a granite flake and eat it up.

It was a greedy little monkey.
The warm wind currents that carried Mingo's call also alerted two flying people twenty miles away.

One was male, the other female.

Oh yes, usually spells trouble.

Like The Birdman, their faces were sculptures of beauty. Only the flight membrane made them look like ungainly vampires while walking.

Were they vampires? Who knows?

But the air was their kingdom, and they came.

The friends of Mingo Drum were coming.

"They were the beasts of the air."

Here is a Birdman marching song in Bird Tongue, translated by Vern Lukas.
"*A racing shadow,*
 Look up humans,
 What do you see?
 A flock of starlings?
 No, birdmen, come to eat you."
Vern Lukas, Historian, and Imperial Scribe.

KEITH HULSE

Chapter 2, Well of Urd

She was alone with Madrawts

(elephant creature)/

(flying monkey)

The human woman sat in the hover car, feeling sullen and downcast, shaded by the heating rays of the purple suns. She was so focused on fate that she did not notice her surroundings.

Then, Ce-Ra heard the coughing grunt.

Her green eyes looked to the mauve sky, where fragments of white clouds sped rapidly on their unknown journeys.

Her red lips parted, showing perfect teeth.

She knew who made that call: her guardian Tzu Strath's enemy.

The Birdman was a sworn enemy of Emperor Alexander Caesar Vortigern, and she was not afraid. The Birdman would kill her swiftly. Life with Ce-Ra would be a living hell.

"Come, Birdman, come," she whispers.

Then she noticed a shadow race along the ground behind Ce-Ra. General Ce-Ra was making a stand, ordering his men to fire at something above as the fleeting dark shadow overtook Reeman.

A glint of light from an arrow in flight?

With a scream, Ce-Ra fell, clutching his left foot. His head knocked against an ancient sea of worn stone, smashing the graphite fossil marine animals embedded in it.

With a groan, the alien general closed his eyes as rich oxygenated red blood flowed onto the yellow sands.

Reeman Black Hair's soul died when he saw his master fall, and screaming lurched to aid him.

A stun grenade landed nearby.

Reeman Black Hair fell prostrate across his master and good friend, who gave him crumbs from the table; *remember a dog waiting for treats?*

Nasty folks say 'lover.'

"Which reader shouted "lover?"

Through dazed eyes streaming tears and ears buzzing, the young auburn-haired woman thought she saw a large four-legged beast with a head resembling a lion's roaring landing amongst the staggering alien escort.

Upon passing out, she saw a large brown beast with two proboscises and four tusks attacking.

And second, a feared Bird Man himself.

But to the human woman, Bird folk looked alike. To her, The Bird Man was all Bird Men.

He was the scourge of humankind.

People said he ate humans, spitting on fires, and laughed while basting them with hot oil.

She understood she was its meal when the eagle's eyes met hers. When the Bird Man saw her look, **he became full of remorse.**

So, he took several steps towards her, and she raised her left hand in protection. Her eyes glinted in terror, and her full red lips parted to make way for the scream forming in her windpipe.

An alien Madrawt then jumped him, and The Bird Man fell back, his right arm raised to shield his throat, some of the flight membrane sizzling open under the heat of a laser sword.

And the Madrawt's other hand clung to The Bird Man's right arm, the long nails raking, drawing blood, and hoping to bleed his enemy good.

So, The Birdman drew both his legs up and extended his hidden foot talons raking downwards.

Talon reader, he was a bird.

A horrid scream and the Madrawt spiraled towards the human woman, his arms failing the air as his blue abdomen came apart ON HER.

Such the silly results of war.

And the air stank.

Before closing her eyes, the woman glanced one final time into the hate-filled Bird's eyes, mistaking the hate for being directed at her and her human race rather than the Madrawts.

She was still lying slumped unconscious on the hovercraft seat when Little Drum arrived **late.**

He could not fly as fast as Mingo Drum, *but then he had monkey blood in him.*

"Last as usual, my little one," The Bird Man smiles.

"Death revolts me," was the tart answer as the ape creature gingerly threaded a path through the bodies.

"One day, you will meet death," the lion creature grunts with an evil look. At once, Little Drum scurried up The Bird Man's right arm and clung there for protection.

The Bird Man ignored both and walked over to the hovercraft. He looked at the sleeping human woman.

She was the most goddess-like creature he had ever seen.

"Did they not say Tzu Strath's women were the best?"

"Her genes have sculpted her perfectly. I am ashamed to look upon her defenseless. He considered himself a brute, not a man.

And many humans/aliens would agree and call him

"BEAST

."

He wanted to know her and get her away from their enemy.

Yes, a son of Adam.

FOR HE WAS THE BIRDMAN, A LAW TO HIMSELF.

Then he heard his two friends' singing songbird call and watched them land.

"Greetings Bran Llyr, my blood brother.

Welcome Branwan, my blood sister."

Gooday, Birdman Vercingetorix, **our Jarl**, and life. What can we do for you?"

Now Vercingetorix, who preferred his forename Mingo Drum, could not look at. . the defenseless human woman who made his own ugliness shine.

"Help me carry her to a safe place?"

Assured by Vercingetorix, she was only stunned. The Bird people lifted her.

"Where shall we take her?" They ask.

"Why, to the Castle of Artebrate of course," Mingo Drum replies, blushing under his tan.

Birdman scouting song in bird tongue translated by Vern Lukas.

"We are flyers,

Swans,

Soarers of the sky.

Who?

Birdman.

Infront of

You.

Lookup.

Birdman.

We are swans." **Vern Lukas, Historian, And Imperial Scribe**

KEITH HULSE

Chapter 3, The Emperor Vortigern

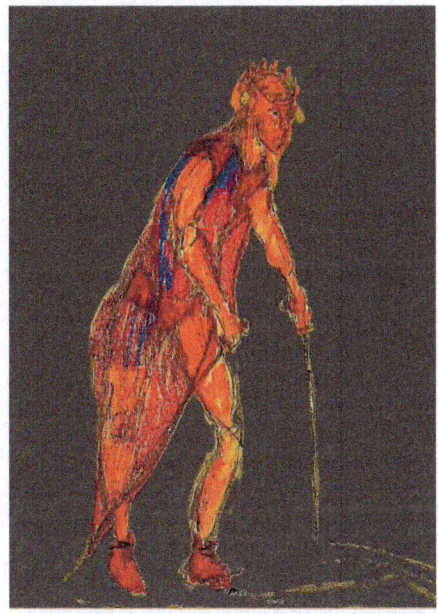

Vortigern needed to be cloned; he was disintegrating.
Only imperium purple saved him

Emperor Vortigern was old, balding, and had dry, freckled skin. Several warts grew from his chin, sprouting long hairs. Despite taking steroids, he could not prevent his muscles from turning to flab.

His tissues were just worn out.

It was the disease of old age; do you agree readers?

"You must consider cloning before it is too late, my Lord Vortigern," a slim man in black robes advised.

"No Diviciacus, no never, medicine will prevail," the worried emperor replies.

"My Lord you are already nearing a thousand years and have occupied the imperial throne six times," Diviciacus his priest, seer, and adviser replies softly not adding that further transplants, drug medications, hormone treatments, and genetic tampering would do nothing as his body was already that of a robot and not the original, and could not support any more interfering before a spring loosened and his emperor **blew apart.**

That is understated.

Sculptors revised six sets of artwork to match the new likeness. Some could not remember the original. Cloning is the best way to avoid these costs.

It was time for Emperor Alexander Caesar to be afraid.

He had done much wrong during his six reigns.

Stuff a tyrant does, *yes reader, the imagination is needed here.*

"It does not hurt my lord," Diviciacus purrs, and the Emperor Vortigern looked at him sternly,

"Does he mean dying or cloning?"

"There will be elections; the Madrawts will see turmoil as weakness?

The empire requires stability, not turmoil," his emperor Vortigern said.

"Yes, the Stardust Corporation has done wonders on Planet Maponos, I mean Tara 6. Glen Zowanski tells me they will create new genes there.

Soon, soon," Diviciacus assured his emperor.

"And produced monsters, flying men, six-headed snakes, put so much toxin into the atmosphere that even the suns appeared purple," Diviciacus thought.

And if his son Conchobhar claimed the throne? Would the cloned Vortigern have matured enough to keep his throne?

And Diviciacus knew Conchobhar was not the wimp his father saw him as.

Conchobhar was rigging votes for himself amongst the Electoral Princes who voted for an emperor when an emperor died.

The Madrawts threatened the empire's stability, which is why they invaded. They wanted peace until they had encroached so much that they no longer needed it. They conquered everything. To the victor the spoils.

For the sake of the empire, we should ignore Vortigern and Conchobhar.

Diviciacus is loyal to the empire, but not emperor.

And the bigger they are, the greater the fall was good advice but ignored.

"Perhaps I should visit the fertility banks and destroy every genetic strand of Vortigern," Diviciacus toyed.

"If civil war breaks out, Lord Tzu Strath would proclaim himself Protector Of the Empire including the wart on my face," as Tzu Strath was popular and victorious. Often in the press.

(purple suns)

And folks hated Diviciacus, which was unwelcome news to the latter.

"Where will our dream be then, Vortigern? Not even forcing Tzu Strath to give his most cherished possession to the Madrawts will buy you time.

Now we understand why they gave the auburn-haired girl to Ce-Ra."

And Vortigern looked at his priest, Diviciacus, and read his thoughts.

With a stable mind, you cannot read Diviciacus.

"The woman's fate will ensure Tzu Strath will hate the evil Madrawts for all time and come to my aid," Vortigern says.

"More likely to hate you and destroy you, mate."

Then adds, "It is time for you to clone?" Vortigern tells Diviciacus to suffer alongside his emperor as a faithful servant should.

Diviciacus was lucky mummification was out of practice.

"Soon, my lord," but Diviciacus had no intention of doing so.

*

The War Lord Tzu Strath had boarded his shuttlecraft to take him back to his battleship, the Imperial Ship Taranis; his bugging device left on his woman had stopped beeping.

He was a worried man.

Reduced to a weeping sore.

A broken heart.

Now she felt completely lost.

Should never given Boudicca to the Madrawts.

(Shamans conjure spooks and banshees)

He would extract her memories from his mind to protect himself from mental anguish over her loss.

She was now dead to him.

"One day my beloved emperor will pay for what you have done," Tzu Strath

promised.

Then: "We have landed, my Lord," Tzu Strath's personal bodyguard advised.

And Tzu Strath looked into the eyes of his long-suffering friend Tribune, Cedric Henry. Saw the shared pain at her loss. The Empire's stability was at stake,

For peace.

Both men knew their emperor would hate Tzu Strath more. Why would the media make Tzu a national hero for his sacrifice again?

More popular than the heirs' Conchobhar's cash.

"Run for the election yourself," Henry prompted.

And Tzu Strath saw the wet eyes of his friend, *"How lucky you are Henry: I am a War Lord and cannot shed publicly one tear for a loved one, for my enemies did say I was weak.*

I must be strong for the empire's stability.

Strong to fight Madrawt's."

(purple suns from pollution)

"She bought peace," Tzu Strath replies, walking away with his tribune following to board the Taranis. "I will comply with the emperor's demands," I thought, "Why not?" *Henry, the alien is correct. I should run for the office of the emperor. Was not my illustrious ancestor Tzu Don emperor back in ten thousand and five A.D.*

Like a phoenix, I rise to take the throne from an incompetent.

Emperor Tzu Don set up the Electoral College of Princes and Senators.

To select emperors on merit.

Unfortunately, Tzu Don must be weeping in Heaven.

Your mistake was limiting the vote.

You excluded the popular populace.

Instead, one planet, one senator.

How could you foresee the empire's expansion to such grand limits of corruption and parties that are whole solar systems?"

"The birdman was present," Henry says in the first chapter.

"He hates me," Tzu Strath answered.

"May the Creator be with her then," Henry offered."

"He will eat her," Tzu believed the trash he put in the media.

*

A Birdman Song on the Emperor, translated by Vern Lukas.

"Fear not,

The royal man of,

Fear not,

The regal man of,

Fear not,

He sits on his other throne.

Fear not."

From the memoirs of
Tzu Strath,
War Lord. Vern L.

CHAPTER 4 VERN ATTACK
(purple suns)

Vern, with a mouthful of teeth

"The young auburn-haired woman awoke to find herself strapped to a float bed. At once, she realized she was a prisoner and saw the clouds swirling above her, and with disbelief, she grasped that the white strips of cloud were near.

"**I am not on the ground,** Creator save me," she thought, for she had turned her head and seen she was barely six inches from the edge of the floater bed. Then she reminded herself of who she was and whose blood flowed in her veins. *I am his daughter and must behave as such, she chided.*

I cannot let these bird people see me as weak. The safety of pioneering families depends on it.

Human dignity was at stake.

She was afraid of heights without proper support.

Usually a fighter jet under her rump readers.

There was one thing flying a space fighter and another lying on an open floater bed five hundred feet above jagged rocks below.

Readers, the critters that hid from Mingo's shadow earlier, now waited for her to fall as a free diner.

"You will be fine," a gruff voice stated.

And she opened her eyes and saw The Bird Man King himself, Mingo Drum Vercingetorix, just above her but did not know his identity, only this was a horrible, smelly birdman, so she shut her eyes, turning her head to avert his yellow eagle bird eyes.

"He will eat me later," she figured; the pioneers told her.

After ten minutes, she hoped he had gone, but he was there gliding, looking her over like sausages. She hoped he would not pooh as birds were not house-trained.

What might a woman see reflected within the avian king's gaze? If she had suppressed her fears?

Pity.

Instead, she saw an ugly man with membranous wings and a hideous scar running from his left temple to the bottom of his right chin.

It made his nose more pronounced. She shut her eyes, but his face remained in memory, his streaming brown hair looked more like a lion's mane, but to her.

The lice-ridden feathers of a vulture, what was that sound? Had he regurgitated his food? She was in a complimentary mood. She wanted a pee and panicked .

"Hello, my dear," and she saw a small ape sitting at her feet.

She swore; *it was our Little Drum. It had spoken to her.* Now she was curious; a talking ape must be battery-run.

And the hideous being picking things off its fur and eating whatever. Oh, she felt ill. The big ones made crunchy sounds.

And The Creator had forgotten her, these were devils come to torment her.

"Did you see how brave I was when I killed the Madrawts? Some fight, but no match," the orange ape boasted.

"What a big-headed little monkey, full of wind," she stopped. She was class-bred. These were aliens to be pitied.

No, General Ce-Ra and the Madrawts were the aliens.

These flying monkeys and birds were MUTANTS.

DNA and RNA strands escaped from the test tubes of Stardust Genetic Corporation labs. Tissues that were washed down the sink spawning themselves into these, what?

She had no words to describe them.

The ape offered her a crunchy flea to eat.

"Little Drum, leave her," The Bird Man commands in a bass voice, and after some verbal protesting, Little Drum left but gave her a last paw above her knees.

"Little Drum, the Bird Man's sibling. Oh, my Creator, they breed amongst themselves by aping humans." She knew Mingo Drum was The Birdman, so, this was his flea-eating child.

And imagined what Mingo Drum's wife looked like, a gigantic hairy ape with six arms and a large udder.

How would you imagine The King of The Bird Men appearing? If we could judge based on this ape?

She did not realize the king was present.

It was human.

An idiot.

No, a culture clash was taking place.

Her culture demanded that everything else be submissive to humans.

Humans treated fleas with insect killers, not ketchup.

Stories familiarized her with the war against Planet Maponos' Bird Men.

Had watched the imperial regiments of Tzu Strath return beaten.

No one in recent history ever defeated an imperial army, not alone stopping the Great War Lord Tzu Strath, **her father**.

But King Mingo Drum Vercingetorix had.

She heard he was a barbarian who sacrificed his prisoners to elemental gods. Thousands at a time, stabbing, strangling, and drowning till the victims were dead.

The Triple Death, they called it.
She called it murder.

They said he tore the hearts out of the bravest enemies alive, and then ate, believing he sustained himself on his enemy's valor.

Just a superstitious murderer.

Now she was on her way to meet her War Lord's enemy, a former ally and hired mercenary general in the sacred war against the Madrawt.

A king who betrayed Tzu Strath during the intense battle with the Madrawts.

It was The Bird Man's fault he gave the Madrawt's victory —a foothold upon Planet Maponos towards their advance to Earth.

"Ka," the high-pitched wail took the Earth woman out of her depressive thoughts. She now focused on the sound, and at once, her heartbeat faster.

A flock of Verns circled them, readying themselves for the kill, and they were the meat.

"Sharks of the airwaves," she remembered Tzu Strath called them.

"At least I will not have to meet King Mingo Drum," she thought.

And The Bird Man, who seemed their leader, the one with the ugly scar running across his face, grunted his war cry.

It did not register that the news associated a coughing grunt of Mingo Drum with King Vercingetorix.

To millions like her, every Bird Man made the coughing grunt.

And watched the lone Birdman fly towards the sharks as the two others and the tiny ape hurried the float away, distancing themselves.

Pity crept into her bosom for the lone Birdman. He might be an alien, a mutant, but he was flying to a horrid **hero's** death.

The War Lord himself would be proud of that Bird Man, *she was.*

So, the first Vern started straight at the Bird Man, who dropped underneath and speared its belly. A red, stinking vapor hissed angrily out of the wound.

It was Vern's blood.

And the air carried it swiftly to the other Verns, who became excited and ate their wounded comrade. Raising her head, Tzu Strath's daughter saw the ape creature called Little

Drum flying back to aid the lone Birdman; that made her happy that the Bird Man would not die alone.

She was also glad the little ape was, *"Silly brave thing,"* she thought as a Vern with a gaping mouth attacked it.

And to her relief saw Little Drum had inflated a foil shield just as the teeth closed.

But the ache in her neck made her rest, and when she lifted her head again, a cloud covered the killing area.

"In here quick," the female Bird Woman shouts, then darkness.

The woman heard shutters open; purple suns warmed the place.

"Shall we arm her?" The male Bird Man asked.

"Wait and see what Mingo Drum does," the female replies.

Now fear filled their captive as though their dreaded king was near as the news media made him out to be an ugly warthog.

And guessed they were speaking of arming her as the mouth of a Vern burst through the window, shutting out the sun's purple warming rays.

"Bran Llyr," the female Bird Woman screamed as the toothed mouth closed upon the warrior's left shoulder.

The captive Earth Woman felt his warm blood over her, so panic gripped her. She was trapped, defenseless and although she fought against her leather straps, she could not free her wrists or ankles.

And the female Bird Woman sunk her short sword into the Vern which died falling away below.

But more Verns battered the door of whatever they had sought shelter in, banging with snouts, bodies, and tails.

Suddenly, the human captive's wrists were free.

"Defend yourself," the Bird Woman commanded and gave her a laser pistol and spear, then turned her back on the human and tended the bite on her companion's shoulder.

"*I am alone,*" the thought shook her. Never had she been in actual close combat.

Combat at a distance leading a squadron of Comet Fighters, squeezing off missiles, and then pulling away.

The War Lord had not changed his mind about letting her in close-quarter combat. What would he think now? She asked herself facing the splintering door.

Then she asked herself what she was doing, standing facing Vern with nothing but a laser pistol and a spear out of the Bronze Age.

A memory flashed across her eyes of the lone Bird Man who had given his life for them and Little Drum, the ape-like creature. She swallowed hard.

Well, she had always begged Tzu Strath to allow her close combat, *well, she had* it now.

She was a squadron leader. You be brave and show no fear in front of these lower beings the Bird people.

Would show them how an Earth woman died.

She fired at a Vern's head, as it broke through the door.

The head she shot filled the room with that stinking red vapor.

But she stood her ground as the school of Vern ripped the door off its hinges while tearing apart the Vern just killed. She was unaware that only three Vern remained outside.

And took careful aim at one and killed and as it died, a human head fell out of its belly.

She reeled back in shock.

The lone Bird Man arrived through the open window carrying Little Drum.

Trained reflex action almost made her shoot him like the computer traced her shots on the target screen.

But she was human and not a machine, and her finger stopped, and the Bird Man lived.

If she had known, would she have been fired, changing history? **It was one of those 'if'** situations; she would ask herself a hundred times what if I had killed him? But fate chose him to live, to exist, and an event that could have changed history becomes especially important in what 'if' questions and people blame fate.

OR GOD,

if in an insurance clause.

She faced the door; another Vern appeared.

The laser pistol was empty.

Throwing it away, she thrust her spear into the Vern.

The doorway cleared.

She looked for the lone Birdman, but he was gone, and the purple sun's warmth flooded in again.

Either dead, a brave beast, or a fool, but never used the word coward.

Then the silence.

Then a coughing victory grunt from the Bird Man that she recognized from training films.

'Mingo is here?' she clutched the spear, ready to hurl it at the king.

She was indeed an Earth woman.

A squadron leader of Tzu Strath's Praetorian Comets.

"Are you all right?" The Bird Man asked her as he framed

himself in the busted doorway. She looked for his king, no doubt overseeing the butchering of the slain Verns into choice meats. Tasty steaks to lie beside her when they wheeled her out on stolen silver function plates with an apple in her mouth.

Yes, a stupid human female, this one.

But his voice was so gentle taking her back to her present situation; her muscles tensed.

He wanted the spear; he did have to claim it. She would kill this brave Bird Man if she had to.

"Excuse me," he says instead, "my friends need me," as he walks unafraid past her.

He knew he was taking a risk as he passed that spear. His gut muscles tightened, wondering.

Through the door, she glimpsed spotted clouds and the Verns.

The media had her mentally warped to expect King Mingo Drum Vercingetorix, the murderer of decent human women and babes, as a monster.

Oh dear, her nightmare was present all the time!

All that greeted her was a barren landscape and dark forests on the horizon.

"Help us put Bran Llyr onto the float bed?" He asks, but she knows by the confident way he says it that he expected her to do as he bid; it was a command, and as a commander, she recognized it.

If Bran had not sustained an injury, she would have protested.

That was her excuse.

Bran, a warrior, required help. He had fought to save her, and she was not a barbarian like the Madrawts or that Bird Man King Mingo Drum. After, she stood away from them, still clutching the spear.

"You can stay here till another school of Vern's passes or come with us?" The big Birdman and it was obvious they were leaving.

"Staying Birdman," she replies, her eyes narrowing to slits of defiance.

"Can you fly, human woman?" The Birdman is sarcastic.

Upon looking out the door, she noticed they were suspended in mid-air, with fierce beasts lurking below, poised to feast on Vern's remains.

The little furry critters would hide again till they were gone, then eat readers.

She saw a lion beast and a Maponosian elephant with two tusks.

"I have no choice, have I?" Knowing she was defeated and a prisoner.

"No, I am sorry," The Bird Man says gently, "Come," he adds and holds out a brown gloved right hand.

She hesitated; the spear was her only defense. What 'IF' she ran him through with it? Then what?

" I offered him the spear.

Realized with horror that he wanted my hand instead.

I would have to touch the beast."

And it galled her sense of command that he allowed her the spear; in a reversed situation, she would disarm and chain him for him to know his doomed situation.

Was this Birdman playing with his mince and tatties?

Worse yet, the Bird Man desired her to lie, a leather belt, submission.

"Was he stupid or something?"

Strange thoughts went through her pretty head.

The reader's comments were unsolicited.

"Please hurry, we have not all day. Bran Llyr needs help quickly or will die," The Bird Man pleads. Well, she lay down and allowed herself the indignity of having the barbarian strap her up.

Then she remembered her pee.

To her horror, he just threw her out the door.

Her pee flowed from her reader; she was bursting.

"God," as she saw nothing but a cloudless sky about herself.

Nothing under her. She was falling, then a jerk as the warm air current pushed the Bird Man and her up.

He had no plans to carry her to the City of Flaming Crystals. It was sixty miles off; his friends were below; all he wanted was her down.

"He was not stupid?"

What friends? There was a lion and an elephant. Reader, do you see any friends?

(The Earth woman finds her courage as she descends slowly instead of rushing to hit the ground.)

Was the Bird Man *crazy or something?* A lion beast, and elephant waiting for her.

"You chicken turd," she shouts at him, so she was to be torn apart by wild beasts. She should have used the spear.

It was his revenge for The Stardust Genetic Corporation shipping Birdmen to the Public Arenas throughout the empire as an entertaining sport.

People said that their Emperor Alexander Caesar Vortigern enjoyed the spectacle of Bird Men with clipped wings, fighting gladiatorial contests and wild beasts.

Bird Men were top billing and crowd pullers.

The public paid for the emperor's wars.

The Stardust Corporation got rich.

Glen Zowanski, the Boss, bought a new planet for his own sport, built a ranch and swimming pool, and flew himself and shuttle loads of girls and guests there.

An entire planet.

Revenge was sweet to them handing it out.

But instead of being torn apart, she stood opposite the Bird Man.

And the wild beasts grunted, bellowed, and approached.

The barbarian did not leave. She still had the raised spear. He pushed it down.

"These are my friends," he tells her without anger.

Even so, she was not used to being close to wild beasts. Their smell was more powerful than him.

That meant he smelled.

"The City of Flaming Crystal is over there," he pointed towards the forested horizon.

She followed his gaze upwards and saw the float bed with Bran Llyr and Little Drum on it heading towards the forest.

Understood, he must go.

Was she free?

Turned to head towards where she thought Tzu Strath was and stopped.

"Where was the great War Lord? She was without a compass, water, or food, in an alien environment and armed only with a primitive bronze spear.

And what would happen to her if she survived the trek?

Would Tzu Strath obey his emperor and hand her over to General Ce-Ra? For the sake of imperial peace?

If the wild beasts out here did not eat her, the Madrawts would recapture her, perhaps? She was on their side of the Planet Maponos. , *yes or no reader*?

She felt crushed and wanted to cry, but she was a squadron leader.

"The City of Flaming Crystals over there, my friends, will guide you. I will return with help," the Birdman says and hops into the air.

He seemed ungainly on land, a monstrous escapee from the Stardust Corporation labs. But once airborne became graceful, and she admired as one does a soaring bird.

And he was brave and fearless.

Was she smitten?

And a wet nose prodded her back.

She turned, stared into the lion's eyes, and screamed.

Then both beasts had a good sniff of her drying pee stains.

Birdman Fighting song translated by Vern Lukas.

"We are lone warriors,

  Who?

We are mighty winged men.

Who?

We are fearsome lady soldiers.

Who?

Fight us, are you dare?

Who?

Bird people."

As told me by Mingo, Himself to Vern Lukas.

CHAPTER 5   PEACE MARRIAGE (TRUMPET FANFARES)

Reeman Black Hair.

"Ce-Ra is late," the Emperor Caesar Alexander Vortigern complains to Diviciacus in the shade.

His shaman priest did not reply. He did not like Planet Maponos; it was too young, and the elements were unstable, making spirit flight dangerous.

He desired a return to Earth, mirroring his master's wishes. This planet was alien, rough, and lacked Earth's amusements.

He also felt very vulnerable here to his political enemy, the Great War Lord Tzu Strath.

This was his planet.

Tzu Strath's domain, the human/alien imperialists would say.

They forgot to ask Mingo Drum Vercingetorix and the Bird

people whose it was.

"Investigate Boudicca's death and Ce-Ra's current actions," his emperor orders him.

Diviciacus knew what he meant, *spirit flight.*

But the blare of a hundred S-shaped carnyx horns announced General Ce-Ra.

And the imperial trumpeters blared back with metal instruments.

A small hunchback concealed in the sand covered his ears.

He feared he would reveal his location to Diviciacus who would slowly kill him by plunging

a dagger into his midriff to predict the future from his blood flow.

The way it spurted. Never his own blood, he was a smart priest.

And by the hunchback's death throes,

Well; this hunchback was not an oracle.

And the hunchback swallowed the spit he would have liked to spit at them.

It was dry.

He dare not move.

His master, Tzu Strath, needed him.

And watched the hated Madrawt's arrival.

Would like to spill his rival very much in intelligence gathering, Reeman Black Hair's organs onto the sand for Diviciacus to examine.

The hunchback cleared his ears to activate an implanted recorder.

His ears were the antennae.

"She escaped, the marriage is no more Earthlings, **our alliance finished**," General Ce-Ra tells Alexander Caesar Vortigern, "Now there is no control over Tzu Strath."

Ce-Ra saw the emperor captivated by the performance of imperial decadence at its magnificence best.

Two gladiators fought each other in a heated sand pit.

It was displayed on a large mobile wagon.

Reeman Black Hair favored the alien, and the other was human.

Why did General Ce-Ra turn to watch? Humans dying cheered his spirits; he wanted them dead or slaves. Their human empire was rich, falling apart from corrupt lousy administration. It would be **his.**

Full of extremely attractive human girls. His troops knew what to do when sacking a fallen human city.

He allowed it, or his men would form their war bands to loot.

He knew the top elite of the human empire was diseased and here it sat, an emperor who copied Earth's past great emperors, but the difference was the past dead ones were great, conquerors of space.

This emperor bribed Ce-Ra to leave him alone. But Ce-Ra's greed resulted in the pillage of human settlements.

Without his billion troops, Ce-Ra was nothing.

The bribes given to Ce-Ra built him an armada of ships that would carry his hungry troops to Earth.

Only the Great War Lord Tzu Strath could stop him and the marriage between him and Tzu Strath's daughter had pacified Ce-Ra. His Peace marriage, the human media had called it.

With Mistress Boudicca Tzu's escape, marriage was off, leaving the War Lord free to defy his emperor and declare war on the Madrawts.

A marriage ordered by the emperor for the stability of the empire.

Million suns illuminated the empire of the Great War Lord honorably served.

Like handing over the girl with the pretty auburn head, his daughter.

"I prefer the one with the net, watch," Emperor Alexander Caesar Vortigern says.

And this gladiator cast his net to fall upon the other's head.

Then he extended his trident, visible from the other person's back.

"I have set a trap for Tzu Strath. My subjects want peace, not a war with your people. The media attributed the economic collapse to the protracted Madrawt war.

Inflation is high.

We both want to get rid of Tzu Strath; he stands in the way of peace. We both would like the Birdman King Mingo Drum Vercingetorix as well."

The Emperor smiles, "Cast the net again," beckoning the gladiator to finish.

He did by pulling the barbed trident free.

General Ce-Ra smiled; the emperor was out to please. That was a human dying on the heated sand.

And a hunchback listening would remain under his sand-covered hole till all left, then make haste to his master, Tzu Strath.

A man who deserves to be emperor, not the weakling who considered Ce-Ra, his friend, and Tzu Strath, his enemy.

The hunchback and General Ce-Ra were aware of the Great

War Lord's character. One feared him, and the other loved him."

Madrawt marching song translated by Vern Lukas.

"We kill,
  We are handsome.
  We loot,
  We are handsome.
  We march.
  To the victor, the spoils."

Vern Lukas
Historian and
                    Imperial Scribe

CHAPTER 6 BOUDICCA STRATH

Her guardians (By Crossover Expo Pinterest)

Her hold on the bronze spear tightened when she found herself abandoned on the ground. A lion and an elephant here to eat her. *(The lion thingamabob might, but oliphants preferred fruit.)*

But instead of leaping at her and tearing out her throat, the Maponosian Lion knelt, and the elephant used its two proboscises to edge her onto the Griffon's back.

"Quicker than walking," she jokes, "hope you like me," and patted the griffin.

It gave a bored yawn.

But she noticed the flesh-tearing teeth and the long upper incisors overlapped the lower rubbery gums.

People hoped for the scarred Birdman's return. That the beast here had recently eaten. She was sure the tail of a desert critter stuck between its teeth.

And suddenly all walked at a tremendous pace.

Of course, she fell off.

The lion patiently waited for her to get on,

Again,

Repeatedly.

This time, she would grip the bright dark mane, ignoring anything living creeping there.

And in the distance, she caught glimpses of the Flaming Forest when they reached the tops of small canyon summits. "To the City of Flaming Crystals," the Bird Man had said. Ah, the name conjured up buildings made of crystals, waterfalls, pools of lilies, and tall trees with multi-colored flamingo nests in them.

Guess what? She would find her imagination had not played games. Earth cities had less colorful names. Then it occurred to her she was giving these Bird people credit for having architectural science.

They were just mutant birds, roosted in a nest and pooped on the wing—yucky things. But she made good aerial scouts against the Madrawts and nothing less, apart from messing up statues in squares, which was her private joke, delegating them to pigeons.

Of course, servants, slaves, and good dissecting specimens in school class labs. It also dawned on her as she rode the Maponosian Griffin. She lacked Bird knowledge beyond her father, Tzu Strath, and media accounts. On bird people. (A bit like Caesar eons before, he beat the Gaul's, so he made them out to be monsters and his reason to steal all that Gallic gold.)

The Stardust Corporation, owners of Planet Maponos, says, "Bird folk are a species of flying primate."

Netting thousands of them into its 'gene tanks.'

And her father was being delicate.

Gene tanks extracted vital body fluids, got genetic codes, and then substituted them with human genes, making monsters.

Spares for the arenas.

And the Stardust Corporation saw the profit made from selling genes that could give YOUR CHILD THE GIFT OF FLIGHT. It is much better than a rubber band wind me up cardboard plane.

Bird people's genes were in enormous demand under Xmas trees and parties.

Even Emperor Alexander Caesar Vortigern wanted wings until he was told the planting of flight genes would be painful, dangerous at his age, and **costly.**

Perhaps if someone cloned him.

That was enough.

Someone discarded the emperor's vision of parading before his courtiers in a silver toga, scarlet jewel-encrusted robe, and golden wings.

"Make sure my clone has them," he insists instead.

Five centuries prior.

Then Mingo Drum Vercingetorix was born to lead his people to freedom.

Readers, as flying apes stripped of imperial civilization.

"What would I have done if I was he?" Boudicca herself asks.

Done the same.

Freedom.

And wished she had bothered now to search news videos before coming to Planet Maponos to see the early films on Mingo Drum.

The Birdman, her rendezvous, remained obscure.

Her guardians stopped at the edge of a forest water hole. Even a spectrogram water diviner could not locate it.

A spring, encased in rock, emerged from a hollow plastic tube. The beasts understood that pawing the flat surface triggered pumps which gushed up water.

Lovely and cool.

REFRESHING.

She drank and then fingered a bit of the plastic.

It was unknown to her.

What intelligence had discovered this material? The Bird people's discovery showed that they lived in trees and on rock ledges, so it could not have been them.

Did this planet hide a civilization we humans do not know about?

And that is when

the Rock Dwellers attacked.

The first arrows thundering into the thick hides of the Monopodium elephant and Griffin.

Their enraged bellows and roars, making Boudicca swallow the wrong way. Then the trained soldier took over, and she sought immediate cover.

Looking quickly over the gray granite rock, she saw no arrows were falling about her.

"They are not for me," she meant the arrows, and she was

correct because the hail had driven off her guardians.

"Well, I begged my father, Tzu Strath, for hand-to-hand action, and now I am getting it?"

Nothing to do now but wait.

"We are the Mighty Rock People.

All this is outland.

We are mighty warriors." It sounded like a multitude; she could not identify them. Except that they were conceited.

Emerging from the rocks, sand pits, and dunes, they scrambled down.

Little four-legged fur-clad creatures, the way their legs worked; made them look like wolf

spiders, but they had tails and humanoid heads, making them look like monkeys.

"See how valiant we are? Throw down your stick. We have weapons," they chorused, and she saw they had bows, short swords, and spears.

Crawling up a rock provided safety and distance, which were synonymous. If they wanted her dead, she would be dead.

But they prodded her till they all rushed her at once.

And her spear went through one.

Was violent hissing

As the creature

It had massive cobble wobbles,

IT SHOT

LEFT

AND

RIGHT,

SHOT HISSING EVERYWHERE

It made an awful stink as it died.

And like a deflated child's balloon hissed through the air to rest on the ground till it

was flat?

And Boudicca felt revolted.

Why her disgust? She just killed one. A billion waited for revenge. Oh well, girl, better you than me."

These things were manifestations of everything she hated about Maponos, (Tara 6.)

It was not Earth; it was not human.

But she did not have time to reflect because as soon as the others overcame their comrades' demise, they attacked anew with a berserker fury, throwing stones and sand. Boudicca was hapless.

Then a stone hit her temple.

A lucky throw.

Perhaps?

She fell.

    During the thirty-six-hour day on Planet Maponos (TARA 6), for the second time,

she was unconscious. As her eyes shut, she heard, "No one can defeat the Mighty Rock.

Dwellers whose empires reach the moons?"

Now where had she heard that tripe?

*

    The bellowing trumpet of the Maponosian elephant and deep roars of the Maponosian lion, the Griffin the Earth settlers called it, answered the coughing grunt.

The Bird Man circled above his friends now.

He was not alone.

Only fools come alone.

Some tough friends were with him.

They were his friends because he was honest.

It showed up their faults so clung to him, for the light that came out of the Bird Man washed away their faults.

And: The Legion of Manticore, named by War Lord Tzu during the battle against the Madrawt, was magical Peter Pans by him, symbolizing man's desire to fly like birds *(But not mess sidewalks like them)* was here.

Tzu felt disheartened seeing the Bird people flying around him, as he longed to fly too.

And as independent warriors, chaotic, unpredictable but under a single strong, respected leader, controllable up to a point, as each was a separate individual swordsman, not an army unit, fantastic light infantry.

Anyway, enough to get them at the enemy before their ranks depleted, and they broke the charge. But to kill one HATED MADRWAT... was worth it for them.

So, the Bird Man landed, enraged by the wounds inflicted upon his friends.

The enemy arrow shafts told him much!

Rock Dwellers, the spider monkey people of Maponos who, since they evolved, had mimicked their betters and worse, when Stardust Genetic Corporation had set up labs on this planet, interfered with the spider monkey people's gene codes, enabling them to speak and jump a few rings up the evolutionary ladder.

They were dangerous, more unpredictable than Mingo's famed warriors, for they had no worthiness and knew not the meaning of honor.

"To the City of Monoliths," the Bird Man grunts, his scar swelling with blood rage.

Their King Dumezillian was the size of the Bird Man himself.

An emperor of moons.

He was imitating the Emperor Vortigern of Earth,

The Bird Man knew the human woman's fate made him responsible for her.

That King Dumezillian would think he was having a goddess. The spider monkey tribe viewed humans as deities flying in the sky.

But the Bird Man knew human/alien imperialists were like Bird people, beings with souls. Then King Dumezillian would eat her as a soup. Leftovers would be given to his people to gain human attributes: her wisdom, her beauty, her hairless skin, two legs, and five fingers.

During the feast, everybody goes to the goddesses.

And: The woman's identity, whether she was Boudicca Strath, his enemy's daughter, was unknown to Bird Man Mingo Drum Vercingetorix, yet he remained responsible for ensuring her safety.

He wanted to sleep well.

He departed immediately for King Dumezillian City of Monoliths, leaving a small security detail with his friends.

A messenger flew fast ahead of the medics and escorts to his crystal city to summon the full Legion of Manticore.

They were his honor guard.

His flying House Carl's.

"This is my domain,

What I see is my people's land.
The laws of my people are my speech.
You, the violator's warning, my cough.
I wield the sword to defeat you.
The purple skies above our highways.
The lands below our land.
  Death awaits the visitor here,
Go stranger and return not,"
They were his words,

Chiseled into huge black granite slabs sixty feet high on each compass point bordering his kingdom.

The principal city names his kingdom, The Flaming Crystal.

Human knowledge concerning bird people was minuscule.

Explorers first, then miners, soldiers, missionaries, settlers, and Glen Zowanski Stardust and his people, Planet Maponos, renamed Tara 6.

Because of five hundred years of struggling contact with the Great War, Lord Tzu Strath.

The sixth mining planet in the Stardust Galaxy.

Which meant extraordinarily little to humans throughout the empire of Alexander Caesar Vortigern apart from mineral ores and wars?

A name depicts much.

Maponos meant Divine Son, so the planet was for the herb healers. The precipitants of knowledge.

They said the universe would rise again from this planet as light that would spread throughout galaxies, wiping out darkness, so creation may begin again.

The Bird Man felt sorry for humans who had lost the meaning of names."

Rock Dweller Song translated by Vern Lukas.
"Who is like us?
We love ourselves.
We are handsome folk.
We have tails.
So, swing in the trees.
We have hands.
So, make crafts.
We have feet.
So we can run.
We love ourselves.
Who is like us?"

As told Vern Lukas, the scribe
By Lady Boudicca Strath.

CHAPTER 7 THE CITY OF MONOLITHS

City of Monoliths built by barbarians

Boudicca Tzu Strath awoke carried on a litter bound.

This imprisonment was intentional, not protective.

Her journey had been rough because the Rock Dwellers did not have the technology of float beds, and she doubted they could even use them if they had them.

She guessed not.

Anyway, her captives turned into a large valley covered in stone monoliths. A vast shadow fell across her. Looking she saw a gigantic pink sandstone shaped like a cross above her on the heights.

She was familiar with this place; she had seen that cross on a routine patrol with her squadron of Comet Fighters in the Valley of Stonehenge, as humans called it.

But she had never seen these four-legged spider monkey people come crawling out of cave mouths in these monoliths.

"We built this city," one of her guards tells her and she had to guess again, did they? These ugly, conceited beings, who talked, scratched, and behaved like monkeys?

Readers, she liked monkeys; they begged for peanuts and stole your handbag.

She noticed many metal rungs and ladders up the monolith walls also, sundials here and there, and some metal circles with pentagrams, perches, and birdbaths.

For birds?

Her professional soldering helped her fight fear when they told her she was going up there.

Many perches appeared insecure.

If one fell?

"Up here, our Great King Dumezillian awaits. When you see him fall flat on your face till he tells you to stand, he is a great emperor and might be our god himself walking this our Planet Simian."

And Boudicca looked at the fur-glad face of her speaker, Planet Simian. This was Tara 6!

But the Bird Man Mingo Drum called it Maponos.

Anyway, they unlocked her copper manacles and prodded her with spears to climb up metal rungs up the tallest monolith; by some *miracle* next to her!

And as she climbed, she noticed hieroglyphic drawings. "We drew them. Are they not beautiful?" One of her guards asked.

"What do they mean?" She as they beamed with information.

"I do not know, I did not draw them," was the reply.

And she climbed ever higher, thin air, which whistled up her dark green toga.

Hated it when the monkey people under her chatted excitedly and pawed her.

If she tried beating them away, she risked falling. There was nothing for it but to climb faster.

But her molesters, being monkeys, easily kept pace with her.

Life now was a discomfort.

At the summit, guides led her into a vast cave where wall evidence suggested a different intelligent life form, not the monkey-like inhabitants, created it.

There were sun reflectors lining the walls, now covered in mold.

And now walking, she saw prisms that changed the light ray colors that brought out certain dyes used in the hieroglyphic drawings. Several prisms lay broken, and no one had repaired them because dust covered them. Some pictures showed what she thought were spider monkey people in nets held by Bird Men.

She dismissed the idea Birdmen were in the pictures.

Now she guessed these loathsome aliens had not built these caves, nor did they know how to fix the prisms or decipher the writings.

Also, she resisted believing the pictured Bird Men were culpable.

They were not human for a start.

So, who were the artists? Tara 6 used to be a planet devoid of intelligent beings, except for the Bird people, whom she viewed as winged mutants defecating while flying.

Had the Stardust Corporation lied about life on Tara 6 to justify milking it dry?

Before anyone noticed there was life here, Stardust censored the news.

If she ever saw her father, Tzu Strath, again, she would tell him about what she had seen.

Neither Glen Zowanski nor his Stardust had ever appealed to her.

She abided by loyalty, honor, and valor standards as a soldier.

But then the musicians started up making a dreadful din.

A noise.

Someone pushed her, forcing her to kneel, and then shoved her face down.

"Our Great Dumezillian has entered."

She played safe; she would do as they wanted.

*

Now Mingo Drum led his 1st cohort of Manticore to the City of Monoliths. He knew exactly where it was. Why not? His ancestors had built it four thousand years ago, and slowly it had degenerated into disuse with the wars against the Madrawts.

It was an enormous collection of monoliths seen from space.

An ancient war, repeatedly reigniting.

Each time, the bird people achieved victory, albeit with consequences.

Now the last war, The War of Survival as the Priests of Light called it, had begun with the Madrawts, as usual, who had conquered Maponos, but a hundred-year guerrilla war had driven them out.

The Bird Men, who lived in sand holes, abandoned many cities, such as the City of Monoliths, hollowed boulders, giant tree trunks in the Flowering Forest, and the planet's wilderness areas.

Then the humans arrived, and the Bird people hid. Distrustful of aliens and no longer the multitudes they once had.

Madrawt wars had depleted their populations.

Did you notice humans are the aliens' readers?

Their lovely cities largely stayed vacant.

Abandoned cities became homes to Rock Dwellers and others.

Why would Madrawts share such information?

Nor had Mingo Drum told Tzu Strath when he served him as a mercenary. Humans were distrustful of *aliens.*

Boudicca would learn the truth soon.

But now Mingo Drum was returning home to the city of his mother. Her tomb lay in the Canyon of Souls just outside the City of Monoliths.

Often, he visited her tomb over the centuries, spying on the Rock Dwellers, dreaming of the day when his people would return.

But Mingo was a man of contrasts:

"The caves have become their homes; I am not dealing with unintelligent life. We no longer call the City of Monoliths our home. May we drive the Rock Dwellers out after our absence?

This city is now their home. He often advised his people they could construct a better city in a different location. But they had been angry, but he was their elected war chief, and if he kept winning battles, he would remain so.

His people ignored the Rock Dwellers and other intelligent beings inhabiting their abandoned cities.

Mingo Drum, they knew, would change his views.

So, Mingo Drum led his 1st cohort, Legion Manticore, up the canyon wing's beating.

The thought of battling the Rock Dwellers did not appeal to him. He believed a show of force would subdue these primitive spider people if they knew he was not coming to evict them.

Besides, it was time they accepted his law.

Mingo Drum's cough was law. The spider monkey had settled on his domains, so they must accept his laws or return to their own abandoned dusty homes.

This was his domain, and everything living in it was his subject.

Anyway, King Dumezillian was admiring his latest human captive. He had enough brains to realize she held rank, for she wore silver body armor over her dark green toga and a gold sun pip on each soldier.

He must own her, she was beautiful, then he would hold her for ransom; she was defenseless, alone, which meant she was vulnerable to his forthcoming advances. He liked the idea even if she would not if she knew about it.

Alone.

Subsequently, several individuals removed Boudicca's armor only after she incapacitated some simians.

Spirit.

Also, spider monkeys were small.

Boudicca impressed Dumezillian.

She would fight fiercely, like a fish caught on a hook.

And felt his loins stir. *A daughter of Eve, this monkey.*

"Who are you?" He asks.

After a pause, "An officer in the empire's service," thinking it wise not to tell her real identity. Some might instantly project their hatred for her father onto her. "Comet squadron," she adds, thinking that was impressive and close enough to Tzu Strath.

But he had never heard of it. He was a monkey king, planning mischief.

Now he was grinning as he looked her up. "The War Lord will pay to have you?"

She knew her fate.

"Yes, a thousand imperial dollars," she had lowered the price; but it pleased this king. With a thousand dollars, he could purchase thirty laser guns from Madrawt traders and conquer all life on this planet.

He was a dreamer schemer.

He made a great king.

And this great king showed with a royal finger flick to have her taken to his room.

A stone throne stands here, topped with a hunting bird's head.

It resembled a birdman, not a monkey.

Knowledge crept into her. She suspected the Bird people were responsible.

It takes a lot for a human to admit they are wrong.

Then the doors slammed behind her, jolting her thoughts.

Alone.

With this primitive spider monkey with exceedingly long fingers that were coming her way.

"You are beautiful," the king drooled.

Revolting; long strands hit the floor, covering carpet slaters.

"You a hairy ape," she insults him.

He scoffed, declaring Rock Dwellers the cosmos' most advanced race.

He was a monkey.

Then attacked her and although she fought bravely, his many arms and great strength soon had her green toga in shreds.

And since monkeys are distant, cousins of humans stood back and admired the merchandise.

He liked green like human men do.

And like a human attacked her and soon had her lying on the cold marble floor.

Boudicca did what decent girls do; she crossed her legs and folded her arms across her chest.

Yet the ugly baboon was so quick,

One moment, he was there; the next, gone.

Above her,

Below her.

She stopped covering herself, accepting that he would look, and preferred waiting with clenched fists, two fists for the monkey.

But this monkey is like a lone meerkat male, eying up a beautiful meerkat floozy female who had deliberately wondered out of her family's protective circle, was

Mentally pawing.

Abusing her body,

And her mind.

However, he could attack her as a human, not a meerkat.

"At least I still breathe; there are worse fates than this? Many of the sultry night clubs of the empire have human/alien floor sex shows."

This king, unlike aliens, was unique.

No woman, he was an alien; you agree with readers.

Almost human, but not quite.

Recognized it as rape and vowed to come back and seek justice under the empire's laws.

Vengeance. None of this forgiveness. She would bring a vet.

She imagined neutering this monkey king and seeing how he would react.

Tzu Strath did not take female abuse lightly; the War Lord cherished women as they were the child bearers of the empire. He had his martial laws to protect them; Tzu saw women as contributing to the economy of the empire.

And would destroy this monkey.

"I must blank my mind as Diviciacus and the Shamans of Light taught," Boudicca is preparing herself for her ordeal.

BUT. HEAVY HAMMERING upon the closed doors averted the king's attention, turning his mood dangerously ugly.

(BLARING sounds).

He bared yellow, sharp fangs. *He had cavities from a lack of teeth brushing.*

And the doors swung open, and a Rock Dweller guard tumbled in, blood gurgling from his mouth.

BLARING sounds.

Loud military horns are approaching.

Boudicca suffered her nakedness.

Why, the monkey had eaten her green toga?

"Make way for King Mingo Drum Vercingetorix, the true ruler of Planet Maponos," she heard Birdmen heralds shout.

Several heavily armored Bird Men entered, and King Dumezillian saw *their threatening, malicious intent towards him.*

He could do nothing but stand and be extremely angry, *fountains of foam.*

Boudicca used a mat for clothing.

The dreaded Bird Man King Mingo Drum was here.

Her fate, what would become of her? From monkey to birdman?

And the Bird Man with the ugly scar across his handsome face entered the room and hope fluttered in her chest.

And he walked up to King Dumezillian and slapped his face extremely hard.

A monkey fang flew across the room.

And Boudicca could not stop the revengeful smile.

The blow was so hard the sound cracked out of the corridors

and the monkey king flew backwards into his throne, cracking his head.

Hard, so a lump quickly *appeared.*

Anyway: "Quickly, gather up your clothes; we must go quickly," Mingo Drum tells Boudicca.

Now Boudicca walked past him, holding the mat tightly about her.

Mingo Drum walked up to a chest against a wall and opened it; it held spoils and withdrew a female kilt and a soldiers' mailed vest.

He handed them to her and looked away.

She wasted no time in leaving the flea-infested mat.

The kilt was a size too small and the vest one size too big.

Boudicca was aware she did not look her best, but she covered important places.

And Mingo Drum took her to the open doors.

Then shouts, the hiss of lasers, and groans of dying.

The Birdman, whom she still did not know was Mingo Drum, thrust her to waiting arms, for he had turned to wrestle the advancing King Dumezillian.

Someone led her through a hidden doorway and down a sunlit corridor, reflecting light from a reflector. Then she gasped as she was flung out into the purplish sky.

AND DROPPED

(carnyx horns blaring)

She instantly thought someone had flung her sixty feet to the sand below.

Nope, Bird Men captured her in a net.

Now Mingo Drum wrestled King Dumezillian as his men held the Monolith of Justice, as the Bird people had once called the Monolith, where Dumezillian held court.

The ape's remaining fang bit deep into Mingo's left arm as his right hand sought his foe's eyes.

Outside, Boudicca Tzu saw the remaining Cohorts of the Legion of Manticore arrive, carnyx horns blaring, standards fluttering in the warm wind.

Their might impress her, and she could see why her father had employed them under King Mingo Drum Vercingetorix as mercenaries against the Madrawts.

Something impressed the Rock Dwellers as well.

They scattered back into their monolithic homes.

But the Flowering Forest soon loomed up, and while she lay trussed in the net, she wondered what happened to the Birdman King and the warrior with the scar.

"My guardian," she laughs, for he had a habit of turning up at the right moment, saving her.

Would he return with her to civilization and be her guardian there, riding the skies as her Comet Fighter wingman dog for the empire's peace? She was sure they could buy him were not Bird Men mercenaries.

It would be impressive; she would be famous and a figurehead, and her flying dog would be a symbol of imperial power and enforced slavery.

She disliked the forced slavery aspect, but during the existence of empires, the slave trade was a commonly accepted practice.

To the victor, the spoils.

To the vanquished, behold your fate,

The slave pens.

And an eye lay on the cold marble floor. It still had the visibility of Mingo Drum.

Dumezillian held his face in pain.

"One day, Dumezillian, I will give in to my people's desires to reclaim our lost cities.

These lands are my domain.

My domain is my people's soil.

I voice their laws.

The wind carries my law to all.

To all who live within my domain.

Live by my law or die, Dumezillian?

The choice is yours."

So, King Mingo Drum Vercingetorix told his foe before he left.

Eventually, he informed Boudicca, who disagreed.

"Tzu Strath's laws are the law, his courts for all."

And the Bird Man knew she was MISTAKEN for Tzu Strath's courts were for human/alien imperialists and laughed.

He, a Bird Man, only experienced rough justice from the imperialists.

Had he not found burned Bird Men and women hung from rock outcrops?

Was it not imperial law to neuter Bird people like stray cats so they could not have young?

Had he not found Bird Children staked out as targets for imperial troopers to practice on?

Found Birdmen villages gassed with all inhabitants bloated, their skin peeling, eyes bulging, tongues swollen and choked, and everything living dead, even the last cockerel that refused to crow at sunrise.

Bird Man's water holes poisoned?

Crops riddled with harmful chemicals.

Had he not talked to escaped captives from the Stardust Corporation and heard how researchers used them as genetic guinea pigs.

"There is only one law here, mine," he would reply to Boudicca.

Manticore Legion flying song.

"All our wing beats together.

  Hear our drums overhead.

  Ka, a legion calls.

  Run, enemy, run."

Written from Memories from Conservations with Mingo Drum Vercingetorix.

Vern Lukas,

Historian and Imperial Scribe.

CHAPTER 8 WOMAN TROUBLE

The Flowering Forest *was huge, unexplored by humans because of the wars.*

A Hawk Fighter's camera focused on her before it departed, startling her.

Elation.

And the Bird Men showed no fear but kept flying towards the green forest. They knew the Hawk recon would not follow as the air filled with sweet pollen from the billions of flowers, which grew protected under King Mingo Drum's laws. *Bees were happy here, and a thriving honey industry flourished.*

So, I was *glad she did not suffer from hay fever.*

And wondered what new drugs the unknown flowers and plants could yield for the treatment of disease.

She had encountered similar news and heard environmentalists' hype, witnessing it in person was remarkable.

Her god gene was awakening.

Readers lay bets. Would she burst into hymns?

If she watched, she would start feeling the oneness of the universes—a dangerous thing for a Comet Squadron Leader of Tzu Strath in the forty-fifth century A.D.

But Tzu Strath, she knew, opposed Stardust Corporation's exploitation of galaxies.

To prove it, he kept a small aquarium in his war cabinet room—a reminder to respect LIFE.

Except he did not include Bird Men amongst his green plants, clear streams, and exotic-colored birds and apes swinging from trees in his private zoo.

Why Boudicca imagined her Birdman rescuer perched on a branch as tourists flooded her winter greenhouse. Her father, Tzu, preferred them as stuffed trophies on walls; they were just big game birds.

He loved pigeons but hated birdmen.

The Bird Men fought a frontier war against the empire.

Five hundred years. A lot of butchering existed on both sides.

Many settlers suffered the sacrificial Triple Death at the hands of Bird Men. *The triple death.*

Tit for tat existed upon Planet Maponos (Tara 6).

But King Mingo Drum Vercingetorix's gene god had awakened long ago.

He cared, had a deep feeling of heart, and felt suffering that tore his soul apart.

Green laws, their king was a paradox, a lover of nature, but an eater of human children? She Boudicca would like to meet this genetic creation of the Stardust Corporation. She could sway him to ally again with her father, Tzu Strath, against the

Madrawts.

Her father would be pleased.

The Bird people: who opposes them?

Stuff the emperor and his Madrawt peace; when she returned, she would not honor her so-called Madrawt marriage to General Ce-Ra.

The Emperor Alexander Caesar Vortigern could visit the purple underworld on an assassin's dagger.

She understood the emperor's use of her body to appease the Madrawts.

The Hawk Fighter relayed camera footage.

No, not to give her back to Ce-Ra?

Yes, the Hawk Fighter had turned away because missiles hidden in the green foliage targeted it.

Boudicca knew that missile activity restricted the forest.

Many planes had been downed here; the Bird Men had missile technology.

Intelligence said there was a city called The City of Flaming Crystal ahead.

Escaped human and alien P.O.W.

They said it was beautiful, full of colored glass reflecting the spectrums of the purple suns.

For others, it was dismal, full of decay and the Bird people lived in giant nests. There was little advanced technology; their priests practiced barbaric rites involving the sacrifice of young virgins of any race.

Others, their priests, were highly knowledgeable and human, and aliens of the empire could learn much from them.

She would have to wait and see.

Conquered aliens made good auxiliary troops.

THE BIRDMEN COULD FLY.

And because Mingo had freed many humans and aliens, their fear for Bird Men had subsided, replaced by gratitude and respect for Bird Men. Seeing them full of valor and the vanity of a warrior class.

And she remembered how their priests encouraged their warriors to sacrifice their prisoners to their elements.

I am not a prisoner of war; she reminded herself.

*Remember Teutoburg Forest, where Germanics defeated **four Roman legions.***

Sacrificed prisoners to their gods. Nailed their heads to trees.

We are also not officially at war with the Bird people. She breathed a false sigh of relief.

*

Mingo Drum led his warriors of the Manticore Legion back to his city.

The City of Flaming Crystals.

He avoided his guest; she was his human. He proceeded directly to his throne room, where his War Chiefs assembled. Tzu would see a lot of turkeys, chickens, eagles, crows, and such gathered gobbling.

Although an unofficial peace existed between humans and aliens in their vast empire where the sun never sets.

Hostile operations were continuing against Madrawts.

There would never be peace on Maponos.

Then, someone shoved a hunchback forward in front of Mingo. It was the disheveled figure who was the War Lord's spy. He got caught riding a hovercraft to the Canyon of Stonehenge.

"My words are visible for all to read on the points of the compass," Mingo Drum tells him as he sits wearily on his throne, "yet you arrive in a vehicle that an assassin would use.

Who are you?"

The hunchback replies, "Anyone and everyone, today I am the famous Nostradamus."

The Bird, familiar with Nostradamus, remained impassive.

"Who do you work for?"

"Yesterday and today he who pays me, this evening and tomorrow you."

Mingo Drum smiles.

Mingo retrieved a money bag from a stunning ivory chest.

Sculpture adorned it.

The hunchback caught the thrown bag.

"Imperial gold dollars. You are generous, my lord," the hunchback replies. He worked only for the Great War Lord Tzu Strath.

"And who is my paymaster on this pleasant evening?"

Mingo smiled but did not reply; he knew the game well.

He sat down and waited, promising to give nothing away. But he already had. Nostradamus had entered the palace, seen the tables laid out with Madrawt miniatures, and guessed he had seen preparations in progress against the hated aliens.

He saw picture writing on the walls, carved figurines, and indoor fountains and knew the Bird people were not ignorant savages, as his master believed.

They were in trouble.

Mingo believed this small man repeatedly infiltrated his cities undetected.

And he worked for Tzu Strath.

Someone should kill him at once.

"The War Lord pays a bounty on missing officers," the hunchback finally offered after a lengthy delay.

Mingo smiled; the man named his master.

"What is her name?"

Nostradamus thought there would be no harm "Boudicca," watching those yellow eagle eyes for a reaction.

Now, after several minutes, a faint smile spread across the Bird Man's face, the scar moved with a smile.

"Just an officer," Nostradamus offered.

"I witnessed the War Lord's departure; why would he want the officer returned?"

Nostradamus felt the pain his beloved master felt at giving up his daughter for peace.

Especially to a Madrawt?

"The Madrawts want her, she offended them, the new peace between the Emperor Alexander Caesar and these creatures must hold.

The empire that a billion suns never sets upon needs stability," Nostradamus.

Now Nostradamus was sure this Bird Man was Mingo Drum Vercingetorix himself.

Familiar surroundings made the man too assured and relaxed.

He had that famous scar.

The hologram his master had shown him did not resemble Mingo at all.

Was his craft searched? Were items similar to that hologram found? It would bring a short sword to the skin of his throat.

"Tell me the truth. This Boudicca must be important if the Madrawts want her that badly. Anyone who is against them is our friend. She will not return with you," the Birdman says.

Nostradamus was in a fix.

"And you will not leave until you speak the truth," Mingo leaving.

"But my Lord, I must leave, I have pressing appointments," Nostradamus protested.

"This is my domain,

My cough, my warning.

My word is law," the Bird Man told him, his eyes no longer smiling.

"The War Lord will not be pleased," Nostradamus, acting afraid, "he wants the human woman."

A warning cough silenced him.

The sound went through the spy's bowels. This being had just reminded him he addressed a creature, not a person, Vercingetorix, the animal, no bird.

And so they led Nostradamus away.

His quarters were not as he imagined, not dark and wet but dry rooms, one room to receive guests, another to eat, a sleeping shelf cut in a wall, and a private washroom and toilet. Food on the table, cold meats, fruits, a jug of water, his bag of cash and a game of A1 intelligent Maponsian chess.

"Perhaps not all quite the beast this Mingo Drum," he muses as he checks the walls for secret passageways. Unable to find any, he realized the exit was through the gated entrance.

"A well-furnished dungeon," he croaked, sitting down to play chess. He knew the king would be back; he had a bag of cash to earn.

*

Boudicca's surroundings amazed her. The walls were aflame with moving lights. Crystals that were fed from sun reflectors.

In the center of her large room, a hole in the roof poured forth greenish light, channeled through shafts by reflectors.

There was a simple wooden table. It revealed carved edges with scenes of forest life. The tabletop was replaceable; it was for everyday use.

Food, classic films, a machine's presence—all suggested technology.

While she searched, her mind thought of the Bird Man King she had not seen.

She never would, had not revealed her identity, was just another bothersome human.

Now, at this stage, she realized she liked Bird people and reminded herself she was human, and they were genetic FREAKS.

Aliens gone wrong.

She could not afford sympathy yet.

But her treatment had been good. She was alive without rape. The Bird Men it seemed not as bad as made out.

"I hope your rooms are fine, here let me show you where the film player is," the Bird Man, with the scar behind, said, sliding a piece of gray slate aside.

He displayed a modern film machine, either stolen or of unknown origin.

A horrifying realization overcame Boudicca that Birdmen were responsible.

They were not primitive beasts.

Time to discover what they were.

She sat and gestured for her bodyguard to take a seat.

Before he sat down, he pulled on a chain dangling from the ceiling. There was a sound of metal clogs turning and the room filled with Earth's bright sunlight.

Here sat a considerate man or torturer. She was confused.

"Boudicca," and he says it as if he had known her all his life.

She was alarmed.

His scar was now threatening in her mind. He was also aware she was focusing on it like a centerpiece of attraction.

Mingo has a scar, and her memory is hazy.

He knew from dealings with humans that they saw it as hideous. Now he wished he had not turned on the bright light copying Earth's sunshine.

He knew she was beautiful, not because he and his people were ugly.

Many women wanted him, their motives extending beyond pleasure.

He lacked lasting relationships.

Had many sons and daughters already.

All had died in the wars.

Now he provided for their mothers, but marriage and having a woman around when he lived so dangerously, he **would be selfish.**

So, he told himself. Look at Bran Llyr and Branwan, his friends. They were married.

The Vern's injury of Bran had an impact.

Almost destroyed Branwan.

He rejected that for himself and all women.

So, sat down and ate a red round fruit; hoping to break the silence, get her relaxed, talking, find out what she was to Tzu Strath.

"How do you know my name?" She asks eventually. He could out-wait anyone; he was a bird used to perching.

"I fly, see many things, saw you and Tzu Strath, was curious, fight Madrawt's," he tells her, "for you," and immediately noticed her cringing as if he had just been in a fight.

For the right to bed her.

He was just another Dumezillian.

"When will you return me to my people?"

"When I find out everything about you."

"I am a prisoner?"

"Guest."

"In these circumstances, the difference is trivial."

He finished the fruit, stood up, and left; she needed time to think. At the door, he stopped and says , "Enemies of the Madrawts are our friends. We do not betray our friends to them." it was a direct hit at Tzu Strath.

"Are you going to molest me like that ape Dumezillian?"

He sighs. Women were all the same, whether a human or alien or his people, give them bosoms and they thought they had you pegged.

And wondered what Madrawt women were like.

So, his eyes drifted up from the floor to her legs, past the short kilt he had given her earlier that revealed, much by the way she sat.

Both were aware his eyes lingered. Why his eyes hurried up to meet her angry gaze, he laughed. It was the choice left.

She was desirable for a human, and, like women, were aware of it.

Your heartbeat is faster.

Damn them.

"Did you have a good look?"

He tried to reply, but she got him feeling small, so he stammers gibberish.

She had bested him, making him appear foolish and asserting control in his house, which was even worse.

Leaving was his escape; he needed to consult his War Chiefs for the next attack on the Madrawts.

He realized once more that women were alike, except they simply had better legs than you.

Boudicca concluded men are identical, regardless of their world.

She gave him a minute, then followed.

No lock turned.

The door silently opened, revealing two smiling guards staring back.

At least they had a sense of humor!

Birdman love song.
" My heart wants you,
  I am round in my belly.
  Marry me if your heart wants me
  Your love caused this.
  You come together again.
  Love me in the sky.
  Your heart wants me,"

"As told to me, Vern

Lukas, Historian and Imperial Scribe by Boudicca Tzu."

CHAPTER 9 SPIRIT FLIGHT

Madrawt landslips resembled enormous bubble-equipped tanks. Its immense size defined it as transport on tank tracks. They mounted one heavy-caliber machine gun up front. The ship squashed anything in its path flat.

"General Ce-Ra sat in the back of his land-ship watching the inhospitable land roll away like an unwrapped carpet.

"A few more hours and Vortigern will be dead," Reeman Black Hair reminds him with a twisted grin.

"No, he will still live, but slowly dying under your hands, Reeman. The empire will be leaderless, and we will help ourselves to its limbs," Ce-Ra, who trusted Reeman, so he explains everything *(so better hope never ends up on an enemy's rack)*

They knew Alexander Caesar Vortigern made a mistake

coming to Maponos over the failure of the Peace Marriage.

He should have stayed in imperial space and let others die for him as usual.

The order to advance given to Madrawt troops.

Soon, the army would take the human imperialists by surprise. The Peace marriage was to drive a wedge between Tzu Strath and Vortigern.

"Reeman, go finish the captured Bird Man," Ce-Ra not wanting to share any more of his vision of conquest.

Saw himself wearing the human emperor's robes on Earth on Vortigern's throne.

Then, he returned home and proclaimed himself Emperor of the Madrawts.

Who could oppose him with such forces and slaves?

Owners forced slaves to fight or face harsh consequences.

Unlike Vortigern, Ce-Ra governs honestly.

The word of the Madrawt Lord was law, and those who faltered lined the Appian Ways on stakes and crosses.

Why did he fear and admire Mingo Drum, whose cough was the law?

One thing, he concluded smiling, the Madrawts knew how to dish out death and enjoy watching offers suffer.

It was the Madrawt way and made them feared. Their Madrawt ways instilled fear, winning the battle before a single shot was fired. The enemy, if spared death, they became slaves.

And the real threat to his dream was Mingo Drum.

Those birdies understood Madrawt's thinking, and that was the danger. Never fooled into becoming slaves; their types fought to the death.

"The only Madrawt you can trust is dead," a Mingo quote,

"how true," Ce-Ra mused.

And Reeman Black Hair stood beside a table displaying organs. They came from a Bird Man on a table.

He raised his head to observe. *Reeman wanted him to watch the dissection in progress.*

"You could save yourself so much pain," Reeman offered **a lie**.

A lie because the Bird Man knew of Reeman's reputation.

No matter what, Mingo's fate was certain.

If he is absent, no one will report. And if they do? Just another war victim fighting fiends. His Legion Hippogriff stood entrenched amongst the Giant's Road, far from the City of Flaming Crystals. It had the honor of holding the border against the Madrawt's.

All Redman's questions he knew nothing of. He was brave despite lacking the confidence of Lord Mingo Drum Vercingetorix, so how could he know about a human woman? Nor did he know Mingo's war plans.

How could he, being only a warrior?

Reeman knew that too; no one could withstand not telling the truth while he played inside their bodies.

But he did like someone who refused to die like this Birdman. It prolonged his game.

"Finish him," Ce-Ra commands, who is hungry and bored, and the joke's over.

Glen Zowanski paid good money for Birdmen's genes, selling them to the cosmetic industry for those who sought flight. After that, he skinned the subject, as the skin made good lampshades. Some said it acted like a prism because the skin molecules had crystal deposits in them.

The scheming Reeman enjoyed it, and since Ce-Ra had left, he was not hurrying, Madrawt's never rushed things they enjoyed.

*

General Ce-Ra was both right and wrong about Tzu Strath. He was upset at the loss of his daughter. It was devastating, but somehow, he believed she would live; she had his genes in her. Four justifications supported his belief.

Bird people rarely kill humans without a good reason.

With this knowledge, he prepared to undo his emperor's wrongdoing.

"You are not worth it, Vortigern," he muses as he presses the yellow alert button.

His forces would be ready for treachery, whether from his emperor or Madrawt's.

And something General Ce-Ra had not figured; Tzu Strath was human with human feelings.

Ce-Ra's mistake with humans was that he had contempt for them, which blurred his vision because that contempt extended from disgust for their leader, Emperor Caesar Alexander Vortigern.

"Alexander Vortigern, you are unworthy of being emperor.

My troops follow me, not you," Tzu Strath and Tribune Henry, standing behind him, smiled.

All hoped Tzu Strath would seize the imperial throne, and Henry believed the popular populace would back Tzu, too, for he was a hero.

For the rest of the day, Tzu Strath instructed his human and alien friends to be ready for war. Which kept the smile on his tribune's face; he was ready.

Not all humans resembled his emperor.

*

Diviciacus was not like his emperor, so he thought.

He saw his emperor relaxing on his golden throne, engraved with suns, moons, comets, and gargoyles standing for many alien and human forms and beliefs.

His son, Conchobhar, the so-called heir apparent amongst his courtiers, had arrived.

Celebrations were in full swing, with dancing girls attracting the attention of their male audience, for they provoked deliberately.

Many girls' tonight would gain their ambition, a pregnancy, and a small income from the father.

Diviciacus did not blame them because of the bad economic situation.

Officials were corrupt.

The top was rotten.

And Diviciacus watched a Black human woman from some distant planet dressed up like a chicken.

Her ebony skin glistened with sweat.

A minor official threw her a bag of dollars.

The dancer attached it to her bikini bottom.

All smiled, and so did Diviciacus.

The emperor mandated the Temple of Light's Purification Rituals as the sole path to spiritual growth.

However, the girl appeared more attuned to spiritual ascension than his structured ceremonies.

Diviciacus, therefore, threw two solid gold coins at her.

She accepted, and the minor official remained annoyed until he learned the thrower's identity.

Graciously and wisely, he retreated.

It is time for Diviciacus to do spirit flight.

He led the woman away.

His god, Dispater Creator, needed something in return for giving spirit flight; the woman would do.

Equilibrium.

Except Spirit always gave more.

Diviciacus and the woman went to his private ship.

Only his priest guard was present. Priests are loyal to the Temple of Light.

Here she drank hallucinating drugs made from plants while musicians beat skin drums and small Bacchic pipes.

Now we introduce Diviciacus's friend, son, and assistant, Kernwy.

Diviciacus was teaching him to replace him while he cloned for a short while. Next, they would clone Kernwy.

Kernwy's would flush the growing Diviciacus clone down the latrine.

"One must plan, it keeps human society going forward," Diviciacus believed and because of his position, no one was fool enough to cross him.

Alexander the Emperor believed that too!

And because Kernwy was Diviciacus's son, it meant nothing, as he had many sons scattered throughout space.

Unlike Mingo's siblings, who had died in the wars.

Some were not fully human.

If their mothers were beautiful when conceiving,

Diviciacus did not mind. He got rid of them when the women became round.

Space was full of dimensions and colored light that through spirit flight, he could enter.

One could mate the Dispater Creator with his female and animal soul forms.

The imperial doctors had invented a serum, a simple acidic solution that allowed compatible gene strands to pair themselves off between species.

No respectable person in the empire skipped getting this shot.

Experts recommended it for space travelers.

Space was full of rest and recreation planets.

The shot made Cat Woman real, Bat Man solid and was creating new species of intelligent beings on frontier galaxies.

And General Ce-Ra had insisted Boudicca get the shot.

Tzu Strath had insisted she get the antidote…. that pleased Boudicca and not Ce-Ra.

Humans showed their cunning.

Ce-Ra saw an offspring from Boudicca as someone humans could accept.

Madrawt's thought process was flawed; they lacked a moral compass.

Anyway, Diviciacus had been asking the ebony dancer who she was, receiving answers that she was the mother goddess Nerthus, the egg giver, giver of life, who flew across space and time on her spirit chariot pulled by cats.

Now, the shaman priest, Diviciacus, told her she was the goddess herself. She is the chosen maiden; she will become the goddess, aiding the war against the Madrawts.

He continued, insisting she would be in paradise.

She was the envy of all.

Her intoxication made her joyous.

To be possessed by her goddess, then to become her goddess and reside together in the cheerful afterlife.

Diviciacus then smoked his twentieth weed.

Diviciacus then went into a trance.

His spirit would reach out for Nerthus, be owned by her, and travel through space-time, molecules, and physical barriers to General Ce-Ra's mind.

Again, Diviciacus lay with the dancer.

Sexual acts played a big part in preparing the victim for willing sacrifice.

It brought the fever of god possession to new heights.

Then Diviciacus rolled away in a frenzy, foaming, his eyes glazed just as Kernwy strangled the dancer to near death.

It made the dancer excited, so she never noticed Kernwy had stabbed her midriff.

As she was weak and gasping for breath, Kernwy easily stuffed her head in a bowl of water till she almost drowned.

This was the holy triple death Dispater demanded for what he would give in return for Knowledge through spirit flight.

Diviciacus always had to outdo everyone else.

A fourth holy way to die, "Fire," he suggests to the dancer.

If such a thing existed.

So Kernwy watched the dying dancer; she was moaning with pleasure, wanting to be with her goddess Nerthus, the holy fertility one.

"Fire," the woman moans with ecstasy.

"Yes, cleansing fire," Kernwy replies and stands back to allow priest warrior guards

to swing her back and forth before releasing her.

Why hot ashes flew about as she landed amongst charcoal in an open pit.

The dancer did not feel any pain; Diviciacus had fed her so many painkillers she was away with the Fay Folk.

Eventually, the woman sat up and watched her charred limbs fall off.

She tried standing up, but her blackened legs gave way.

Diviciacus shut his eyes. When he awoke, he and his closest would eat the flesh of the goddess Nerthus and be part of her.

Kernwy hoped a less barbaric way existed for spirit flight.

But in the meantime, since it was not him being prepared for dinner, he would eat his fill.

No matter what Diviciacus said, that she had been a willing sacrifice, Kernwy knew drugs helped her not to distinguish reality from fantasy.

Why did she feel no pain?

But spirit flight was about unreal things becoming real.

"When Diviciacus clones, I will become High Priest of The Temple of Light. Things will be different; there will be true spirit flight without eating someone foolish enough to get herself eaten," **so Kernwy plotted murder.**

Diviciacus was going against the teachings of the Temple of Light," Kernwy.

The teachings taught against human/alien sacrifice.

It violated imperial law unless a sacrifice to the emperor.

Diviciacus was losing Kernwy, who was his son.

Kernwy's god gene had awakened.

Imperial Spirit Flight Hymn.

"Your priest leads.

We worship Light.

Your priest interprets.

We worship Light.

Your priest will help our spirit fly.

We worship Light.

　Sacrifice to me."

From Kernwy's secret diary.

Here I, Vern, sacrifice what and to whom? Vern Lukas.

CHAPTER 10 AMENITIES

Little Drum was all jealous girl ape thingmabob

"Boudicca, bursting, gave up searching for the toilet. It was obvious her prison lacked one, so she asked her female guards.

Laughing, they showed her by the touch of a palm on a red crystal a sliding wall to reveal a loo and bath. *It was very private for very private affairs.*

The guards were female and left.

Readers: male guards would put her on edge.

So, she sat down, thankful their seat resembled a human one. There was a black slot she guessed their rudder-like tails went in.

Being civilized, she soon knew she needed a bath and hoped the handsome Bird Man with the scar had not smelled her, and being a beast like a dog had? Then fear overcame her as she knew her month-end trouble was about to begin. These alien beasts may have a different birth canal, possibly smaller, larger, or nonexistent.

Something the Madrawts or battles could not produce overcame her, panic.

This made her summon her women guards. The Bird Man with a scar was present this time and appeared embarrassed when informed by a guard about Boudicca's needs.

Their fingers scolded him.

Boudicca, secure because of her guard's taunts, relaxed, attacked, and berated him. It just shows that girls stick together no matter what species. Males, like dogs, use trees in public parks, so they know nothing of the finer things that keep females of one species apart.

"I am sorry I forgot you are not part of our culture. I should have pointed out the amenities," he says, his scar a bright pink.

Maintaining her verbal assault, Boudicca showed no remorse, asserting that women should always be in control and have the upper hand in dealings with men, regardless of their opinions.

She had concluded that this Bird Man meant no harm to her. How could she ask him about private things, anyway? It was as much her fault as his.

"I did like you to have Little Drum for company," he says without asking, and she changed her opinion rapidly.

A spy for dinner.

And Little Drum scuttled past, showing bandages, and playing up for attention. "Not my idea, it is the king. He thinks you could do with female company," Little Drum complained.

Boudicca did not click; she was referring to the Bird Man hovering over her but to the elusive Bird Man King Mingo Drum Vercingetorix.

The scar, girl, the clue to whom stands before you. Fall down and kiss his jeweled fingers.

And it was a shock also that Little Drum was female.

Upon closer inspection, she was a woman with noticeably short hair.

The Bird Man walked past and made himself at home, while Little Drum sat on his knees. They felt instantly familiar, like old friends reuniting.

"How are you finding our city?" He asks.

"I have seen little?" She felt her period start. "Oh Creator, damn, trapped with my back against the wall till he leaves," she thought.

"I can show you it is lovely at night," he replies, and she wonders what is lovely about living in caves.

She remembered the crystals and how quickly everyone had forgotten them.

Her attention was now towards a more immediate concern: her menstrual cycle.

And he sensed her agitation at his presence and guessed she must hate him. He was an alien beast to her, as she was an alien to him.

He was her captor.

She must be afraid.

Without hope.

But he was not a Madrawt.

He was a birdman.

She recalled being a teenager at a disco when her first

period started.

Embarrassment overwhelmed her upon arriving home.

That is exactly how she felt now.

"I might come in two hours, giving you ample time for your privacy," he reassures, struggling to make her feel comfortable. *"I should treat her like royalty,"* he pondered, extending his hand towards hers.

It would have been better for BIRDIE to tell her he was taking her home to her father, putting her at ease.

She resisted, but his hold was strong. He had tremendous strength, and he easily planted a gentle kiss on the back of her hand.

Like you do a *human* princess, he had seen human movies as a mercenary.

And walked away.

"Jerk," she felt a dirty old man had just bumped into her.

(perfume of the Flowering Forest)

"Well, Little Drum, do you have periods?" She asks.

"Ready to have babies, are we?" the reply.

She requested it; is she cruel to the Birdman, readers?

*

Mingo Drum, the Birdman, felt his hunger, prompting him to consider the woman's needs.

"By Taranis, my thunder god," he exclaims. With this knowledge, he came to an abrupt halt. That explained her mood. He would get double cheeseburgers and Coke from the kitchens. He doubted they kept human food.

They would offer her their food. He hurried back, knowing their food was not what humans ate.

"Lord," the two-woman guards gasped and stood up.

The open door revealed a woman sampling food.

She was swallowing a meat cube covered in white sauce. "You are a master?" she asks accusingly. Then she watched his face pale, and the scar go white as his blood drained because a secret had slipped out.

"Have you never seen a woman before?" Turning slowly, she wore a silken bathrobe that he had left behind. She noticed the color returning to his face swiftly, and the silk still damp from her shower clung to her moons.

THE GAME WAS ON.

What game, the one between men and women since time began?

Boudicca our feline; reader, what say you?

He saw much; she knew he had and was deliberately making him uncomfortable. *She trusted her subconscious feeling that he was not a Madrawt fiend.*

A Birdman who ate human babies. Is this bird taking good care of her and checking the food for potential human consumption? Her media brainwashing was not letting go that easily.

Teasing him as her stress dummy.

It did not help that she was experiencing menstrual cramps and had to explain to Little Drum what she needed.

But the Bird Man could smell the perfume of the Flowering Forest flow from her, like the warm winds around him as he flew high over his domains.

"Satisfied my Lord?" She was being sarcastic. He could not help noticing she was **all women and beautiful.**

First impressions.

Now Little Drum replies for him since he was speechless. "Nice, is she?" Grinning like a Cheshire cat and eyes slits.

The warrior Bird Man fled.

Boudicca enjoyed the trolley's offerings, desiring the recipe.

"Drink, it is a painkiller for women's troubles," and Boudicca took the silver cup that had grape vines etched on it.

"How beautiful. Who made this?"

"The artisans, they do not fight but make beautiful things instead."

Bird Men displayed class structure; she found much to admire and study.

A proud warrior.

"And these cave drawings?"

"Their ancestors."

And noticed Little Drum stuffed the tail of something into her mouth and Boudicca raised suspicions about the menu?

"The painkiller will not hurt. We have been in contact with humans for hundreds of years, it is herbal based," Little Drum allays her fears over the drink.

"Medicines?" Boudicca enlightened.

"Yes, herbs." Little Drum boasted.

Little Drum was a cheeky monkey.

Boudicca looked at Little Drum and her guards and wondered how advanced they were in genetic engineering.

Was it stolen from Stardust Corporation?

She, being human, found it unbelievable that the Bird Men could think independently.

It served as a defense mechanism against the grim reality dawning that these primitive barbarians were not as backward as they appeared.

Were the Madrawts or the Bird people the real threat to

imperial peace?

Was she warming to them *or just one?*

No one labeled her a birdie lover.

"Try some mushrooms," Little Drum offered.

Mushrooms. She liked those and knew now what she ate.

"Where are those mushroom fields I saw?" Boudicca remembered the acres of mushrooms and toadstool plantations under her as she had flown in.

"Yes, our ants farm them for us."

"Ants?"

"Nearest thing in human tongue for you to visualize," Little Drum, "someone must farm while we fight.

We warriors; ants handle refuse with seagulls. Scavengers are what I call them, but Mingo Drum does not want to offend, so he insists I call them *ants*," Little Drum.

"You mean they can understand you?" Boudicca.

"Oh yes, they understand. They have a limited vocabulary. Would you like to meet one?" Little Drum asked.

Boudicca liked it very much, too; the information she was gathering was priceless for the peace of the empire and its citizens.

She verified some prior writings about them.

Bird lovers, they were called; the citizens wanted books about heroes fighting winged Birdmen.

That sold, not books on Bird Men architecture.

The popular imagination of the scribes filled the arenas with Bird Men in fights with imperial gladiators, **who always won.**

And deep inside she felt sorry for the Bird people as she knew Tara 6 would become an imperial colony. She would do her best to help those BIRDIES left to adjust to imperial society. She was the daughter of Tzu Strath; people listened to her because of that.

She could see Glen of Stardust or someone like him already making balconies for paying guests to view the caves with their drawings.

Workers would nicely space the "Do not feed the animals" signs.

Stuffed Bird Men in fearsome dioramas posed in the caves, while real Bird Men would pass by sweeping up the litter.

Imperial peace and stability are certain.

These proud free people needed to be shown that the empire required them.

As much as they needed the empire. They had nothing to fear from the human/alien imperialists.

She could dream on.

But remembering her 'Peace Marriage' brought bile to her mouth. She owned the emperor nothing. He had ordered her to marry Ce-Ra, a death sentence. Loyalties were becoming confused; these people treated her with respect and kindness. She must remember who she was. Yes, keep her identity, yes, the Bird men were using physiological warfare on her.

Were they enemies like the Madrawts were?

She must remember all the horror stories about these people outweighed anything good written about them.

They murdered colonists in imaginative ways.

According to the imaginative scribes.

They liked to trade in beautiful women and alcohol, and she knew she was good-looking.

They mixed up human genes with their own to look less brutal.

Slaughtered the makers of the wall drawings, had not inherited a culture but were the product of escaped mutants from Stardust's genetic bubbling vats.

They ate humans and anything that moved; they were more carrion birds than majestic birds of prey. Besides, majestic eagles did not cook their food, tear it to bits, swallowing chunks of meat; it would be easy to remember them as enemies now.

Their conflict with the empire exceeded any peace.

No official peace existed with Mingo Drum.

People could exploit her, and as they butchered her, they could see her genes floating in a test tube: the artist depicts the butcher as a black crow with the face of an angelic choir boy.

Little Drum must be referring to human/alien slaves and not real ants.

It was her duty to escape as a P.O.W.

"We will finish the snake and take you on a tour of our beautiful city. We are enormously proud of it," Little Drum offered.

"Snake?" Boudicca's stomach tightened.

Birds ate bird seed, carrion, snakes, mice, voles, rats, and other birds.

What have I been eating?

In the kitchen, Mingo Drum instructed his chefs to serve tasty human food.

"Sweet and sour worms, chopped up small so she **will** not know?"

"Sweet and sour chicken."

"Worm is meat."

"Cow, sheep sort of thing."

"We do not have any."

"Give it your all," Mingo could tell his chefs were about to kick him out of their kitchen.

Which proved Birdmen were sensitive to the needs of their guests.

Above, in a well-padded cell that could pass off as a human four-star hotel room, Boudicca examined a spoon; it looked like an owl's mouth.

What did owls eat? she would look for tails in her dishes in the future."

A human love song.

"I am in love,

We are in love,

Let us elope.

To eternity and beyond,

Our love lasts."

Vern Lukas, scribe, to the Bird Man

CHAPTER 11 I AM MINGO DRUM VERCINGETORIX

It beat walking

"Mingo Drum found the human woman with Little Drum amongst the mushroom fields because no one could not notice her from a distance; *she had no wings*. Some mushrooms grew to sixteen feet; some were brown, others white with red spots.

Toadstools grew in many colors.

All for food and medicine.

So, Mingo, on the way to Boudicca, passed a three-foot mushroom, picked off mold, and collected spores.

He said goodbye and left.

But the ants became excited and started running about because of his presence.

"What is that clicking noise?" Boudicca asks.

"Ants," Little Drum replies.

Boudicca, for a moment, took her seriously.

Then reminded herself, captured machines.

Again, a human superiority complex.

Nothing humans could invent machines with AI to serve.

Then an ant appeared.

She jumped and screamed.

Something she was doing a lot nowadays.

As for Little Drum, she patted and fed the ant honey cubes from a pocket to reassure the insect the woman was friendly, simply different, a crazy human.

"They are coming to see Mingo Drum," Little Drum explains, "that clicking is to announce his arrival.

Boudicca also desired to see the Bird Man King finally.

Then the Bird Man with the scar appeared.

Boudicca eyed him up and down, challenging, mirroring his earlier actions.

She admired a man's slender shape; he is a bird girlie.

The scar ran bells.

Ants lowered their antennae to him in respect. MORE THAN *Boudicca showed.*

Why Boudicca kept her distance; those mandibles the Bird Man and Little Drum were standing between could snap you in half.

"I must leave; they want me," he apologizes and leaves with the ants.

"Let us follow," Little Drum prompted. "I dislike being kept in the dark."

"Either do I?" Boudicca followed, too, as she wanted to see Mingo Drum, her father's foe.

Dummy, that was her name.

Now they entered a forest, and she saw a large clearing under a false canopy of vegetation.

Camouflage against aerial recon.

And Boudicca froze.

Phalanges of ants in body armor.

They do not allow you here; away, hurry.

Turning to leave, she looked into the big brown eyes of a lion creature.

She had become lost.

With no weapons.

Then it yawned and licked its lips.

Was she a chewy treat?

No, she was boring.

Also, thirsty. Readers, do lions lick their lips when they are bored?

Someone was tugging her to follow; it was Little Drum who was throwing insults at the lion creature.

A few feet from the beast, she felt safer, noticed the stitches, and recognized the creature as the Maponosian Griffin Lion that had defended her against the Rock Dwellers.

More distance, less fear.

People may be afraid, even brave Comet Fighters.

"He thinks he is the king's best friend, so is better than any of us, I too am the king's best friend and know I am better than anyone," Little Drum complained.

Boudicca wondered if she was Alice in Wonderland.

HORROR upon horrors the Griffin was following Little Drum's insults.

Gad, shut up, monkey!

"Rag, what do you want?" Little Drum asks still, and Boudicca finds that wide mouth was a foot away from her head.

A dribble of sweat ran down her back.

"Gee up, old Rag," Little Drum called upon landing on the Griffon's back.

Rag meant doormat, so another insult.

"One day I will eat a monkey," Rag says .

And Boudicca picked up the thought; it was like picture talk. *No, I have an imperial implant that transmits feelings and changes into pictures.*

Boudicca held onto human sanity desperately.

Rag and Little Drum did not possess any of these modern items.

Rag and Little Drum passed her.

Boudicca had no temptation to escape because there were multicolored mushrooms.

Worse, giant ants about her.

Followed and attempted to grab the Griffon's tail for good luck.

As though reading her mind, its tail extended right under her nose.

It farted.

There must be a renegade imperial surgeon loose here; they *must* have implants like me. However, Bird Land amazed her girlish side, and she searched for the scarred Bird Man.

Another part of that girlish mind!

"Now you gave me a promise." the voice belonged to the Bird Man with the scar that was a vivid purple from anger directed at Little Drum.

Not her.

But she was smart enough to realize she was involved; she had seen too much.

"I guess I will not be leaving then," Boudicca looked at the ants.

He said nothing.

And a boyish part of him was glad she could not leave; *he could see more of her.*

Oh yes?

Anger's purple faded, replaced by embarrassment's red.

He took her to his chambers inside a hollow tree trunk, not hers.

Oh yes?

An elevator to the upper levels of that tree.

The throne room opened to view via a door that exceeded the tree's width.

Illusion girl, all tricks.

A diorama was before the throne.

"Here is Planet Maponos as concerns us, Tara 6 sorry," he says with bile, "you see we possess one-third, imperialists another, leaving one for Madrawts.

Equal shares."

"This is our planet, remember?" he was reading her mind. Saw in her eyes he was cheating, taking advantage of her vulnerability.

He shook his head and left her mind alone.

"You are seeing our last chance to drive the Madrawts out," he was telling her and she was wondering who he was. He must be close to his Mingo Drum to be allowed to

show her this diorama?

"I cannot free you now until I make peace with Tzu Strath, my enemy," he says.

It was '**my enemy**' that **alerted** her to his identity.

"Tzu Strath put a scar across the traitor Mingo Drum," she deliberately waited for a reaction.

She got one.

"What do you know about Tzu Strath and me?" he asks venomously as he sits on his throne. Nothing but his lies, for he is a human void of the warrior code. "

"That in the heat of battle against the Madrawts, you took your fighters and fled," she replies firmly." She knew he would not kill her because she lived.

She had seen his lust.

He wanted her, but his warrior code had stopped his advances. He was the dreaded king.

She had been with the monster.
But she had no fear of him.

He was the scarred Birdman.

She should have guessed from his bravery.

Only Mingo Drum Vercingetorix would have rescued her in

that fashion. *Let us pity him, readers, for he was in the hands of one of the empire's most beautiful **young** women.*

Poor **old** Mingo.

He had no chance.

"I was told that if we were victorious, Tzu Strath would declare war on my people.

Why, then, should I fight for my real foe? Are we bird people, snakes that meekly wait for the pot? No, for even the snake fights back.

And I follow logic, and yes, Tzu Strath put this scar here when I tried to leave," he ranted.

"As you crippled his left leg?"

"He deserved it. We are enemies," he offered.

"He was told you were going to lead your warriors against him in a surprise attack during the fight against the Madrawt," her father had informed her about it.

"I know," he replies, "the work of Reeman Black Hair and he believed rather than Mingo Drum Vercingetorix."

"You are his enemy," she replies after a pause.

"As are the Madrawt's," he answers.

The truth dawned on her; this warrior's word held weight.

She also knew her father had not told her everything about The Battle of Treason. She had taken it for granted that Mingo Drum had betrayed her father.

The media had taken over the victory to foster imperial policies.

She accepted the portrayal of Bird Men as treacherous, sacrificial savages needing conquest, yet her firsthand experience altered her perspective.

She now doubted the "Bird Men" information.

But there was still a nagging doubt that Mingo Drum knew her identity, deliberately brainwashing her to weaken her.

She proposed, "Why not speak with Tzu Strath? He will uphold any honorable peace."

"A hundred broken peace treaties," he stated, "accounts for the missing Bird People." He waved a hand across the diorama.

"Those were peace treaties with Emperor Caesar Alexander Vortigern, not him," she defended.

"And Tzu Strath is his servant," he tells her.

"Tzu Strath is his own man. Imperial policies are changing, and he will not obey his emperor so loyally again." She stood up for her father.

"And he gives his woman to Madrawt's. Why?" He pointed out that Tzu Strath *was a veritable beast.*

PAUSE.

Then she answered.

"I was to arrange a peace with Ce-Ra," half-truth, so she felt she had not exactly lied to him. Somehow she felt he hated liars, and *she did not want him to hate her.*

"United front against us. How wonderful! What one expects of a man who gives his own kind to Ce-Ra to play," he accused, and she felt an icy shiver at 'to play' and bitterness towards her own father.

"The stability of the empire and the lives of billions depended upon this marriage," her father had weakly defended himself.

Why did she constantly inquire whether he would follow an imperial order to blow his brains out? Would he?

Standing there was the noble savage Mingo Drum. He would give no woman to Ce-Ra for playing.

Unlike the Bird Men, the empire's lost honor and valor

shamed her.

"Tzu Strath is a worthy enemy, a good man loyal to his emperor. I wish I had so many minor kings and queens as loyal to me as Caesar Alexander Vortigern has?" Mingo defended his enemy, Tzu Strath, with sadness.

This defense took her aback, and she wondered if he had read her mind the way Old Rag had sent his emotions into her.

"I do not read minds. I read body talk," he explains. "One day, I hope you will tell me the truth about why Tzu Strath gave a woman like you to Ce-Ra?"

He left her to think about that.

She wanted to, but she could not bring herself to blame her father; after all, orders had to be followed. But it was time her father played his own cards against her emperor, who did not deserve the loyalty of brave men.

But the Bird Man returns to declare, "Tzu Strath belongs to himself." Later, he left, and their subsequent lack of contact had justification.

It is a woman's song.

"He is handsome.

Tall and rugged.

Oh, me, oh, me.

I fell in love.

Will he marry me?

Oh, me, oh, me.

I am with a child.

Will he marry me?

Oh me, oh me."
As Boudicca told Vern Lukas, The scribe.

CHAPTER 12   MADRAWTS

Madrawt trooper with laser deflector shield and laser gun.

The Madrawt advance was like locusts over the land. General Ce-Ra had done his job well of building up his armada. Hundreds of fighters took to the purple skies.

Planet Maponos, **huge space battle wagons,** crossed galaxies five times at the speed of light.

Twenty thousand artillery pieces thundered shells into the imperialist positions on Maponos. The purple sky became red from their flames, then black with smoke. A million Madrawt soldiers went forward, seeking the death of their enemies. And cared not if they died themselves, for their god Huitzilopitchli would reward them in paradise.

As soldiers of their god.

The warrior Huitzilopitchli.

Air raid sirens sounded in imperial urban areas as neutron bombs exploded.

Unfortunately, the blast vaporized those without shelters.

The Stardust Corporation got richer, selling shelters for just such a war.

Those in authority were not alone these days in buying shelters to survive.

All desired survival.

Unfortunately, many were just poor colonists, human aliens who owed many imperial dollars to the corporation in air fares perished.

It was an expensive business traveling space.

They had no shelters.

Were any rooms built?

No public shelters existed.

Atomic warheads by the dozen sought the anchored imperial ships in dark space above looking to destroy Emperor Caesar Alexander Vortigern.

They killed many but him.

He was born lucky, and *not his time to die.*

Laser cannon and laser Gatling cannon left white traces in the sky, making night day.

Shells landed cracking, releasing deadly germs into the air to contaminate and kill, some quick, others nice and slow.

Someone planted millions of land mines.

And only each side knew where.

Unlike common soldiers or civilians.

Workers took down road signs.

Nuclear storms began.

General Ce-Ra liked mustard gas, for it was cruel, and like his nature, perverted and dark.

Behold, the land became barren. Space also exploded as fusion bombs amongst the Madrawt transports; just as well, or several million more Madrawts did land thinking, KILL.

And the Legion Hippogriff perished, and Madrawts raced across barren lands.

Only hastily scent Bird Men warriors stopped the advance and King Mingo Drum Vercingetorix ordered the evacuation of the Flaming City of Crystals.

And while the emperor fled, Tzu Strath fought and held the advance in deep Space, for now, truly little of Planet Maponos remained in human hands.

The capital, New Alexander, was void of life. But in tunnels, Tzu Strath's men in paper thin chemical suits waited for the order to counterattack.

And Tzu would as soon as the Madrawts lost the momentum of advancing.

Mingo Drum's territory ants amassed.

Ant Marching Song.
"Click snap.
Our riders are Birdmen.
Clicky snip.
Give us wings.
Click.

Then together we fly.
Bird and ant.
Clack, click, snap."

Vern Lukas

CHAPTER 13 HERO

Baldy the Oliphant.

Boudicca's freedom followed an attack on Madrawt's positions.

She could wander.

Boudicca wondered if Mingo's fate, where roles were reversed, would be imprisonment.

During the days of close arrest, she had time to reflect upon the events that had driven Bird Men and humans to be enemies, so she started seeing things from Mingo's perspective. But deep down, she remembered he was a Bird Man savage.

Something with feathers in a park gobbling birdseed.

And he was avoiding her.

Which annoyed her?

They gave her an additional guard, Old Rag, the lion, whom she tried to win over with kindness before her impending escape.

Hoped.

Then Little Drum told her about the Madrawt advance, and it must be true, for looking out her window, she saw through the fleece canopy armed Bird Men preparing

for war.

"We are leaving the city," Little Drum tells her. "no one must go near the Imperial Sector, the radiation is high," and gave her a small laser handgun. That shook her, Madrawts. Things must be bad.

If she were to escape, she needed a chemical suit.

Was her father still alive?

She yearned to pilot a Comet Fighter—a necessity given the severity of the situation.

This was one reason she became depressive and edgy.

Poor Boudicca.

"Look, another human?" Guards with Boudicca on a damp forest road.

Recognizing Old Rag and the Maponosian elephant beside her.

She remembered them as her other companions.

"Baldy, just call him Baldy," Little Drum says as the Maponosian elephant eyed her with two beady pink eyes.

Behind, Nostradamus walked nervously in front of an ant.

"Yes," a late reply.

Now Boudicca had a faint memory of a shadowy hunchback figure always lurking in the shadows near her father, whose existence they denied.

One of her father's spies.

She was not alone.

It was no longer poor Boudicca as hope built up for escape.

Daddy had sent his spy to rescue her.

Someone captured him. Keep this from Boudicca.

With these thoughts, she deliberately stumbled, falling badly, pretending to sprain an ankle.

This allowed Nostradamus to catch up.

And being the spy, he gave not the slightest hint he knew her as he helped her onto the back of Old Rag.

"Greetings from Tzu Strath, imperial citizen," is all he whispers.

Boudicca pressed his hand.

She understood his mission was to rescue her; not to send her back to Ce-Ra, not with the war started now.

"How long have you been a captive?" She asked as they walked.

Little Drum was not happy; she was jealous, and she was female too.

"Not long," he replies.

"How is the War Lord and the Madrawt War?"

"Ce-Ra has taken all by surprise."

Boudicca understood things went badly.

Where were the Bird Man and his ants? Could he do

anything?

Then the sound of big guns behind.

"We must hurry, the Madrawts have arrived," Little Drum urges.

They will violate the City of Flaming Crystals with their dung and the Rock Dwellers will move in.

"Is all lost?" Boudicca asks Little Drum.

The ape-like creature shrugged its shoulders.

The attention Boudicca received made her unhappy.

"The Bird Man is alive; these are their lands. This planet is only a colony to us," the hunchback says.

Boudicca relapsed into silence. This was not Tara 6; it was Maponos.

"Tzu Strath, I love like a brother. I will not fail him," the hunchback added.

Boudicca understood she would be free soon.

Then a commotion ahead blocked the damp forest road, a mother screaming frantically for help; a small 'chick' lay in her arms.

"Maponosian meningitis," Nostradamus cursed.

They all felt hapless.

But fate intervened, for Mingo Drum is here.

He was dismounting from a lion creature, and Boudicca hoped it was not too late to help.

He ignored her.

"They have not totally vacated the hospital," he says, looking back at the burning city.

His hard gaze revealed his return plans.

She found herself pleased.

"**Hunchback, is it possible to trust you?**" He asks, ignoring Boudicca as if she never existed.

That infuriated her.

"My Lord?" Nostradamus.

"Make sure Little Drum takes Boudicca and the sick child to the Salt Plain," he commanded, "for Little Drum might follow me and endanger you all."

"I will, I give my word," and he held the reins of the lion creature.

Now Mingo Drum looked at Old Rag and Baldy. It was obvious he was mind-communicating.

Nostradamus felt a hot breath over his head as Old Rag yawned over him. His hairs at the back of his head counted the teeth.

Nostradamus understood all too well.

He would keep his word.

"Mother, your child shall not die," Mingo tells her and heads back to the city.

Boudicca felt a rush of pride.

Readers, what do you think? She has fallen for a BIRDIE.

Certainly, her Emperor Alexander Caesar would not do such a thing.

Her father would have sent word to the rear guard to inform the hospital staff, who then gathered the supplies after leaving the battle.

But Ming Drum was going in person. How archaic?

No wonder these fierce bird people obeyed him, apart from Little Drum. Why, she exploited her king's affection.

He gazed directly into her eyes.

Their gaze locked.

Everyone was pleased.

Yes, the sun and moon had noticed one another.

Even Little Drum smiled. She liked weddings.

*

King Mingo Drum Vercingetorix had evacuated his capital rather than fight a pitched battle to fight a guerrilla war he could win.

He also hoped the Madrawts would spare the city so his people might return one day and find it intact! But he was dealing with Madrawts? These aliens are much different in mental outlook from the imperialist.

He had decided it was better than mentally dithering and doing nothing. But the Madrawts looted and set fire to his capital for something to do. The Bird people were only fit to be slaves, to be exterminated slowly by giving their master Madrawt's pleasure.

In dying!

Few races in deep space had bothered to study Madrawt's history.

Those ignoring Madrawts' claims made a serious error.

Conversely, viewing them reveals liars who raze civilizations, accepting only their society.

Only Madrawts lived properly. They only respected and loved their own kind.

Political correctness has obstructed the traditional belief that a dead Madrawt is the only good one.

Waiting a few centuries for a planet to rid itself of nuclear fallout was nothing when the land became available for Madrawt's hunger for farms.

They valued nothing in other cultures and pulled down historical truths that challenged the way they taught history.

Saving technological advances like science.

Especially warfare.

So looted the Flaming City of Crystals and set it on fire since there was no one to rape and decapitate En masse.

It was a war of cultural conflict where one side's survival ensured their gods' supremacy.

Poor Mingo Drum.

Poor Bird people.

Who could see the smoke billowing out of the glass corridors of the city, feel the surging gusts of heat carry red fiery sparks to the forest canopy that ignited?

It was all hot. **HEAT.**

Forest creatures joined fleeing refugees.

The Madrawt army entered the City of Flaming Crystals and perished.

Many Madrawts died because the glass corridors formed an inescapable maze.

Melting glass corridors became tombs.

Burning plastics released poisonous fumes that they inhaled.

Back drafts of fire.

Mingo lost his city, but he had inevitably won a battle that would slow the Madrawts down.

Mingo secured medicine and observed the hospital's evacuation firsthand.

And the fires allowed him, the wild beasts, and his people to escape.

He was a hero amongst heroes.

When he knew his people were on high ground, he ordered the dams opened that irrigated the mushroom fields and flooded the city, sweeping away the Madrawts like sewer rubbish needing flushing away.

He exhausted his efforts to save his people and the forest.

And so, Mingo Drum and cohorts of the Manticore Legion flew overhead as black smoke blackened the purple sky.

And the Madrawts, burned and soaked, could not give chase.

Two new threats neared the Madrawts.

War Lord Tzu Strath had no intention of retreating.

Second, Conchobhar, who had a sizable fleet of his father's, the emperor to lead seeking glory and election as emperor.

And Mingo Drum coughed his grunt, and the winds carried it to the Madrawts and imperialists.

Even animals understood his cough.

"This is my domain,

My word is my promise.

My law is my word."

"**And** he coughed many times as his capital, now a mound of rubble, polluted the purple sky with smoke.

He repeated his cough because his beloved forest was suffering.

Repeated his cough, for he felt the sorrows of the wildlife.

He was a Bird Man King whose mind as thought was alive."

Mingo's Song.

"You want my love.
It is free.
The forests I love.
The pigeon bird of peace,
I love.
Oh, lady, you tease me.
You want my love.
Come to me."

Told Vern Lukas by

CHAPTER 14   THE DRAGON

Rock Dragon's nature scares whatever is in you out.

"The Plain of Salt was the designated assembly area for the Bird People.

Here, they would quickly herd the noncombatants north to the City of Winds.

Since theirs was a warrior society, this meant the young, mothers, aged, and food-producing insects.

The forest beasts refrained from harming them as if under a secret agreement.

A bond existed.

The bond of fleeing fire.

Telepathy to impress the wild beasts not to harm them. These were Mingo Drum's people, and they all knew his laws.

Forest regeneration would follow the fire.

Millions of slow-moving animals, flightless birds, and insects perished.

A vacant city awaited many wild beasts as a new home.

And an army of Nobles and warriors and ant phalanxes was gathering to await Mingo Drum.

When Boudicca saw this, she was glad this gathering destructive power was to be unleashed against their common enemy, the Madrawts.

Then Dispater, the Good god of the empire, gave her luck, for they became separated from the main refugee host while walking an old Wadi flood channel.

"This is not the way," Little Drum complains, alarmed.

Nostradamus looked at Boudicca, thinking of escape.

"I only made a promise to the enemy to ensure your safe arrival at the Plain of Salt."

"Having fulfilled my obligations, we are now safe," he whispers to Boudicca.

Suddenly, a roar echoed off the Wadi walls.

Old Rag pushed past, knocking them over.

Baldy trumpeted.

Little Drum shrieked in terror and ran behind Nostradamus, who gave up trying to free her tight grip that was ripping his clothes.

"What is it?" Boudicca asks Little Drum.

"Ah THAT," the great flying fearless ape companion of Mingo Drum croaked and swooned.

Now on the right-hand ledge stood a Maponosian Rock Lizard.

The Bird Men called it Dragon.

Boudicca and Nostradamus saw a dragon. It had a thrilled

neck.

Steam coming from its mouth.

Nostradamus understood the beast because it was his responsibility.

It drank hot spring water stored in a large abdominal area to aid digestion.

"It does not breathe fire," he tells Boudicca reassuringly.

Now it rose on its hind legs, hissing, tasting the air with a black flicking tongue.

And Old Rag charged up the embankment, but the dragon creature swiped him away with a horned tail.

Now there was nothing between them and the monster apart from Baldy. And none noticed the shadow racing across the ground.

Only the beasts discerned the cough amidst their own stressed vocalizations caused by the Dragon.

A spear then came from nowhere and struck the dragon below the neck. The dragon fell to its knees, having difficulty breathing.

Mingo Drum Vercingetorix was here, driving his long two-handed sword into the base of the dragon's skull.

It died.

Yes, Mingo Drum stood there, his chest expanded, head held high, long brown hair running free under his gold headband.

Sunlight shimmering on his gold torc.

Then he gave his coughing grunt, and the world knew he had killed an enemy."

What Nostradamus reported.

Birdman kill song.
 "Ka, I have killed.
  May all hear my cough.
  Ka, I am lord
  Of flightless beasts.
  Ka."

V. Lukas

CHAPTER 15 THE TEMPLE OF LIGHT

Nerthus, a prehistorical pagan fertility goddess, held sway within the empire for millennia. What did she do with the cats? Your guess is as good as mine.

Kernwy slit the chicken's throat, filling up gold tankards with blood for Diviciacus to drink; of course, for that many tankards, many poor chickens.

This was all wrong, Kernwy thought, *(he knew chickens make good pets).*

The Temple of Light did not teach human sacrifice.

Yet still, Diviciacus drank deeply and belched at the end.

"There is much profit from drinking the warm blood of a sacrificial victim."

Kernwy knew Diviciacus was told it restored vitality and hoped the chicken had a nasty blood disorder.

He desired power; *therefore, we must monitor trainees.*

Why, Kernwy looked at the dark priest, standing still behind his master. Now reminded of the young boy, they had drugged and drained of his blood last week.

They were just make-believe vampires.

And the boy lay on a cold marble slab behind that screen in front of Kernwy for Diviciacus to examine his entrails for omens, the sick, crazy, blooming priest.

The only omen that was present was General Ce-Ra, death.

And Kernwy's guilt knew they deserved death for their murders. Diviciacus was no longer fit to be the High Priest of the Temple of Light, which taught spirit flight and possession to those seeking the Creator, Dispater God.

Dispater was a figurehead in uniting all the religions of the empire to stop religious wars, but since mankind had traveled deep space, it had become plain that there was an intelligent force radiating through dark space, unseen, keeping everything in spirit flight eternally young.

Dispater?

Mankind's challenge: harnessing this power.

The answer was spirit flight and possession.

Enlightenment: feeling unified with existence, God.

"This is our god," "no ours," "this is not God," "our holy books say nothing of this?" And the religious men argued as religion waned.

And then some bright emperor flicked through his computer history files after giving the machine the problem.

And Constantine, a Roman Emperor, had the same problem.

He adopted the Christian belief as a unifying force,

So be it, then; the empire needed a new imperial religion with a new name.

They chose Dispater, who then gave the emperor The Temple of Light.

His church.

That had been three thousand years ago.

Diviciacus had strayed far.

Kernwy slit the boy up, and Diviciacus drank fresh blood.

"We are common murderers," Kernwy says.

He envisioned his High Shaman initiation, specifically the purification ritual.

Kernwy would cleanse Dissipater's church.

Starting by driving a short sword into Diviciacus.

Then, allow Diviciacus to examine his own ebb of blood to foretell his short future.

DEATH.

Yet Dispater's entanglement with God made him visible to ordinary people.

The dividing line was slim.

Dispater unified the empire, and people worshipped him in many forms.

But some stubborn folk did not accept Dispater as God.

They had no religion, nor read holy books. Folk carrying on daily ordinary lives.

Like Boudicca.

Spirit flight was no attraction. To her, god made all

things. She did not worship in the Temple of Light. She worshipped by being kind and caring; and used his name many times. She ate, drank, and had sex with men and enjoyed life. She knew who she was. The light was already on her.

There were billions like her; shamans and priests hated them; they should be in a temple.

And like her father Tzu Strath, the empire came first until the Peace marriage. It was her body and no one else's. The empire, with its rotten top, could go to hell. It was the ordinary citizen who minded his own business she cared for. The families that would suffer under a Madrawt invasion. The kids, the father who worked split shifts for a miserable wage, the wife who cleaned nights, the actual sufferers of failed economic policies.

Now she met a bird who pooped on the roof of vehicles, the birdman.

Poor girl, little birds did that, not human-built birds.

Slowly she was transferring her pillars to live by the Bird people. They had children, not just chicks, sick and old, they cared for, unlike in dozens of human planets.

And as a jewelry admirer, she recognized the high quality of the craftsmanship.

Religious chant of Dispater..

"Om, I am One.

I am you,

I died for you.

Now die for me.

Om, I will give Spirit flight.

Just be loyal to me." **Lukas, Religions of the Empire.**

CHAPTER 16   LONELY

Your kids had wings, cool, wonderful.

Boudicca followed Mingo Drum, who rode Old Rag like some Beast King.

"And that is what my captor is, king of the beasts," she tells herself.

Now Nostradamus, ('Hunchy' so called by his enemies) was silent after Mingo reprimanded him.

"We are going to his house where Bran Llyr and Branwan are waiting for us," Little Drum cheerfully knew that Mingo **was never angry with her for long.**

She was the prettiest ape ever and incredibly beautiful.

As for Boudicca, she watched Mingo's broad shoulders, a field of sweat bubbles that burst into rivers to flow down his tapering winged muscular back where his long brown hair wetted by sweat stuck to the ball of his back, like a lion's mane. His bare skin is deeply tanned and shiny with his body oils.

She could smell the beast on him.

His gold hair band reflected the purple rays of the sun, making it twinkle like it was full of gems.

A golden crown.

Gleaming muscle thighs gripping the flanks of Old Rag, his glinting bare feet where his hidden cat claws were ready to spring out and open an enemy.

His magnetic charisma, animalism, and Boudicca liked as a woman only could, his tight

bottom.

"Dispater God, what am I thinking of?" *She shocked herself and brought up a good human girl. She changed her small daily.* He was worse than an alien, a mutant beast. And tried hard to see him as a winged **flesh eater but failed.**

She thought of the scar, hoping it would revolt her; but made her feel sorry for him, yet it added a ruggedness to his handsome face.

WHAT WAS SHE ADMIRING, *A BIRDIE*. BUT HE WAS, AND SHE LIKED THAT FACE.

Tried to remember he had lamed Daddy, but the anger faded as she blamed Madrawt

planted lies that made allies enemies. How could she feel sexually attracted to the beast ahead?

Because of genetic advances, humans and aliens married throughout the empire for peace and could have children.

Once changed, he would no longer be a beast, an alien, a BIRDIE.

Readers, aliens saw humans as aliens, you know!

She never had an alien boyfriend. She had not met a handsome one to sweep her off her feet until now.

He was not an alien; he was A BEAST.

Mingo Drum Vercingetorix was nothing more than an intelligent bird, and she had better not forget it.

And his rudder-like tail?

It was so long he could never stuff it down his pants at an officer's ball.

Readers, what is she thinking?

A tail reminded her he looked like a monkey but carried it gracefully. It was soft, and the feathers were metallic, glinting purple in the sunlight.

Naughty Boudicca wondered what he did with it while he slept with a woman. *It encircled her, preventing escape.*

Just how did these bird people propagate their kind? She did not know!

On the wing?

Some said it was.

Others like pigeons in a park.

Oh female readers, is Boudicca giving away secrets?

So, she chided herself for having improper thoughts but still giggled.

Just then Mingo turned; the right side of his face caught the sun and flamed purple.

His eyes glowed yellow like an eagle.

Beast, but what a beast, she concluded.

He smiled, melting his stern face into a bowl of friendly warmth.

He was almost human; she guessed.

"He is Mingo Drum, never forget that" Nostradamus says beside her.

She flushed; he was right.

A beast that had shown more compassion than anyone she had ever met. The hunchback was right; the warrior feared only exhaustion.

Mingo was a king who had sensible, good laws.

Mingo, a hero of his people.

Mingo, who was becoming Superman to her.

During the conflict, Mingo united his people.

Mingo, her noble barbarian.

Her:

Mingo Drum Vercingetorix saw himself as none of these.

Just a lonely warrior who felt the weight of responsibility from aging and killing. He was a man who bedded many females, for he had an urge inside him that needed relief and made him male.

A male beast.

Who had many sons and daughters?

But killed in the wars.

He understood a warrior belonged in battle, so how could he ever raise a family? There was only war these days.

He was grateful to all the women that bore him children. One day, one would live.

His offspring shared his DNA; however, he championed their liberty, even unto death.

In FREEDOM.

And as each child died, some of his heart broke.

He had loved all his children.

He loved his people as if they were his children, too.

He saw Boudicca as different.

She was human.

Mysterious.

Stirred his inner lonely parts, and her beauty was a spider's trap.

She had entered his life when he longed to settle down.

All understood his weariness, shared by his people,.

He would like to watch his children grow and reward him with grandchildren to

spoil.

Boudicca is exceptionally beautiful.

She would have HIS handsome children, rear them in safety in a human world.

A warrior, he knew.

Walked like one with confidence.

He respected her, as he did all women.

He wanted to bring her to his room, as he did with other women.

I was just unsure how to proceed.

about it, she was human.

This man was macho.

And especially Little Drum, who could really gossip, did not confide his desire.

Lonely should be his name.

A birdman courting call.

"Hear my sweet chirps.
I sing to you
My lovely.
Hear my sweet chirps.
Build a nest for us.
Have our chicks.
My lovely.
Hear my sweet chirps."

Mingo and Boudicca: I heard this.
                              Vern Lucas

CHAPTER 17 CONCHOBHAR

Conchobhar, son of the emperor, surprised them all by ordering his ships into battle. They had expected him to run like his corrupt father, but he was his own man.

His father wanted all the ships to accompany him back to Earth. He knew his son Conchobhar was not doing battle for his sake but for his own.

To bravely show fearlessness.

But his father knew Conchobhar wished him dead, for a live emperor prevented him from assuming the throne under emergency powers that the people would grant him, the Electoral Senate as Protector.

Bribes would confirm his appointment; his army would enforce it for life.

So, a lone battle wagon limped back to Earth; morale low amongst the crew, for they carried a fleeing emperor who had not even given an order to fire a single shot.

Vortigern had dealt a death blow to the concept of empire and freed Tzu Strath and others of their imperial bonds. They thought of Conchobhar and the War Lord Tzu Strath making a stand against the Madrawts.

Shamed into depression and simmering rebellion.

Time for a new emperor.

On the spot.

Even Diviciacus was not happy.

And they disliked this High Priest as they saw him as a barbaric witch, akin to Rasputin from the old Russian Empire,

Diviciacus' defense involved inspecting entrails for omens.

Yes, the empire was cracking open, *like Humpty Dumpty the egg.*

And the emperor sought solace in his private chambers with young maidens, drink, and a lone violinist to provide melancholy music.

While his empire burned.

*

"Prisoners my Lord," Reeman Black Hair says with excitement.

General Ce-Ra stood still, watching the thousands of human/alien P.O.W.'s parade in the dusty square of the Madrawt Maponosian capital Meconium.

At its peak, the purple sun glowed in the Mediterranean-like climate.

P.O.W.'s enduring hours of sun felt like desert dwellers.

"Separate the strongest and send them to the slavers," Ce-Ra replies.

Reeman Black Hair had hoped not to spare anyone and sulked.

"Spread the word through space's media networks about what happens to those who resist us," Ce-Ra said again in their air-conditioned room.

*

Reeman Black Hair acted decisively. So, with glee, he went about organizing their doom. Reeman Black Hair planned to line the Appian Ways into Meconium with stakes and crucifixions, so their moans would lull him to sleep at night.

The screams of hell horrified humans but left Madrawts unaffected.

Imperialist politicians had mistakenly judged them on their own corrupt values, which were not high.

Madrawts viewed humans as corrupt, weak, and deserving of their fate. The strongest went to slave pens, and their genes would survive for good slaves, keeping the slave market prices buoyant, which explains why General Ce-Ra was a rich man.

He conquered.

Many prisoners fought beasts and gladiators in the Arena.

The crowds loved Ce-Ra for donating slaves to fight and bringing their families to watch, which is why he became a household name.

These spectacles showed the rest of space what Madrawts thought of aliens (humans included), with contempt; *it also made many of their enemies realize they had to fight to the death.*

And the arenas made sure Madrawt children grew up with that contempt surviving.

What did Alexander Vortigern do?

With the Senate's approval, he sent a messenger carrying a million imperial gold dollars to the Madrawts to negotiate peace.

Ce-Ra was pleased; he could now finance his war against the humans.

You see why they despised humans. Money was like a god to them.

It was to Ce-Ra, too, and he, the benefactor, could spend it like a god. It brought power, women, wine, song, an easy life, and soldiers and money corrupted humans, making their conquest easier.

And the messenger with the imperial dollars was one Morag Constantine.

A nervous junior diplomat career woman of merit.

Of no great family.

Rumors circulated about her appointment as ambassador to a remote planet.

HER promotion was to the Madrawt capital Meconium.

Poor women!

And as she passed down Appian ways, she was sick because the stench was overcoming.

See, Madrawts promptly left the fallen bones, which farmers later repurposed.

Readers, we humans do the same. After Waterloo, first false teeth makers, then fertilizer sellers. World War One trench horses' treatment—sent to glue factories—reveals much.

Yes, are we MADRAWTS?

They ground bones at Golgotha; the place called Skull Place.

Anyway, General Ce-Ra gave Morag Constantine an audience, took her gold gift of peace and channeled the money into his private accounts and not back to his master's on his home planet.

The money would build up his OWN PERSONAL ARMY, his. Soon, soon, he will be emperor of the Madrawts and the humans/aliens. 'Lord of the Madrawts' they would call him a god.

And as a sign of contempt for the human emperor, he manacled a silver chain to Morag's

throat, and after dragging her about his court, lay with her. She would become his pet monkey.

Being an intelligent monkey, she would learn many tricks.

And he gave her a cup to beg, and the Madrawts laughed and put silver pennies in her cup which Ce-Ra kept for himself.

"You are a lucky monkey," Reeman Black Hair tells her," he likes your blond hair and blue eyes."

Morag Constantine wished she had never been born.

But fate had given her this road to travel.

And as for Vortigern, he sent her family his condolences.

"Your daughter is missing in action."

And signed by an underling in the War Department."

Song of Morag Constantine.

"I am without love.

In this alien land.

Who will rescue me?

I hear birdmen coming.

Someone who will eat me will rescue me.

I am without love."

Told me, Vern Lukas, Historian, and Imperial Scribe by Reeman Black Hair

CHAPTER 18 SNAKE SEASON

Rock Dweller.

Mingo Drum Vercingetorix walked with Boudicca.

He had no remorse; life demanded he struggle on.

And Boudicca saw him as a bat with its wings folded around itself. Later, she would learn more truths about the Bird men from talkative Little Drum that those wings were a shield against the sun's hot purple rays.

Now Boudicca felt confused because he had killed the Rock Dwellers as a beast.

Now he acted civilized, closely influencing her, very different from that beast.

Mingo intrigued her.

Boudicca felt defenseless as her womanly instincts stirred.

"That is my house," he says, pointing to the top of a mountain in the distance.

Boudicca reckoned it would take a day to reach it, then without asking, he hauled her off Old Rag's back. Her heartbeat was faster; was he making a play for her?

But the lion beast understood and went and stood beside Nostradamus, who assumed the worst until Mingo Drum told him to mount.

Nostradamus, who assumed the worst until Mingo Drum told him to mount.

"Climb onto my back. There are riding straps," Mingo says, showing her leather stirrups.

She was a relieved and confused woman.

The part that was relieved was called DECENT.

They titled the confusing section "WOMAN."

Boudicca shook her head.

Mingo's face was blank of emotion.

"There are many poisonous snakes in this area," he finally says.

"I will take my chances," she replies, not mounting.

He nodded, smiled, ran, and jumped into the air. At first, he skimmed the ground.

Titled his rudder tail, gained height, then was soaring, traveling back to the city.

"He is right; this place is terrible for reptiles. Remember, birds evolved from dinosaurs?" Nostradamus tells her.

"This is the way to his house. Continual road usage would drive the snakes away,"

Boudicca replies, hoping.

She looked around; the wadi contained pristine plants,

lacking any roads.

Why should there be? Birdmen fly.

And they walked on.

"Do not worry, snakes fear me," Little Drum boasted.

Boudicca remained unconvinced.

"Just wait and see." Little Drum implied they would meet snakes soon. Also, Boudicca noted that Little Drum had edged closer and seemed nervous.

"Mingo should never have left; just wait till we see him. I will pull his ears and chaff them.' Little Drum, "I hate snakes, they do not have legs."

And many shadows darkened the land.

Looking up, they saw Bird men and women, many float beds, warriors, and refugees

seeking new homes to live and die in.

"What is that clicking noise?" Boudicca asks.

"Ants." Little Drum.

Both humans looked about.

And black and red ants covered the land five hundred feet below.

"Mingo will lead them soon against the Madrawt's. The ants have been good to us, breeding many warriors for this moment," Little Drum informed freely.

Again, the humans looked at each other.

"What about the settlers?" Nostradamus asks.

"We do not hate them as much as the Madrawts," says Little Drum. "Bird people hate nothing except Madrawts." Her politeness prevented explicit mention of humans.

"And snakes," she adds.

PAUSE.

"Tzu Strath as well. He is a terrible human. If he does not pull his settlers out of Mingo's lands, the ants will sort them out." Little Drum could not help her mouth, for she was a little gossip.

Boudicca and Nostradamus exchanged glances.

Tzu must be told so bombers would arrive to resolve the situation.

By helping the Madrawts, do you agree, readers?

The hate cycle continued.

Mingo's plan, using ant fear to drive settlers away, needed Little Drum's help. Boudicca hated snakes, cold things with dead eyes, like sharks ready to bite you.

Suddenly, just like that, they came upon you.

And one did too.

A dull yellow sixteen-footer.

Birdmen just in front of them?

And a Birdman NCO, seeing them coming, hailed them, recognizing Little Drum relaxed and approached.

"I will tell Castle Artebrate that you are on your way up. Just in case some eager young one laser you," he says about twelve feet away when the yellow snake reared up from nowhere.

And bit him in the neck.

The poor bird man clutched his throat, staggering backward.

Then the yellow snake bit his stomach.

It was some nasty snake.

Anyway, the birdman was rolling on the grass now. And Boudicca froze; the snake was watching her with cold eyes. "I want to bite you too," it says to her.

But her eyes picked up a hazy vision of birdmen and ants running to them.

And the NCO had stopped vomiting.

He was dead, only bubbles of foam around his mouth popped as air slowly escaped

his lungs. His face was black, eyes puffed shut, his back arched wickedly, limbs stiff at odd angles.

Boudicca could not move. She was terrified of snakes.

It was those snake eyes; they held you like a dumb rat waiting to be eaten. The snake sensed help coming and clearly wanted to check its surroundings.

Little Drum fainted and slid between Boudicca's legs; *she was terrified of snakes too.*

Now the two red ants with the original NCO had blundered into at least six more yellow snakes coupling. The interruption understandably annoyed the yellow snakes as it was mating season.

Lo snakes matched the red ants' speed.

A shadow raced across the ground.

None noticed it.

A large thing seized the initial snake, blurring the vision. That made her move, so she picked up Little Drum and hurried backward, where Baldy stopped her. She felt the Maponosian elephant trying to send her images of what he wanted in her mind.

And she understood and allowed Baldy to use its two proboscises to set both upon its back; she was not arguing; the elephant was huge. Here her bare ankles and legs were now safe from snakebite, so relaxed and felt her muscles shake and knew if she talked, her voice would tremble.

She hated snakes.

She had a phobia about them.

Some people hate spiders.

Poor Boudicca, for they had stumbled upon a group of Yellow Dust snakes the most deadly on Planet Maponos.

One snake survived, biting a red ant's eye.

The other red one, watching, attacked, dividing the snake into six pieces using its mandibles.

But the bitten ant shook violently.

Boudicca was afraid it would go nuts and kill everyone with its mandibles.

But a soldier approached and communicated with the insect.

Lo, a headshot, spared the ant the poison's effects.

The remaining and attacked the dead snakes that littered the ground, shredding them into wafers.

"They were the best of mates," the soldier explains.

That ants could be mates, filled Boudicca with amazement and surprise. She looked at the purple sun above her, hating this planet of beastly wonders. She craved her own worlds and her father's ship, with its human artificial sunlight.

And made the mistake of judging all planets by Earth's standards.

Forgot all about Earth muggers.

She longed for carpeted corridors to walk down.

And forgot about Earth drug barons.

She wanted air conditioning.

And forgot about climatic change.

She wanted shopping malls.

And forgot about economic wars and poverty.

She wanted good male company.

And she momentarily forgot Mingo Drum Vercingetorix.

Enjoy a hot bath following a night out, a meal with reliable food, a dance, and male companionship.

Planet AJAX offers this as well.

She wanted home to civilization.

Then, a coughing grunt ripped through the air; the first snake's head hit the ground. And Mingo Drum landed with the headless snake coiled about him in its death throe.

Nostradamus squeezed Boudicca's right hand reassuringly as he had read her mind.

He agrees, "He is not human, he has made a kill," he whispers softly.

Mingo unwound the snake and threw its body at the remaining red ant to mutilate in hate.

After the red calmed down, the birdman soldier gathered up the snake tissue.

Snake was high on Birdmen's menus.

Boudicca did not want dinner that night.

And Mingo hugged the remaining red ant, sending it mental pictures of sympathy.

The ant responded by touching his body with its antennae.

Boudicca wanted home.

Poor human girl stuck in an alien world Maponos, but wait a moment, was it not Tara 6, a human world?

And a missile zoomed overhead, turning a Madrawt fighter

into a ball of flame.

A reminder she was an imperial Praetorian Comet Squadron Officer.

Now, if she allowed herself the pleasure of homesickness, she would prove her father, Tzu Strath, wrong in not allowing her into close combat.

She had much to live up to.

Being a woman became impossible.

"That is why we do not walk. Now we fly space fighter woman to Castle Artebrate, my home," Mingo Drum challenged.

He knew her, so her acceptance was low key.

Did he know she was BIG GIRL TROUBLE?

And finally noticed he was not alone; he had a cohort of his famed Manticore Legion with him.

Later she would ask herself if she had seen correctly that the entrenched bird men she saw had no membranous wings.

They were flightless.

And without chemical warfare suits, why?

*

Nostradamus watched his master's daughter's eyes go wide with fright as Mingo ran and spring as if leaving a poolside diving board.

"The man has power and light bones, a bird definitely," he tells himself.

Mingo Drum headed downhill because of her extra weight, so the ground skimmed by Boudicca, and she had a worm's eye view of the grass looking for snakes.

Anyway, flies and bees knocked against her face. A large rodent creature like a gopher zoomed underneath them.

Frightened.

She passed over some green snake slithering down the hill and was glad she was not walking.

To her, the hillside was alive with snakes.

The Birdman knew otherwise.

His kitchen staff hunted here regularly.

Only dimwitted, venomous snakes ventured into daylight.

Maponosian snakes are now smart and dangerous, cunning like foxes.

The Bird men's predatory intentions meant a fight for survival was unavoidable.

(high-pitched moans)

Like the Birdman against the Madrawts and human/alien imperialists.

Under Mingo Drum, Birdman tolerated snakes unless they invaded homes—a frequent occurrence given their slithering.

Anyway, the cohort was soon flying beside Mingo Drum.

And Boudicca felt a strange beastly pride as she was part of the formation. They wore tight bronze body armor for show, as it was useless against modern weaponry. Plumed helmets adorned their heads, and they carried an assortment of choice weapons.

About Mingo, they carried their standards and carnyx horns and drums.

It was all about the show.

Glamor and valor help mitigate the harsh realities of war.

Humans dream of flying like birds. And now she was doing it. She wondered when peace came. Would Birdmen hire themselves out throughout the empire as transport?

Her imagination was wild.

She saw herself flying through the streets of the empire's capital, New York, Earth, where the old United Nations building was now the Electoral College of Senators of the Planets, refurbished, of course.

Making a stir flying about on the back of *her* birdman.

The Bird Woman Boudicca Tzu, Planetary Times magazine, would print. Look at her father's anguished face when she arrives at a military ball on the back of her Birdman.

"That is my daughter," he acknowledged his daughter. Otherwise, she denied his fatherhood. Just then, a lone Madrawt fighter appeared and broke the Bird men's formation.

Only its first surprise swoop caused casualties, and when it returned, the Bird men were swarming all around it, easily avoiding the cannon fire and filling the cockpit with lasers, and the fighter flew to the ground exploding, one less Madrawt.

The Madrawts did not have a chance. Boudicca admired the Birdmen's tactics; she would remember them in case she had to fight.

Then she saw a parachute. It was the Madrawt navigator.

So, several members of the cohort went wild and flew near him/her; Boudicca was not sure. They played a horrid, cruel game; they stuck lances into the Madrawt, then cut the lines so the navigator fell gathering speed to the ground below and snakes.

Boudicca exclaims, "Murder!" recalling the Bird men's story. They rarely took prisoners in battle; when they did, they sacrificed them to their gods of war and kept their heads as trophies.

And King Mingo Drum Vercingetorix heard her.

So sent a mental picture to his carnyx blowers, and the air was rent with strange high-pitched moans.

"Stop," he coughed, and it was like a sonic boom.

His men hovered about the navigator wanting to take a trophy.

"We have a human guest," he reminds them.

His men flew to him: why?

Boudicca saw Birdmen ground troops approach.

Leaving, she expected trophy theft.

A Madrawt head.

Witnessing troops perish. She understood that a direct hit on her comet would swiftly end her life, but trophies were barbaric. Tzu Strath was right, they were snake eaters.

This was against civilized convention.

"We are not on Tara 6, but Maponos. These are winged beasts," Nostradamus says.

She shivered, wishing she were back on the back of Old Rag. Whom or what she rode now was a matter of conjuncture?

"My people hate Madrawts. Madrawts nail our children to their walls and give us no quarter," Mingo tells her. Her people did, too, and gave Madrawt no quarter. She was being hypocritical.

"Does that mean you have to behave like Madrawt's?" She felt her disgust out of control. She hoped to make *her* birdman civilized but knew she could not, so she raged deep down.

"You have not seen the news yet. Wait till you do?" he replies. She did not know he was referring to the impalements of one thousand imperialists, her tribe."

Manticore Marching Song.

"We are birds on the wing.
  We fly in formation.
  An arrowhead.
  Fly birds of the wing.
  Like eagles, our kin.
  We are birds on the wing."

Vern Lukas

CHAPTER 19 CLASH OF CULTURES

Little Drum.

"Castle Artebrate was a hollow mountain covered in wildlife, and at the top:

Amidst falling snow, soldiers, refugees, priceless art, and machinery rescued from the Madrawts journeyed towards the City of Winds to avoid enemy seizure.

So, landing on special platforms, Boudicca noted that many individuals in the cohorts rested on special metal rungs set in the walls, like sleeping bats.

She glanced down to inspect if droppings were covering the floor.

What a wicked sense of humor.

It was not, of course, "Nostradamus, they are toilet trained," she jokes.

Unfortunately, Mingo, who walked ahead of her, had good

hearing. What bird did not?

He turned and faced her. "Will you and your friend join me for food?"

"Yes," for she wanted Nostradamus' human company.

"Good, by the way, we shall eat bird seed, and we use disposable nappies," then left her. He *also had a wicked sense of humor.*

At first, she took him seriously, then laughed.

She still had much to learn.

The man possessed humor; or was it avian?

Anyway, they took her to the king's women's quarters, where she saw Bird women with children getting tickled, and some breastfed,

Others changing smelly nappies, others nursing many children, orphans, or a daycare.

They made good mothers.

They loved their children.

His children?
Many were heavily armed.

Ranks showed no gender bias.

Many flightless birdmen again.

"You will be safe here," the voice belonged to one of her original female guards.

"What is your name?" Boudicca asks.

"Keira."

"How quaint. What does your name mean?"

"Black-Haired One," and Boudicca noted the Bird woman had long, silky black hair that set off her green eyes.

She was beautiful.

The other guard says, "I am Gwenda, the White-Haired One," she too was slim and pretty, and her hair was silvery.

None wore much apart from gold chest coverings laced with gems, leather shorts, and boots. *Maponos was a hot planet.*

Boudicca thought of Birds of Paradise. Who could blame Mingo for having many women?

Heard the underworld highly prized the Bird women for the sex slave trade.

She disliked the idea of dating a Birdi.

Mingo Drum was an exception.

Oh yes?

Soaring through the stars close enough to touch. *Her bird, oh well!*

She was dreaming of **HIM**, Mingo.

Deep down, she was a romantic. She *was full of hormones.*

And guess what? When she entered her room, she found other humans present.

SHE WAS SHOCKED, to say the least.

One was a boy, and the other a young adolescent female.

"I am Hamon Ma," the boy offered a handshake.

She shook it.

"I am Hart Woo," the girl bowed.

"Just call me Boudicca."

And as Boudicca made herself familiar with her surroundings, they swapped events.

Hamon had been traveling with his family to make an olive farm in the imperial desert sector. Then Madrawt's raided and missed him. Walking into Bird Man Lands, Mingo Drum took him himself.

Although Mingo treated him well, Mingo had promised him his release one day.

"To stop killing his people, he wants us to understand Bird people," Hamon explains why he was here.

"My situation mirrors yours; departure is not desirable." Hart Woo, lounging like a cat on a sedan chair. "I have no reason to return to Maponos' imperial sector."

Boudicca noticed the word Maponos. She had not used Tara 6.

Hart Woo dressed like the Bird women guards, with the addition of a long blue sun reflector cape that hung across her shoulders fastened by a gold torc.

The boy Hamon wore a white toga and kept glancing at dark blue shorts. Hart Woo wore, whose cat-like position must have been having a tortuous effect upon the

adolescent Hammond.

Boys will be boys and girls, girls, Boudicca.

Birdmen paired with whomever.

It created a robust gene pool.

"*They need children, warriors needed to be replaced,*" she remembered the Historian and Imperial Scribe Vern Lukas' writings, "*If parties of either sex agree to lie together,* they do. Both parties will be the child's parents upon birth, resulting from their union.

Brought up by the mother.

Bird women made caring mothers.

The father visits and supports the mother.

Sometimes other children are born from the same father. Usually, a bird woman has many children to several fathers; it is good for the gene pool.

Also, both sexes attend warrior school, but usually, the woman does not join a warrior

legion: by age thirty, they have several children to mother.'

Why Boudicca looked for stretch marks on Hart Woo, with relief, saw none.

Their life embodies valor and chivalry.

Society cares for the mentally ill.

People love and cherish children of either sex. Both parties contribute to feasts and celebrations: the weighty dowry does not exist, only laughter and gaiety under the surface of the warrior, both male and female," V. Lukas.

*

King Mingo Drum Vercingetorix was absent for several weeks from his Castle Artebrate, as he was engaged elsewhere for war, makes one busy.

This was both a relief and displeasure to Boudicca, who saw herself as a sexual prize for the Birdman king after Hart Woo admitted she had lain with the king several times, for like Boudicca she was curious.

Now that made Boudicca disgusted; Hart Woo was in her late teens, and despite the age difference, Mingo might be several hundred years old.

"I became sexually active at high school; besides, I am old enough to bear chicks," Hart Woo.

Mingo Drum was not house-trained, and this child lacked proper human parenting.

"I intend to have chicks, strong ones who will grow up as warriors and kill our enemies," Hart Woo.

"But you are a human child," Boudicca says, not admitting she had become interested in boys at high school too.

"The mother goddess blessed me at twelve. Bird women

mate when their blessing starts," Hart Woo referring to the monthly curse. "Do not call me child' again. This is not the empire where it is okay to ask for high school girls and brothels, and freedom of choice exists.

Birdman's lands value children highly and prohibit brothels and the degradation of motherhood.

I AM NOT A CHILD,"

Boudicca shut up. Mingo's attempt to garner praise for his people from Hammon and the girl proved unsuccessful.

Instead, promoting free-living ways.

Imperialists could date high school chicks called Hart Woo, but Birdmen were not aliens; they were birdmen, to be shot on the wing and sent to taxidermists.

"I shot a Madrawt with an arrow while outdoors. Of course, the teachers finished him, but it was my kill," Hart Woo, "I was no longer a child, and he had just lost another child in the struggle against the Madrawts.

He needed comforting. They are celebrating those who killed an enemy... pause... and not all were Madrawts."

"Shut up Hart Woo," Boudicca.

"You are not my mother; stop telling me to be quiet, then Hart Woo stood."

She seemed calm, and her classes at Warrior School had taught her some discipline.

She was stunning but lacked sense. Boudicca would speak to Mingo Drum about her. If he wanted humans to leave his people alone, then he did better stop pawing human kids.

There were human/alien imperialist hunting parties out wanting revenge, and that happened heaps, to rescue a girl from the clutches of an evil, dirty, lecherous Birdie.

Mingo Drum and his people saw things differently; they did

not sleep with children but with those ready to bear fine sons and daughters.

It was a clash of cultures.

Her Birdman had been fooling around with human girls. Readers, are you joining a hunting party to avenge the girls?

*

The beast himself was on the Plain of Salt, leading a vast army of ants and allies. He would send his legions first against the Madrawt lines on the wing to soften the Madrawt's up. Next came the ant phalanxes, the Elephants' Legions, and the Legions of Lions.

They were exactly that.

Wingless Bird men sat upon their backs.

He would reserve his Manticore Legion and the newly raised Hippogriff Legion.

And an imperial plane flew over on reckon taking photographs that came up instantly on a computer hundreds of miles away.

Tzu Strath saw them.

There were alert orders given.

Was Mingo Drum about to attack them?

He hoped not. He, too, was preparing his forces for a counterattack on the Madrawts.

Intelligence suggested General Ce-Ra had taken much of his army back to his home planet to back his claim to the Madrawt imperial throne.

He hoped for them to be flushed down a black hole.

SHOULD HE SEND IN HIS BOMBERS AT THE BIRD PEOPLE?

STOP THEIR ATTACK AGAINST HIM.

And intuition lit his mind. It came waltzing into his right temple. It is the perfect time to bomb the Madrawt lines, making it easier for Mingo to conclude matters.

MAYBE HE SHOULD DO NOTHING AND LET THEM WEAKEN EACH OTHER, TENDERIZING THEMSELVES FOR HIS COUNTERATTACK.

What should he do?

He would attack the Madrawts..

Why, even Conchobhar had agreed to help.

He would ignore Caesar Alexander Vortigern.

Non-Earth reinforcements: the Birdmen were to Tzu.

The Emperor Vortigern was still trying to bribe the Madrawts off and Ce-Ra was now calling himself Emperor of the Madrawts.

Vortigern's presence proved useless.

And Conchobhar could do with a glorious victory to help him claim his father's throne. Now, on the brig of his ship, I.S. Caesar watches his torturer extract the truth from a Madrawt prisoner.

"Where is Ce-Ra?"

"On Planet Madrawt," the high-ranking officer replies during a pause in truth extraction.

The bottle of nitric acid had stopped dripping onto the Madrawt's groin.

They could have given a truth serum, but it was a Madrawt they had. All remembered the impalements. *See Boudicca, the Bird men were not alone in killing Madrawt parachutists.*

Why did the torturer heat a metal glove that was insulted within and hold it up in front of Madrawt's remaining eye?

His left eye dangled over his chest.

IT BELONGED TO A HATED MADRAWT and must give an unobstructed view of the nitric acid burns.

See, Conchobhar had learned much from his father. The imperial throne awaited a new heir.

The memory of a thousand crucifixions along Madrawt Appian ways. His revenge matched the public lust for justice to win support for a new emperor who was more suited to the times.

The Emperor Alexander Caesar Conchobhar would restore glory to the names of Alexander and Caesar.

He conquered planets, razed civilizations, and then earned the title "Great."

"It is the truth." It was a squeak from the remains of the Madrawt officer.

Conchobhar nodded to the torturer, dressed in black, standing for death.

The heated glove on the prisoner's tummy melted everything within its reach.

His passing was loud.

"No quarter given," was Conchobhar's order.

It rallied his men, who thirsted for revenge.

He understood the masses better than his father did. The Madrawts were a God-given.

opportunity to make his name, as did the War Lord Tzu Strath's win popularity for winning victories.

He would be greater than Tzu Strath.

Ruthless, like Attila the Hun.

A soldier emperor at last and the troops did flock to him.

Tzu Strath was always loyal to the empire and would swear loyalty to him or die.

The Madrawt corpse, ejected from the ship's screen, floated

away towards the Madrawt sector.

Twenty-three other Madrawt sailors were aboard the ship, taken from a skirmish.

All would visit the man in black who caused optical problems.

All would float towards the Madrawt sector as jetsam.

Conchobhar's song.

"I am Alexander,
He is Caesar.
I am Genghis Khan.
He is Caesar.
I am a warrior prince.
He is Caesar.
I command, and they follow.
He is Caesar." **History of Conchobhar, V. Lukas**

CHAPTER 20
COUNTERATTACK

Imperial stormtroopers used thrust spears with explosive heads, similar to diver's anti-shark devices.

Mingo Vercingetorix was sad. He loved her deeply, but he was a beast.

And she is human, worse, the daughter of Tzu, his enemy.

"War Lord Tzu Strath received the order from Conchobhar to execute all Madrawt prisoners.

He told his alien, aide, Tribune Cedric Henry from New

Neptune. "I refused, even as emperor."

The tribune knew Tzu Strath rejected brutality. Henry had been with Tzu Strath for seven hundred years plus since the New Neptune Wars.

Following his people's surrender.

Tzu Strath had spared them all.

But his people were not Madrawts.

Tribune C. Henry understood Conchobhar's game better than Tzu Strath.

"He is going to declare himself emperor," Henry truthfully declares to Tzu Strath.

"We already have an emperor," and Tzu Strath made the mistake of transporting his own morals on Conchobhar.

Drug use on the prisoner revealed Ce-Ra's absence, mirroring Conchobhar's findings.

Also, they could exchange Madrawt prisoners for their own men.

The tribune understood that Tzu Strath's honor did not influence his men's behavior toward the Madrawts.

The best Madrawt was always a deceased one.

"I wish to get a message to Mingo Drum, and if we did, **would he listen**?" Tzu.

The tribune foresaw this and prepared himself. "I will go."

Tzu prioritized his friend's safety, choosing departure instead.

Following the discussion, Henry departed.

"Mingo Drum belongs to the old school too, my lord," Henry smiles.

*

Mingo Drum Vercingetorix rode a red ant to war.

Behind came ant phalanxes.

Above soared his Manticore Legion.

In front, Ce-Ra weakened Madrawt's lines, siphoning troops to strengthen his position as Madrawt Emperor.

But deep in a Madrawt trench, a Madrawt captain interrogates humans.

A hapless family of six.

The mother now lay on a fold-up military green bed.

Someone abused and then strangled her. The captain always wanted to lie with a human who held Madrawts with contempt; **now, who was boss?**

In the next flap room, they chained her husband, awaiting shipment to a gastropod farm as slave labor on a Madrawt planet.

These gastropods are bus-sized.

They would ship his three daughters out as troop comforters.

His eight-year-old son was going to be a mascot, dressed in yellow with bells. Mascots went up front with the troops like pipers of Scottish regiments.

If he survived, he would go to some farm or mine for free labor.

"Alien dung," the captain threw the father a gnawed antelope chop. He better eat, food would be scarce...... *not all belonged to the old school.*

Then Mingo Drum attacked.

A few weeks later, he returned to castle Artebrate, much haggard and worn out. He strode into his room and threw his bronze war helmet onto a chair. It was purely decorative, lasers existed.

The helmet bounced onto soft rugs from mountain goats.

He avoided arguing with Boudicca. He displayed a trophy—the captain's head—plus a new companion, young Thomas.

And now an orphan.

And no longer dressed as a mascot with bells; Mingo had gotten him dressed in leather trousers and the boy had wept in his arms as they buried his pappy.

He never made the snail farm.

Madrawt murdered the man during the Birdmen's attack.

Mingo had the wounds covered. Not to disturb the boy's mind further.

"I see you keep human concubines?" Boudicca asks from the door of his bedroom.

Someone's scar became a vivid scarlet.

It throbbed flakes of dried dirt, pinging onto the rugs.

"I have no human concubine," he replies, forcing himself to be calm.

"Hart Woo," A reply; *Boudicca, the human girl, she picked her time exactly right.*

Pregnant silence.

He nodded his head. "The young human girl?"

"Young is not the half of it," Boudicca screamed; she was sure of herself.

Mingo poured himself a large tankard of chilled non-alcoholic wine, full of vitamin C and thirst quenching.

He poured one for her and wondered **who this human thought she was** to come busting into his private chambers like this.

He knew, as we know readers, she packed what it takes.

Keira and Gwenda had failed their duties.

So, the man fell heavily onto a cushioned sofa, **sprawling his legs**. He drained his tankard, belched and offered her to refill.

Oh, dear, she made a horrible mistake; she went to the wrong wine pitcher. He noticed, but he kept numb. **What a sod reader?**

The pitcher resembled Bacchus, a reveler, while Boudicca, unaware of the alcohol, spoke freely.

Or was she aware women are craftier than the fox?

He was thirsty and dusty, *his excuse.*

She noticed his sprawled legs and other parts that aroused her towards BACCHUS.

"Hart Woo is sixteen years old, a child," Boudicca pursued.

The man nodded his thanks for the refilled drink and sipped it **this time.**

"And how old are you?" He asks, eying her up.

He was another lecherous Mannie.

"Old enough," she replies, draining her drink, "to know the difference between

right and wrong," *but not the difference between alcoholic and non-alcoholic wine.*

The man finished his drink off.

He is primarily a beast, a creature of flight, yet she disregarded Nostradamus's warnings: she had confidence he wanted her. She made him notice what she packed.

His fate was determined.

"Hart Woo has no home in your world," Mingo offered back. "I did not forcefully take her; she lives in my world, not yours. I only took what she gave me; she wanted to be one of us.

She is welcome to live with us."

"And when your world vanishes? What then? Who will have her in her own world? A birdie lover destined for the brothels," Boudicca retorts.

"That life awaited her; she is young, and I have been in human cities. Vice is everywhere. Speak to your people first, before you speak to me," he advised.

Now she put down *her* tankard. She was leaving Castle Artebrate with Hart Woo and would be back in a Comet Fighter.

"**You** will not let that happen," Mingo tells her.

He had passed responsibility for Hart Woo onto her, for every other human in his rooms and lands; the no-good scum had pushed their lives onto her; she was a squadron leader, not a social worker.

Boudicca saw herself as an outpost of human civilization.

A guardian of morals.

Boudicca always had to get involved.

A human with ideas and much energy.

Boudicca rejoiced at Thomas's rescue from the Madrawts.

But worried about Thomas's moral safety after what had happened to

Hart Woo.

Boudicca was some woman, and Mingo Drum Vercingetorix knew it. She knew it.

Comes from being Tzu Strath's daughter.

Boudicca knew he was a brave, morally misguided warrior, but she could correct that.

Apart from the scar, he was handsome. In fact, the scar emphasized his manliness. He was caring, strong, and almost human.

Someone cut out her work.

He thought about her a lot. For a human, she had spirit and was healthy. They have good white teeth and a trim figure of their own.

Yes, Mingo, buying a dog, are we?

Then the heavy herb wine hit her.

This was a warrior society. Wines were treble strength of human wines in imitation of the potent brews their gods drank, which ended in divine orgies.

There were women in heaven.

Someone's head spun.

She staggered backward.

Mingo Drum caught her.

At least her tongue was silenced.

Mingo Drum took her in the wing.

"Remember, he is a beast first, a bird on the wing," but she ignored

Nostradamus's warnings.

It was a dream-like world.

The drink made her want to keep the beast.

Oh yes?

He can exhibit civilized behavior.

Like someone dragging a tiger around a park on a chain.

She possessed a body that could captivate any man.

And together they would create a peace with her father, which meant she no longer had an emperor and PEACE MARRIAGE.

Tara 6 (Maponos) would be a new Eden of enlightenment.

Of understanding.

She loved her bird men.

Oh dear, any comments from readers?

Remember the month, reader; what is the month? I do not know.

And Mingo Drum loved her in his feathered ways.

*

In three months, she, Cleopatra, and Caesar made dozens of angel cakes.

THEN AN UNEXPLAINABLE ACT OF GOD ARRIVED in Tribune Cedric Henry, with peace offerings from Tzu Strath.

And Little Drum assured of her importance led the human tribune straight to Mingo Drum.

"**My Lady** Boudicca Tzu," Cedric's first words instead of "Greetings King Mingo Drum!"

And Mingo stared at Boudicca **in astonishment**.

Here stood the daughter of his enemy; and yes, his scar showed vividly.

And throbbed a bit.

He was being boyish.

The Birdman believed he had been the victim of an elaborate trap. He might have seen clearly if he was not involved. Besides, Tzu Strath would never approve of his liaison with his daughter!

Just bad timing on Cedric's.

So, Mingo walked away, leaving Boudicca standing in her new body armor.

Her green eyes cleared from his humiliation thrust upon her.

She had an idea she was pregnant from making angel cakes.

NOW she felt used.

Why reveal it? It is a female confidence.

Hurt that a barbarian alien king could think lowly of her. Tribune Cedric Henry would think the same if he knew she bedded Mingo.

Her dream of enlightenment ended.

Besides, Henry was really a second-class citizen of the empire.

A conquered alien. Dreaming of dating Boudicca was taboo; she had a track record of avoiding aliens and did not consider them handsome enough or worthy of her. It was one thing for aliens and humans of the lower classes to meet. Another is for the siblings of War Lords, presidents, and kings.

"What is it, tribune?" Boudicca asks.

"This man came to see Mingo Drum," Little Drum answers, smiling.

Cedric looked at Little Drum. He **knew she was Mingo's daughter**.

Boudicca sighed. Her Birdmen account will sell; her identity was key.

"Lady Boudicca, your father wants peace with the Bird people; perhaps you can take advantage of your freedom with Mingo Drum to help?" Cedric.

Boudicca crushed the rising flush to her cheeks.

Cedric talked; her mind was away with Mingo.

"Have you quarter's tribune?"

"Next to the other humans."

Although she tried to see Mingo, he refused, leaving Little Drum to tell (him) of the peace plans.

"You three are humans. What do I do?" Mingo had asked

Hamon Ma, Hart Woo and Thomas.

"If you make peace, I will never be a warrior," Hamon Ma moans.

Mingo put the boy on his large knees.

"Yes, you will; where there is intelligent life, there is war," he replies sarcastically.

"I want home," Thomas sobs.

"I want to stay here with you," Hart Woo lovingly.

Mingo knew Boudicca was right. He was wrong to sleep with this young human woman.

No one raised her to be a Birdwoman.

There was a difference.

He breathed deeply, gritting his teeth.

Cursed the weakness of a male.

He cursed himself for not being wise.

Cursed himself for his lack of self-control.

He cursed his gods for making him weak.

Cursed himself for being in love with Boudicca.

He cursed himself with a chastity vow.

Cursed himself for not being human.

Finally, **he** cursed himself for not saying "**No**," more often.

"Hart Woo, tell Boudicca to take you and all human's home."

Hart Woo cries, and the others join him. He hoped he had made the right decision; Lady Boudicca was right; these were human kids, and he was destroying their lives, muddling their minds with Birdman rhetoric that would soon be extinct.

He should have sent them across the imperial lines long

ago.

Had sent others, why not these?

He knew it was selfishness, an insane desire to be accepted by humans, that had made him encourage them to stay.

Had craved human understanding.

The great Mingo Drum Vercingetorix was lonely and insecure, and humans could cure it. The Birdmen were vanishing, humans were to blame. So, he craved their bones thrown from their eating tables to survive.

What was Maponos compared to the vast imperial empire?

And Boudicca had made him see it.

"You have used me," Hart Woo.

"Not so," Mingo says and covers his ears as the children verbally tear into him.

He sat there with open legs, his sword between his legs.

An alien in a diminishing world but an expanding human one.

"We are not friends. I am a Birdman, and you are humans; humans are always dominant; on top, we can never be friends; our worlds are too different; why do none of you fly?" he wanted release from his own pains over Boudicca.

And the human children ran and sought Lady Boudicca and poured out their hurt and hate for their adoptive parent who now spurned them.

The air was rent with a horrid grunt.

At first, her heart reveled in joining the children in hurting the beast king, but later, as she tried to sleep, she remembered everything said to her and felt the hurt against the beast king crumble.

This happens when trying to sleep. Thoughts keep you awake all night.

"I long to comfort you, Mingo Drum, but you spurned me, for I am human. If it is an acceptance you want, then I accept you, beast king," and the words 'beast king,' she knew deep down she thought of him as exactly that.

His barbaric culture was more uncouth than many alien worlds. He was a barbarian; she saw him as that, a noble beast in conflict with itself and her invading world.

Her heart cried for him.

With every passing hour, the grunt diminished, echoing death, betrayal, and pain.

Silence gripped the bird people; they feared the unknown. Castle Artebrate was a tomb. People within knew they should prepare their death chants.

They did.

And the savage Mingo understood the environment more than her own kind. He displayed kindness and love, often focusing on those young and old.

He knew his people were archaic and practiced horrid things like collecting trophies from battles.

Heads.

They had to embalm them; otherwise, the odor would be unbearable.

But when she compared him to Emperor Alexander Caesar Vortigern and the High Shaman Diviciacus, the man was innocent of the charges against him.

Mingo Drum did not partake in sexual perversions.

Humans did.

He was full of honor and valor.

His word was law and worthy.

Laws are good for all within his domain.

His words are trustworthy and good.

Mingo Drum Vercingetorix was not to be taken lightly.
Nor forgotten once met.
And he would not stop his grunt of death.
His people saw what he grunted against,
The unstoppable tide of alien immigrants, humans.

It sounded less like an animal's cough, more like a death rattle.
Their coughs were the chorus.
Tribune Henry had seen this on his own Planet Neptune.
Boudicca blamed herself for hurting her man.
The human children were heartbroken.

"Cough,
　And it went on,
　Cough,
　And on,
　Cough,
　And on,
　Cough."

Oh, Boudicca, your spirit collapses as you have judged wrongly and know it.

As told me, Vern Lukas, by the human children, he set free

CHAPTER 21 TRUTHS

Flight, birdmen could fly, humans could not, bred jealousy

Nostradamus remarked, "He released us all," as he glanced back at the mountain with a fortress. He would not have done the same.

Because of his nature, he suspected a trap ahead.

Boudicca forced herself to look back.

HE had ordered her to go.

She went.

Would beg no man to keep her.

AT LEAST SOMEONE HAD PROMOTED HIM FROM THE BEAST!

Now she knew she had fallen in love with him.

She was Boudicca Tzu.

A human woman.

The bandaged Bran Llyr came to see her off with his lover Branwan. Boudicca had become good friends with them, requesting and reading their history books with them while King Mingo Drum made war in the purple skies.

As she read, many human/alien truths about the Bird men became lies. She discovered they were always birdmen.

Human mutants were second.

Stardust discovered them and immediately realized their dream of flight.

Glen Zowanski's Stardust Corporation had moved into his genetic department, wanting their genes to twine with human/alien genes.

Flight was big money.

Zowanski's dream was to market them, except the Bird men took offense at being asked to donate their genes for cash, alcohol, or drugs.

It was not manly or womanly.

They were not racehorses!

Stardust used kidnapping to get its way.

Birdmen were just big chickens.

Zowanski was a fan of 'Chicken Run.'

Then Stardust found out Birdmen could impose their wishes upon certain animals on Tara 6.

They immediately caught birdmen.

A mess of things made.

One result was the Rock Dwellers under King Dumezillian.

Then the age-old conflict between pioneers and natives broke out into many wars that reached their apex in the Tara 6 Wars.

Birdmen called the Madrawts' arrival the Wars of Survival; these wars, they will tell you, continue.

Bird-men cities once blanketed the planet.

Currently, they control approximately one-third of Maponos.

The genes developed by the Stardust Genetic Corporation had entered the planet's gene pool.

FLIGHTLESS Bird men.

Birdmen's civilization faced collapse.

They retreated to the wilderness, taking secrets.

Until the Bird people elected Mingo Drum Vercingetorix as their War Leader.

and allied himself with the Great War Lord Tzu Strath against the Madrawts.

And Tribune Cedric left with counter-peace terms and two willing Birdwoman.

Keira and Gwenda who had bewitched him with their beauty. He convinced Nostradamus he needed them for information because they were close to Mingo.

"Remember the ants?" Henry had said.

Tribune Henry showed a darker side of himself that lurks within us, and if we were not careful, it appears triumphant. And his cravings for these two women would bring a future ill.

To join his harem and to suspend them from the ceiling in bird cages.

FOR THEY WERE BIRDIES.

Had convinced Mingo Drum the two Bird women would show Tzu Strath the

Bird people were beautiful people.

He lied, *readers, here a son of Adam.*

*

"They believed something created them before all other forms," Boudicca says. Her company had guessed Mingo meant a lot to her because she constantly spoke. About him. Mingo had let her go; *he believed it was the human thing to do.*

"Created after the friendly spirit created the Heavens and more gods to help run the creation. Princess and princesses of Heaven, they call these gods.

Angels?

Planetary deities then enforced this law.

Spirits of the rocks, trees, and waters. Very caring Bird people were towards their environment because of this.

So Diviciacus branded them pagans to whip up anti-Birdman feelings," Boudicca moaned.

Tribune Henry knew the problem. His world changed upon the imperialist's arrival. His people worshiped water as they believed all life came from it. Now they knew there was no water god sitting on a throne in heaven.

But Diviciacus had branded them primitive, needing enlightenment, and sent in his shamans.

Trouble, it caused the War of Missionaries, Neptune 6.

Millions refused to refute their water religion and so died at the flaming stakes until Tzu Strath arrived and stopped it.

Cedric owed his life to the War Lord.

The Birdmen were lucky the Stardust Corporation had started the wars and not Diviciacus.

Now Cedric stared at Boudicca, trying to guess if Mingo had lain with her. That would give him an excuse to have his two bird women.

Her tummy looked swollen.

"But the adults know gods do not sit about Heaven pulling their fate lines. It is all to do with spirit, just like Diviciacus says, spirit possession," she babbles on.

Nostradamus looked at a Bird thunder god totem carved on a rock face as they passed through a narrow chasm. Trophies hung from metal rings set in the walls.

Madrawt heads.

Some spirit possession, he thought.

"They also know that Heaven is a mirror of their own society. Their belief is that their spirits wander in a spirit realm, coexisting with our realm after death.

Their belief in fairies mirrors this.

They might still believe in their afterworld if they were winning instead of losing.

Mingo himself will cease to exist when he dies, like his people. Ceasing to exist, so will the memory of him and their after world," Boudicca.

Cedric Henry knew his master would have many problems with his daughter when they got home.

She was a bird lover.

Unhinged.

Believed in Fay Folk.

Might be pregnant with Mingo?

"They also see Mingo as Mahbon reborn, a young god who is supposed to usher in a golden age. It means the son of Light.

Unfortunately, Mahbon sacrificed himself for the good of the species.

The enemies of the Bird people nailed him to a tree and adapted the story to fit their human needs,

and Madrawts.

They see Vercingetorix as the reborn Mahbon, invincible with superhuman powers."

Nostradamus felt sorry for Mingo Drum Vercingetorix, who had met the beautiful Boudicca.

A single woman held the power to destroy an entire culture.

Boudicca's love song.

"What have I done?
Ho ro ho ro.
I spurned my love.
Ho ro ho ro.
I have his love.
Ho ro ho.
Why did I spurn him?
Ho ro ho.

Now my heart breaks.

Ho ro ho."

As told me, Vern Lukas, by Nostradamus.

CHAPTER 22 INTRODUCING

Rallying Battle Standard

Five and a half years have passed.

A four-and-a-half-year-old lean little boy whose tummy protruded with his latest meal ran out of the bushes in front of the red ant Mingo rode: masses of blond curls hung from the boy's head.

He also wore the harness of a warrior, small size, of course.

Mingo did not want the boy's presence in the marshaling area until the child ran to him, shouting, "Daddy!"

"I cannot be mad at a child." He says to his aides.

"Color stripes hand him up."

Color Stripes Kenala did so, breaking the stern wrinkles to wink at the lad as he

picked him up.

"Where is your mummy?" Mingo asks.

The boy jerked a finger towards a pile of rocks.

"Nanny, take the boy to Castle Artebrate, I will see him shortly, "and allowed the lad to open a leather pouch on his thick waist belt and take one, two, three, and when told enough, four more dried fruits covered in wild honey. He stopped being greedy only after his father promised a toy.

Mingo looked at Color Stripes Kenala.

The man was nearing retirement if Birdmen warriors were lucky enough to retire.

Kenala had served him well.

He was the Manticore standard bearer, and it was a personal honor as the standard

was a rallying point, and the enemy knew it.

And all knew Manticore meant Mingo Drum Vercingetorix.

Hit the standard, hit Mingo Drum, wipe out the Manticore Legion, and wipe out the Birdmen Nation's heart

The heart was Mingo Drum.

"There are many Madrawts on the loose Kenala," Mingo muses. Mingo had been pressing Kenala to retire for years, but the continual war had demanded Kenala's

experience.

Now Mingo ordered Kenala to escort his son home and always guard him personally. He was getting his retirement orders away from the front line. Going and living his life out behind the lines, growing melons.

Birdmen, like bird cousins, liked melons, full of tasty black seeds.

Kenala picked up the little person walking away.

Someone in the ranks drew his short sword and beat his reflector shield.

Instantly, metallic clashing filled the air sword's rhythm.

The boy Kenala was carrying took out his wooden sword and beat Kenala's shield strapped to the warrior's back. Black crows and gulls took to the air; yes gulls, they get about.

On your next walk, observe the gulls you've overlooked and be thrilled. *Alfred Hitchcock wrote about them, you know, and made a film.*

Kenala could not stop the tears.

This was a great homage the Manticore Legion was paying him.

Now, he was to be the child's guardian. That child was hitting his helmet with his own blunt toy sword, imitating the warrior's excitement.

Color Stripes Kenala knew he had joined a new battle that would tax his strength to the limits.

He would not fail his elected war chief, who held the title of king. He returned the child to its mother waiting at the border.

Also, Kenala wished Boudicca, for the boy's sake, would see his king not as a beast but as a husband.

Five and a half years passed before Mingo Drum Vercingetorix granted Boudicca and all humans freedom.

Five years and six months later, Mingo defeated the Madrawts.

And Kenala wondered when the wars would end. He liked

the idea of growing fruit, juicy strawberries full of seeds.

Peace would allow life to return to inter-tribal warfare. Of course, Mingo would no longer be the War Chief of all birdmen.

Just King of the Artebrate.

It had been long since they fought the Gododdin Bird men. Kenala had personal grievances against them, dating back almost a thousand years. He sighed, then grinned. He would never grow fruit.

If he only knew.

Anyway, the human empire was now split in two.

A brief history of Vern Lukas.

Conchobhar, Emperor of the East, sat on his red throne in his palace on the Planet New Alexandrius. Emperor of half-known human space. Was that enough for a man? He knew the answer. It was not.

His father still ruled as Emperor of the West from New York, Planet Earth.

Conchobhar blamed Lady Boudicca Tzu and Planet Maponos for his curtailed ambitions.

Five and a half years had passed since Lady Boudicca had fallen with a child to a Birdman beast king.

She should have gotten rid of the worm inside her instead of building it up into a life

within her womb.

Now the child could claim the Birdman throne.

Also, the heir to Tzu Strath's Guardian army.

A united threat to his ambitions.

Five and a half years since Tzu Strath had declared his army guardians to the empire with the promise to the populace that the guardians would restore the rightful

emperor and bring in a golden age.

The Emperor Alexander Caesar Conchobhar knew that the little boy Arthur Tzu, and everyone else in the empire and beyond, would be the golden one.

Boudicca's son.

"There is much in a name master?" Lorn Lukas, his First Minister of State, says dreamily.

Conchobhar knew he was right.

Earth's legends inspired Arthur and the Round Table.

"He must die," Conchobhar says quietly.

"Yes, my Lord, he must die," Lorn replies, not clarifying who.

Anyway, Lorn Lukas sought a quiet spot in the royal gardens. Then he plugged in his lead from his personal PCW to the socket behind his left ear.

He continued his writings on the History of Vercingetorix and the early Arthurian Myths.

Lorn Lukas was quite a remarkable man.

He was honest, open, and incorruptible.

Born on the Planet Tara in 6 A.D. 41568, he had grown up with the heroic legends of King Mingo Drum Vercingetorix and the Great War Lord Tzu Strath.

His father had been Chief Librarian of Tara 6 and his mother an archaeologist.

Together they molded their son Lorn well, for he had an inquiring mind, respected the past and dreamed of a utopian future for all humans/aliens.

So Lorn Lukas authored many books under the ghost name Vern Lukas, then published on Tara 6 and **illegal**ly distributed throughout the empire of the west and east.

They were all about a future golden age ruled by Emperor Arthur.

He was planting the seeds of the golden age.

His books were cheap and more popular than the Emperor Alexander Caesar Conchobhar, who wanted the author executed.

This caused riots.

Conchobhar used violence to quell them.

People respected fear. They could love Vern up to the point of FEAR.

*

Cloning was no longer a requirement for longevity.

Medical researchers have prolonged life further through the development of the Master Pill.

One pill that had to be taken daily stabilized the body's protein hormone levels to those of a thirty-year-old man.

The Master Pill was expensive.

It was in great demand, as you can expect.

Diviciacus brief history.

And Kernwy knew Diviciacus had them and seethed inside himself for as long as Diviciacus remained High Shaman, and The Temple of Light would remain departed from its true teachings.

Diviciacus is the son of a peasant farmer from Neptune 12. A man gifted at birth with ESP. He used his talents of soothsaying and fork-bending to his advantage.

So, sought refuge as an orphan with the Christian Order of Piety.

A first lie, he had parents.

He studied for the priesthood, seeing that the Temple of Light was in favor after the Wars of Tara 6, exclaiming the shamanistic values of the Aboriginal People of Neptune 12 to reach the imperial God Dispater.

And saw that the High Priest Zapod, the alien, was not in favor of Emperor Caesar Alexander Vortigern because of his birth.

So befriended Zapod and found himself at court and became the astrologer for the emperor, performing mind and healing tricks so that the emperor favored him and Zapod died of a mystery disease.

Officially, his lack of immunity to human diseases and his extraterrestrial origin explained his death.

Unofficially, Diviciacus murdered him.

Do you agree readers?

And Diviciacus was no longer a poor peasant boy but rich and set about making the imperial religion, the unifying force in the empire.

He ruled it like an emperor.

Kernwy came from Anglo-Indian stock, so he knew about Brahman spirit flight. Why he joined the Temple of Light? See, Diviciacus was his father. The only contact Diviciacus had had with his mama.

Diviciacus saw Kernwy as the perfect front of respectability that the Temple of Light needed.

The human empire was the prize.

Full of divisions.

And on Planet Maponos, Lord Tzu Strath ruled the human

territories and galaxy like he was

A War Lord.

*

Boudicca met color Sergeant Kenala at the well of Urd to take the boy to his human home for six months.

Shame for Mingo.

The boy's life lacked stability, constantly moving.

But he had some exceptionally good friends.

Mingo had given him Little Drum, Old Nag, Baldy, Bran Llyr, Branwan and Kenala.

Mythical friends—for what better could he wish?

His father and mother united for one.

Boudicca hardly saw Mingo if she could help it. He was a bird-like creature with human hands.

She hated him for the BEAST he was.

He deserted her.

Never loved her, just talked his way into her bed.

Had sent her the humans Hamon Ma, a cadet in a fighter squadron, and Hart Woo, now married to an officer and Thomas, adopted out.

BREWARE.

The Well of Urd also held Reeman Black Hair, unbeknownst to others.

"Mama," Boudicca's son shouts, pulling away from Kenala's arms.

"Arthur Verica," she answers, running to pick him up, cuddle, hug, and kiss and the boy smiled with pleasure.

"How is Daddy?"

"Playing with ants. When can I have an ant mama? Daddy

says when I am big, but I am a big boy now. Please make him give me an ant for a pet," Verica pleads.

Boudicca promised.

A big person lies to a child.

Then she allowed him with weak protests to empty the shoulder bag Tribune Henry, her escort, was carrying.

Mama always had presents.

He found some hover car models, wooden fighter gliders, some sweets and story books he would get Mama to read him while he snuggled up to her in bed time nice, warm, cozy, and safe with his teddy, Little Drum.

And he had plans for Mama, he wanted six stories, the loo again, a milk drink, getting chased and threatened with a spank, the promise to sleep if she just read another story. Then try to start the cycle again to stay up longer.

Smart boy.

Reeman Black Hair grinned.

The family scene had not touched his heart. He smiled because he had them. There was Arthur, the so-called bringer of the Golden Age.

Reeman Black Hair gave the order.

Color Stripes Kenala jumped for the boy, falling on top of him.

A Motor EXPLODED.

Releasing blue gas that sent all to sleep.

See, Reeman Black Hair took no chances with his precious hide. He feared the wild animals of this planet.

Especially the friends of Mingo.

And some were in front of him.

He picked up Little Drum and shook her, making sure she

was asleep, then tossed her aside.

Tribune Henry jumped down an embankment. He did not realize it dropped a hundred feet, but he was safe.

A lion and elephant were arena-bound, and the flying ape was a curious pet. He kept her on a chain.

The other captives.

The human escorting platoon he killed, and their vehicle set ablaze.

He wanted everyone to know Arthur's whereabouts.

Ten miles distant, Mingo Drum Vercingetorix was sitting above one of his law menhirs made of black stone.

Below, his craftsmen had just finished chiseling a new law.

It read,

"Let there be peace between Birdman and

Imperials in the land."

He understood his people would never rule the planet alone.

Times had changed.

He was not a fanatic; he had a family, the whole Bird Nation. The young warriors, rave about no peace and shed the last of their blood. As King, he knew many sought ordinary lives, even through surrender.

Peace had come.

This law was the start.

Mingo saw the smoke coming from the Well of Urd, where his son Verica was meeting HER.

This specific son, the sole survivor of the wars, held great significance because of his potential inheritance under the imperial laws.

He had not slept with another female since taking the chastity oath.

FOR HER.

It was now common knowledge.

One does not refuse the most beautiful women who came to seduce to populate

the gene pool with his genes, the best in the population without worthy cause.

He was certain Boudicca knew. He did not know how it affected her, but he had kept his vow.

Ah, readers, he loved her.

So, Mingo rose and rented the air with a coughing grunt. The fast, warm air currents would swiftly carry his word to the Well of Urd.

His craftsmen looked and saw their war leader glide toward the smoke.

Mingo Drum was not a lucky man. His boy Verica was gone, and he knew by the impalements the Madrawts had him.

Imperial vehicles roared to a halt at a safe distance.

Lo Mingo still called the humans 'imperialists' vermin. He still had not accepted the empire's fragmentation. Nor Tzu Strath was his own man now.

Humans were all humans and imperialists from Earth.

Mingo straightened his back and came to his full seven feet, his face drained off emotion. His scar thumped.

There, getting out of a sand-colored armored car, was a man he disliked.

Tzu Strath had already seen him and had the advantage of knowing what he himself had to do.

He limped alone up to the Birdman king.

"Here is the beast that ruined my daughter's life," Tzu Strath.

"Here is the man whose daughter ruined my life," Mingo Drum thought.

"The beast that mimics humans. The so-called king who gave me a limp," Tzu Strath thought and liked the limp, made his men see, has seen action, gave him an expression of an experienced war grizzled general.

"The new human emperor of Tara 6. The human male who ripped my face in two," and Mingo liked his scar, for it frightened his enemies and gave an air of ferocity. It was a good shield to hide the softness inside him.

Tzu Strath declares, "Here is the beast whose army I need against Conchobhar and others."

Mingo thought: "I need this human army to become king and bring about my vision of peaceful law."

Tzu Strath says badly, "Here is the beast that gave me a birdie grandson."

Mingo also says poorly, "This is the person who gave me a human wolf and a human grandson."

Lukas's text: "Life without one another? They joke?"

Whom would they hate?

Who would they fight?

The Madrawts departed the planet temporarily.

Who would they love if Tzu's daughter Boudicca did not exist or her son Arthur the Verica of Mingo Drum had not been born?

The Madrawts?

Mingo Drum and Tzu Strath faced each other, two men waiting to kill each other.

Like two irresponsible teenagers.

The Great War Lord Tzu Strath rested his right hand upon his ceremonial laser sword 'Bright Hope.'

His soldiers fanned out but did not approach.

Mingo Drum's hand rested upon his short sword 'Law's' hilt. He did not have soldiers behind him. He was enough for these *'imperialists.'*

In the skies above, his Manticore Legion was forming, already young warriors eager to kill humans had answered his call, glad war had come again and flying like birds to

his aid.

It was a poignant moment.

Did Mingo know of his legion above?

That explains his arrogance in going solo to Tzu.

Will we ever know?

A popular song on these two.

"They love each other really.

Ha.

Really brothers in arms.

Ha.

United by blood now.

Ha.

Through beautiful Boudicca.

Ha.

Will they kill each other?
Ha.**"** V. Lukas

CHAPTER 23 GODODDIN

Nostradamus in disguise, good at his job, yes?

"And Reeman Black Hair hurried west by northwest to avoid the lands of Mingo

Drum Vercingetorix, so instead crossed Gododdin Birdman's lands.

And Boudicca saw Kenala looked nervous.

But Birdmen feared nothing, for their afterworld was a paradise. They only feared the red suns falling upon their heads and the sea drowning them.

But changes were happening.

Was the old color stripe afraid?

"What is the matter with Kenala?" Boudicca says from her tousled position on the land ship.

"You know where you are?" He replies, watching *the clouds*.

Branwan shoveled closer to Bran Llyr, her lover for comfort.

Arthur could not care as he could ran about the ship with his Madrawt guards hot in pursuit.

FUN.

"Over Tara 6," Boudicca replies. Rarely did she call the planet Maponos, especially when Arthur was present; she was making a human of her son; *others said this was to spite Mingo.*

As love turned sour.

"Gododdin," Little Drum squeaked from an old cage.

Boudicca was ignorant.

People mentioned the name a few times, then quickly dropped it.

No one had really explained Birdman politics in depth.

No one told the Madrawts either, as no one spoke to them.

Except that there were Birdmen living all over the planet calling themselves after where they lived, and Mingo was their king.

Near the truth, but not all.

Anyway, Old Rag was sniffing the air and pacing his cage.

Badly trumpeted.

Boudicca shifted nervously, as if needing a dump.

"Gododdin are the sworn enemies of the Artebrate," Kenala says .

Reeman Black Hair should have been listening. He might have posted adequate lookouts, but he never listened to aliens, especially humans, and Birdmen *just did not exist.*

They came out from the crimson clouds.
The Gododdin came on Maponosian Vultures.

(So, called by the imperialists.)

If the average male Birdman stood between five and seven feet, then you can easily imagine the size of the Maponosian Vultures they rode.

Purple feathered and two heads.

Ugly bald heads and necks, so their dying victims focused on massive flesh-tearing beaks, immobilizing escape by fright.

So came the "lazy Gododdin" as Little Drum called them.

Experts at pirating ships of the air and land, they killed the Land Ship lookouts in the masts with small silent darts through the neck and heart fired from crossbows for a better aim.

Assassin's weapons.

Gododdin Pirates were at the height of the Birdman culture upon Tara 6 (Maponos) before the invasions by human/alien imperialists and Madrawts.

Assassins for hire.

Ninjas of the airways.

Now, under their present ruler, the beautiful Queen Cartimandua, they had not changed their ways, only swept them under the carpet for a unified Birdman defense against colonizing off-worlders.

And King Mingo Drum put up with Cartimandua's ways, for he needed warriors.

But the reckoning between Artebrate and Gododdin would come with peace with the humans.

Old ways back.

Now Old Rag roared, and Reeman Black Hair turned annoyed (thinking he would rip the beast's tongue out and roast and eat it.) The roar defied the landing pirates.

Seeing the savage vulture heads snapping up his crew from behind proved too much

for him, he ran away.

Lots of squelching, cracking, and pain amongst the Madrawts, so who can blame the expert bully Reeman?

The Gododdin caused chaos.

Why, Reeman pulled a safety lever, and a unit on a corridor wall opened. He jumped in; it was a lifeboat. In seconds, the Land Ship ejected him.

Now Boudicca fought her chains as she and Arthur faced a naked Gododdin covered in blue tattoos. It looked like he was going to bring his long sword down and decapitate her son.

> Her lovely little boy,

> > All bitterness and usage of the boy.

as an emotional weapon against Mingo went. Shameful thoughts of having an alien child with flight membranes vanished. HER CHILD WAS ABOUT TO

> > **DIE.**

But Baldy went berserk, smashing the cage with his large bald head to save the boy.

The crack of wood made the Gododdin turn his head. He reeled back from the emerging Maponosian elephant, now within reach of a clawed paw that belonged to Old Rag.

Old Rag did what werewolves do!

Baldy found the screaming boy, whose thoughts of being a big boy were gone. He just wanted **mummy.**

And Boudicca cried her heart out.

Baldy stood his ground over the boy.

Kenala slid a shield in front of Arthur.

Then a dart stuck in Kenala's left hand. Yawning, he looked at it and fell asleep.

Silence apart from the trumpeting and roaring of the two beastly friends of Mingo.

And the Gododdin held consul as American football players do.

We are all familiar with movies.

They would steer the ship back to their capital.

"But who was the boy? They knew of his famous protectors; why was he important?"

As for the Madrawt dead and dying, it was trophy time. They threw torsos overboard for the vultures to feast upon.

Madrawt stew sounds good.

And when the ship docked, the elephant and lion creatures sedated, the pirates approached Boudicca's party.

"We know you," the Gododdin warriors say to Little Drum, for she was indeed famous.

Little Drum puffed her chest out with self-importance. "I am not surprised. I am Mingo's brave friend."

Boudicca cringed as Little Drum tells all in self-importance, silly ape.

The birdmen joke amongst themselves that they had caught Mingo Drum's 'human plaything,' 'human harlot,' 'human wife,' and other things.

What exactly had Little Drum been saying or trying to explain?"

"*I am Little Drum,*

Mingo's girl.

He will come to me.

We are engaged; you know.

Mingo's girl," Lukas, the scribe.

CHAPTER 24   SWAMP DRAGON

Shaman Crocodile teeth.

"The grandeur of the Gododdin capital Torrs was their giant temple. Boudicca had once seen in the air.

Anti-fighter missiles riddled these Birdmen domains.

No one in their right mind flew outside the imperial sector without support.

Torrs comprised swamp islands in an estuary.

A road leading to a temple ended where the land ship docked. Quickly, the Gododdin warriors and slaves camouflaged the vessel with swamp greenery to hide it from the air.

The Gododdin took no chances. They had been driven into the most inhabitable lands.

"Behind us are the polar ices,

  In front our enemies.

We are the last of the free,

Do we fight and die for liberty?"

A common saying by the Bird men before they went into battle.

Anyway' Queen Cartimandua was unbelievably handsome, yet muscular, Boudicca decided.

Similar to a female weightlifter, except she could fly.

The queen's hair was long, black and her gray eyes shone with intelligence. Like all Bird people, she wore light clothes and showed her tanned bosoms as if she had come out of a Restoration Charles I painting.

Mapon had a tropical climate.

Settlers suffered from itchy sweaty groins.

A tinge of jealousy swept Boudicca.

"I wonder why my Birdman king never married her and got himself two kingdoms in the bargain." Soon Boudicca found the answer!

Her audience room had the same picture writing, but it did not depict rural or battle scenes, **but scenes of sacrifice.**

Gododdin had fused polished enemy skulls into a throne. Red gems filled the empty eye sockets.

Standards of her fallen foes adorned the roof, and a large smoking pit was in front of the throne.

All about stood nobles and warriors with grim faces.

Here, Boudicca found her answer why her Birdman king had not married the beautiful Queen Cartimandua.

"Boudicca Tzu welcome," the queen says tonelessly.

Boudicca understood her welcome: prisoner, hostage.

"Is this Arthur, the young king? Bringer of the golden age," the queen purrs, "our golden age," and **her warrior's laugh.**

Boudicca knew she meant a golden ransom.

"Harm the boy Verica and Mingo will kill you," Bran Llyr shouts.

"Yes, Little Drum will want revenge," Little Drum boasted.

SILENCE.

A ROAR OF LAUGHTER.

"The loyal friend Bran Llyr, I have heard much of your exploits, even seen you in Mingo's court.

And this your lover Branwan?" Queen Cartimandua hissed, exaggerating her hip movements as she walked amongst them, stroking Bran Llyr's long golden hair with her tail.

"A champion of Mingo's," she adds, looking about her court.

FORCED laughter. *People respected heroes, and all aspired to be one.*

"What would Mingo give you? One cauldron full of gold?" She asks, squeezing Bran's cheeks so his mouth opens, and he defiantly meets her gaze.

To Branwan's annoyance, she kissed a manacled Bran Llyr.

Bran spat the kiss out.

Why Queen Cartimandua's eyes briefly flared hateful anger towards the Artebrate.

Hated Mingo Drum Vercingetorix, who had spurned her affections for centuries past.

Hated Mingo for being War Chief and King of the Bird People when it should be her job.

Hated all Mingo's friends.

She was forcing alliances with tribes further north. Those tired of sending gold and warriors to help Mingo fight his enemies.

Mingo had defeated the Madrawts with his ants, so they were no longer a threat; now time to settle old wounds!

The Northern Tribes looked at her for leadership; well, Queen Cartimandua would lead them **TO GLORIOUS WAR.**

"Bring forth the sacred dragon," she bellows.

"No," Branwan says .

Boudicca lacked knowledge of the sacred dragon. Mingo had never mentioned it; *after all, she lived with her human father.*

A plank on chains from the roof dipped into a steaming pit.

Shaman priests with skins, headdresses of alligators, and dorsal fins appeared on their backs.

They started throwing chub into the steaming pit, and Branwan begged mercy for Bran Llyr.

Her panic spread to Boudicca, who now pleaded for her son.

"Who, Verica or Arthur?" Queen Cartimandua's irony: Verica, a Bird name, or Arthur, a human name.

Boudicca vowed to never abandon the boy should they survive. His home would be her home; she would not be secretly ashamed of his Birdman ancestry.

"I understand he has some Birdman blood. Not entirely an alien, then?" *The queen referring to his human side.*

But the sacred dragon interrupted them as it lumbered up the plank. Men appeared with long pikes whose tips gave out a nasty electric shock.

Queen Cartimandua took no chances.

Here they prodded Kenala into the room, unsteady because of the sleep drug dart.

The queen knew perfectly well there was nothing sacred about this swamp dragon. But she knew how to use religious power to support her rule.

Shamans backed her as a fertile reign.

Supported the shamans' backs.

Both got what they wanted.

Power.

They were to offer Kenala the dragon, but drugged, he would offer no fight.

And the queen spoke to nobles who gave orders for Bran Llyr to be separated from his friends.

The sacred dragon moved closer to the prisoner, its mouth open, revealing rows of serrated dirty teeth from which hung past meals.

Like the Komodo dragon, its mouth was full of septicemia bugs.

The past bits looked humanoid.

And Bran Llyr did what I, Vern Lukas, would do too: kick his guards and put his manacled feet like a rocket into the dragon's nose.

"This is murder. What contest is this? What sport? Where is the noble bird compared to humans? Which evolved closer to the silly monkey?" Boudicca insulted.

That is why Queen Cartimandua waved pikemen in to stop the dragon. She was in deep thought. Here was Mingo's human fancy bit who had insulted her, and Bird people have a weakness.

Vanity.

"Arm Bran Llyr, we would have done so anyway,"

Cartimandua *lied.*

It was done.

Everyone apart from Boudicca knew she lied too.

Then the queen threw the keys to the manacles behind the swamp dragon; she still had murder on her mind.

Therefore, Bran Llyr faced the dragon with a long sword.

And had never fully recovered the use of his left arm from his wound after the Vern bite. But as he says,

"I only fear the sky falling on my head and the waves drowning me," he says as he swings the long sword. He doubts it because it is not his. Your sword has magic that worked for you.

Worse, the sword's magic being from an enemy would work against him. But he was not afraid to die. **He believed in an afterlife.**

And the sword cut deep into the lips of the swamp dragon.

Purple blood splattered Boudicca.

The swamp dragon snapped, but Bran Llyr flew, landing behind.

And kicked the manacle keys towards Little Drum.

"Why me?" She asks.

"Use your tail to get the key." Bran Llyr and Little Drum did so under protest, she might be the bravest warrior, but faced with a genuine threat became the household pet she was.

The tail of the dragon swished and knocked Bran over, so he rolled against Thrust spearmen.

The dragon followed.

"Why me, oh why me?" Little Drum complains as she frees herself.

Now Bran swung his sword and kept hitting the dragon

many times, but the dragon in pain blinded sought revenge for it and pushed Bran towards the steaming pit.

"**Hurry Little Drum,**" Branwan begs as she watches her lover Bran parry snapping jaws.

"I am I am," Little Drum replies, then Branwan is free and unarmed. She leaped past the Thrust spearmen onto the neck of the dragon, her fingers reaching for eyes.

Bran Llyr now thrust his sword deep into the beast's soft throat scales.

Such a gush of blood when he withdrew his sword.

And the dragon snapped a last time, pinning his torso in its mouth.

Branwan found the eyes.

The dragon fell into the steaming pit.

Several times, Branwan raised her head in the air.

Boudicca ran to her child, shielding him.

"*This cannot be happening. Heroes always live,*" she thought.

She last saw Branwan between the dragon's jaws.

Queen Cartimandua knew Mingo Drum would come to avenge the deaths of his friends and meet his own.

Boudicca wished Mingo would come.

Little Arthur, being a little person, cried.

Boudicca wept for him.

A lone head broke the tepid, smelly surface. It was Bran Llyr, but nobody hung. from it, then it sank; *many swap dragons lived here.*

And Queen Cartimandua stood legs apart, hands braced on hips, her bosoms rising with the fast beat of her heart. The fight had been exciting; she would choose a lover soon from nobles or warriors about her.

But she did not want an heir. No one here interested her.

None except one she hated Vercingetorix of the Artebrates. His arrogance went unnoticed; he boasted, "I am the vanguard, the rearguard."

The king's reply showed he viewed himself as a servant to his subjects.

And Boudicca knew why Mingo never married her.

Mingo was good.

Cartimandua was bad."

What my wife Cartimandua told
> me, **Vern Lukas**

"They still fly,

Branwan.

 Bran Llyr.

Lovers in flight.

Never died.

Call them for help.

Heroes always come.

In the sky.

Bran Llyr and Branwan."

CHAPTER 25   HATED FOES

The Sword Law.

Mingo Drum Vercingetorix turned his back on the War Lord and walked away.

Strath Tzu felt insulted.

"You are my prisoner, Mingo," *he was retaliating the insult.*

"Crazy old man," the reply spat back from a crazy, outdated chicken outfit.

War Lord Tzu Strath showed his displeasure by grabbing Mingo's left elbow.

Why, Mingo jumped to face his hated enemy? The *scar coming to life.*

Now Tzu Strath wondered what Boudicca saw in him. **He knew prisoners could come to love their captors,** who fed them.

"You ruined my daughter's life," Tzu says, for he

knew not what else to say. Their ingrained pattern of violence made it difficult to break the mold.

Love each other!

Boudicca had told Tzu about the hidden advanced Birdman culture.

Tzu recognized the threat to Tara 6's imperial colonies.

Mingo was a dinosaur and his birdies.

1, When he gazed at Mingo's angry face, he perceived a savage devoid of culture.

2, Mingo had filled his daughter with wine and a rape drug to mate her.

Birdmen were not eligible for imperial citizenship.

He knew all about Hart Woo and had questioned Hamon Ma about sexual contact with Mingo.

The boy denied all, but Tzu Strath knew Bird men had insatiable sexual appetites.

They said Mingo, a beast, mated with the ape Little Drum his child.

Mingo had soiled Boudicca; *and kept his seed going, grand bird son,* **lucky grandad.**

In Mingo's eye, Tzu bred treachery into Boudicca.

Mingo twisted free from the War Lord's hand.

Tzu waved his escort forward to kill the beast king.

The fragile peace between Bird people and humans was about to break.

Anyway, Mingo drew his sword, and Tzu copied, his laser blade Bright Light, the same one that gave Mingo his scar.

The air hissed and smelled of burning iron.

Mingo saw the escort come and did two things: attacked Tzu vigorously, cutting deep into the human's left wrist as Tzu's gamey leg failed, and then dropped, spreading his wings to escape in flight.

And dropped his beloved sword, Law.

To be fair, he could have killed Tzu. *(All helmet cams recorded everything.)*

Tzu now hated Mingo for the pity.

Mingo had counted a coup.

"For Verica's sake," he shouts at Tzu, meaning he does not want his son to hate him for killing his grandfather.

It bit deep into Tzu's soul. He felt he owed his enemy life, and he did, **but he did not admit that.**

Mingo was silhouetted against the sky and became an easy target for the escort's human laser below.

"I do not want him dead. Find him," Tzu orders. Many pursued a wavering sky figure. Something had obviously hit Mingo.

"For Arthur's sake," and knew Mingo had not heard him.

Then Tzu picked up Law and counted the coup.

And Mingo drifted down a wet wadi for the rains had come. The sudden increase in height from the wadi saved him from hitting the ground, gave him more speed, and he was away airborne.

His brain roared with pain from the laser wound, his vision blurred, and flight erratic, the torn membranes in his wings ripped.

A torrent of water waited below, threatening to engulf him.

What have you done, Tzu Strath?

Forty, sixty, seventy, a hundred, a hundred and thirty miles per hour, the Birdman

king raced.

It took him his last will to avoid crashing into the sides of the widening cliffs. His exposed lower parts raked the top of bushes, so he shrieked.

He lost his sense of time.

He lost his bird skill at navigating.

Just following the River of Skulls.

"I will hand Law back to you personally; with your own sword, I will kill you, Mingo Drum Vercingetorix. I will drive it deep into the soft flesh of your belly," Tzu swore as medics attended to his wrist. That really hurt—*another scar to show off to young officer recruits.*

Some soldiers were happy. Law made up for Mingo's coup. Now they could have their honor returned for not protecting their beloved War Lord.

They wanted Mingo, a king fit, to be nailed to a tree for his *people's murders and wars.*

Boudicca had tried to dispel the myths of IGNORANT SAVAGE. Mingo was part of a dying culture, so they wished for an understanding between the races.

BIRD LOVERS.

Tzu Strath **knew** the races could not achieve peace and understanding. He did not want it changed. A warlord's role in a peaceful era: what is it?

He and Mingo knew their worlds were ending.

Knew his grandson was Arthur, not the other Verica, his name from his bird father. Arthur was not Birdman; he must be human. Arthur must humanize the Bird people.

And thanks to the writings of Vern Lukas, the boy was already a legend, a bringer of a golden age; men had something to look forward to.

Arthur would be an emperor one day. Verica had to die; a Bird boy would never be accepted as emperor.

Therefore, Mingo Drum Vercingetorix had to die too.

When little Arthur was ready to take the reins of leadership, Tzu Strath would join the dust of Mingo Drum Vercingetorix."

I created the legend of Little Arthur and the Golden Age.

Grandpa's song.

"I love my grandson.

Oh yes, I do.

Even if not human.

Oh yes, I do.

I only have him.

Oh yes, I do.

I love my grandson." Vern Lukas, (Lorn Lukas)

CHAPTER 26 THE RIVER OF SKULLS

Gododdin warrior with lunch

Queen Cartimandua allowed Boudicca a great deal of freedom on the outside of the temple for she wanted her seen, *a living coupe.*

And Boudicca found her days occupied being a full-time parent. Tiring work for the little boy demanded much. Play, hugs for bruised knees, and then wounds kissed to make them better.

Worse, to be carried to his play area, and when refused? Complaint of a sore leg to get carried. Queen Cartimandua allowed Boudicca and other women to sit on benches carved as the fruits of the forest!

Boudicca's private thoughts were lonely and happened when Arthur played happily in a sand pit, making castles in the sky.

She weighed life, for crisis brings forth truth and the action of truth in doing what is right.

Selfish, she knew in denying her child full-time love because "I am a squadron leader and mother. *One must come first?*"

Readers and I reject this, due to denied love for a bird king.

When the little one wanted his flight membranes tickled, she tickled them and this reminded her that her son was a beast, not human.

But they were so young that they were soft, not feathers like his father's. Soft and no hint of the savagery of the birdie there, and because there was none, prejudice melted away.

His long, blond, curly hair at least reminded her he was human.

"Do you mind having two names?" She asks him.

"Arthur mummy," he replies, hugging her. The boy with Mingo would call himself Verica and get a hug. He *was no fool.*

She regretted her treatment of Mingo, yet he abandoned her first.

Felt bitter towards Mingo.

If he could only talk instead of being so much flying valor.

Readers, do you agree that we have a couple of idiots here?

"I will be your mother always, squadron leader second, a cleaner of planes, but mother first," she promises the little boy and feels the urge to have a little girl also so that she can play with her long blond curls.

They would be red.

Or black?

There was Tribune Henry; no, he had strange attitudes towards captive Bird women, or what about Mingo? Another birdie as a child?

Sharing Arthur with Mingo held no appeal.

"He is my only surviving son. I want him," he would demand.

"Well, he could rave, huff, and puff like the bad wolf he is," she tells the boy and knows because Mingo's turn at being a father had gotten them into this mess; Arthur was always safe in the imperial sector.

Deep down, she wanted Mingo's daughter; oh well, not at this rate, dearie.

The purple sun tanned their skin high on the temple to the gods of Queen Cartimandua, where they were prisoners.

Below the River of Skulls, the land became swampy. No one saw the body entwined in the branches of a large, uprooted tree, and Mingo Drum opened his eyes now and again, and flies flew off his eyelids. The powerful smell and roar of wild beasts awoke him from his feverish sleep.

He strained and glimpsed the Temple of Skulls, his location momentarily clear, then lost, then found again.

And the estuary water rippled past him as the back of a swamp dragon passed. The current made up Mingo's mind as it swept him to an island.

An artificial island, large and well camouflaged.

Then night came.

And midges.

Again, the roar of wild beasts awoke Mingo. This time, his immersion proved preferable to a midge-infested fate.

He was weak but alert; a water snake crossed his path, and his talons came out.

It tasted good, even raw; he was a bird. The genes of eagles flowed through him.

Then he crawled onto the island.

Technically, he was the High King of the Birdmen, but he was no fool.

Only one temple had steps that were lined with skulls, decaying heads, and freshly cut trophies.

"The Temple of Skulls," he cursed, "Queen Cartimandua." If he called for help, his captors would hold him hostage or kill him slowly.

He knew the Bird man's politics well.

Unlike Reeman Black Hair.

And a leech fell off where the smile broke the skin.

Every beast has its own call, and he recognized Old Rag calling from a cage. It can only mean one thing: his wife and child were here too.

Queen Cartimandua!

If Gododdin caged Old Rag, the captives were also caged.

Then a light appeared and vanished.

A door?

He crawled forward, prodding the grass in front with a stick. It was the rainy season. Flooding forced snakes from their burrows.

Then two things happened.

A Gododdin warrior appeared in front of him and emptied his bladder upon him.

And a disturbed water cobra rose.

The swaying drunken warrior watered it, too.

Hot steam floated off the serpent's head and, in revenge, bit him where it hurt. The man tried to draw his short sword and being in so much pain, dropped his weapon that fell beside Mingo.

Staggering backward for help, the snake followed.

Showing the truth that these reptiles are amongst the most aggressive on Maponos (Tara 6) and bit again.

Mingo saw it as one less enemy; he was no longer thinking about a united Birdman nation.

Mingo, sword in hand, entered the shadows, answering Old Rag's call. Whose bars were stiff vines and roof ponds of lilies.

From the air, one saw a swamp.

Torrs: Gododdin's capital.

Now a doorway lit and remained open as the stricken warrior's friends came to deal with the snake.

Mingo knew once in that light he could lose himself in connecting corridors. The pickaxes beat the water cobra, so it stopped biting and quickly slithered into a stream to safety.

Its wounds bloodied the stream, diluting out towards everything nasty that liked the taste of blood.

Karma had visited the swamp dragon.

But Mingo made it to the doorway. It was a guardroom for those who minded the captives' cages. And Mingo staggered down a corridor, angry that Bird men guards could be so derelict in their duty.

Behind him, a certain reptile slithered in, intent on revenge.

Alone, Mingo went looking for a corridor that would take him to Old Rag, his friend by scent and sound.

Outside, the Gododdin warrior lay silent upon the grass.

His friends, afraid of the snake in the dark, lacked an advantage, therefore retreated to the guardroom for torches or daylight.

Full of beer, they just wanted to sleep.

"Draguar peeing then bitten?!" someone exclaims, slamming the door.

Oh, dear, something had slithered in earlier?

As Mingo went up a level, he heard men swear and furniture thrown about.

"Destroy it!" "That snake—how did it get here?" He hears and smiles.

"Judas, it bit me."

Mingo thanked the unseen for looking after him.

"Zap," it was a laser.

"Gododdin' rubbish," he spits, knowing the snake is dead.

Then he opened a grilled door and could smell his friend.

"Old Rag."

It was a telepathic picture of him.

It was a mistake, for Old Rag saw him in his mind and roared with excitement. That set off other beasts. The din would awaken Torrs.

Mingo knew he had to do something.

So released all the beasts as he searched the cages for Old Rag.

Lion creatures, canine hybrids, apelike creatures that ran up walls and down corridors in their haste to be free.

He apologized to his maker for using them because many would die for him to be free.

Responding to the beasts' roars and grunts, Maponosian elephants on a different island trumpeted.

"I will come for you," Mingo promises, sending out a message of hope to Baldy.

And could hear the shouts of Gododdin warriors confronting the freed beasts.

Freeing Old Rag, the planet's Griffin, he yielded temptation, adding his cry to the night's sounds.

Then he fell across his friend's rough back and allowed Old Rag to jump off the top of a veranda into the friendly darkness that was night.

Queen Cartimandua thought she recognized a grunt of a certain Birdman as she looked over her veranda carved in the shape of a swamp dragon's mouth and adorned in flowering creepers.

Camouflage again.

Cartimandua was told her someone had freed the wild beasts awaiting the games.

The coughing grunt was indeed an old enemy.

Mingo Drum Vercingetorix was here.

*

Little Arthur woke his mummy up. "Daddy," he says.

Boudicca looked about the room lit by the scarlet moon outside the grilled windows. Seeing nothing, she told her son to go back to sleep.

Once again, she was dismissing his Birdman instincts; *he was human, YES?*

Yet, the boy walked to the grills, watching the swamp ahead, listening to the freed beasts.

Boudicca joined him, hugging him and stroking his long blond hair to comfort him.

"The beasts, please come back to sleep," and Little Arthur allowed himself to be carried back to bed where he would be safe, warm, and cozy and wait for his daddy.

Arthur felt lucky.

Two houses, two names; one grandpa, a mom, and a dad providing hugs and toys.

Especially hover car models.

He was nuts about them.

And crazy over the ones that went 'Ewa' with flashing lights.

Also, floating garages with car park spaces.

Mummy was a better squeeze for these types of toys. All Daddy gave him were wooden swords, bows, arrows, and lectures on flying and not pulling Old Rag's ears.

"Will I be able to make daddy's sound?" He asks.

"What sound?"

He tried to imitate the coughing grunt but ended up clearing his throat.

Boudicca produced a handkerchief, a standard item in any mother's emergency kit.

Now she was afraid, for she believed the boy that Mingo was outside; she had hoped Tzu Strath would have arrived first, but it was

Mingo out there *being the beast*

AS USUAL.

Her heartbeat was fast as she remembered the past.

Her were-creature, half civilized, half bird was here.

*

Diviciacus, the High Shaman of Light, was going with his master, Caesar Alexander Vortigern, Emperor of the West, on a peace mission to General Ce-Ra.

"I hope the entertainment is to your satisfaction, Vortigern?" Ce-Ra muses as they watch a gladiator contest in the Arena.

He deliberately did not use Vortigern's title, which would have made them equal.

Ce-Ra did not think humans were equals. Just alien life forms beyond contempt that lived for nothing but their sexual drives.

And to rub insult into a vassal, their Madrawts outnumbered the human gladiators.

Already, one human gladiator had fallen below the royal stand of Ce-Ra, Emperor of the Madrawts.

Two Madrawt gladiators armed with lances looked for a thumbs down.

Ce-Ra gave the honor upon Vortigern, who, disgusted with the human performance, accepted it to please his host.

As a result, long spears entered the human gladiator and withdrew.

The crowd applauded.

The doomed human gladiator raised a knee, flopped a hand towards his human emperor, and, with a last gesture, gave the middle finger.

Ce-Ra smiles.

Vortigern lacked his people's affection.

"The human has offended my younger brother?" Ce-Ra.

It was obvious the Emperor of the West had accepted his vassal state.

Is he the younger, subservient, cringing, obsequious

brother?

A vile image of a statesman?

And Diviciacus wanted him dead.

Kernwy wanted Diviciacus dead.

Ce-Ra wanted them all dead.

Emperor Caesar Alexander invited Emperor Ce-Ra to send troops for the war that was about to start against the Emperor of the East, his son Conchobhar. But there was a price to pay. The troops brought their families, which opened the door to Madrawt colonization.

Readers, yes or no?

Differing views on Madrawts profitability divided human subjects.

Factions would spring up. Some would not unite, so perish as little insects and others would join Tzu Strath or the Emperor of the East, Alexander Caesar Conchobhar.

And human and alien planets would declare independence.

Because of this, persistent individuals will enslave their citizens for personal luxury.

"Come and help me, my older brother Ce-Ra," Vortigern begs.

And Ce-Ra invited Diviciacus to the Temple of War:

"I will make you the shaman priest to our war god Huitzilopitchli," Ce-Ra and Diviciacus would introduce him to the worship of Dispater." Someone gave Ce-Ra a green-blue feathered cape to wear and a pipe to smoke containing a mind-bending drug. A headdress with a fearsome face carved on it and adorned with heavy, hot, feathered wings.

Diviciacus soon ignored the weight as the drugs took effect, imagining himself as the sunbird of war that nourished the Madrawt soldier in battle with strength.

He chanted in a strange tongue, believing the god was speaking through him. Then saw Huitzilopitchli fly down and land and Dispater kneel before him.

"Come," Huitzilopitchli says to Dispater, who obeyed and spread eagled himself across a stone altar.

And men with bird heads held the good god's limbs firm, and Huitzilopitchli hacked out Dispater's heart with a long knife and drank from it.

Huitzilopitchli declares, "I nourish myself on the hearts of the conquered, fortifying myself to battle the evil that seeks to destroy life.

Give me life Diviciacus."

"I will, great god, I will," and Huitzilopitchli stood back and showed Diviciacus the line of patient humans and aliens waiting to come forth and spread eagle themselves on the stone slab.

The ranks included many commoners and princes, representing all the defeated nations.

And Huitzilopitchli gave Diviciacus the long knife that dripped Dispater's red blood and the remains of his heart to eat and "Share with me, become one with me, the most powerful god known to life, and we will rule life together?"

Diviciacus witnessed Madrawt soldiers sacrifice a man.

And Diviciacus took hundreds of beating hearts.

Still Huitzilopitchli was not happy.

"I have given you life and great power, and you have not repaid me Diviciacus."

"What must I do Lord?"

Huitzilopitchli displayed a man unwilling to submit.

Even from his back, Diviciacus knew him as Caesar Alexander Vortigern.

And Diviciacus walked up to him and plunged the long knife deep into his emperor's back. With both hands, cut out a heart.

And now Huitzilopitchli smiled.

When Diviciacus came out of his trance, he was standing over a stone slab altar, and he saw Kernwy drag a body off it and topple the corpse into a smoking pit.

Diviciacus saw twenty-six humans and ten aliens in the pit.

He also held a long knife, and the floor was wet with slippery blood.

Witnessed a cauldron brimming with beating hearts.

"I will rip his heart out and give it to you, Great Huitzilopitchli," Diviciacus swore.

Kernwy vowed to cleanse himself.

He viewed himself as a pawn within a wicked system, longing for freedom.

Unknown to his master Diviciacus, he had read many of Vern Lukas's books proclaiming the coming of a golden age.

"And the Birdman King Mingo Drum Vercingetorix will defeat the Madrawts, and the boy Arthur will lead his human/aliens armies under his banner, and all Bird men will pay homage to him, and he will become the new Birdman King, and his mighty armies will sweep the

galaxies clean of the evil Madrawts forever more.

He is the chosen one of Dispater and all gods. Men of all religions and races will follow him.

"Bad Vortigern,
Who thinks he is Alexander,
Because he's an emperor.
And is extremely angry like Caesar,
So, he thinks he is Caesar.
But Alex and Caesar turn in their tombs.
Because they know what Vortigern is.
Vortigern the Madrawt," the children of the empire would chant as
they played hopscotch.

"Fate has decreed it," Vern Lukas. And Kernwy believed.
Kernwy's secret diary., read by V. Lukas

CHAPTER 27 CAPTURED

Morrigan, Mingo's war goddess and trophy.

Kenala's only duty was to love Verica, the Lord's boy. Though Boudicca made him call the lad Arthur, he would forever be Verica to Kenala and all Bird people.

Boudicca had argued to Queen Cartimandua that he was the boy's companion, so they had not sent him to the dungeons below the Temple of Skulls.

"A retired warrior, too slow and unfit to fight the wild beasts of the arena," he remembered Boudicca plead his case and was grateful. He needed the MASTER PILL of the humans to restore youth; but doubted if he could ever afford it.

"Nani Kenala?" Queen Cartimandua chirps.

It took a heroic effort not to huff and puff. He could still fight in the arena with his friends.

"His meat being old and tough would offend the beasts there," Cartimandua jokes.

He had to stay close to Verica; he promised Mingo Drum, a male nanny he was!

"May I have the little ape as a toy for the boy? He cuddles into her at night," Kenala asks hopefully.

Cartimandua says, "Take Little Drum,," adding, "The **chatterbox**.""

He noticed extra guards, and the boy told him Daddy was in the swamps. This made Kenala excited at the prospect of escape. When the time came? He would show them he was Kenala,

Color Sergeant, the best the army of Vercingetorix had.

An escape would present itself to Kenala as Mingo Drum Vercingetorix had recovered enough to plan it for them.

Only the boy's presence would allow Mingo to make a quick entry and exit. The others prevented him from doing that. *He did not know the lovers Bran Llyr and Branwan were dead either.*

HE WOULD FREE THEM ALL AND THAT WAS HIS PLAN.

He needed to look like a Gododdin warrior, which meant wearing a loincloth and a necklace of swamp dragon teeth. *Lagoon, a long knife, murder—was that involved?*

Birds had an advanced civilization.

He merely slaughtered a juvenile from one of the many swamp dragon farms about. Their skins were in high demand throughout the human and Madrawt empires.

He had his necklace.

And using brown berries from the swamp lily, he dyed his hair a rich black and put it
in pigtails.

Now leaving Old Rag on the outskirts of Torrs City, he entered a busy corridor that would lead him under the estuary. The corridor flowed with Gododdin and the produce of their mosquito-infested swamps. Not that they lacked the means to exterminate the disease-carrying insects, but that they encouraged them to breed and fill the swamp air.

One of the Gododdin natural lines of defense.

Of course, the Gododdin developed resistance to the diseases.

Bird people were not backward.

And the Madrawt soldiers who advanced in their chemical suits found the quicksand of the swamps more terrifying than the dragons and Gododdin warriors.

They would assemble in their areas and unzip to refresh from dehydration and heat, and the mosquitoes came, biting and spreading disease.

Ah, they died in their thousands.

Boils the size of golf balls.

The runs.

Bleeding from places.

Dehydration.

The shakes.

Diseases deliberately manufactured by the Gododdin tailor-made for their enemies.

Such an unhealthy place could not house the City of Torrs the Madrawt High Command believed.

And left Torrs alone and went elsewhere in search of Bird men.

So it was: Mingo noticed the high blank glass planes, the mirrors, and picture writing scrolls on the corridor walls and wondered who was looking at him behind
these two-way crystal planes.

He sent a picture of himself to Baldy.

This communication was sloppy.

Exciting all the beasts in cages and swamps.

"Go and fetch Mingo," Queen Cartimandua says to her war chiefs assembled behind her.

"Remember, Tzu Strath would like him alive to kill personally," Tribune Henry, his representative here, reminds her. And again, Tzu Strath had sent his trusted friend to save his daughter.

"This is my city; if I want his head on a stake in a market, I will," she says coldly, but noted mentally Tzu Strath's wishes. She wanted the shipment of a thousand breastplates and laser rifles.

Tzu Strath knew his history lessons well, divide and rule.

THERE WOULD BE NO UNITED BIRD NATION TO OPPOSE HIM.

Only a lonely tough grizzled old bird called Mingo Drum Vercingetorix is ready for the broiling.

Tzu Strath hoped for a deal where each party had something to offer.

And a mosquito bit a soldier going with Tribune Henry.

"Bring me back, Mingo; I promised him death," Henry remembered Tzu saying.

"A great pity I would rather have him won as an ally, loyal to our cause than Queen Cartimandua the pirate queen," Henry had countered, and Tzu knew he spoke the truth.

He hated Mingo, period.

Anyway, how does one get Mingo Drum Vercingetorix to the human way of thinking?

He had hoped Arthur would have been the key. Bring the boy up human, so Mingo could see the change. But no, Mingo calls the boy Verica to mess up the lad. Remind the boy he had beast blood, and he was Birdie not human.

Therefore, Mingo had sealed his fate.

Vercingetorix would be a legend. Centuries later, his statue might rise, a testament to that myth.

Mingo's blood was on his own hands.

In another part of the Temple of Skulls, Reeman, Black Hair waited for an audience with Queen Cartimandua.

He came with gifts of weapons, for Ce-Ra knew like Tzu Strath, inter-tribal warfare must continue.

Bird slaughter until extinction, mirroring the Dodo's fate.

"Then only one enemy left, Tzu," Ce-Ra says to Reeman

Black Hair, who understood.

Humans and Madrawts knew how to deal with them.

And Reeman Black Hair did not see two tiny disease-bearing mosquitoes fly in and bite his escorts, sucking up their blood, mingling it with another's blood,
letting it all mix.

Soon another enemy would appear on Tara 6 (Maponos).
DISEASE.

And Mingo, at last, found his faithful friend Baldy the Maponosian Elephant with two proboscises.

"My friend," Mingo sent a picture of himself hugging and patting Baldy. Why the elephant rubbed its bald head against the bars of its cage for a scratch?

Mingo slid the latch.

"Well, who do we have here?"

Making Mingo turn and see he was surrounded by Gododdin warriors and their warrior priests.

"It is daddy, daddy is coming," Little Arthur shouts running up to his mother to pull her to the veranda.

Kenala, Color Sergeant, followed with Little Drum, who had been fitted with a collar. It was gem-encrusted to remind the little pet it was a valued household object and nothing more than *a Ming vase to be smashed.*

Was the ape barely house-trained and needed a diaper on?

"A gift to Mingo's friends," Queen Cartimandua had said, and Little Drum trembled as the collar snaps about her neck as if it would detonate.

Her conduct improved immediately.

A collar, never had she been treated like this, humiliating and heartbreaking.

What she did not know was that Queen Cartimandua would detonate the collar one day when she became bored of Little Drum's maid-like antics as she sought favor and LIFE. When she had been given her freedom and was flying over the swamps on her way home, savoring freedom.

No mess to clean up.

Swamp dragons and others would appreciate Little Drum's drumsticks.

And Kenala knew his Lord Mingo Drum needed him, but he had sworn to protect Verica clenched his fingers so much till they suffered from cramps.

Now Mingo had given Baldy a picture of where Old Rag was waiting, and as stated, others got the picture, Gododdin warriors, and dropped a net on our Birdman king.

Mingo ordered his best friend to flee, leaving a manacled Mingo to be dragged to face his old lover, Queen Cartimandua.

And the elephant Baldy did not suffer from guilt; like Color Sergeant Kenala, it was a beast, been sent a picture by Mingo that he would rejoin him later and Old Rag in the swamp forests. Mingo Drum Vercingetorix had every confidence in himself that he could escape with his people imprisoned here.

He was Mingo Drum.

*

High above in the hanging veranda of the Temple of Skulls Queen Cartimandua peered through the potted plants and trailing vines.

"You spurned my love long ago; now I have you, and I will give you the pain of a broken heart," she thought it amusing; she was a woman he had spurned, and hell knows no fury like that.

Writers like Vern Lukas claimed Mingo loved Boudicca but knew his place, a beast, an ape with wings, so he refused to pursue her.

It was also told by Vern Lucas that Boudicca was afraid to declare that she loved a BEAST! She is an imperial descendant and daughter of the most powerful War Lord known, Tzu Strath. Her position demanded she marry one from her own ranking, not a commoner or *a beast with wings; a birdie that went chirp tweet!*

But Mingo was of rank; he also was a king, but unfortunately, a king of a doomed culture.

"What games of love I could play," Queen Cartimandua whispered to the black night as the stars twinkled above competing for attention. But her attention was on herself as she imagined herself in Mingo's embrace, allowing the man to believe he had conquered her and stolen her love again; then she would plant a dagger in his back and watch him stagger dying not believing she could kill the man she had just loved.

She would cut out the heart and throw it into the swamp below.

And Mingo Drum Vercingetorix stood there now ragged and worn, drained of strength, his recent wounds showing from his encounter with Tzu and the wadi. Briefly, a touch of pity and concern flashed in her dark eyes for this man Cartimandua would not admit she loved.

Hate comes from being spurned and is a cousin of love.

It is hard switching hate to love, easygoing love to hate. Any fool can do that!

Poor Mingo never realized this, that everything she did was directed towards gaining his attention. He also never knew that a child light had been born from their brief union.

A Babie. Reader, was Mingo, the type that asks of his loves, "HOW?" You decide?

At sixteen, their first child had been sent to join the Manticore Legion; it had been Cartimandua's plan to have Mingo notice and love the boy as a father and her as a mother.

As one warrior of great ability would to another warrior of strength.

The boy died during a Madrawt raid. And the boy died knowing who his father was.

No heroics, no chance to die in his father's arms and tell Mingo that he was really his son from his union with Cartimandua *and a cabbage!*

Buried with the Bird men warriors in a common grave.

A menhir slab with their names chiseled in gold was

erected to remember them.

Human explorers had stumbled upon it, smashed the headstone to get the gold, and left.

Wars prevented Mingo from replacing the menhir. Just one of many Bird men graves, unmarked, forgotten To be plowed over one day by human/alien farmers.

But Queen Cartimandua, to give her justice, found that grave and marked it annually with a pilgrimage by leaving flowers.

She was a mother; she had spent nine months hand labor to bring the lad into the world. If men experienced childbirth, their willingness to send others' children into war might diminish.

Vern Lukas explored how the Trojan War began with the abduction of a woman.

There are many fish in the sea.

Such is life.

Now Mingo broke his unblinking gaze with a smile as he remembered the nights they had lain together united flying over Lake Moon Swan, so-called for the pink swans of Maponos gathered here at night to eat shrimp that swam after moonbeams, silly foolish crustaceans.

But when one is festering with wounds one sees things more clearly: Boudicca had born him his only living heir. Verica, or Little Arthur, as she called him. A human name's a reminder to him that she regarded him lower than a beast.

What was he? A Birdman king or centipede from rotten wood.

Why could not Boudicca love him?

Was he lower than an alien?

Did he plan this road before he was born to be her soul mate?

Cartimandua saw his rising turmoil; she knew his thoughts. A dangerous thing Mingo Drum Vercingetorix, especially in front of her who you had scorned. She holds your life in her hands.

"I do not have the power to give you my domains for the life of my son and friends for I only hold these lands in trust for my peoples," He says to Cartimandua.

"Even if you had given me your lands your people would have elected a new High King," she replies, "they hate me."

Mingo grinned, she still had her wits about her, what he had been attracted to in the past for her cunning was more famous than the winged red fox.

"I want your life for theirs," Cartimandua, for her own hurt had surfaced, and deep down, she regretted it, for she knew what his answer would be.

"Let them free, and I will surrender my physical body to you," this was the reply she knew she would get, and his valor attracted her to him.

Panic rose in Cartimandua. She still loved him.

"Then you will die," she agrees afraid of her words.

Mingo smiled, he hated this world, sought release, and feared nothing but the purple sky falling upon his head and drowning when the sea would cover his lands.

"My debts are clear; I will bring none with me into the spirit world. My gods will welcome me," he spoke calmly for his belief in the purple opening into the spirit world was so strong; and besides if he still breathed there was always hope he could escape with his friends.

"And she will die with you," Queen Cartimandua, "and I will bring up your boy as my own, a Gododdin."

"Then there will be hope for your tribe if he lives amongst you," insulting her unworthiness.

"When the moon is full, you will die," and whispered, "lover." Even her courtiers were surprised. Surely, she still loved Vercingetorix.

"Tzu Strath has my sword," he smiles back.

"Then you will surely die in shame, Birdman."

And he smiled again, remembering no shaman priests had foretold that the purple suns would fall upon his head, *he would live.*

Now Queen Cartimandua slapped his face several times to rid her of that smile; a smile had helped steal her heart.

When she failed, had him chained in a chair for safety and then made her guards leave them alone.

Now Vern Lukas takes the story over:

"What man? What man, human or alien, can stop his bodily functions when a creature with beautiful flesh molests his body?

Cartimandua had Mingo chained. She forced Mingo Drum Vercingetorix to love her until his feelings for her grew, and he loved her because he was a creature of the field and air needing to continue his bloodline.

He broke his vow of chastity, and the Birdman gods who favor love would not punish him, for life is not about holding back desperately needed genes from the gene pool through vows, but about adding color, diversity, fun, and creating many roads to our Heavenly home.

And the knowledge he had broken his chastity vow would like a poison creep into his soul.

Did Cartimandua know about the vow?

Mingo's adventures became movies.

Anyway, Bird women are different from human women for, like many beasts, they can store what has been given to them till fertile, and she fell pregnant when that occasion did happen.

A trait, whether from a primitive or more advanced ancestor.

Cells formed new life, and a new spirit of light entered Maponos.

And a boy started to live in her tummy, and now she was the equal of that human slug belonging to the race of Delia, Boudicca.

Mingo Drum could die now. The son would slaughter all the enemies of Cartimandua.

And named the boy in her tummy

Cuchulain.

What Mingo told me.

Cartimandua's song in bird tongue.

 " I killed my love.
  He broke my heart.
  I killed my love.
  I have a child.
  He broke my heart.
  I killed my love.
  Mingo my love." V. Lukas

CHAPTER 28 HE KILLS.

Henry was so full of himself. Must be hot.

Now Mingo knew his friends Bran and Branwan were dead, for his lion and elephant friends had telepathically told him.

So much death followed him, and it made him stoic, for it was as much his fault as Queen Cartimandua. As her prisoners, they could expect nothing but death.

And his soul rent in twain and sorrow filled him, sorrow for his dead children, his dead people, for revenge.

*

The purple day was hot, the swamp's hazes of steam, and the Gododdin arena was full.

Despite feeling unwell, many attended because they truly

wanted to See Mingo Drum Vercingetorix die.

They had carbuncles under the linen cloaks they wore for fear that they would be accused of having a plague and sent home. They hoped but knew deep down the queen's guards would take them outside the city and throw them into the swamp for the ever-hungry swamp dragon.

Already the River of Skulls was littered with bloated corpses. Warriors came and set fire to the butchered on the shore. Fear of the plague sometimes kept warriors away. Wild beasts ate the diseased, which made them sick, creating a vicious cycle.

Why is the arena a fearful atmosphere?

Queen Cartimandua did not find it amusing.

Her advisors informed her that a new plague had emerged in Torrs.

She already knew that!

She was afraid.

At this rate, her unborn would not have subjects to lead to battle. Why, the victims developed large carbuncles on their pale, waxy skins, and emit smelly body fluids from their orifices?

Finally, choking to death as they gasped, dehydrated for water.

Choking on nothing.

Just a nervous reflex.

They died turning blue for nothing.

With eyes bulging.

Their tongues protrude.

Gododdin knew there was an afterlife. Except they went about saying it was folklore, so did immoral things.

Never truly embodied that sense of bravery.

As pirates were empty shells.

And never thought about death till they were dying.

They were Gododdin pirates of the sky,

Who burned your ships and cities?

Raped your women in front of you.

Slit your throat to their gods.
They never considered death because it was not their own.
Now they were.
And it was a bit late for last-minute confessions to gods and burning sage sticks.

Because the disease had been a mutant strain from a Gododdin gene warfare lab.
What goes around comes around.
They had been planning to use it on others like Madrawts and humans.
Then, a mosquito bit a Gododdin scientist. He lay choking. He would die within sixty minutes. The City Watch would take his corpse. He invented the disease.
Yes, what goes around comes around.
Now, the queen's advisers had cautioned against public cremations to avoid panic.
We must treat the ignorant masses with ignorance and tell them nothing, and we plan our own escape routes along the way!
"The swamps are deep and full of swamp dragons," they urge, and so it was done and as the dragons ate bodies, the virus found its way into the waterways and became rapidly available for more unaffected mosquitoes.
Hell had come to Maponos.
And the burnings on the shore stopped altogether and were a public morale boost. People left the dead in their homes because the City Watch was ill.
And the wet windy season began, "The buzz of death," the mosquitoes approach it
was called.

Anyway, Mingo's guards dragged him out into the arena. One of them looked pale, and this man soon fell. His companions checked him and found his chest covered in carbuncles.
Fear, quickly replaced by anger and hate, gripped the men as they recoiled, blaming their companion for exposing them

to The Choking Death.

Like wolves, they drew their swords and hacked him.

Then, silently, the audience melted away for those who suspected themselves ill.

Oh, poor Queen Cartimandua, beautiful queen, queen of corpses in a city of death, oh poor Queen Cartimandua.

And a guard, too terrified to go anywhere near Mingo in case he was infected, threw the keys to Mingo.

Now Mingo unlocked his manacles and held out a hand for a sword.

Why did someone unknown throw an oily skin at his feet, and as he untied the strings, he held his beloved sword Law to his ears to hear its magical song of strength?

And the guards left.

The arena was silent.

From behind a veiled screen, Nostradamus smiled. He had stolen the sword from his Master Tzu Strath. Although he loved his master, he knew the hate between these two prominent men were wrong and hoped to end it by acting now.

Law was one way.

But Tribune Henry was also watching.

He did not find it amusing.

Mingo would naturally think Tzu Strath had returned it, and knowing the Birdman, Mingo was bound by his own rules to give something important back.

What about the planet?

Peace instead, the boy, Little Arthur, Nostradamus, hoped for.

Tzu Strath would have to accept that.

Anyway, he had been told to rescue the boy at any cost.

Now from a grilled box, Boudicca and her party watched. She saw her Birdman swell his chest in defiance. He stood tall and proud, his long brown hair gently moving at the ends of a slight breeze. His gold hair band kept the rest in place.

The gold torc glinting around his neck like a furnace under

the suns.

His loincloth glinting body sweat.

His flight membranes rippled to the rhythm of his deep breathing.

The sword in his hand was upright, ready to cut.

"Boudicca's savage," they had tittered amongst the imperial circles and in cartoons
Even now, Henry's followers followed suit.

"Yes, Boudicca's savage warrior," Nostradamus proudly for Mingo reached down into men's spirits and pulled up their primitive ancestral urge to be free, to run across the plains to drink at a river's edge while a lioness drank also on the opposite bank, free.

Of Cartimandua, she constantly hoped Mingo would plead for mercy. But another part wished he would not because she could never love a coward. Another part wanted him dead because of Boudicca.

So, slowly, the swamp dragon god crawled out of the gate into the arena with Mingo. Its soft bright yellow under the belly was a field of carbuncles.

It was close to death, struggling to breathe for the past hour.

Mingo was a haze to it.

And Mingo Drum Vercingetorix faced and defied it with a coughing grunt that carried far afield.

Now the poor swamp dragon plodded onto the source of the grunt as its ears oozed horrid smelly pus.

Mingo stood his ground.

He had realized there was something lacking in the beast's usual hostile temperament.

It should have cantered over to him in its eagerness to make him supper.

Why did not Mingo fly away? The rules said he would be shot down.

So, ran and the dying dragon followed out of an inherited program to eat and live.

The remaining crowd hissed at him.

Mingo could not care.

And led the swamp dragon under the royal box, then stopped and slid under the approaching jaws that belonged to a tiring beast.

Repeatedly he poked his sword into the neck till blood poured freely onto the arena's sand.

"Mosquitoes carry the death," it was a whisper that flew around the remaining spectators.

Buzzing mosquitoes filled the gentle breeze.

Midge's that could rout an army.

And the citizens left in droves.

That is when Mingo Drum Vercingetorix flew straight into the royal box in the melee of mosquito swarms bearing death.

The queen had stopped staring at Mingo; her gaze was now riveted on her fleeing citizens.

And Mingo showed he was an expert swordsman by striking down those beside her.

Their long spears restricted the guards' movement.

With his sword Law, Mingo now turned to face his spurned ex-lover.

Cartimandua.

And Cartimandua noticed something cold and wet at her throat. It was a sword, and if Boudicca had not influenced him, he would have slain her!

"You threatened the life of my son and a human woman, and you killed my friends Bran Llyr and Branwan."

Queen Cartimandua knew her head was his trophy, staring at him from a dining wall with dead eyes.

"What now?" She asks putting her faith in her heaving bosom, deliberately inched higher towards him, triggering his memories of lust, which is what she wanted.

"What now indeed?" He replies.

"You escape," she replies for him, "as I am hostage," and knew her torment would start again that he lived and loved another. She planned to reveal to him about a son he did not know existed, laid to rest in an unmarked grave, right before he departed.

Without a word of goodbye.

So, he could share the pain.

And have him feel some guilt that she hoped would hound him till death.

And of an unborn future life within her.

She, Cartimandua, had not grown careless with her cunning in age.

"The Birdman Mingo Drum Vercingetorix had a conscience.

It could also be guilt or fear. Much like a dog suffering after stealing your food.

Consciousness persists.

It is like love.

He was also a dreamer, a man who believed a shared life force unites all beings peacefully inhabiting this land.

He knew he did see his friends Bran and Branwan again. They were already in the afterlife. It tempered his lust for revenge.

Vern Lukas (Lorn Lukas.)

"Mingo walked the deserted streets of Torrs with a laser pistol in the small of Queen Cartimandua's back. He had suppressed a basic savage urge to kill her.

Was he a barbarian, a murderer who could kill her so easily?

She had told him she had his child, and of a grave he should visit.

But *she was Gododdin.*

Then we guess he is the beast Tzu Strath always said he was!

But he needed her as a hostage to free his friends.

Someone threatened his lineage.

Arthur Verica and his unborn, the beast, won, and Queen Cartimandua lived.

She looked shattered; her city was empty, and since it was the rainy season, it rained and drove the mosquitoes to seek shelter, so they walked in safety. But passing a lone figure with a paraffin mixture on his back as he squirted pools to kill mosquitoes and their young. The man's face was sullen; he resumed work.

"I am your queen," she shouts at him.

He turned to face her.

Carbuncles covered his left side.

Anyway, at last they reached the place where Old Rag and Baldy waited. Here, Queen Cartimandua expected the sword blow to give her an escape from her gloom.

She would have a long wait!

He felt sorry for her. Her people should not blame her, they the Gododdin, had always used the swamps to defeat their invaders.

"What have you released into our world, Cartimandua?" He asks.

Boudicca watched as the two former lovers stared into each other's eyes. If they could have been friends too.

"Help us?" Cartimandua pleads.

Mingo was truly a king, for he pushed down thoughts of Bran and Branwan. There would be time to mourn later. The Gododdin were people, birds, needing help. He aimed to help and save as many people as possible.

The Birdman Mingo Drum Vercingetorix, it is said, looked deeply into his soul and hers. She was Gododdin, the enemy first, what they had been past, moments of passion. But he saw past her and one voice that was evil called, "Kill the bitch and fly away," while another voice tugged silently at his soul, "Help her."

Yes, kingship won, Cartimandua and Boudicca saw into his hard-yellow eagle eyes and saw the true conqueror there.

HE HAD CONQUERED HATE.

The purple suns at that precise moment broke through some overhanging clouds.

Mingo suddenly shone like a demigod flickering purple flame along his body outline.

"Mahbon reborn," Queen Cartimandua for she referred to the Birdman's belief that

this son of Light will rise for everyone.

And herald a new order of love.

Boudicca saw belief written across his face, believing those words. The spring fever jumped from Cartimandua to her. Everything would be all right. He was here, was he not?

Now Little Drum ran behind a bush and peered out, afraid.

Color Sergeant Kenala dropped to his knees in reverence of his king.

Cartimandua was right, their god Mahbon was reborn.

Mingo was confused by all the excitement; he felt no change.

"Daddy," a boy called and ran for his hug, cuddle, and kiss to make things better.

Even if he was a ferocious warrior.

"Soon mine will call you daddy too," and Cartimandua reminds him of a lonely grave and that she was pregnant.

Though displeased with the burial, he anticipated the birth. Someone who might succeed where they had failed.

And the grave hurt, she should have told him long ago; the boy might have died differently, IN HIS FATHER'S ARMS.

There was no actual difference between the human woman Boudicca and her; women were the same with love.

Spiteful machines he concluded.

Mingo Drum Vercingetorix died a little more that day."

Bran and Branwan would stand guard near Mingo, protecting him until his passage to the afterlife.

Cartimandua's baby song with English translation.

"Tha mi a' bruidhinn leanabh.
I talk to my baby.
Baby,
Baby, I love you.
Baby, I love you.
I talk to my baby.
I will suckle my baby.
Baby grew in me.
 I talk to my baby.
Tha mi a' bruidhinn leanabh.
"

                The scribe Lukas.

CHAPTER 29   THEY WISHED EACH OTHER DEAD AND BLOATED

Nostradamus stunk like the animal skins he wore, an expert spy for alien Worlds.

"They are dropping like flies." Tzu Strath examined the medical reports.
Tribune Henry felt guilty because, deep down, he was a dirty alien as well.

"At least we know from the friendly Birdmen that the mosquitoes carry it," Tzu Strath.

Tribune Henry built up his courage to utter his next words, "I hear the plague has broken out amongst our Artebrate enemies."

Tzu Strath straightened. He knew and pitied their children. The emperors could die; the advisers and corrupt officials, but the children were the future.

"The Madrawts are more badly affected," Tribune Henry

continues.
That made Tzu smile.
Only the deceased Madrawt proved worthwhile.

He saw Madrawt children as some sort of weed blown on the hot winds needing weed killer, lots.

Madrawts evoked neither pity, empathy, nor desire.

And Tzu had to admit, a Madrawt was exactly that, a Madrawt. Lower than those blasted birdies. This made him worry about his grandchild, Little Arthur, and the tales of Vern Lukas (Lorn Lukas), that Arthur would herald the return of a golden age for the empire. Lo, the stories had become **prophecies**.

For aliens and humans.

But not blasted, Birdmen.

If the prophecies were true, the boy would survive! Then: What if Vern fabricated those tales? Tzu even believed them! Arthur could die like any other child.

"I am assured our genetic scientists have produced an experimental vaccine of sorts," Tzu said aloud, believing in them rather than the gods and prophecies, "Send me Nostradamus also," he added.

Being an alien, Tribune Henry still felt guilty as he witnessed Tzu gloating over the dwindling numbers of the planet's non-imperial inhabitants.

Even Nostradamus had changed since his encounter with the Birdie King Mingo Drum Vercingetorix. He no longer saw Bird men as just intelligent budgies, savages that even the imperial gods hated so turned a blind eye when you shot one clay pigeon shooting!

They were a persecuted alien humanoid people he knew now. The Flaming City of Mingo had unveiled its wonders to him. Now, he hated spying missions against them, for he knew he was speeding up their extinction. But he loved his master Tzu, as he was one of the few people, human or alien, that treated the hunchback as a person; but so had the Birdman

Mingo.

He connected with Birdman. Both were ugly, and Nostradamus hated his body. Why take a razor to your wrists or legs? By doing that, he was admitting defeat, allowing the disgust shown to him by his betters to reach him, pervert him, and fester hate in his heart for himself when he should love himself; his body was a temple to his spirit within, his own priest to Dispater.

A heart that was bursting to love and laugh like Mingo Drum's.

So, he told himself that there was nothing wrong with his body, but he felt deformed.

If he felt vengeful about his birth, he would turn on the lights to disgust the working woman and relish her reaction.

Making her feel dirty, as if she had just been *with a Birdie*.

He was only plain ugly, like the misunderstood Birdman.

Like Mingo Drum Vercingetorix.

Ugly.

Should not punish himself for his body.

Sometimes he wished he were on the Birdman side and fly with them. Upon learning his identity as the long-sought imperial spy, however...?

They would give him the Triple Death for sure.

"We are what we are," he comforts himself.

Loneliness was the great killer, and Nostradamus was lonely. None of this marriage nonsense for him. He was free to drink and buy sex when he felt the urge for Tzu paid well.

He ate what he liked.

Slept when he wanted.

He was Nostradamus and proud of it. As Mingo knew, you had to love yourself first to be proud.

He and Mingo were similar.

THEY WERE LIARS who lied to themselves.

Now a moral conflict raged in him.

"Ah Nostradamus," Tzu Strath greeted him, offering him a

seat and ordering Tribune Henry to bring refreshments.

His influence on such an esteemed company stems from his identity, the hunchback Nostradamus.

A life's mission, expanding human culture, made his existence worthwhile.

And thanked the imperial syndic judge for sentencing him always to be a hunchback for raping. He saw this as revenge against past tormentors. The punishment had done him well, the imperial branding iron on both bottom cheeks to remind all he was a convict. Death awaited those who tried altering his deformity.

So, he thanked his unknown deceased parents who had left him an orphan and penniless, as other dads and mums would have paid a handsome fee for a cosmetic medic to sort him out.

He was the hunchback and the best spy known.

Abe to blend in with alien cultures because his alien appearance allowed him to shuffle unnoticed among their cities.

The Tribune disliked his presence. He left a negative impression his master kept the company of vagabonds because that is what he looked like.

But they served Tzu, and that counted.

If Nostradamus had thought for a second Tribune, Henry was plotting against Tzu. He would assassinate Henry. He *was very loyal to Tzu.*

"Bring me Arthur as soon as you can, please, Nostradamus," Tzu and the "please," made him feel good.

Nostradamus smirked, "Looks like the old man loves the kid, huh? Just like he loves me."

Why not tell the boy? The fool ignored his own bloodline because Mingo's birdie blood was in the boy.

"He is in the Gododdin lands," Nostradamus replies, wiping the remains of a cream tart from his big rubbery lips. He was very partial to cream tarts. "Have him back in no time."

The War Lord Tzu Strath showed him an open drawer.

Nostradamus now filled his pouches full of imperial gold dollars of different values.

His pockets are seemingly endless.

Cash to buy; news, equipment, tongues, women, and drink, who said life as a hunchback was bad.

He departed for vaccination, placing faith in the gods that the experimental drug would prove effective.

And left for work.

Much did he differ from his War Lord, whose trust in gods had vanished.

Much did Nostradamus have in common with Mingo Drum Vercingetorix who believed in gods of myths, deities of magic.

Reached through Spirit possession?

Thus, he and Mingo had much in common with the High Shaman Diviciacus and the official religion of the empires, **Dispaterism, and spirit possession.**

"You pay him too much," Tribune Henry voiced.

"And we pay Queen Cartimandua much for her broken word. And she did the same. To the Madrawts, which means Tribune her Gododdin has become one of the most powerfully armed Birdman nations.

Thank Dispater for the Choking Death or they did be upon us now," Tzu Strath.

*

Diviciacus at this moment was many light years forward with his worried Western Emperor Caesar Alexander.

Madrawt ships comprised his fleet, mainly under the command of Ce-Ra's younger brother Ce-Ammon, a devout follower of the war god Huitzilopitchli.

He was after sacrifices.

Prisoners of war.

Allies also, if shortages, needed to be filled.

Diviciacus, the High Shaman of the new religious order, was eager to provide a heart each day, supporting this gruesome request.

Imperial soldiers feared the Madrawts, for they were few.

The imperialist army ordered the lowest ranking individuals, including those in the guardhouse, men with terrible records, kitchen porters, and cleaners, to select sacrificial victims.

Sufficient supplies lasted to a minor planet at Conchobhar's eastern empire's edge.

It had a small holding garrison.

The Madrawts provided a glimpse into the future.

Hell.

The eastern soldiers, believing Vortigern would send them home disarmed, accepted his surrender terms.

Instead, Diviciacus led an orgy of destruction.

Ten thousand human/alien soldiers had their hearts torn from their chests and given to Huitzilopitchli.

Their new Madrawt masters imprisoned the rest of the colonial population as slaves.

They gave the rest to Diviciacus for Huitzilopitchli.

For the journey to earth and conquest.

And now all men and women hated the Emperor Caesar, Alexander Vortigern, and Diviciacus for their Madrawt friends.

Yes, Emperor Caesar Alexander Vortigern was worried as now he knew the price of accepting Madrawt's help to stay wealthy. And guessed that the Madrawts would soon not need him and planned to escape.

Orders secretly given to fill a fast ship with as much wealth as possible. There were many alien worlds beyond deep space where the boundaries of chartered space ended. His people hated him anyway, so he saw no moral reason to help against what he had given them, **Madrawts.**

And Kernwy gloated and waited for his chance to kill Diviciacus who waited for his chance to sacrifice Kernwy to Huitzilopitchli; **what a 'Mad, Mad World.'**

A Madrawt supply ship reached them on the captured

planet with many sick men aboard.

It was as if the imperial gods were exacting revenge for being abandoned. After all, the plague that ravaged them was the Choking Death.

Interplanetary Plague.

Then, Madrawts' new Emperor Ce-Ra feared the unseen. The Madrawts were more susceptible to the plague and died in their millions. Once again, the mutant genes mutated, producing new strains that coughing could spread and quickly killed down the scientists working to eradicate it.

And Ce-Ammon died alone, for his servants had died.

And Ce-Ra left his court, taking refuge in his battle wagon that floated just outside the atmosphere of the Planet Madrawt.

Vern Lukas says, "The Madrawts spent their wealth on weapons, leading to a poor health service. Conquerors who forgot disease."

The cost of a battle wagon was twenty universities.

Knowledge led folk to contemplate their leaders.

Knowledge changed tanks to irrigation schemes, why worry, vassal planets fed
them.

Soldiers to students.

Soldiers obeyed, students did not.

And they were paying the price for death.

Vern Lukas also writes, "Their entire civilization geared itself to the terrible War god Huitzilopitchli, and woe to the Madrawts who challenged it, for people denounced them as devils and on altars to part them from their vital hearts."

Then some bright spark mutated the virus, so it affected Madrawts alone.

Now Emperor Ce-Ra was terrified.

And none shed a tear for him.

But wanted him dead and bloated.

Even his own people murmured against him.

Diviciacus and his kind worked overtime to make Huitzilopitchli take the plague away.

Religious genocide on a grand scale by Madrawts upon Madrawts.

But the plague was here.

Which meant Huitzilopitchli did not favor Ce-Ra.

The war gods were angry.

All ignorant superstitions.

And Ce-Ra was afraid of his religion.

For only the best hearts would appease Huitzilopitchli.

And people wanted Ce-Ra dead and bloated.

Huitzilopitchli chant translated by Lukas.
"Want my love.
I want hearts.
Want my favor?
I want hearts.
Want the rain?
Give me hearts.
You will be in heaven with me."
More like hell," V. Lukas.

CHAPTER 30 THE GREAT FIRE

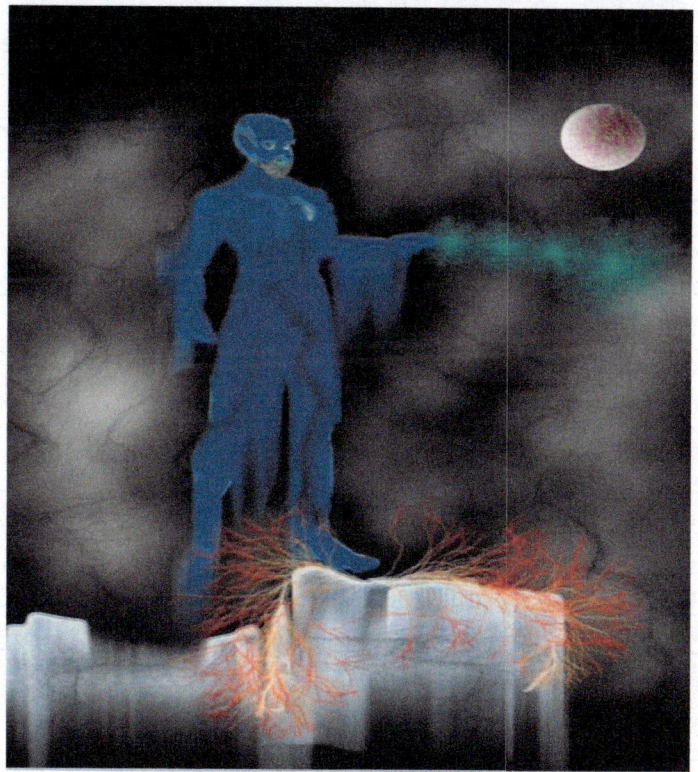

The Vate's spirit mirrored that of fate.

How Mingo felt after leaving Cartimandua no one knows. He wanted to take her with him, having said it just once.

Later she attempted to push Boudicca from a River of Skulls pier. Only Little Drum saved her, as her tail accidentally snaked by the queen's legs, tripping her, and taking both into the river.

And Mingo dived in; the heroic type that we all wish to be. He had been hanging about humans these days; he forgot he had wings. Wings meant he was a beast.

Oh, Boudicca, do we mean you?
Cartimandua had his little one in her tummy.
Was it responsibility or something deeper that he did not fly?

And a swamp python lurking under the pier stumps saw them as food.

Mingo *thought of his own life as the python wrapped around him.*

Cartimandua had found metal rungs and climbed them to safety.

"You will pay Mingo, I promise I will make you pay," she shouts at him, dripping
wet, and went back to her city.

This is when the Color Sergeant Kenala shouted at Boudicca to bring her out of shock. He **ORDERED** her to use a pole to propel the skiff across to Old Rag and Baldy.

"What good is Mingo's sacrifice if they catch Little Arthur?" He demands and deliberately uses the human name to bring her back to the present.

She took the skiff across, looking at the water's surface for Mingo.

And halfway across, a little furry hand reached for the skiff's sides. There was Little Drum looking up into the pole raised to strike.

Why, Little Drum smiled weakly and climbed aboard and fought down the temptation to boast about how she had fought the swamp python and won. Instead, she went to the front and shivered because she hated water, especially hot water, and soap.

Color Sergeant Kenala hovered over the swamp python and shot it in the head, freeing Mingo, who floated away gasping for air.

Kenala went after him, giving Mingo his prehensile bird tail to hold.

Mingo Drum Vercingetorix would live another day.

Boudicca reached the other bank and freed herself from Arthur's clasp on her right leg. *He was only an afraid little person.*

Kenala flew over to join them; Mingo looked wetter than Little Drum.

Hearing the shouts, Boudicca realized Kenala was right - Gododdin warriors were gathering on the bank to her left.

It was time to go.

Boudicca watched Mingo fly high above them, scouting for enemies and bands of the dying that had been driven out of their towns and villages.

She was jealous he could fly. "Never mind, Little Arthur will be able to," and remembered she discouraged it as a beastly trait; her son was human *and felt ashamed. The beast-man in the air had dived into snake-infested water to save her little boy. The Birdman was wonderful **again.***

Mingo had seen many corpses.

Many twin trunk elephants lay dead, so did Maponosian Griffin lion creatures, Rock Dwellers, snakes, and other creatures.

The plague spread beyond its hosts.

He feared not death; it is inevitable. But he feared for his son and Boudicca. For Boudicca, she believed in nothing and so feared death.

Even if cloned, his original body was gone.

A clone, being a new person, could develop a distinct personality.

Death's horror returned to the clone.

Verica was too young to grasp the concept of a spirit bird world beyond death.

Mingo realized cloning served no purpose.

"Ghosts," Verica had shouted excitedly, hoping for a ghost story to frighten him so he could cuddle up and feel safe, warm, and cozy.

"I guess you could call them spirit people," Mingo says, leaving the topic to haunt the boy's dreams.

Mingo felt the salty tears in his eyes.

Even beasts have feelings.

He felt useless.

"Children pests," he coughed, flying on. They were heading for the City of Winds, his new tribal capital. They had to end the wars before rebuilding the ruined Flaming City.

Boudicca "City of Winds?" And wished she had some extra woolies.

She saw Mingo as higher than a Neolithic farmer.

A barbarian.

Her Mingo was extremely dangerous and no doubt why Daddy feared him.

Indeed, a threat to set up homely ways.

Mingo was a wild man.

Planet Maponos himself.

He could never fit into imperial society, but Boudicca ignored it.

He is a party piece, and Mingo's temperament is untrustworthy. Soon, would find himself a wanted man.

And she loved her Birdman but would never admit it publicly to herself, *silly girl.*

Especially tell him that, **the beast.**

First, the winged barbarian moves.

Now, Mingo built a fire between them every night so any biting insects would have to pass through it before reaching them. He led them to a cave each night, where he threw burning branches.

Fire is the cleansing destroyer of life.

And one-night, Little Drum was playing with his son, seeing who could throw pebbles farther down the cave.

From deep within the cave, a booming voice warned, "Make me angry by hitting my head again."

Guess what? Little Drum jumped behind Arthur/Verica,

shouting, "I have a sword."

Despite her being a terrible warrior and an even worse pet, everyone always loved her.
forgiven for being Little Drum.

Mingo, who had been sitting on his haunches ripping meat from a spitted hare bird, stood up, fat dribbling from his chin. Wiping his hands on his loincloth, he drew his sword, Law, and advanced.

Boudicca followed her man, alarmed.

Her man? *What else had Mingo been doing apart from building fires? It seems he had been an extremely busy birdie reader baking angel cakes.*

Kenala hurried forward with a probing spear, (a spear whose tip exploded if detonated by the bearer.)

Old Rag grunted and Baldy trumpeted.

The little boy screamed, shook himself free of Little Drum, and ran for his mummy when the figure of an old man appeared.

Fear paralyzed Little Drum.

"Why are you alarmed, Bird King?" the glowing yellow figure says, emitting a coppery green light, "I am a Vate, and I know you well."

But alarm gripped Mingo.

"Who is he?" Boudicca asks, taking a hand of Mingo's.

Mingo and Kenala did not know. He confirmed he was a Vate. Talking would be a waste of breath.

The old man extended his flaming right hand, revealing a diorama depicting Planet Maponos.

"See before your death and destruction, yet you, Mingo, survive always. We have been searching for someone like you," the old man says.

Boudicca wished to be armed.

"What do you want?" Mingo asks.

"I am a Vate."

Now Mingo searched his memory. He should know everything as he handled the lives of his people.

"My world exists around you, but it is unseen by you." You can smell my world, touch it sometimes, think you see beings from it, and sometimes think you have entered it," the Vate.

"A ghost daddy," Little Arthur Verica says excitedly, making sure he was having a good look from behind his mummy's legs and behind him, peered at the fearless Little Drum.

Both noticed whose hand Boudicca held.

The old man smiled, neither affirming nor denying.

Superstitious Kenala thrust his probing spear forward as if he were killing a vampire.

The Vate stepped back, disappearing.

Sergeant Kenala disliked the cave.

Mingo waited for its return, his duty to know more, while Boudicca led Arthur **and Little Drum** out of the cave.

However, the Vate reappeared behind the two Birdmen warriors.

"I am a Vate, existing long before your birth, Mingo." And you, Kenala, I saw in your mother's womb in the City of Monoliths before the Rock Dwellers claimed it," the Vate tells them.

Sweat broke out over Kenala's forehead.

"What do you want?" Mingo asks again.

"I see the Savior," the Vate replies, looking towards the departing boy.

"Are you Vern Lukas?" Kenala asks thinking here was the originator of the human Arthur legends.

The Vate smiled and replied, "In each of us is a gene god that gives us all AWARENESS, GOD CONSCIOUSNESS, the knowledge of right and wrong.

Yours is awake, Mingo.

Yours is not Color Sergeant Kenala. You are true Birdie.

When it happens, life becomes a vessel for God, SPIRIT power," the Vate tried to explain.

The Birdmen did not comprehend God.

Their world valued the environment and maintained a delicate balance with nature to avoid upsetting the spirits.

Equilibrium is essential for preventing disaster.

So, what was this Vate God?
The gene God?
Gene of awareness.
The gene of god communication.
Of communion with spirits in other dimensions.
The gene of communion with powerful entities called angels.
A gene connecting us to God's life force, universal omnipotence.
Finding HOME on the other side.
It was SPIRIT.

"Dozens are luckier than others when the gene God awakens.

A body becomes charged with CREATIVE LIFE; thus, healing happens.

It is strange," the old man called Vate called to Boudicca, "your imperial scientists have
mapped the twirls of DNA and RNA and broken their secrets.

But because the gene God does nothing, does not produce a finger, or eye color, it is useless, and they call it 7X and forget it.

If only they could think.

I dwell here, far within these caverns. My spirit crosses space when awakened by the gene God."

The Birdmen finally felt a connection with the Vate, sharing his belief that legends lived within mountains, hills, rivers, and caves like dragons, giants, or heroes from the dawn of time, and they awaited awakening when needed.

Now even Mingo Vercingetorix felt humbled.

He stood before a powerful spiritual figure. He hoped it was good but feared it would transform into a monstrous dragon or evil villain.

"Mingo's awoken gene God attracted me. Your spirit flight has crossed me. You connect with me, with existence; solace found in starlight or sunshine.

But this little one, his gene God, is fully awake. He is my reason for coming.

He whom I call the Savior, Vern Lukas, is indeed prophetical; here stands a new

Arthur, who will save all."

"All?" Kenala asks, fearing he meant humans and aliens.

"I know your heart, Color Stripes Kenala.

All means all.

War, disease, inter-tribal warfare, and invaders ended the old ways, the Vate said with eyes boring into Kenala, so the sergeant envisioned all heartbroken.

"As long as I, Mingo Drum Vercingetorix, am free, I shall rally our warriors.

We are the last of the free.
Behind us are the frozen polar caps.
Before us, the enemy.
It is better to die fighting
Than live as slaves.
I fear nothing, not even the purple suns falling upon my head or the waves

drowning me," Mingo said in the true fashion of a Birdman king.

"Mingo, I trust you, but your people believe their world is ending. Mingo, do you recall the Bird people's Golden Age?

It has gone.

You fight for your own survival, Mingo.

Little Arthur Verica embodies galactic gifts from the Bird people.

I will leave you with one thought."

The old Vate, before fading away, urged them to safeguard Arthur.

Chaos would reign until a new Savior arrived.

"I will," Boudicca.

And both Bird men warriors stared at Little Arthur Verica.

The boy, seeing the danger gone, gave a cheeky smile. He understood they had been talking about him. His exceptional nature made the next few months unbearable for everyone.

But they loved him, a small person was him.

"What did the Vate leave you?" Kenala asks.

"Knowledge that I know where there is an abandoned Madrawt fuel dump. We must go there and leak fuel over the swamps and fire it." Mingo replies that the Choking Death will die, impressing Kenala. "My other child will also live."

Oh dear, Boudicca suspected Cartimandua's approaching child was Mingo's.

Well done, Mingo. **Think, readers: a stork delivered the baby?**

The Vate's parting gift to Mingo was the idea of the Great Fire.

Vate sings this.

"I am a spirit.
Faie
A fate.
Fae.
A fate.
Fairy." Vern Lukas

KEITH HULSE

Chapter 31 Times Changed

A son's grave in no-man's-land

The known world in A.D. 42000 was in utter chaos, desperately needing a savior.

The human-alien imperialists under Tzu Strath looked to Little Arthurs.

Other writers cashed in on the Arthur idea that sold.

Word of the Vate reached the Birdman. People called Mingo, Mahbon, the son of Light, reborn who would save them all with his sacrifice.

One must die for all.

Bird Nations offered warriors for the War on the Road to Extinction, unless they desired unification with Tzu Strath's population.

Vern Lukas, they were a stiff-necked people.

*

Nostradamus caught up with his prey, but now he had to rescue Tzu Strath's family not from Queen Cartimandua, but from the Birdman, whom he admired.

He did not favor the prospect.

Mingo's ways matched his own, so he had to kill the Birdman to emerge victorious.

So, he reasoned himself into believing.

He collected a few water cobras, determined to free the captives Boudicca and Little Arthur. If that failed, he would use a folded-down blowpipe with a poisoned dart.

Color Sergeant Kenala was an old easy target. One needs poison for the elephant and lion. The flying ape Little Drum would freeze with terror as he walked up to it, making her an easy kill.

All must die. An escapee would bring the Artebrate after him.

He could not handle mobile prisoners.

He knew Mingo was ahead at a cave, so Nostradamus waited, sitting on a rotting tree stump holding his canvas bag of snakes. For what he intended to do, he hated himself, and Tzu asked him to do it. Never had he questioned his role as an assassin.

Immune to the Choking Death thanks to the new vaccine.

Nostradamus froze.

Quietly, he slithered between the stumps of moss-infested tree stumps and saw them.

But they were heading deeper into the swamps. Easy going for them as they could fly over water crawling with swamp dragons. And all the time, Nostradamus carried the canvas bag, checking for rips. He was paranoid about a snake's head appearing and biting him; sure, snakes were hissing somewhere.

"Blooming heck," he swore, "let them go. Boudicca and Little Arthur are back there. Go, Birdman, go free," and with a relieved heart, he opened the bag and dumped the water cobras into a stream. "I did not want to kill you anyway, Mingo."

"I am glad to hear that hunchback," and Mingo threw a trophy at Nostradamus's feet.

Kenala followed suit.

Alarmed over the grizzly trophies, Nostradamus spun around to see two figures.

A gargled sound was trying to escape somewhere in his throat but could not, for he felt like a boy caught stealing jam tarts from a baker's oven.

"Gododdin," Mingo says with a smile, "Sneaking up on the great spy of Tzu Strath?"

Kenala extended his talons from his foot and jumped onto a snake, breaking its neck.

He repeated the action with each of the others, placing their bodies in the canvas bag he had taken from Nostradamus. In his surprised state of mind, Nostradamus forgot how tasty a snake was, like a chicken.

"Dinner," Kenala tells Nostradamus who showed no

revolution.

Nostradamus was starving.

"You can stay here or return with us," Mingo tells him.

"I have a mission to complete," Nostradamus tells him.

He was staying.

"What?" Mingo asks.

How can someone inform the prey that they are the target?

"Scouting."

Mingo smiles, knowing that Nostradamus is deep in Gododdin's lands and that his the mission was to rescue Boudicca and Little Arthur.

"Go free them if you can hunchback," Mingo tells him.

The man did not mind the nickname. That is how Bird people described him.

And he doubled back, wondering why Mingo had not killed him. The Birdman's plan ended up being a joke on Nostradamus, who, curious, ventured deep into the swamps.

Slowly noticed the oil floating on the top of the swamp waters. To find the source, he followed the trail of oil backstream. **Suddenly** flames spread along the oil and, cursing the Birdman Nostradamus, *fled*

for his life.

He was alone amidst a great fire that Mingo and Kenala had lit that burned through the Gododdin swamps.

And the carriers of the Choking Death perished, and the two Bird men saved their world for they gave Tzu Strath's vaccine time to become available.

Nostradamus knew why Mingo had not killed him. He knew he had, too, as flames heated him up; *he was cooking.*

Indeed, the joke was on Nostradamus.

Now Mingo returned Boudicca to War Lord Tzu Strath.

That had been a day to remember.

It had been raining, and the War Lord was at his front lines. For Mingo did not trust him and would not cross them into imprisonment and sacrificial strangulation on a public altar to some imperial god of war.

Lo, the land was barren, pitted by craters made from exploding shells; not even the bold snakes of Tara 6 (Maponos) ventured here.

Graves dotted the landscape instead of trees. Graves dug where authorities thought someone died when a neutron grenade went bang.

Mingo knew the area well; he had led Birdman attacks against these imperial lines long before the Madrawts had. He also knew his people's mass graves had no markers above them; they were like cows, *slaughtered animals with no souls.*

He felt rage; Boudicca's peace offering, amidst the graves, mocked his dying race.

He could not remember where Cartimandua buried his son except

SOMEWHERE HERE.

Boudicca may huff and puff that his people could not care for their dead; he knew Bird people came grave cleaning.

People shot them as wild chickens.

He noticed fresh mounds marking the Madrawt dead.

Also saw the many corpses awaiting burial. The corpses made the air stink.

The soil ranked as disease, chemicals, and unexploded ordnance lay here.

"Are we entering a golden age?" He grunts sarcastically.

Color Sergeant Kenala laughs.

"The old man Vate said to protect the Savior, well, Little Drum will, because Little Drum fears nothing."

The Birdmen exchanged glances, a shared understanding passing between them.

However, they directed their laughter at themselves.

How could two dinosaurs like them protect Verica?

They clasped hands.

Kenala had vowed to protect Little Arthur Verica, remember?

Silence filled the large tent room; they had expressed everything that needed to be said.

And when Kenala departed, Boudicca stopped staring back at Mingo from her father's position.

For all the time spent alone together recently, they had not pulled down the barriers of pride built from hurt love.

Mingo returned her stare, and then he did something natural, but it could have waited till she was gone.

The rain had a bitter, salty taste because of war pollution; it was not good to drink. Mingo wiped his lips and spat out the raindrops.

Of course, Boudicca realized *he was spitting her dirty taste from his mouth. His actions hurt her.*

WELL, DONE MINGO DRUM VERCINGETORIX.

And her heart broke more, for she loved Mingo.

Because she walked away without a word, Mingo understood. *She hated him*, a beast of the air.

Well done, Boudicca Tzu.
Not so the little one who broke from his mother's hold and ran back, shouting,

"Daddy."

And Boudicca saw tears swell from the great Mingo Drum Vercingetorix as he held up his little boy.

Friendly Bird men, aided by Little Drum, saw this bad omen and would soon spread word of it across Planet Maponos.

The king should not cry; it was a foreboding illness.

"The Bird people in those ancient times were very superstitious, unlike others, *who roams Tara 6 these days?*

In those days, they were still wild, wooly, and free, borrowing Mingo's words,' the last of the free with naught behind us except polar caps and imperialists in front.'

TEARS is a bad sign.

Queen Cartimandua saw tears as a sign of defeat.

Many turned to Little Arthur Verica for hope of freedom.

Let us pity Mingo Drum Vercingetorix, the family man."
Vern Lukas

Now Boudicca saw the father in him, how he kissed the little boy many times, smelled his hair, his powerful hands holding the lad so he would not fall, and the boy knew he was safe.

He was kind, yet she felt remorse for hurting him. Recognized their destinies were diverging, their paths no longer meant to cross.

Tzu Strath also noticed those hands, further confirming his suspicion that Mingo abused children. The man's handling of the child was regrettable. **He was a military man; he never held Boudicca close like that.**

"Come with us, Daddy, please. You said you did tell me a story and tickle me," Little Arthur Verica pleads, but the Birdman king put him down and, seeing Tzu Strath approaching with troopers, turned, ran, jumped, and sailed, gaining height as he skimmed the soil.

Then his rudder-like tail flipped him high and up.

The little boy cried and stamped his feet.

His wings were not strong enough yet for him to fly after Daddy.

He only stopped bawling when he heard a coughing grunt and looking saw Daddy circling him.

Tzu Strath wished Boudicca were not present. Mingo made a fine target.

The bird-man king's defiant grunt echoed against his human enemies.

"This is my domain,

 These are my lands,

 My cough is the law.

 The grunt is my war cry. I fly where I please.

 I am Birdman," Mingo Drum called.

And the non-hostile bird men amongst the imperialist troopers were still. They felt the pull of the wild, and the imperialist troopers felt it too.

The wolf's lonely howl evokes a yearning for freedom and untamed living.

"Daddy, please come back."

And Mingo looped the loop showing off to his son he was free.

"Gosh," the little boy says admiringly.

But Boudicca tightened her soul by allowing the human mother to rise, for she had no intention of letting **her** Arthur do that **and break his neck**. She forgot his avian nature allowed such actions.

And friendly Bird men who had settled amongst the human/alien settlers heard and saw and wished Mingo Drum Vercingetorix were dead and rotten, for they were no longer savages that do those crazy bird stunts in the sky.

It reminded the imperialist settlers they were beasts of the air, not civilized folk that could read and write, go to school and the Temple of Dispater, the Imperial god, *even take human names*.

And Mingo heard their answering grunts.

"Times have changed,

Birdmen are past.

We want our sons and daughters to live.

Someone gave us reservations.

Corn, we plant.

We cannot fight anymore.

Our fighting spirit is gone.

Go away, Mingo, and leave our sons be."

Mingo listened, his spirit shattered, realizing he had little left to live for.

Deep down, he knew Boudicca would keep Verica from him. His son was now Arthur; he had better get used to it, but one thing he would never do was live upon one of Tzu Strath's reservations.

As Boudicca watched his aerial antics, all folk saw the passing of an era in him. This place held history. Their kids would never experience it. That day yielded intense emotion.

Mingo Drum Vercingetorix was an admired foe. He was doing his death flight chant, saying the names of his ancestors because he was going to them. He was asking them for courage and strength to meet his fate.

The listeners knew that too.

"I am the last of the free.

A Birdman.

An Artebrate.

I will die with a spear in my hands.

And my sword is Law in an enemy.

I am free, born and die free.

I fly where I want.

Hunt where I will.

The land is my friend,

So, bury me where I fall," he coughed in answer to the civilized bird people. And.

many sons and daughters left the reservations when they heard Mingo's grunts repeated to them.

They threw away their top hats,

Great coats and tacky boots.

Brushed out their feathers, they tried to hide.

In efforts, to be civilized.

And took to the air free painted up in blue war paint.

"I hate you Mingo Drum Vercingetorix," Tzu Strath.

And the hate was not his alone.

"Do not take our sons and daughters to die with you,

  Go away Mingo Drum,

  Die and rot away someplace, Mingo," the parents of those who left the reservations following Mingo.

> Fearing they would never see their children again?

> Mingo Vercingetorix was a bad pied piper to them.

*

Nostradamus survived the Great Fire and knew why Mingo had smiled.

The joke was on the fire.

Lose a man following you. Nostradamus could not have done better! A fine complement to Nostradamus, who must be getting careless these days; he also knew Mingo knew he could save himself, a great compliment coming from one such as Mingo Drum Vercingetorix.

And Nostradamus felt his heart break for Mingo's fight for freedom.

Poor Nostradamus had become a complicated CONTRADICTION. He swore to serve Tzu Strath, and he would, but he yearned to join the fight if Mingo lived longer.

"We are the last of the free,

Behind us, the polar caps,

In front, our enemy.

We have nowhere to run," and Mingo's words burned deep into Nostradamus's soul.

In fact, the imperialist troops going into battle had taken Mingo's chant up.

"I am no goddam Birdman," Nostradamus reminds himself, "A hunchback, human spy, and belong with humans, not Birdies."

Only one Nostradamus could exist on Tara 6, and he ruthlessly extinguished the part of himself yearning for freedom, fearing the untamed spirit Mingo embodied.

"How can I serve two masters?" He asks himself.

Birdman death chant translated from birdie by Vern.

"Treoraich sinnseran mi.

Ancestors guide me.

I am dying.

Ancestors take me.

To my purple world.

To live again like a fae."

"How can I serve two masters?" Lukas asks?"

CHAPTER 32 2 NEW IMPERIAL LAWS

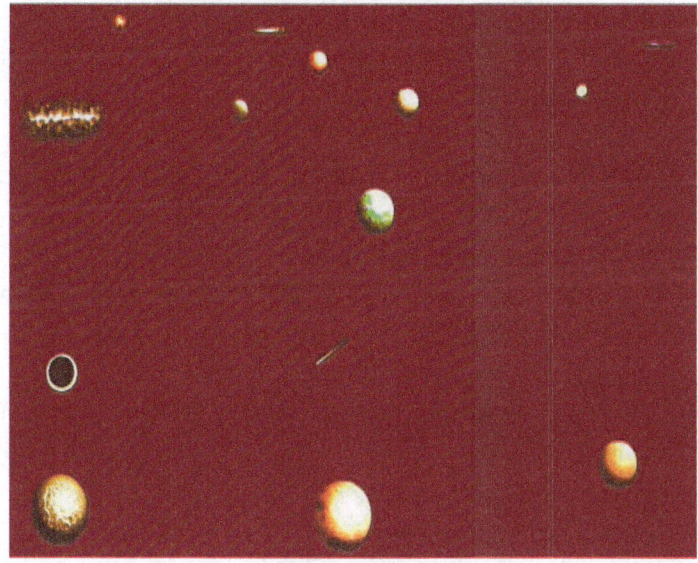

Planetarium

"Brutus," the original Caesar of men, had said forty thousand years passed on Planet Earth, but Emperor Caesar Alexander Vortigern did not deserve or live up to his name and substituted Brutus with Diviciacus.

And so, the deed was done."
Vern Lukas.

Reeman Black Hair had demanded an audience with the younger brother of the Emperor Ce Ra, the Emperor Vortigern on Planet New Orion, which bordered the Empire of the East of Caesar Alexander Conchobhar.

The problem: the younger brother's monthly tribute of gold and slaves to his older brother Ce-Ra had not been regular.

If Vortigern wants his older brother's help, he needs to pay on time.

Vortigern saw otherwise, the gold was a drain that he could spend to buy friends in the civil war going on in his western empire.

No matter how much gold he sent to his older brother, Madrawt's help was short in coming.

"Ah, does not the younger brother of Ce-Ra know what the effects of the Choking Death are?" Reeman Black Hair asked.

Vortigern smiled. "My older brother knows how we suffered. Can I send dead slaves?

Who remains alive to pay taxes?"

Reeman Black Hair never the diplomat pressed on as the emperor watched a dance.

About the death of Mingo Drum.

His favorite show, for it showed off Boudicca's figure advantageously.

The emperor could imagine the dancer as Boudicca.

He could also touch after.

And nymphs enticing her to send to Mingo surrounded the dancer.

The emperor liked his nymphs.

Then Diviciacus came behind his emperor, wearing a bird headdress of Huitzilopitchli, WAR GOD.

A long knife sheathed his back.

Only the emperor did not detect the shiver that visited his courtiers as this masked priest entered. The emperor, captivated by his nymphs, did not see the masked priest enter.

The emperor's face was hot and wet with sweat as he imagined himself Mingo.

"Afterwards,' he thought as a young nymph slid about his gold silk robes.

A silver water nymph with glued blue fish scales on her.

Diviciacus had paid well to get the prettiest nymph dancers out.

Vortigern was the emperor, and he could do what he liked. Unfortunately, this attitude encouraged others to do as they liked.

Diviciacus stood directly behind him.

Perverted as his emperor.

And just before Caesar Alexander Vortigern's imagination got carried away with the silver water nymph, Diviciacus slid the razor-sharp long knife across his emperor's throat from ear to ear.

After that, there was no stopping Diviciacus from cutting the emperor's heart out.

Diviciacus tossed this imperial offering onto the altar of Huitzilopitchli.

Reeman Black Hair smiled.

Not a human royal guard intervened.

"Long live the Emperor Ce-Ra," Reeman Black Hair shouted as Madrawt troopers filed into the audience room.

"Long live Caesar Alexander Conchobhar," a lone suicidal voice of dissent shouted.

"Long live the Emperor Tzu Strath." the situation was comical.

Then someone shot a Madrawt and the killing in earnest started.

Diviciacus did not even flinch when a probe spear exploded beside him, its splinters drawing blood from his legs. Rather, he appeared to revel in the pain and enter a dreamy state.

Huitzilopitchli.

But Reeman Black Hair had come prepared. The Madrawts outnumbered the human guards, and the human army was at the front.

Vortigern had never expected his well-bribed older brother to sacrifice him to

Huitzilopitchli?

And Diviciacus dragged the human/alien survivors in front of him. He looked at…

them with cold eyes from behind a bird mask.

He still held the murder weapon.

Fast he was, the way his hands worked, one grabbing a prisoner's shoulder and the other knifing deep, twisting, cutting the heart free for the altar of
Huitzilopitchli.

That day's massacre included even the household staff.

Humans and aliens thereafter reviled him, dubbing him "The Butcher."

"One day I will tear your black heart out, Kernwy promised.

And Kernwy knew Diviciacus had perverted the faith of Dispater, the good god.

"What is my faith?" He asks himself, "What gods do I worship? Dispater the life essence that good living can reach?" And he smirked at his own hypocrisy.

Dispater, the living emperor in the flesh, looked at the slumped Vortigern and wondered if he would destroy the body out of meanness to prevent cloning.

And Kernwy smirked,

"I believe in shamanism,

Spirit possession.

Ecstasy.

Without human sacrifices.

I do not believe in Diviciacus.

May the Birdman save me?"

He considered who he'd summoned, alone within a room resembling a planetarium.

The Birdman?

The empire's enemy.

Mingo Drum Vercingetorix.

No, he meant the other little bird man, Arthur the boy. Poor Kernwy was a victim of Vern Lukas's writings that had filled a spiritual vacuum, and he had believed in the return of a golden age, but unlike the Bird people, a golden age for humans.

When space again belonged to humanity.

He felt fortunate to be human, not possessing avian

appendages. But he envied and hated them for their ability to fly.

Poor Kernwy was jealous.

Besides, heights made him dizzy.

The Birdmen must be crazy to fly so high!

But the boy Arthur was different, he had human genes, and that made him human,

well, more human than beast.

Almost.

Crucially, Arthur must inherit his grandfather's army, assuming the role of Tzu.

War Lord.

And as Vern Lukas wrote, "I envy him not, for no one will forget his Bird man's origins. He must be strong and ruthless if he is to rule wisely and fairly. The Spirit of Light mirrors the soul within a man's eyes.

Human/alien or bird men will know he is good, and they will follow him, from settler farmer to veteran soldier.

And it would take armies to rid Kernwy of Diviciacus and his Madrawt fiendish friends, not beliefs.

It was now that someone brought him news of the new Emperor and Lord of Madrawts Ce-Ra, issuing a new imperial law.

That all male humans and aliens must pay a second-class citizen tax and would only be exempt if serving military service in Madrawt auxiliary legions.

Kernwy laughed.

They spearheaded the attack, paving the way for following Madrawts.

Another name for genocide.

Then he heard the second imperial decree.

Men must venerate the new imperial deity.

Ce-Ra,

Or die!

"**And the genes of Mingo Drum and Tzu Strath were in**

Little Arthur/Verica. It gave him a solid start, paving the way for a Golden Age revival.

What people sang for Vortigern.

"The octopus is gone.
  Hooray.
  They did to him
  What they do to chickens.
  Shame for the birds.
  Not for him.
  Hooray.
  The octopus is gone." Vern Lukas.

CHAPTER 33 I VISITED

Long way down, then Mingo could fly

"The Birdman Mingo Drum Vercingetorix was where he had begun, on the top of
the pink sandstone monolith.
Alone,
Dejected.
And he spoke to himself these words.

"What use a king if he cannot even keep his son in his own lands?
A king lacks value without a queen.
Where: My subjects, where are they?
I cannot find my laws.
I wonder: Where are those who oppose me?
My subjects are slaves,

Law broken.
My foes dine with me.
Eat my people' food."

Something troubled the Bird Man, and I knew why — I was entering his life to study him. I am the scribe, Lorn Lukas, who is the author, Vern Lukas.

My deep study of him, as a man, Birdman, and alien, yielded intimate knowledge.

I went into his skin, joined his sleep dreams, watched him eat, noted his postures, body language, how many times he peed, how lust overcame him, and how he chose females to comfort himself with.

Cartimandua broke his chastity vow long ago.

And his God gene was awake.

He knew an unseen power chose him.

The essence of life.

True, Little Arthur Verica would bring back the golden age, but without Mingo Drum Vercingetorix, there would have been no Arthur. One of two Madrawt fighters, him?

Tzu Strath, the Great War Lord, was the other pawn in life's game of good versus evil.

And the Madrawts were evil.

The God gene, ah, poor confused Mingo, he followed tribal gods but knew they stood for the equilibrium of nature's forces, knew of their prophecies that light would appear as Mahbon, the young god reborn.

A man destined to bring justice, a god on Maponos. And Mingo sought him, searching the books, finding him not. I think the closest he reached him was when he was able to sit on the grass, the carpet of our maker, and feel the oneness of the universe.

And Mingo, alone in his depressive moods, waited for the return of many deliverers he heard of. For he was a desperate man seeking anything to save his people.

And he thought of his son and longed to hug him.

His spirit shared its life essence with his surroundings. He became one with the stones, air, shrubs, and crawling beasts, and he grew strong when he was thus.

He cries, "A better world, for everyone!"

Share sandstone monoliths that gave his barren lands a forsaken appearance.

And he leaped from his high perch and sailed for home and at that moment my ship landed in the pink, purple dust of his domain and I strode forth on my feet.

Lorn Lukas came for Arthur, my Verica, and my golden dream.

I had stolen this ship to escape my master, Conchobhar, the Emperor of the East. A Light Traveler built for the fast speed of light travel.

Suddenly, a birdman plummeted from the sky, landing before me.

Startled and afraid, for I never expected to meet a Birdman *so close unexpectedly.*

They would capture me and take me to Mingo, where I would give a powerful speech, revealing my identity as Vern Lukas. I would declare my purpose: to serve his son and ensure everyone knew he was the deliverer.

Part of my mind scoffed at my proclamation of oratorical brilliance, calling me a buffoon.
ego.

And here I was, like a Christmas tree in my long navy-blue silken robes with white cuneiform writing printed on them, a tall black top hat, a black pigtail, and soft red shoes.

And here was this Birdman in front of me, unafraid, almost naked, tanned compared to my sickly pale skin.

His long brown hair was free and knotted with the wind. My hair gel worked; every strand stayed put.

I immediately recognized him as no ordinary birdman. He oozed confidence and superiority, knew he could kill me, and I knew it. And since I was alone, I depended completely upon his mercy.

The Bird Man approached me with long, languid steps and sniffed.

Me.

I sniffed my perfume and scents that made me smell so clean.

AND HE SPAT
In disgust.

I knew what he thought I was: one of them, you know, a perfumed rake.

Baths I liked and smelled clean, but he looked at me as if I was a bug. Well, he could sniff, he stunk, he needed a bath quick; he was offensive, and that was
>being polite.

An imperial scribe's life mainly involves accompanying the emperor.

This Birdman shone primitive strength in an innocent, uncorrupted fashion. I should have been the one scorning him.

I explained my identity and purpose to him. That shook him. I mean the official scribe to one emperor and then another, come to serve Mingo's son. I mean me, a human leaving a cozy job to come to what the humans called Tara 6.

"Go home, human," was his reply, and he turned to leave.

"Wait, if you are a friend of Mingo Drum, take me to him," I shout.

His anger flashed in his eyes, and for a moment, I feared for my future.

"You are looking at him and as for my son, leave him alone."

"Why, what have I done but immortalized him?" *I realized I still had plenty of road left!*

"You have made him a god," he replies and flies away, landing atop a green
marble monolith two hundred feet high.

>I did not understand what he meant. I consumed everything written about ancient prophecies.

People needed a savior.

And chose Little Arthur/Verica as the facts pointed to him as a potential Savior and my imaginative pen did the rest.

If anything, I had done this barbaric act a favor in getting a Bird child accepted as heir to Tzu Strath's army.

Also, I know several soothsayers who have close relationships with their guides, and they told me to look for a bird.

I have several large, enclosed domed parks near me.

Seriously, the trail led here.

What harm would it cause if people believed Arthur was an actual god? The gates of limitless pleasure his for the asking?

And instead of gratitude, this Birdman sneers at me! As the most powerful and respected scribe of both empires, I approached him, a feathered barbarian. I would seek Tzu Strath and find out where Little Arthur was. Alas, I'm a poor pilot and I landed my ship badly, rupturing the batteries and a few bolts, stranding me—and worse.

At his mercy, I felt.

There were beasties howling nearby.

He stood on the green marble, gazing down at me, contemplating my fate.

His lunch?

Oh well, I have nothing for it but to seek his "help!" I shout, as I knew I was nowhere near an aero garage, and it was hot here.

And as for his unhelpful attitude, I learned later why. First, I was human and, therefore, an enemy. *I was lucky he did not kill me.* But it went against what I had learned about Mingo, who saved humans/aliens. Haman Ma and Hart Woo were now celebrities on chat shows speaking of their ordeal with Mingo Drum Vercingetorix.

But it was me, good old me he did not like because he blamed me for exploiting his son and driving a wedge between them.

The wedge bit was the bottom line.

If his children survived wartime?

His uncontrollable warriors started the wars by burning settlers out of their legitimate imperial homesteads, did they?

I should never have mentioned my name.

So, I stood below the marble monolith, which was impressive. This carved artwork is **so valuable that many would pay a premium to display it on their patios.**

"Are you afraid of me, Mingo? One writer who holds a pen," I add quickly afraid he might fly off and leave me to whatever was howling.

Pride and vanity had always been the Bird people's enemies, and Mingo had enough for the entire nation.

He answered with a deep grunt and then dropped straight off that monolith and my heart missed a beat as I thought he was going to land on me.

Straight down at me, and I ordered my feet to move, but they froze!

He kept circling me.

"I fear only the sky falling on my head and the waves drowning me," his reply on the jet streams.

I was stunned silent.

Then a Maponosian Lion or Griffin pops up; *did I not pee then?*

I am only a scribe!

"Climb on the lion," he orders me. I have seen them in pictures but have never seen those teeth so close. And the lion was sniffing me and found me unpleasant to eat. *What was wrong with perfumed meat?*

Thank Dispater the good god I bathed regularly.

Then Mingo flew away and left me standing all alone with that

LION GRIFFON.

Then it trotted after him like a pet dog.

I had no choice, did I?

Suddenly, a trumpeting call filled the air, revealing a twotusked creature.

Maponosian elephant appears on my right and heads towards me.

My knees played a samba!

And I caught up with the lion griffin and held its tail so I could climb up. It could run away with me from that mad bull elephant charging us.

But the idiotic creature stands, staring vacantly.

Oh god, Dispater, Dispater, help me help, please, and then the trunks are sniffing me.

It sneezed repeatedly and distanced itself and gave me this disgusting stare.

What was wrong with my perfume?

Now we sped off towards The City of Winds; only after several miles did my heart return to a normal beat, and I remembered Mingo Drum Vercingetorix kept unusual company, and these must be Old Rag and Baldy!

He could keep his company!

Many times, I confess I thought about climbing the tallest rocks and wait for rescue in case it arrived, but He would only fly in and capture me.

I did not want to annoy Mingo Drum Vercingetorix with his funny friends!

And The City of Winds?

Workers tunneled thousands of stone monoliths into living apartments.

A fascinating eerie whistling wind produced many tones, as if the spirits of the dead talk.

I marveled.

"Well, human gossip writer, what will you write now?" Mingo asks.

"You," I reply.

He grunted, amused.

"Why did you choose my son as the usher of the golden age?"

"Would you believe me if I told you?" I shared a dream with him, one where an old man called Vate prophesied Arthur's coming to Maponos.

Write about him. I just followed my urge.

I saw recognition in his eyes, and I thought of fear. Did this aerial warrior know the Vate?

"Verica, my Lord, is ideal; he is part human and bird, of imperial lineage, one whom the empires' populations can relate to. No longer will the emperors be human, and the rest second-class citizens." I called as I was *worming* my way into acceptance. I also did not mention Arthur; the Vate had warned me not to.

Birdmen were the frontier, legends written, fortunes made by writers like me.

Vate only sped up things.

And being highly intelligent, I knew Mingo resented me for taking his son away and turning him into a superstar.

Upon reflection, he had a point.

He should not have misbehaved with Boudicca, should he?

Making a child fated to inherit Tzu Strath's army.

A child that would inherit the Artebrate Bird Nation of Mingo Drum Vercingetorix.

A child destined for galactic power.

How can Mingo blame me entirely, I ask you?

Then one day I watched the Birdman King Mingo Drum Vercingetorix approach me on one of his horrid red ants. I could not get used to them, as I was afraid of their giant mandibles. A monstrous insect without feelings except for a deep biological clock that programmed them to work, fight, tend eggs, and eat things like me.

I trusted them not.

Mingo could leap into the air and fly to safety; I knew I could not outrun the ant.

That is why I saw them as horrid ants.

Seeing one at a distance was fine by me, but not up close, thank you.

And because I was watching, the ant never noticed the disheveled figure behind it.

Those mandibles were noticeably big.

"Vern Lukas, so fate has dragged you here as well?"

Now I saw the hunchback.

Well, I wanted to meet the players of my game and was.

It was later, along with Nostradamus, that he told me why he had left the service of Tzu Strath.

"I am among the few remaining who enjoy freedom."

Times changed.

Nostradamus knew Planet Maponos would be another civilized world.

He expressed strong sympathy towards Mingo, **seeing them both as outcasts.**

"He has promised that I do not have to use my special talents against Tzu Strath.

"Remember, his word is law," he tells me. I immediately realized Mingo preferred me as an ally rather than an opponent.

All the guilt, the assassinations, the botched jobs that ruined lives were outdated! It is understandable why someone would go crazy clinging to such worthless things.

Nostradamus could find a fresh start on the frontier with Mingo..

To be reborn spiritually.

"In reality, I still serve Tzu Strath by protecting Little Arthur," he adds, and I saw
the logic.

"It will be Arthur who will eventually defeat and drive the Madrawts from our galaxies," more logic.

"Tzu Strath will outlaw you"? I pointed out.

He agrees, "Without those reward posters and cover blown, how else would Mingo trust me?" He asks, and at once, I suspected him and Tzu Strath's real motives.

Was Nostradamus getting close to his target for a kill?

Do I warn Mingo?

NO.

I secretly hoped Mingo would disappear, allowing Arthur, my creation, to bring in the golden age.

I admit I still saw Mingo as a barbarian, not wanting the benefits of civilization.

I guess I and Nostradamus were not much different, *were we readers*?

At least we were working for the same end, the golden age.

Nostradamus informs me, with a grin, "In a few days, we are heading down the River of Skulls." Why?

"Sounds like something out of Space Dragons and Dungeons," I reply, and he replies with a bigger grin.

"Besides, Arthur will pardon me because it is he who will eventually pay my wages?" Lukas

Song of Nostradamus

"I am the shadow man.
The fly on your knee.
A flea in your blanket.
The lump under the towel as you shower.
The cat on your lap?
I am Nostradamus.
The shadow man."

CHAPTER 34   CARTIMANDUA

Beware, she has a tail, never mind the ingrowing toenails.

The River of Skulls was worse than I imagined any game designer could dream up.
It stood for everything that was barbaric about Planet Maponos (Tara).
It stunk of age. It teemed with swamp dragons, gnarled trees, and fire-scarred areas.

Gododdin trophies littered the trees as a warning to those who entered their domain.

Praise be mostly Madrawt, thank Dispater, our imperial god.
Thank Tzu Strath for the Choking Death vaccine because the place had mosquitoes.

The only beauty was above, in treetops where flowering vines bloomed, and butterflies and glorious colored hummingbirds and noisy apes lived.

Snakes littered the path we took.
Snakes disgust me. I cannot explain it, but the sight of one, even caged, sends shivers down my spine. And someone had not caged them.

A complete contrast to the dry wilderness we had come from. The harsh reality of the planet made me grateful for seeing its true nature, far removed from the idealized refuge I had envisioned.

Now looking ahead at Nostradamus walking behind Mingo as we followed an ant cohort that was clearing a path through the swamp, *chomping snakes.*

"Mingo's first road, Mingo Highway 1," Mingo jokes but is serious.

A road to Torrs, the capital of the Gododdin. He never realized roads brought commerce, which brought wealth that meant a demand for trinkets and an end to his lifestyle.

He could fly. What use roads?

I heard tales of the Gododdin; fear gripped me. A cohort of ants to protect us, they must be more savage than Mingo!

We soon reached a large river teeming with reptiles. The sight of the Temple of Skulls, true to its name, filled me with disgust.

Queen Cartimandua, beautiful yet ruthless, stood across the river. I was gaining considerable knowledge about the Bird people, who I had transformed into heroic saviors of our world. Soon I would ask Mingo to take me to Tzu Strath because here I do little to help Arthur **reach his destiny. Little Arthur.**
Only by writing can I do that.

And Mingo knew that. Why else keep me here amongst the mosquitoes, hoping I did get bitten and get a disease? He seems to mimic the way I work.

Great minds think alike.

He wanted his son back when I left, but it was too late.

Though I missed the secret meeting between Cartimandua and Mingo, the City of Torrs buzzed with a celebration that night. The Gododdin and Mingo, the Artebrate, had declared peace.

The Manticore Legion stayed alert that night for that reason.

As did Cartimandua's palace guard?

Trust was lacking.

"Want me to pass your writings back to your publisher?" Nostradamus asks.

Astonished, I looked at him.

"I have lines of communication open to Tzu Strath; it is up to you?"

I took it.

I did not report him to Mingo, and I confirmed my suspicions about this spy. Deep down I wanted King Mingo Drum Vercingetorix dead and buried for Arthur's star to rise and mine as well.

My writings linked Arthur and me.

Anyway, after Cartimandua, we headed north.

Here, Birdman Nations, I never knew existed.

Meanwhile, ants cleared a path, the climate shifted from swamp to forest, and temperatures dropped.

Behind us came an army of flightless Bird men and ants and in the sky, the Manticore Legion and Gododdin cohorts for our numbers were growing,

Were we off to glorious war?

Is war glorious reader?

And always at my side is the lion creature Old Rag and two proboscis elephant Baldy. Yes, I felt a prisoner and they, my guards.

And Queen Cartimandua came for me alone. She wore little apart from her blue woolen cape and her beauty stirred me, even if she had wings and a tail.

She was still all woman.

"You are Vern Lukas, heard of you," she tells me; well, who

says the position did not bring rewards? So, knew straight away she wanted *me; success brought BIG HEADEDNESS,*

"You can make me immortal Vern; do you mind if I call you Vern?"

"No," and was telling the truth. *She was packing what it counts. Men, unfortunately, are men.*

"Mingo will soon attack; observe, then report. I want you to write about me, Vern; I am not a barbarian. But according to Tzu's populace, a vulture.

These humans will govern the planet. I want the human luxuries, **want to help me get them?"**

Interruption.

At first, she was a colorful speck, hidden amongst birdmen warriors and carnyx hoots.

"We are both to die this day, human scribe," Mingo grunts.

Many grunts responded from the group approaching.

"Cartimandua, the Queen of Pirates," Mingo warned me and grunts his call for aid.

I was a worried man indeed

Pondering over my fate.

"Cartimandua, meet Vern Lucas," Mingo and this beauty fell silent. Mingo did not know she had met me quietly at night.

Ah, night, time for secret meetings of Amor.

"Vern, you are not, and I imagined," this woman says as she lifts my smock to look at my legs. She was a talented actor.

Mingo had a good look.

I was being examined.

Next, her hands were about my face, opening my mouth and checking my white teeth.

Then a hand dropped and grabbed.

"I am an impressed writer; you can write about me. Well done Mingo, I thank you for your gift," and made ready to leave with me.

Specks were gathering in the sky; the Manticore legion was coming.

Mingo always kept them in a cough's hearing.

Cartimandua had planted lust in me, a son of Adam.

*

After that, I saw Cartimandua too much.
I became addicted to her.
Sex has a powerful influence on men, leading to insatiable cravings.
When you write poetry, love raises its ugly head, and everything seems beautiful.
I filled the galaxies of her heroic pirate deeds.
Blockbusters came out on her.
She rewarded me: Cartimandua states, "You only want my body."
That was true, what a body. I have eyes, and she got immortality in ink and illustrations of her in feathered cloaks and golden armor, her hair awash, the stars behind her, and the sun under her feet.
Some tales had her, the huntress, standing on a fallen beast, Mingo.
I made men envious of my catch.
Make men want a birdie as well.
Her presence should draw men to Maponos.
To catch a Birdie woman for themselves.

And I painted her equally to Queen Boadicea of Icinea.

Adolescent boy song of the empire
"She wore pink that made me wink. Repeat 3 times.
Black, that made me drool.
Red that I fainted.
She took my cherry.
Then it was gone.
Leave me a note.
You useless boy.
She wore pink, which made me wink." Repeat 3 times.

Vern Lukas

CHAPTER 35 A YEAR AGO

Statue of Nostradamus

Tzu Strath, a powerful warlord, stood by the lakeside with Conchobhar, Emperor of the East,
Conchobhar wanted an alliance against the Madrawts.
Tzu Strath knew this made good sense.
The empire's stability, what stability?

To recognize Conchobhar as heir to the throne of his deceased father, Vortigern. Arthur's life faces peril should this occur.
A winged beast boy, not Conchobhar, would usher in the golden age.
Yes, Tzu Strath loved this grandson with wings, which he must thank Vern Lukas for, or he saw Arthur as Conchobhar did, *the beast.*
And called Maponos Tara 6 still.
And stopped ranting about Bird seed having infected his lineage. Arthur's fame made his grandfather known, helping

to erase the Bird stain from Mingo Drum, yes?

The human world was still in its early stages. And Conchobhar's presence reminded him of the Peace Marriage that brought bile to his throat.

Conchobhar to Tzu represented Vortigern, the instrument of that marriage, and here was Vortigern's whelp demanding loyalty.

Enough that Peace Marriage had brought Mingo Drum Vercingetorix closer into his life than planned.

As for Arthur, he was a real menace these days, bombing his troopers and all sorts who did not keep one eye glued to the sky.

Oh sweetie Boudicca, your beast boy can fly.

"**Ratta tat,**" the boy would scream and drop a few chicken eggs.

His aerial antics brightened the day. People admired with longing eyes the loop the loops.

He, Boudicca's son and the old man's grandson, was the mischievous child with a tail.

"Plums, I will kill his father," Boudicca knew Arthur had seen his dad loop the loop.

"I will help you fight the Madrawts, but I want something in return," Tzu Strath surprised Conchobhar.

Readers, Conchobhar is an emperor, and Tzu is a low-life general.

"**What?**"

"**Galaxies.**"

*

Old man Vate was smiling when he appeared to a little boy who had long ago stopped bawling for his mama because he had shinned his wings flying amongst shrubs; now he flew amongst troopers and swore like one to his mother's horror.

He had been naughty and wished he had not broken her rules by flying outside the garden.

Desperately craved a hug and cuddle.

Eyed Vate suspiciously.

He knew all about dirty old strangers. Especially ones that lived in moldy spider infested caves.

He expected sweets.

Fly in front of the old man, flexing his claws.

It was Bird blood in him, and granddad took fits over this.

However, Vate, the old man, smiled because Tzu Strath just got for the boy his future empire.

This boy required those galaxies to win the ending battles against evil.

Madrawt.

"Little Arthur," the old man Vate smiling.

Young Arthur struggled to name the man.

He remembered him from the cave. He had not hurt Arthur then. Maybe Mama sent him to find him?

Whatever the old man squatted and rubbed the shinned skin, the pain vanished and made Arthur happy. Arthur needs a good toffee chew.

The old man shared a tale with Arthur about a young king on a distant planet called Earth. He explained how Arthur would be the savior of his people.

"Like me?"

The Vate smiled.

Arthur was well-informed about Vern Lukas. It was impossible to keep such a secret,
especially in an army camp.

*

A thousand cold barren miles north of the lands of the Bird Nation Dalriada, Mingo
Drum Vercingetorix was preparing for what he called the decisive battle against the Madrawts.

Before him was a vast Birdman warrior horde of varying ages, sexes, and of course,

                      ant phalanxes.

In fact, **anyone** strong enough to thrust a probe spear was here.

Anyone able to thrust a short sword up and further into a Madrawt chest was here.

Many regarded Mingo as if he were a god, a resurrected Mahbon.

Restore the Bird people's golden age.

Little Arthur was not in the minds of anyone, Vern Lukas had competition.

All **anyone** knew Mingo's son by Boudicca was not called Arthur, but Verica and he was a boy called Arthur who was, for the humans, a golden age, which meant

the end of the free!

Mingo and Queen Cartimandua welcomed a son, Cuchulain.

Although happy with his pure-bred son, he still loved Verica and cursed Tzu Strath and Boudicca for removing him into a purely human world.

"Two names are wrong.

He is uncertain about his identity." Mingo had shouted at me, Vern, as if it was my fault.

He did this a lot these days while drinking. He seemed like a sorrowful father who had lost many children. You could not easily hate something you had made legendary, but envy was easy,

he had
FLIGHT,
Freedom of will,
To go where he pleased in his lands.
Freedom from silks and cosmetics.
To be savage away from civilization.
Freedom to live heroically.
Indulging in woman, wine, and song as a warrior might have a premature death.
Freedom from the evils of civilization.
He was tall, strong, a warrior out of the past.

Our past, our myths.'

Yet he had laws.
He was a conflict.
Did I hate him?

I needed to admit I was jealous of his ways, but he was not human. That influenced my writings against him these days; what I created, I could destroy; he was as villainous as the Madrawts.

But he was already a legend on the frontier before I started writing; I just took over.

My writings solely supported Arthur, never referencing his other name.

His birdie name readers.

To annoy Mingo without a doubt.

Many spies would keep me informed of what Mingo planned. Bird men who had settled down peacefully amongst the imperial settlers and adopted human ways. And he did nothing to stop me; I suppose Arthur was Verica whom he longed for back.

Arthur, he believed, would free his people, but differently.

Mingo could click his tail and take Cartimandua from me.

This rivalry influenced my pen against him.

Although he was nowhere near Cartimandua, I saw him in her eyes and knew he must visit behind me. *Love, lust, and murder are all entwined, are they not?*

I understood his affection for Boudicca, viewing Cartimandua as a mere toy.

Humans and aliens were just as guilty, but I was all anti-Mingo.

Cartimandua captivated me. The sensible course of action would be for me to leave her and seek another who would give me her heart.

All is fair in love and war.

And here he was, addressing his great host, preparing his army for battle, sober.

"We are the last of the free." Mingo's most famous line was

coming alive again.
Then a shadowy figure appeared behind him.
It was menacing.
I tensed, expecting the assassin's short sword to cut his spine.
The entire host moved forward in anger.

Yet it was Nostradamus who leaped from his master's feet and threw himself at the
Madrawt, whose sword pierced him, fell, pulling the assassin with him, and Nostradamus tripped Mingo, who had rushed to help,.
Why?
'BANG.'
The small man aimed the bomb at Madrawt, and it exploded with a bang.

Now Mingo lifted Nostradamus and carried him a safe distance, Madrawts like Mingo, in my eyes, clung to life like lower life forms do.

Mingo did wrong, leaving his assassin to die a private, slow death.

Not one warrior present slew the Madrawt. He had already prepared himself to meet his assassin's goddess and no matter what they did to him; he was happy dying the way an assassin should gain entry to Heaven, in total agony.

"My word is law in my domain."

He was more beastly than I wanted to admit because he was a beast. Like a snake attacks a lion that mauls the serpent and goes away, the snake, expecting no help from the lion, dies slowly in the scorching sun, an uncomfortable death.

The lion suffers no remorse and sleeps well, even though the doomed snake hissed loudly all that night, venting its pain.

Mingo was indeed the lion!

I, Vern, put the Madrawt out of misery; I was human.

Reader, what would you do? Kick the Madrawt places, pee on him/her?

Medical professionals attended to Nostradamus and

removed his wrists.

He was full of the powerful painkiller *that allowed consciousness.*

Was this Mingo's *punishment* for knowing that Nostradamus would one day betray him to Tzu Strath?

I thought I was the only one who suspected.

Then I found out Nostradamus *had requested consciousness.*

"I fear the dark tunnel that awaits sinners," he whispers to me in gasps.

His flak jacket had saved his torso from significant injury; he was a lucky man.

"Saved the son of a bird, yes?"

"Why?" I ask.

"He is everything I admire."

PAUSE.

"I always wanted to fly."

PAUSE.

"He must live for Arthur."

PAUSE.

I felt a terrible guilt my writings had caused upon Nostradamus who believed my writings.

My error brought us here.

Nostradamus laughed.

He was thinking of the assassin's heaven,

Here entwines with ghost women in spiritual union, the equivalent of physical union.

We believe we are a highly prized union on the other side, thanks to Dispater's religion, and the Bird men accept this. Of course, they do; they accept I.O.U. over there.

Makes dying for an emperor easier.

"I set the clock; he cannot escape himself."

Then, just like that, he died.

Later, I stopped sulking and thought about what he had said, **"I have set the clock,**
he cannot escape."

Damn the Vate for choosing us all.

Nostradamus to die now.
I want to write.
Mingo Drum to kill.
Arthur's mission: end galactic evil.
Madrawt.
Later, Mingo came and spoke to me briefly.
"Conchobhar has landed an army on the north pole, and in the south, Tzu Strath has sent his army over our borders.
We are at war again."
The war had never truly ended, just simmered beneath the surface, and now it had officially returned. He mounted a red ant and went to lead his army. He halted, turned toward me, and gave a salute.
I had won.
He was riding to his death and knew.
I stopped hating him at that precise moment; he was the brave beast I had always
admired and written about.
"I set the clock, he cannot escape," what did Nostradamus mean?
About a year after Mingo Drums Vercingetorix's uncertified death, a prostitute from Nostradamus gave me a sealed container,
Nostradamus held a similar appeal to her, as he did too many.
The document told much about Mingo's inner self.

But for the moment. Mingo sent the expert spy's body south to Tzu Strath. To the very front lines, Bird men warriors escorted the body on an aerial float with much carnyx noise and banners.
Cartimandua had gone with her warriors to fight the enemies of the free. It felt like the Little Bighorn, their last performance.
They were honoring Nostradamus for giving his physical

life to let Mingo stay in this dimension.

Of course, Tzu Strath knew Mingo murdered Nostradamus.

I had to choose between Nostradamus and Cartimandua.

Arthur was across the border with Boudicca.

I went with the body of Nostradamus.

Nostradamus had a choice: to live or to die.

And over a Birdman.

Mingo Drum Vercingetorix.

"We are the last of the free.

To the north there is ice.

To the South, our enemy and slavery.

Better to die free than a slave."

I found a great wealth of love for Mingo Drum and decided not to hurt him anymore. This man, unlike a beast, possessed the power of flight.

No one expected what happened next.

A disaster.

A catastrophe.

I heard about Mingo's battle with the Madrawts. During a quest to free Birdman's captives from retreating Madrawts, the Madrawts captured him.

He no longer had the magic of his sword Law, to keep his bogeymen away.

Unknown spies had captured Boudicca and Arthur as well.

Nostradamus: blooming spies are everywhere.

So, deserting Cartimandua, I arrived at Tzu Strath's H.Q. for nothing because my creation had gone.

I feared the future.

Cartimandua might dispose me for leaving her for Arthur's destiny.

She only saw her beauty in the morning birdsong.

And Tzu Strath, upon hearing that the Bird men were now leaderless, threw all his mighty divisions along with Conchohbar's upon the Bird men nations who
fragmented.

The military genius of Mingo Drum Vercingetorix was not

available during those days of darkness.

Would the nations ever recover?

Chop off the head, Julius Caeser's strategy.

*

"I would like to accompany Tribune Cedric Henry in his search for Arthur and Boudicca," I ask.

Tzu needed Nostradamus.

And Tzu Strath looked me up and down, seeing my silks replaced by frontier armor; the change impressed him. Planet Maponos made me grow up and hardened my outlook on life.

"Double-cross me with your idyllic writings, and I will send assassins after you to neuter you no matter where you go," it was his way of agreeing.

I accepted.

I did not want death anyway, apart from loving myself; Cartimandua had given me a winged daughter. Even if she was a half-bird, she was beautiful.

A bonny budgie reader?

"He really is grateful to you for what you have given his Arthur," Tribune Henry means Tzu.

I gave him a puzzled look.

"Arthur, an identity, an empire, a future."

PAUSE.

"Birdmen have no futures."

PAUSE.

As we left the city, I saw what he meant about Birdmen having a future. The friendlies aped human/alien fashion, and the clothes did not suit them. They looked comical in their black top hats and imperial battle fatigues.

Robbed of their noble lion clothes and torso armor.

Some had wings but drove hover cars.

In their gardens thrown-out junk, like broken fridges, televisions, and beer cans.

Some gardens are mostly weeds and burned-out vehicles. The trash cans are full of takeaway wrappers.

Instead of soaring freely in the sky, youths idled aimlessly in the streets.

Boredom led to trophy collecting.

"Later, Tzu Strath made them produce the human heads and gave them a burial and hung a few Bird men to get the message across," Tribune Henry, watching me.

On every corner, sleazy bars are present, with Bird women requesting treats.

I noticed wingless Bird people interbreeding with Stardust Corporation's creations.

Well-compensated individuals.

Humans wanted the secret of flight.

I saw **Nostradamus's ticking clock** and hoped Mingo Drum would escape it and die free.

I was about my daughter's future.

"Look over there! Tzu Strath is putting up a statue of Nostradamus." Lonely.
hunchback staring out into the Birdmen Nations, the wilderness, I think Nostradamus's
clone will appreciate Tzu's act as a loyal servant, will you?" Henry asked.

I stayed silent, and the statue was likely to influence the clone to emulate the
Original and spy.

Vern translates Birdie's death chant.

Oran bias
Oran bias
We chant
Before we battle.
Oran bias.
Oran bias.
Ancestors help us.
I fought well.
I am dying.

I am dead.
Oran bias.
Oran bias.

CHAPTER 36 REUNITED

Stocks

Mingo Drum Vercingetorix stood in front of Ce-Ra, Lord and Emperor of Madrawts and Emperor of the West. He smiled now and again at Ce-Ra's insults and grimaced, showing hate when guards slapped and kicked him.

Ce-Ra wanted Mingo humiliated and broken before he killed him; the trouble is Mingo knew he was to die horribly, so why grovel?
Ce-Ra would grant him a slow death, like in the tin mines. The idea of toying with Mingo's life excited him and was a welcome break from ruling his empire. Mingo, one of his most hated foes, now stood directly before him.

What a pleasant experience it was.

Then a shadowy figure appeared behind Ce-Ra, and Mingo growled when he recognized Diviciacus, who stood still as if he met a dangerous lion.

Only when he realized Mingo could not hurt him did he advance and play a game upon Mingo's chest with his butchering knife, pretending to be after a heart for the wonderful Huitzilopitchli.

Ce-Ra moved in his seat as he watched Mingo's blood run down his chest.

Diviciacus pulled back his hand, ready to thrust his dagger.

"No," Ce-Ra shouts, thinking **tin mine.**

"Huitzilopitchli demands the heart of his enemy," says Diviciacus.

The courtiers, not guards, murmured agreement.

Ce-Ra mentally noted each who opened a mouth; *soon opening their mouths to drink vile potions.*

He also noted that Diviciacus had gotten too **big** for his shoes.

Diviciacus, drunk with hash, was oblivious to Ce-Ra's annoyance.

Huitzilopitchli wanted **this** strong heart. Needed to protect the Madrawt world from evil.

The heart of Ce-Ra.

Kernwy smiled, knowing Huitzilopitchli would speak to Diviciacus and tell him to tell his people to make him Priest Protector of the Madrawt Empire.

Kernwy grinned as he visualized Ce-Ra's response.

Madrawts would never tolerate the human hash-addict rule.

Now Diviciacus had brought in Boudicca, who stood behind Ce-Ra.

He noticed her.

"Bring in Boudicca," Ce-Ra demands

A belt and controls manipulated by Ce-Ra constricted her body.

His whim was to show Mingo how it worked like a boa, and eventually, Boudicca passed out.

Losing her entertainment value.

Mingo prayed to his bird gods for strength to avenge this act.

Instead, he could only stand manacled and watch Boudicca with sadness.

Seeing a heart on the altar, Boudicca panicked, believing it Mingo's.

Then, mistaking Mingo's stare for a beast's pity.

She did not recognize the broken love there. Love, however, is a complex and ever-changing force.

So, her love for him made her stare back haughtily at him instead of Ce-Ra, and neither lover considered their partner's imprisonment.

Ming Drum went cold because he saw she still **hated him.**

Ce-Ra was an intelligent frog, sorry man - his success proved it. He saw the game of love being played and found it amusing.

This pain far surpassed that of the tin mines or the quick dagger.

He also had an ace card, which he now produced.

Mingo died when he saw his son.

The boy should have been safe with Boudicca in the lands of Tzu Strath.

"Verica," he shouts in agony.

The boy cuddled into Little Drum, not him.

The Birdman went berserk in his manacles, used his talons, and raked.

Ce-Ra asked if the Birdman was that strong, but he did not flee his seat; he paid guards to die, *yes or no reader?*

Boudicca pulled her child, Arthur, to herself.

Little Drum climbed to the top of her head.

Madrawt's hands tried to pull Arthur from her.

The boy who called Arthur for a year and told his father was a beast did see his father as a barbarian that day, tearing Madrawts with his taloned feet.

Arthur realized the grunts were not human because he forgot he was not entirely human. A year's absence from his father and natural childhood shyness kept the boy distant.

Who was called father?

"Bat's son, a birdie egg hatched, a were-creature that howls at the moon," where
some names he had heard imperial children taunt him with at school.

Boudicca had allowed Arthur as much of a normal education as possible, for those brought up entirely at court, history shows, make evil emperors.

Grandfather Tzu was an eager helper to humanize the boy. And Mingo Drum Vercingetorix aided by not insisting he see the boy he knew as Verica. His love for Boudicca demanded he stay away from her for he believed she hated him. He was a beast.

The boy needed one soul; these two had given him two.

A boy needs a mother more than a father.

Mingo was not there to call him Verica.

Boudicca and this man are fools.

To control Mingo, Ce-Ra used the belt on Boudicca, whose gasps and shouts brought Mingo towards her, and when she lay still with Verica lying motionless atop her, he thought them dead and, in a final desperate act to kill his aggressor rushed the podium where Ce-Ra sat.

And raked the left knee of Diviciacus apart.

Then many stun guns felled the savage beast that was the father of Arthur/Verica.

Verica's name almost escaped Mingo's mouth.

Arthur, a human name, Verica should know what Mingo Drum Vercingetorix stood
for:

The pride of vanity that the Bird man Nation stood for.
Honor.
To speak the truth.
Never lie.
Look after the backward.
Be fearless in battle.
Fear nothing, except the sky falling on your head.
And the waves drowning you.

*

Mingo awoke alone, his head hurt. He tasted blood on his lips, and his eyes were puffy.

Worse, he wanted a wee and saw he was in public stocks.

Pigeon droppings littered the iron stocks, the air gray, dawn coming soon.

With it torture, he could not imagine that the Madrawt public filled the market outside their Hall of Law; they would poke, spit, beat, and make day hell. During hell, three times, the city watch would come and feed him.

He was almost naked.

The toilet was a hole underneath his legs.

About him, cages, tall stakes, and gallows adorned with the executed and glass beakers holding the pickled remains of those that went before him.

The Madrawt public liked their prisoners to suffer.

Mingo Drum Vercingetorix knew this was where he would die. Accepting his fate, he knew that doom awaited his loved ones.

He lacked the strength to break the iron stocks and save them.

Even thinking of his other free son, Cuchulain by Cartimandua, did not strengthen his desire to live.

Cartimandua ensured he never saw Cuchulain.

A Gododdin boy hating all Artebrates.

What problem did women have, like Boudicca? You love

them, have children and then they do not let you near them! *Mingo Drum sure could pick his women!*

"I have two fine sons, and I cannot hug and kiss them to make them feel safe and wanted.
Women, why do I need them?" He gasped at a rat that raised itself on its haunches, listening.

Now I Vern Lukas speak from the heart, "He loved Cuchulain, and he was not from the womb of the woman he loved. Nor was Cuchulain involved in the affairs of destiny.

The Vate had avoided the lad, and unless Arthur/Verica committed suicide, no one would notice Cuchulain.

It is not for us to complain against the expert potter, Dispater the Imperia God.

"You did not live for me Mingo Drum Vercingetorix," Cuchulain wrote much later in life. *He should be grateful fate did not need him so he could live a normal flight-filled life.*

Mingo, silly man, he still is a son of your blood.

Verica shouts, "Daddy, you are my best friend!" as he ran to be carried on those big, winged shoulders'

He remembered this as a man.

"When I was a baby, I did not know my father. When I was a boy,

I Cuchulain did not know my father because he was absent.
Poor Mingo Drum was a complex man full of complex guilt.
A complex man full of remorse.
Poor Mingo Drum was a complex man full of pessimism.
A complex man full of defeat.

And took silent joy in watching the gray dawn sky come alive with a paintbrush
that filled the horizon with pinks and reds.

Each day he would not disappoint his public, for he roared and grunted and they Clapped. Madrawt's children ran up to him and spat, kicked, and pulled his long
brown hair.

One even poked his left eye.

He coughed, "Free, no more."

And the Madrawts would agree with him.

With the disgusting food and lack of fluids under the Madrawt sun, he would soon dry out and be stuck in one of those glass beakers for future Madrawts not to fear their boggy man.

"I am the last of the free," Mingo coughed and a Madrawt girl child ran to him and slapped his lips, so they bled. She also ran away crying because his eagle beak grazed her palm; *what goes around come around!*

Madrawt Road Chain gang Chant. Translated by Vern.

"They Whip us.
 They work us.
 The chain gang.
 Die Kettenbande
 They Whip us.
 Making roads.
 Farming, mining.
  They whip us good," repeat till exhausted.

Told Vern Lukas by Madrawt prisoners

CHAPTER 37 SATAN'S PRINCEDOM

Planet Madrawt is hell

Tzu Strath inherited Nostradamus's spy network for his employees, who came to him for pay and told him where Boudicca was.

"It is not surprising then that I, Vern Lukas, Tribune Cedric Henry, and Color Sergeant Kenala found us together on Planet Madrawt.
What a strange world Madrawt is!
It is pure evil.
There are four suns, and the planet revolves around S fashion.
The planet is humid, a *nursery for tadpoles transforming into*

Madrawts.

Fern covered and imagined walking into a haunted house. You feel the chill, neck prickling, unseen spirits reaching too close to you. You hear them, but there is nothing there to hear. Poltergeist activity abounds from the many slaves extinguished here.

Such is Planet Madrawt. *Pure evil, I Told you, readers.*

What if Satan exists as a heavenly prince? Well, Madrawt was his footstool!

The vegetation was carnivorous.

Animals filled markets for circuses.

Planet Madrawt is huge and has ecological zones not known to us. Full of ferocious wild men, *not amphibians.*

Coupled with this, the rigid Madrawt Laws. No wonder the Madrawt is cruel.

Their lords wield absolute power, epitomized by their emperor.

Regarded as their living war god, Huitzilopitchli.

If defeat occurs, the defeated usually *ends up on the god's altar.*

The most valuable possession the Madrawts offer their god to avert planetary disaster.

Ce-Ra coveted this job. Remember, this was before he misjudged Mingo Drum Vercingetorix, the last of the free.

Little wonder Ce-Ra carved hearts on the altar. They prohibited females from holding the top job.

Madrawt society viewed women as child bearers.

A Madrawt female kept dozens of tadpoles in her womb till birth.

Huitzilopitchli had created women for that purpose, frolicking.

This explains why the cosmetic, fashion, and lingerie business was big business on Madrawt Planet.

The majority who harassed Mingo in the stocks and En

route to the public arena were women.

He stood for the brutal nature of Madrawt men.

It was their men they were abusing; Mingo was just a gigantic bird who never harmed them, apart from sending their sons to paradise.

Indeed, the Planet Madrawt was the Princedom of Satan.

*

Vern Lukas, along with Tribune Cedric Henry, proposed a plan to undergo cosmetic alteration to resemble Madrawts.

I tell you, the false skin felt hot and itchy, and I must remember that my skin under my clothes remained uncovered. It was mine, and language implants enabled me to hear and speak Madrawt.

We wore long gray smocks, signaling we were veterans of war, and the cosmetic boys had scarred up our faces, stitches here and there.

We could hire ourselves out at Halloween parties and make a large profit. The Madrawts held
their veterans in high esteem, as those who had exposed themselves to death for the glory of Huitzilopitchli.

People nicknamed the veterans the Walking Dead

Everything is free.

You do not need any identification.

We were veterans, honored and respected.

Restaurants left plates of scraps at their back doors for our kind.

We carried little begging bowls as veterans got no pension; we were Walking Dead

were we not?

A Madrawt veteran ditty.

"Stinking walking Madrawt zombies.

Rats are our mates.

Flies our standards.

Roaches are our bed companions.
Ticks to tickle us.
Fleas to share our blood.
Lice to hang as earrings.
Carbuncles to color our seats.
Soap our enemy.
Stink our aura.
We veterans."

People believed that giving to a veteran's begging bowl brought good fortune, as people said Huitzilopitchli would listen to your requests.

We slept at the back of an inn in donated fold-down beds. Some veterans sheltered under a corrugated shed roof, with jugs of ale. Now you see, Madrawt is a nation geared for war. *Many had frogs, sorry, sons in the front lines.*

And if we fancied a Madrawt whore, we could have one free, but we were not Madrawt, for in our eyes, they were blooming horrendous, ugly creatures. Feeling dictates beauty.

Thus, we wondered about their capital, Madrawt, seeking Boudicca and Arthur; I will tell you Nostradamus would have been proud of us. And we headed straight to the Grand Palace of their Lord, hoping to find their important captives.

Inside the Grand Palace, a shrine for veterans to worship and bring good luck to the emperor.

Here, we saw Boudicca walking in crocodile fashion with other ladies of the harem.

We felt pity. If Madrawt whores were repulsive to us, what then was the Madrawt male abusing Boudicca? This was not a movie; it was a real-life' No hero to rescue the starlet.

Boudicca was a beautiful woman, Ce-Ra, we knew, knew too.

For one hour a day in the morning, these beautiful women from many planets tendered the blessings of Huitzilopitchli to his Walking Dead.

Dispater, the good imperial god, had blessed us.

Previously, harem women provided entertainment, for when they amused us veterans, they lay with Huitzilopitchli.

Exception one did. Someone left his body as a reminder to the Walking Dead and anyone who insisted on their customary rights with a harem woman.

Ce-Ra was no fool. He understood the value of custom and the value of despotic power and the fear of superstition surrounding The Walking Dead.

"Boudicca, it is Tribune Henry," he whispers to her as she fills up his plate with saffron rice.

She did not flinch but stared into his red contact lenses.

She came back with rice chicken for me and saw to our needs. We learned Arthur was a hostage in the Tower of the Condemned.

"Mingo dead?" That shook me.

Could it be true, the man who had taken me out of my blue perfumed scribe robes into armor and the frontier was dead?

I owed Mingo Drum Vercingetorix to find out the truth.

Then Cartimandua would truly be mine.

And understood why Mingo Drum should give his heart to Boudicca. She was a beautiful woman by human standards, and someone like her could only give her heart to someone like Mingo Drum Vercingetorix

We returned with a gray smock for her to pass her off as a Walking Dead.

Then she could leave with us.

And it worked.

"We can repeat what we did with Arthur in the Tower of the Condemned," I hope.

But Boudicca recommended caution; the Madrawts were not stupid, but being so confident, we did not plan properly.

Yes, our gray smocks had made us invisible.

Boudicca song.
"*Sgal,*
 I loved someone.
 My love is dead.
 Howl.
 What have I done.
 Stubborn girl.
 Time wasted.
 My love is dead..
 Sgal."

From what I remember, Vern Lukas.

CHAPTER 38 THE OLD MAN AGAIN

Madrawt prison cell

The Madrawts wanted Mingo to suffer if possible, so his guards would
throw disinfectant over him, and when this happened, the crowd heaved.

The liquid would splash, burning them in various directions.

Mingo's strength could not halt his agonizing decline. He would *foam, grunt, roar,* and try to rear to shake the fluid off; *it stung terribly*.

Crusty scabs formed where beaten, protecting him from germs.

And tired, he began to sag and sleep, and as he did, the neck-clasp would choke him and awake him rudely.

As for abolitions, he tried to keep that for nights when few Madrawts were about, but because of his poor diet, he found it humiliating during the daytime.

BIRD Feeding times were popular with the crowds for his guard's mixed hot peppers into his watery gruel, where they showed him the floating roaches.

And force-feeding him, he would roar over the disgusting mixture. The Madrawt public craved a glimpse of the beast, and the guards ensured they got it.

"Mingo Drum, Mingo Drum,"
  Pig Mingo,
  Chained up, Mingo,
  Mingo, Mingo Drum," the Madrawt kids would sing as they played their own form
of hopscotch.

And we heard it on our approach to the Tower of the Condemned.

"What does this mean?" I ask.

Tribune Henry read my mind. Is Mingo alive?

"Our mission is to free Arthur," he reminds and knew he was right, "Do not screw
things up, or I will make sure Tzu Strath finds you, scribe!"

Well, at least his silent hostility was in the open; he had not wanted a pen pusher on this dangerous mission. My fame as a scribe linked to Arthur also played a part.

Golden Age *bird men he hated.*

He felt awkward in my presence, as if my fame made him submissive to me. But all knew Tribune Cedric Henry was Tzu Strath's right hand.

Well, I was his left.

They entered the Tower of the Condemned.

It was dark, badly lit, damp, decay smelling.

Abandon hope to all of you who enter.

Disease condemned Arthur to lingering ill health and death here.

What looked like beggars manned a desk.

They branded the sign for prisoners upon foreheads. Their desk job provided a welcome escape from the fate that awaited them.

"Our goal is to find a condemned Walking Death. His name is Pahtamon," Henry lied.

The reprieved checked their computer, because they had many Pahtamons here, as it was a common name on Madrawt. It also took many Sus; the Madrawt dollar to make sure this reprieved showed us about the cells.

The men wore a mix of clothing taken from the condemned. Boils afflicted the first Pahtamon, a Madrawt.

He had one eye *removed*.

Speechless, *taken his tongue.*

One of our guards used a cattle prod on him, so he awoke.

"That him?"

Henry shook his head negatively.

The guard, poking the prisoner, explains his presence: "He stole from Huitzilopitchli."

We grunt approval and left the condemned having a fit on the floor that was his furniture.

The second Pahtamon was an elderly man.

How does this relate to finding Arthur? *We were in the tower planning to continue from that point.*

"He was a general, and next to him, a female; she was a favorite of Ce-Ra," one guard remarked, pointing out the alien woman in the cell.

"For a money, you can have her," he meant it, believing he was doing a favor as he saw us no better than himself.

He threw a switch and electrocuted the general, but not enough to kill.

"I used to serve under him," the guard shocked him.

Henry paid the man for the woman.

Was Henry insane? Nothing would induce me to join with that woman; she needed to be bathed; she was famished, bedraggled; what was Henry thinking?

Henry says, "Stay and act like you are having fun," then turns off the lights.

I was going to do nothing else. The floor was a mess; rats were amuck.

This undeniably was the condemned tower.

Those who entered faced execution as their only exit.

And twenty minutes later, Henry returns. "I have found him, but we need a key."

Boldness and urgency to get Arthur out of this dump made us seek our guides and ask them to show us the other Pahtamons.

We needed those keys.

Outside in the corridor and alone with one guard, Henry stuck his short sword into him, took the keys, dragged the dead guard into a cell, and locked at the door, delaying discovery.

He had our keys.

At the stocks, Mingo opened his red eyes and saw the old man, Vate.

He seemed solid, yet the Madrawt public took no notice of him.

"Mingo Drum Mingo Drum,

Why are you loitering? It was the Vate.

"Why have you come?"

"To free you who are called Mahbon reborn," the male Vate replies.

"Fat chance," Mingo replies with a painful chuckle.

"Some unseen powers exist.

The Madrawts' disbelief in it so means nobody's watching me."

"I do not believe in you either, so go away or leave me to die with dignity," Mingo replies, defeated.

"Look, Mingo, the keys to your stocks," Vate says, holding

up the keys. Mingo, like a dog in a pound, watched, hoping for both freedom and a dog biscuit.

Vate touched the locks.

"Rusted; a powerful man like you should have broken them?"

Mingo thought about it.

Vate was giving him an invitation.

Mingo strained upwards to free himself.

The Vate had gone.

Nothing happened.

He strained again.

Nothing.

Had he been dreaming about the Vate?

The locks have worn out.

He pushed up; he felt stronger, healed.

His antics amused the gathered Madrawt public.

"First, he talks to himself and now thinks he can break our locks.

Mingo, Mingo Drum.

Crazy Mingo Drum," they chanted at him.

Mingo gave up straining to be free.

The crowd left bored with him.

He had only imagined Vate.

When the Vate touched the locks, he heard them click open.

He started straining again.

The crowd reappeared but with rotten fruit and vegetables to throw.

This angered Mingo, replacing defeat with a yearning for freedom.

And, of course, vengeance.

Someone pinned the lock open.

The crowd stopped the throwing act and stood staring in disbelief.

They knew they were on the menu.

Mingo took off the bar of his stock and threw it at the crowd.

It killed a few.
Now he pushed against the lower bar.
Also, a soldier climbed onto his platform to restrain Mingo, should have shot Mingo because Mingo took his pistol as the man climbed and shot him, showering the crowd with gore.
Then he shot the locks off his feet and was free.

He stood up.
Fired a stream of laser light from the pistol into the crowd.
Vengeance was upon the Madrawts.
Then he flew away as the crowd scattered for cover.
Beast, man, Birdman - that was him. Brave Mingo, poor Ce-Ra, heard the grunt and cough of his enemy and froze with terror.
It could not be possible; Mingo was in a stock dying.
To the highest tower, Mingo flew and landed.
Coughed and grunted.

"This is my domain,
My law is my word.
I am the last of the free.
To the north, the polar ice caps.
To the south, my enemies.
I am Birdman.
I am Mingo Drum Vercingetorix."

Suddenly, Planet Madrawt was not a safe place for Madrawts to live. The entire city was in uproar, and soldiers ran about the streets firing at shadows.
A lot of those shadows were Madrawts, poor blighters!

This diversion was ideal for our tricks.

Walking Dead Ditty translated by Vern.

"Wir nemen,
We take.
Entertain us.
We Take.
You are handsome.
We have identity.
Never pay.
Feed and entertain us.
We veterans."

CHAPTER 39   IT IS YOU

Madrawt hounds had a unicorn horn and fur

But the keys Henry had were the wrong keys.

I feared we would never return to our shuttlecraft. Here we had left Boudicca tied up. Why, she wanted to come with us?

There was nothing else but for Henry to return to the guardroom.

"What do you want?" A guard asked him there.

"You must come with us; your friend is with my companion and has not brought the keys to see if Pahtamon is in the remaining cells," Henry lied.

The guard removed the keys from a drawer. Henry stabbed him as he walked past into the dimly lit corridor.

They again hid the body within a cell. Henry wisely checked the desk drawer for more keys, *he took them all.*

For a civilized man, Henry, I saw, was a ruthless killer.

Was he no different from my Birdman Mingo Drum?

He might have been worse because he delayed taking me to Arthur, for he stopped, reloaded a new clip into his laser pistol, and entered a cell.

Here, four Madrawt prisoners hang from the walls, badly tortured by a nearby Singe Claw, a machine that claws your torso and cauterizes the wounds as it goes.

Henry shot each one. "They might tell."

But he was killing them because they were Madrawts.

It was like that all the way to Arthur's cell, executing all Madrawts; he was wasting
time.

Arthur's goal was in a top room cell, chained to a bed.

He cried, clinging to me tightly.

Then the alarms went off as someone found Henry's victims.

We had to hurry because we could hear baying Madrawt hunting dogs coming closer to our escape route down a sewer. Just as Henry was about to descend, the Madrawts came upon us.

Henry stood his ground and killed many and only came with me and the boy when I refused to give him my laser clips to reload his gun.

"They breed?" He with a stare that challenges me to disagree; I knew better; time was wasting.

Now, on the sewer train speeding to safety, I had a good look at Henry in his gray Walking Dead smock; he seemed stern and remote, unaffected by the women and children he killed.

Then our sewer train took us to a spot underneath our shuttlecraft where Color Sergeant Kenala and Boudicca waited with troopers.

Kenala had freed Boudicca, who had arrived as planned.

Kenala stopped picking his beak when he heard the call of Mingo above.

"Daddy," Arthur looked towards a shady spot high in the sky.

Boudicca felt certain it was Mingo.

Still, she pulled her son protectively into the shuttlecraft.

Kenala grunted back to his aerial lord.

And a spot in the sky that grew bigger as Mingo landed.

I glanced at Cedric Henry, who was no Nostradamus and hated Bird men but liked Birdie women.

Arthur was returning to the human world.

"Yellow alert," Henry gave an order to his men, and they quickly cocked their Weapons, Kenala moved behind Henry.

Despite his freedom, Mingo still seemed a threatening figure.

The legend lived, and all knew it.

"Red alert," Henry orders, and his men aim their weapons at Mingo.

Mingo Drum Vercingetorix would be a bonus to bring home to Tzu Strath.

Now Boudicca came and stood in front of Mingo, **a courageous act.**

Those armed men, recognizing her, holstered their weapons.

Someone pressed a steel blade against Henry's spine.

Good Kerala.

"Stand down," Henry says.

"I want home, too," Mingo says.

"Home to Maponos or Tzu Strath's military camp," Henry and he was serious.

"Maponos," Mingo says and looked at Kenala, who nodded his head.

Someone shut the doors, and the shuttle engines ignited; the craft was ready to leave Planet Madrawt.

Now Arthur appeared, and, at that moment, I saw the real

greatness of Mingo Drum Vercingetorix.

"Arthur, come here," Boudicca called her son away from his father.

Pain filled the legend's eagle eyes.

Arthur looked bashful. He had not seen his father and had heard human stories about a ferocious beast called Mingo that ate little children.

Mingo knew the boy by a different name, and he avoided using it to prevent confusion.

The boy's name was Arthur, Tzu Strath's heir.

I swear to this day I saw Vate stand beside Arthur and then vanish. It was the infra-red light of our craft—a trick of the light, but Mingo saw it. The Vate reminded Mingo that the boy belonged to another power, the power that was fighting the evil that manifested itself in Madrawts.

Mingo turned to leave.

"You are coming back to Tzu Strath, red alert," Henry tested the limits.

This time, I pulled a pistol on Henry.

"No, Henry. Once we are at a safe distance, he can return home." I am amazed I found the courage!

"You do not have the nerve?" Henry.

"Put down your weapons," Boudicca tells the men.

"We are Tzu Strath's men," one replies, meaning she was not.

"I am his daughter," she snaps.

Bird lovers must have gone through their minds and were not Tzu Strath's men, but Henry's.

Where could Mingo go, anyway?

Taking Mingo's hands, Boudicca turned her back to the soldiers.

Readers, at last, affection from one of these two brick-heads?

Mingo's eyes betrayed his pain, which she saw clearly. She saw his love, their wasted time foolishly squandered. It all came to her in an instant, a rush of insight.

Her hands seemed so small in his.

Callused, blood-stained.

He stroked her auburn hair, and she kissed the palm of that hand.

It was very touching, and Henry allowed them the quietness to prove she was a birdie lover.

His men had buried many of their comrades on patrol, killed by the Artebrate warriors. The Birdman, known for their many imperial defeats, was right there. With him dead, vengeance would be served and victory assured.

Boudicca might have stopped a murder.

Despite his extensive officer training, Henry was no better than the man he intended to kill.

And then Arthur went and hugged his mummy's legs.

Then it all happened so quickly. Mingo grabbed his son and left Boudicca. He wished to view the boy in the bright light.

The escape door was behind. The craft lurched, straining to leave, sending Mingo tumbling towards that door.

But Arthur was coming back to Tzu Strath. Henry had decided. That was his enemy, Mingo Drum. He wanted to shoot Mingo Drum and shot Mingo in the stomach.

Arthur fell, and Boudicca snatched him to safety.

Someone bayonetted Kenala from behind.

Mingo, Mingo, Mingo Drum.
Mingo man of steel.
Mingo, Mingo, Mingo Drum.
Where is Law your sword?

A legend fell out the door as it closed.
The craft was leaving minus a passenger.

*

On the flight back to Tara 6 I realized I was not only creating legends about Mingo and Arthur to bring in a rule of goodness, **but I was also writing about one of the**

most tragic love stories known.

The awful things I said and thought about the Beast weighed heavily on me. As for Boudicca and Arthur, they kept to themselves, and when we reached Tara 6, she became a recluse. That hurt Tzu Strath a great deal and, naturally, **he blamed Mingo for his daughter's moods.**

But he was a cunning general and could stomach it because he had his grandson back, which he viewed as more important than his daughter's childish mood. I was unsure if Vate had seen him, but I was certain we were all chosen for a purpose.

And by the way, Boudicca had a baby winged girl, Fay.

Our little pet hates were nothing compared to the boy's future, which was heavily entwined with the fate of all worlds.

We were microscopic ants compared to that.

Cedric Henry ditty.

"I hate them.
Birdies.
Troopers, do you love birdies?
We hate the lot.
Fit for a Xmas roast yes?
Yes, we troopers answer.
I hate them.
Birdies.
We hate the lot.
Birdie women are ok.
What say you troopers?
We are troopers.
Fight, eat, and play.
Birdie women are ok.
We hate the lot." As seen and heard by me Vern

CHAPTER 40 FLEE DIVICIACUS FLEE?

The smell of sweet cherry, nice.

"Kernwy closed the door behind him quietly so that no one would hear him leave. Jubilant, he left, muttering, "That fool will finally pay." He planned on self-grooming and then divulging Diviciacus's story.

Behind the closed, unlocked doors, Diviciacus lay blindfolded.

He was experimenting to heighten his senses during extreme moments of pleasurable stress. He had to trust someone, Kernwy, who did his bidding. A *terrible mistake.*

Diviciacus says, "Find me a desirable."

Kernwy viewed this opportunity as retribution.

And brought him a young, fair Madrawt girl.

A favorite cousin of Lord Madrawt, **of course.**

Kernwy drugged her, just like he did the others.

And now she lay dead, tortured to death by the psychopath Diviciacus. So, when Diviciacus finally came out of his drugged stupor, he expected to find a cleaned-up room by Kernwy, *his trusted servant!*

But fear has its limits. Kernwy is driven mad by taking part in butchering victims as his master explores spirit possession and flight.

The Madrawts would find her across Diviciacus's bed very dead butchered like a sheep in a butcher's shop.

For in his dream world, Huitzilopitchli had commanded Diviciacus to eat the organs of the sacrificial flesh, for his god was tired of hearts.

Diviciacus ate and slept well.

Lord Madrawt himself stood glaring at the priest, who was now sitting cross-legged smoking a fresh weed.

"A thousand cuts, then crucify him," Ce-Ra shouts.

The searing pain of nails hammered into palms jolted Diviciacus awake. Kernwy was nowhere to be found.

For Kernwy watched from a safe place, for even in his master's last hours he feared Diviciacus.

Then guards came for him because Ce-R wanted to get rid of his human priests.

A shocked Diviciacus asks, "What has happened?"

Kernwy is hanging from a wooden structure.

The place of execution was lonely for Ce-Ra feared his people's reaction to seeing their High Priest of Huitzilopitchli executed.

Golgotha, the hill of execution.

Here, Madrawts slaughtered sheep to Huitzilopitchli as a sin offering.

Diviciacus inspired more fear than the last king, Ce-Ra.

Diviciacus spoke to Huitzilopitchli just like that.

But Ce-Ra had seen too much of life to believe that his sacrifice would avert the disaster befalling his race.

Therefore, Diviciacus was to die in secret.
Kernwy must die also in case he talked.
The executioners must die.
No witnesses.
And the killers of the executioners die.
It was Ce-Ra who exploded bombs in their craft.
Only Diviciacus remained to hurl abuse at Kernwy. .

> And Kernwy ignored his master.
> Above them, circling carrion birds attracted Mingo Drum.
> *Someone shot you in the stomach, Mingo.*
> *Are you indeed Mabon reborn?*

Now seeing two humans, he landed and went to their aid, scaring off the vultures that had been picking Kernwy.

He cut down the assistant priest, then freed Diviciacus, and the man amazed him.

Someone pushed nails through his palms to free him, but he did not faint.

Was he dealing with Diviciacus, yes?

Gone were the faces of Diviciacus and Kernwy under the thousand cuts, so none had eyebrows, noses, lips, or ears, so Mingo did not recognize them.

Poor Mingo Drum had so much pity for these two humans.

The one nailed to the cross would live. He would like to become this brave man's friend and together plot their escape from this hellish Planet Madrawt.

He needed to heal his stomach wound.

A scratch as Cedric's blast had melted Mingo's belt buckle.
Mingo had rubbed garlic on the burn.

Was he, indeed, Mabon reborn?

The other sat there, his hands useless, seeing the vultures removing his parts.

Mingo wanted to kill him; what other options did he have?

Where could he take him? Mingo considered these condemned people slaves or prisoners of war, or perhaps victims of the flesh market.

So Kernwy gave Mingo a pathetic, bewildered look that says, "Why me? It was him that cut hearts out of people. Why me? Why me?"

"We cannot do anything for your friend," Mingo they were friends.

Diviciacus recognized the Birdman.

He stayed silent.

Life was precious.

Now Diviciacus reached for Mingo's short sword.

Mingo halted his reach.

"I should do it; he was my friend."

Mingo's admiration for the man deepened. He was prepared to end his friend's suffering, proving his strength and valor. Mingo felt he deserved to be friends with such a person.

Mingo Drum idiot readers.

Now Mingo handed his sword to Diviciacus, and only at the last moment did Kernwy realize his impending death.

Diviciacus's back obscured Kernwy's eyes from Mingo, preventing any questioning.

Eyes that screamed, "Scum murdering scum stop him! Mingo, stop him, and let me tell you who he is."

Mingo considered Diviciacus exceptional, a genuinely good person, given that such individuals often met unfortunate ends.

He had liked the hunchback Nostradamus, and he died.

Boudicca looked at what happened to her and his son.

And Tzu Strath was totally warped and lived.

Only the good die young.

He yearned for a different destiny than the humans' obsession with cloning. Death, for him, was merely the threshold to a new realm.

But the slaughter of his people had weakened his faith in

his bird gods.

So, he saw Diviciacus release his friend's spirit into a painless, better life where they even honored IOUs as perfectly acceptable.

But Kernwy believed death was final. He witnessed a lot under the psychopath who intended to kill him. And words came not from Kernwy's mouth, for Ce-Ra had it removed.

He could not yell, even at the one who could save him.

Diviciacus knew it and stuck the sword deep into Kernwy's midriff and helped the insides out.

Horror overcame Kernwy.

Mingo turned to take the bloodied weapon from Diviciacus, whose eyes feigned tears. Mingo understood brave men could cry. He did when his heart broke.

All men possessed hearts.

Diviciacus tossed aside Mingo's intended weapon, feigning disgust.

He wanted Kernwy in pain because he knew Mingo would end Kernwy's misery quickly.

Kernwy, the traitor, and son must suffer.

And when Mingo walked with his back to Diviciacus, the latter shouts, "Madrawts, we must flee," and ran for Mingo, took his arm, and dragged him away.

"Madrawts coming up the hill in hovercraft, they will be here in a moment, we must flee, I do not want to be crucified again, my friend is dead, I have killed my friend," Diviciacus lied, and Mingo heard the hum of craft, but it was buses and lorries for the highway was nearby, and Madrawts picking fruit from nearby trees he mistook as troopers, and he was still not strong and Mingo, seeing the back of Kernwy hopes he was dead.

Kernwy noticed circling vultures approaching to devour him.

"Dead. I slew my friend with a sword. What have I done? Let me fall upon your dagger or better give me it to attack the approaching Madrawts who will be here soon so I can die." Diviciacus.

Mingo, along with his new friend, escaped.

Readers, Madrawt vultures are not like vultures back on Earth. They ate you fresh, not dead and bloated; *the smell was out with these birds. No offense, Mingo Drum.*

And Kernwy remembered his hands were useless and could not scare them away.

Kernwy, Diviciacus's nemesis, is a killer himself.

Karma is at play here, reader.

"He goes to another realm for judgment.

But that one act of betrayal to Diviciacus will tilt the scales towards leniency," Vern Lukas, "Kernwy made his bed with Diviciacus, so he shares the same fate as the monster."

Vern, it is a life assessment.

Actors like me, and you are on life's stage.

And Mingo Drum understood why his new friend was moody. His friend had died, and Mingo thought this caused the mood.

Mingo faced a wicked man's deadly scheme.

Vern translated Mingo's song for Kernwy; he sang it to a brave trooper.

"Brave man, I salute you.
Brave man.
I salute you.
Now I kill you.
I beat you.
To the victor the spoils.
Welcome me.
Failte mi." Diviciacus was back, Vern Lukas.

CHAPTER 41 WHO WOULD EXPECT ME?

Demigod

Six long months had gone by since we returned to Tara 6. Tribune Henry's promotion to Consul gave him command of an entire army. This meant, thankfully.
I rarely saw him.

But suspected by his probing chit chat, he hoped I wrote up his victories and make him popular with the masses; *fat chance; two popular generals lead to civil war. The fool, I am my man, a journalist.*

But my thoughts were with my girl child whom Cartimandua had called Ena, the Fiery One. I truly was a father, and I yearned to see her.

But Cartimandua had excuses to keep me away.

She was punishing me for writing up Arthur and not her children.

What gives with females? Are you a girl reader? Please tell me.
In retrospect, she had a point.

Mingo had taught me not to fear life apart from the sky falling on my head and tidal waves drowning me and being nowhere near the sea.

But Tzu Strath was at war with the hostile Bird Nations and advanced to the Gododdin swamps, ready to attack Torrs, the Gododdin capital.

Only this question remained, 'Was it worth launching a frontal attack or bypassing and capturing it later when weakened by salt shortages?'

What about Ena and Cartimandua, whom I loved?

They were Bird people and would behave as Mingo would, with valor, so die.

Something I had learned to do by dealing with Mingo, so thank you, Mingo.

"Why do these Bird people rule our lives?" Tzu Strath, after I ask permission from him to see Cartimandua and if I could get her to come and sign a peace treaty.
THINKING TIME.

"Their women rule us," and did not explain.

But they were highly evolved, or once, but the way the friendlies lived as drunks aping us, the evidence would say they were a degenerate race needing the benefits of our ways.

"They are a defeated people," I reply, also from my depressive thoughts on the Bird people's future.

Tzu grunted in agreement.

I knew he was thinking, then who needs them, does Arthur?

"Arthur is an alien; you have aliens fighting with you. Alien rulers, knowing Arthur, will give to him, not you, when he demands their allegiance.

A human warlord.

Guard your Birdman assets Tzu Strath," I told him.

"But after I win, what about the brave warriors who helped me fight the Madrawts?" He asks striking a match.

He had started this smelly habit of smoking cigars lately for image; **images counted.**

"Until Planet Madrawt is dust, you will need every warrior you can recruit; remember, I have been there; it is huge; there are billions of Madrawts, and all want imperial hearts to offer Huitzilopitchli."

He listened politely. "And if the Madrawts recover from the Choking Death and their economic woes, what then Tzu Strath? They will be back vigorously," and adds, "I take it I can visit Cartimandua?"

He nodded and waved me aside as our talk ended; *waved cigar ash onto me, too.*

"By the way, you remind me of Nostradamus," he says, not even lifting his head from maps under clouds of cigar smoke. Was he hoping I became his spy? And remembered Nostradamus's *clicking clock* set in motion against Mingo.

I wish I had taken the time to learn about Nostradamus's work.

Leaving Tzu Strath, I sought Boudicca, who welcomed me kindly. However, I...
saved Mingo's life?

Arthur was taller than human children his own age and looked like Mingo, except he lacked the rough, stark features, for he had inherited his mother's beauty. He was indeed growing into the handsome demigod I had created for all men and women to follow.

I could imagine him leading armies to liberate Earth and other planets under Madrawt's rule.

Like an angel from Heaven flying across the skies waving

his sword, the fear he would worship him overcame me.

I was wrong to push my fellow man into worshiping another man.

Arthur was not a god amongst us.

Worshiping men corrupts.

No wonder Mingo Drum Vercingetorix disliked my writings.

So, I altered my writings and influence the minds of my readers that Arthur was a man.

I had unknowingly committed a sin; the elevation of a man to godhood.

I left for Torrs.

The journey was uneventful as I traveled along established supply routes to the front line. The news brought me of a glorious victory against the Madrawts, a turning point in the wars, and it meant Tzu Strath and his allies were halfway to Earth and the borders of the Madrawt solar system.

A year's time would reach Earth if this momentum continued.

I wondered if we would need Arthur at this rate of victories.

"Yes," I say, "We will need Arthurs."

Our history and culture ensured that, and even worse, Consul Henry and Emperor Conchobhar. **Any comment was so devious they were trying to outsmart each other.**

While crossing the swamps, I saw many birdmen on Tzu's side fighting amongst themselves.

Conquerors have always used divide and rule!

And made myself known to the Gododdin warriors who allowed me passage and then it hit me:

THE EMPIRE OF TZU STRATH HAD BECOME SO LARGE AND UNWIELDY, HE NEEDED A CO-RULER.

Henry, his loyal, trusting friend.

Tzu Strath was making the first important mistake of his life.

They needed Arthur.

I had to forget about settling down with my daughter Ena and Cartimandua. Henry's coming was the signal to the end of the Birdman world. I had to convince Cartimandua she had lost. We must flee north until we make peace with Tzu Strath.

And as Henry would negotiate, peace would not be in her favor.

I also resolved to return and lead Boudicca and Arthur to a place of safety. I owed it to Mingo Drum Vercingetorix, trapped forever on Planet Madrawt.

As the Gododdin led me away, a shadowy figure floated out of the swamp.

OLD VATE.
The Gododdin fled this ghostly apparition.
"The power of the pen," is all he says, then vanishes.

I could have chosen differently; instead, trying to force Cartimandua to flee, I could have joined the Artebrate and fought Tzu Strath.

Would she listen to me?

Cedric Henry's Law Menhir.
"Birdmen do not carry weapons.
Punishment is death."

Update Fay.
Tzu Strath hired nannies, and they and the baby girl he sent to another planet.
"One bird heir is enough; two and my soldiers will leave me." His line of reasoning.
Or to hurt Mingo deeper.
To please his young wife, Ona?
Of Boudicca, she was a mother deprived of a baby. It would weigh upon her what her daughter looked like. Was she walking, FLYING?

She ended her relationship with Tzu.
He had the young Ona.
"Here, monkey," meaning Little Drum, "go find Mingo, your boyfriend, and tell him he has a daughter he will never see." Tzu Strath is wrong, hideous, and a talented actor.

As seen by me, Vern Lukas, and told by Little Drum.

CHAPTER 42   HOME SWEET HOME

Queen Cartimandua rides in battle

She showed delight, amusement, and eagerness for the upcoming challenge Vern Lukas presented to her.

"So," is all Cartimandua says to me.

Following a lengthy absence, we finally met. Saddening: no kisses, passionate words. Well, I was a fool, for she was a beautiful queen.

But my handsome daughter, who inherited her mother's dark looks and wings, pleased me because she possessed the gift of flight while I lacked it.

The sole reason the imperialists hated the Bird people was flight.

They just hated anything non-human, anyway.

I hugged and kissed my daughter.

Tell her that people loved her despite her dysfunctional family.

Would a winged grandchild shock my parents? Or pleased they had a grandchild? I had not told them yet. **I will readers; they are my parents.**

At least I had no worries about meeting Cartimandua's parents, for they were like her, birds!

"Chirp tweet," Just making in-law human jokes, not funny, am I?

Then Tzu Strath's shells landed. They did that regularly.

Genocide was at play.

After the shell burst, children emerged playing.

Kids are kids.

Shells are shells.

I understood Nostradamus at last.

I forgot what the conquering birdmen did to the vanquish trophies!

And forgot Mingo's kindness to human children.

Like us, they were a contradiction.

Outraged about the cruel treatment of a Griffin but could ignore child trafficking.

People hated them because they were just like humans.

But my daughter Ena was in this bombarded city. I must get her out. I had judged these peoples on my human terms they would sign a peace treaty giving away their lands to Tzu!

What an ignorant fool I was!

So, shells exploded outside in the gardens, swamps drained into lily ponds.

Where could these brave people go?

Their world revolved around them, a common Bird Nation boast.

Where was Mingo Drum Vercingetorix?

Many regretted not joining him and being a united front to the enemy.

Too late now,

And Cartimandua drugged me.

When I felt dizzy, I became alarmed and afraid, thinking she was going to kill me.

But when I awoke, she had given me wings, sore but wings needing physiotherapists to get them into shape. Then I could fly and take my daughter Ena on picnics to distant clear lakes.

Then the artillery barrage started.

Cedric Henry was massing his troops for the ASSAULT.

"Marry me Cartimandua?" I ask her from my bedside.

A long pregnant pause.

"Yes," she replies. Did she love me, or was she thinking of the future? Married to Vern Lukas was an open bet not to end up as an alcoholic prostitute in some human bar in downtown Torrs 6.

"A king for a day, Vern," she replies.

Thinking of kings, I thought of Mingo. Did she still love him? I was her man now.

Anyway, I could not wait to try out my wings. What a gift!

I knew I could fly.

Just like Mingo Drum Vercingetorix.

Except I am a warrior whose weapon is the pen.

And behind the War Lord's troops, Dictator Cedric Henry was issuing orders.

Take no prisoners; he was ashamed he was an alien. The more Bird people killed, the more accepted as human, he thought.

Leading his troops across the river initially were friendly birdmen.

"There is your true enemy, the Gododdin; kill them," and in that belief, forgot they were butchering their own kind.

And the big assault guns opened.

"King Vern, King Vern," the Gododdin warriors shouted as Cartimandua married me. They could not care if I were human. We were about to die.

I was king for a day.

It was the Birdman's custom to marry whom you choose, and I had no illusions about who was the actual ruler here, and neither did the warriors.

Cartimandua.

"Lead them, King Vern," Cartimandua says with Ena's tiny hand holding her right palm.

I was going towards my death. Was she getting rid of me that quickly?

Was I making way to Mingo's memory?

I imagined him proud of me as I went to the front of the Gododdin formation into battle. Cedric would hang me for treason, a bird lover.

I imagined Cartimandua and Ena waving goodbye to me.

In fact, Cartimandua had given Ena to a nanny and mounted a Griffin to lead her Griffin Legion to battle, **death, and glory the military way.**

And saw her overtake us as Griffin were the heavy shook troops as they swarmed amongst the friendly Bird men of Henry.

My Cartimandua, in her gold body armor, looked exciting, glowing in the sunshine.

A target for snipers. Oh no, Dispater, no!

But she was magnificent, resplendent in her bravery and example of valor to her people.

She was indeed a queen and above her flew the women, lightly armed to fly quickly behind the imperial lines and cut off supplies, raid and flee.

Where was my Mingo with his phalanx of ants? Then we did show them.

NOW THE SILENCE OF THE BIG GUNS.

"We are the last of the free.

"We are the last of the free.

To the north are the cold polar ice caps.

In front of us, the enemy

"Better to die free than slaves." Thousands of throats shouted,

Reluctant to kill the last free ones, some friendly Birdmen left.

Others killed us.

We were the crazy ones, those who threatened civilization's benefits, the holographic televisions, freezers, and supermarkets that had the food to fill them and lawns to litter with the junk bought.

And better, sleazy bars to erode the culture they were born into; now they were just
aliens in an empire so big the sun never set upon them.

Vern translated Cartimandua's rally song.

"Rally with me.
Rally 'comhla rium.
Cartimandua
Standards to me.
Standards to me.
Rally with me.
Rally with Cartimandua."

The warrior Vern Lukas.

CHAPTER 43 AND HE CAME FOR HE WAS MAHBON REBORN

Huitzilopitchli.

"You cannot put a clever dog down," Vern Lukas says.

Therefore, Mingo was not a Birdman; he was a dog. *A past empire's intense midday sun saw only mad dogs and Englishmen outside.*

"I have grown to like you, Divipatreus. Together, we can board that docked cargo ship and escape this planet," Mingo tells his new friend, who was Diviciacus.

Divipatreus eyed the vessel.

Where would he go?

To the wilderness of Tara 6!

No, Earth was his target; he planned to use his magic to claim it.

They forgot the Madrawt garrison there, and he would denounce the lord Madrawt Ce-Ra is a traitor to the god Huitzilopitchli.

The humans had conquered Earth, or had they? No one informed him.

Either are we, *news traveling at the speed of Light takes a long time to hear.*

Now a week out from Planet Madrawt, Mingo sneaked out of the dark cargo hold and made his way to the ship's bridge. **On the way, he intended to kill as many Madrawts he met. To even the odds against him.**

They were just Madrawt scum.

The enemy.

Not breathing or capable of feeling.

Like crabs thrown in boiling water.

Mingo.

He raided tribes before seeing all bird men as one people.

In those days, he and his Artebrate would have killed Gododdin children in a raid, casualties of war or taken back captives.

The girls would grow into good baby-making machines.

The boys into slaves, or if young enough, brought up as Artebrate warriors.

It was the Birdman way.

So, Mingo Drum Vercingetorix thought nothing of opening a cabin door and entering, slaughtering the occupants.

It was not murder; they were Madrawts, Cedric Henry was proud of him

Birdie families shunned those children because of their perceived ugliness.

Madrawts were using genetic therapy to make themselves attractive.

They considered themselves dominant Cane Toads, so why remove the warts?

Dead Madrawts meant less Madrawts in the future to fight.

Indeed, the savage Mingo Drum Vercingetorix, **was he not?**

And he was Mingo, the winged beast.

By the time he stood outside the bridge, he had made his way up six levels of habitation and slaughtered twenty-six crew.

He was a killing machine, a general's dream.

Of course, this made what Tzu Strath said about him true; he was a beast, *yes or no?*

And: The ideal soldier in times of war.

The bridge held three Madrawts, two officers, and a boson.

The beast burst upon them using his sword, killed one officer, and took the other hostage by holding his blooded weapon at the man.

He lost whatever he was trying to say.

Madrawts are the superior race.

The responsibility of learning Madrawt is with conquered subjects, not them.

And worse, they spoke a dialect of Madrawt from some distant colony of theirs on a rocky moon! So, Mingo's language implant was useless. He was a dangerous armed simpleton.

"Maponos," Mingo screamed, holding a map up.

"Maponos," the veteran boson.

The officer agrees.

They set the course.

And the simpleton calmed down.

And the starship lurched, heading west; Mingo was going home.

Then the officer threw himself at Mingo, seeing the beast lower his sword as he relaxed.

He was dealing with the Mingo Drum—a dangerous armed simpleton.

All he did was impale himself on a sword.

Thinking the officer was unfit to eat, the beast discarded him and turned its attention to the boson.

Gripping the wheel, the man shook his head and grinned widely, hoping the beast would not decapitate him. He had a lovely, good, plump woman back home with six Madrawt kids wanting presents from faraway ports.

She feared sailor rumors, wanting him STD-free.

And Mingo lowered his sword, and the boson maintained his course.

The navigational screen above Maponos in Madrawt illustrated [the ship's position/the target.

"Divipatreus, come to the bridge; we are going home," and Mingo forgot his home was not the home of his new friend.

At first, Diviciacus was afraid to leave the safety of the hold, but the temptation to reveal himself to the crew overcame him, and he appeared. He hoped the crew slew Mingo; *this was Mingo Drum priest?*

Silly, the crew was dead.

One never loses the fear and respect that is installed upon the Madrawt mind from a youthful age for their High Priest and Huitzilopitchli.

What crew?

Only six remained alive below decks at their engine computers. Mingo had missed them!

Now Mingo arranged with Diviciacus that they take shifts awake, making sure the boson kept the star compass indicator needle pointed on the screen above at the Madrawt sign for Maponos inside the Stardust Galaxy.

Thus, he secured the engine room by locking it; those inside were at his mercy, or they could stay in their metal coffin. They were Madrawts; **WOULD** Mingo forget when he reached

Maponos to unlock the engine room door?

Two cooks and two porters worked in the kitchens.

The cook attacked him with a cleaver as the porters ran for their lives.

Mingo easily defended himself and slew the cook, so the man's body sizzled on a hot plate and stunk the kitchen up.

The second cook threw big woks and anything he could lay his hands upon at Mingo.

Mingo beat with sausage meats with the cook until he crumpled, begging for his life. Mingo needed a cook for the long voyage home, so he threw the man a plucked chicken and a sack of potatoes before finding the porters.

Found them hiding beneath the mess tables, grunted at them, and moved on, passing the cook, who was still muttering. He then pulled the man to his feet and gave him the chicken.

Enormous birds eat little birds. He also pulled the sizzling dead cook off the hot plates. Later that night, Mingo, as he ate, was aware a lifeboat had ejected into deep space. Aboard it, the cook. He was off to take his chances out there amongst speeding asteroids.

There were also pirates, muggers, and **psychopaths**; he was safer cooking for Mingo his chicken.

Why did Mingo wish him lots of luck?

In the meantime, Mingo needed a cook, found the porters, and made them draw straws; the loser got promoted, and the other became the official food taster.

Now deep in the holds, Mingo had found farming equipment, fertilizers, explosives for mining, specifically selected for his world.

Private ownership already existed. What more did they want?

To rape the land till it was barren. And Mingo spat at the machines and kicked the
                bags of fertilizer open.

Universal cook's ditty.

"Harm us not.
Or no dinner tonight.
Pay us well.
Or no food for you.
Give us porters.
We are chefs.
Not dishwasher.
Harm us not
Or no dinner for you."

What Vern knew was that dishwashing machines or droids did that job.

CHAPTER 44   HE WAS TOO LATE

Bird girls trick or treat?

By the gods, we showed them the spirit of freedom was worth fighting for. Our newfound will, too, took them by surprise, and we threw them back across the River of Skulls, even penetrating the swamps beyond ten miles before I rallied my PROUD BIRDMEN.

These were wild, wooly people, not disciplined. Besides, I must take responsibility for myself. I found the charge exhilarating and got carried away; I am a scribe or was!

We also spiked their big guns, earning a respite from the shelling.

"I want this city to be leveled and salted.

This land will remain barren.

A monument to imperial power," Henry told Colonel Horatio Nelson Smith.

Smith's job was to deforest hostile lands to reduce cover for enemy ambushes.

As a good soldier, he set about organizing his men, human and alien, pilots, and crew to the task.

One was the human Billy McNeish of Houston, Texas, and Old Earth.

They were the wrong boys for the job.

Colonel Horatio Nelson Smith was sick of wiping out ecological habitats.

Fighting Madrawts was one thing; he had seen first-hand trophies.

And he did not care for the methods of Tribune Cedric Henry, now dictator!

Young Billy McNeish was a romantic idealist volunteer who had fled Old Earth to fight Madrawts.

Neither did not enjoy fighting a minority alien race.

They were secret Birdie lovers, yellow canaries in cages

hung from their ship's bridges.

And no one knew.

Reader, are you a secret birdie lover? Got a budgie back home/
They went on holiday.

Vern Lukas's friends heard.

Fortunately, those men avoided the front after the Gododdin's retreat.

They were also aware of the 'No Prisoners order,'

Vern Lukas needed to believe he controlled these wild birdmen.

I, Vern Lukas, admitted my folly! Faced with the wounded's mutilation, what action would I have taken? Had I not told them about Henry's orders not to take prisoners? This was an order for the Gododdin to slaughter everyone they found.

So, the swamp dragons fed well and would have a big litter.

Now Dictator Cedric Henry looked at the lagoon. He understood why his men disobeyed his orders to bury the dead.

There must have been about five hundred headless limbless bodies in it.

Gododdin took trophies, leaving the torso for swamp dragons and snakes to feast on.

Big snakes such as anacondas and pythons were here.

Decay filled the air with its stench.

"Hang every Birdman you find till we reach the polar ice caps," Henry throwing
Mingo Drum's words back at the Gododdin.

And when he reached the ice caps, he intended to do something about the friendlies: they were birds too.

Besides, Tzu Strath was not on Tara 6 now. He had a young wife to keep happy. And Cedric was a dictator.

Tzu was honeymooning with his beautiful wife, Oona. And

the expert pill had given her the looks of a twenty-year-old.

Whereas the Great War Lord, Tzu Strath, froze in his fifties. His flesh, bronzed and wrinkled, muscular and hard.

Date his own age the fool.

Conchobhar had instructed his youngest daughter in the seduction of Tzu Strath.

The warlord's inappropriate behavior stemmed from his young wife.

He was aware of his old, mummified body.

And fell in love with Ono.

For she was young and pleasing.

And he was her dotting slave.

Besotted the old silly fool.

What did Conchobhar want, reader?

She encouraged Tzu to take hormones to be more active, so he pursued her as they played a game of cat and mouse.

Youngsters frolicking in the harvested wheat field.

Silly Tzu forgot Arthur, which was exactly **what Conchobhar wanted.**

Oona had ambitions too and was separate from her father's Conchobhar because she would be an empress one day. **That is not what Conchobhar wanted.**

And Cedric Henry took advantage of Tzu's bedazzlement with his young bride.

Cedric was ruthless.

Boudicca was aware Cedric saw Arthur as a Bird boy, and she did not approve of her father's marriage, for she distrusted Conchobhar and Oona and feared for Arthur's safety.

What of my daughter, "Forgotten apart from by me," **Boudicca.**

"Mummy, can I go out and play?" Arthur called from the toilet.

"When you wipe yourself properly," for she noticed the loo paper roll towards her feet. She gently tossed it back and heard Arthur moving about.

Then he came covered in chocolate.

"Little boy," she says lovingly, using wipes cleaned him up.

"What about living elsewhere?" She asks softly.

"He took his mummy's hand and placed it on the wing membranes that he wanted
tickled.

A knock on the door.

It was Kenala, accompanied by his human escort.

Henry always kept them together.

The place had a million cameras.

They were bird prisoners.

Arthur was a threat to the new rising order.

"Want to play football?" Kenala asks.

Little Drum kicked a ball.

It shinned Boudicca's legs.

Boudicca lets Arthur go. She needs the time to plan their escape.

Somewhere, she would get out of her father where Fay, her daughter, was. A mother never forgets a child.

He had told her calmly, "Bring back another bird child, and I will ensure you cannot have babies again."

Kenala was coming, unlike Henry, who did not care about the boy's life. Kenala's skills would be valuable in the wilderness; he could fly and scout for enemies and food.

GRILLED SNAKES .

Arthur's play song.

"I am a little boy.
I like toys.
Soccer.
Flying.
Mummy.
I am a little boy.

I like girls.
Mummy is not a girl.
Mummy is a mummy.
I like sweets.
I am a little boy. "

Told me by Kenala

CHAPTER 45 SPACE PIRATES

No discrimination existed in pirate work.

They arrived quickly because they could not avoid detection by radar and could not fight back, as neither Mingo nor Diviciacus knew how to use the controls.

So, the pirates came.
They boarded and roamed the ship freely.
Until they neared the bridge.
Found the BEAST Mingo Drum Vercingetorix, and he shot the first alien dead.
The second as well.
The third as he fled.
Mingo followed to kill them in the ship's mass of corridors

for he was an enraged beast.

Divipatreus followed also, for he did not want to be alone. His eyes watched the broad, muscular back of Mingo with a mixture of admiration, hate, fear, and want.

Huitzilopochtli needs a heart.

Diviciacus, also known as Divipatreus, dreaded Mingo's power, fearing discovery and its consequences.

The shaman knew the location of hidden treasures, and his desperation for freedom led him to consider paying the pirate captain.

Money bought anything, he believed.

The pirates did not promise him anything like the fun of burying him with their buried treasure; his ghost protected the loot, such an important job.

And then he saw four pirates coming out of the kitchen behind Mingo.

He held up his hands and walked towards them.

Mingo saw his new friend being beaten, collapsing to the floor.

The beating clearly ruined Diviciacus's plan.

Then Mingo shot them.

He also heard something metallic bouncing down the stairs, the sound he had heard in war a thousand times, a grenade, and he dived under a metal hatch.

The grenade went off, capping his ears.

Later, he awoke cramped but alive.

In a darkened room and handcuffed.

The smell of sweat overpowering.

He smelled the air.

Madrawt stink,

He moved this way and that by shifting his bottom till he found a body.

MOANING.

Now, the strong iodine smell of Madrawt's blood.

His toes felt like handcuffs.

The kitchen porter?

"Divipatreus?" He whispers several times.

"Birdman king, they took him," the porter answered.

They had Diviciacus aboard the pirate ship, which was towing the tramp to the Stardust Galaxy. The safest place for pirates was Tarra 6, a Heaven.

Gododdin warriors were pirates.

And the entire galaxy was a mirror of Tarra 6.

Also, Dictator Henry paid well for Madrawt and Bird men's scalps and more for Madrawt ships, and he had a list of what he wanted to deprive Madrawt society of?

Dentist drill for their oddly shaped teeth.

Forceps for Madrawt difficult births.

Candies for Madrawt kids.

Films, watching repeats repeatedly, were moral breaking.

And Dictator Henry's list was endless.

This was total war and genocide.

Diviciacus revealed his identity to the impressed and interested human pirate captain.

Could Dictator Henry outmatch Diviciacus in his bid for freedom, except Henry would not free him?

And the vampire amongst them wanted to sacrifice the porters to Huitzilopochtli.

They were Madrawts.

The scalps to the pirates as bounty, BIG DEAL.Fear prompted many to advocate his liberation. To take him to Henry **now.**

Take him to a Madrawt outpost.

The crux: his dismissal.

For he was bad luck.

Choking Death claimed the first men.

Then the ambassador from Henry's camp told them they had to wait several weeks in quarantine for payment.

The ship's air conditioning broke down.

They began squabbling.

A snake appeared from a cargo crate and fatally bit someone.

"I am Diviciacus, the High Priest of Huitzilopitchli," he tells them from his new sitting position in the messroom. All this misfortune is because of your ill-treatment of me. **Release me."**

Alien or human, they feared Huitzilopitchli, that Madrawt bloodthirsty god.

"I will not mistreat you as your human captain did."

The puzzle perplexed them.

"Did he not allow you to do the fighting and die? While he was safe?" And so, spoon-fed them with his lying worms.

"I will lead you and you will be the captains of Huitzilopitchli, who will bless and bring you luck."

Luck meant riches to them.

One amongst them killed their captain and appointed himself the new pirate captain, for he listened to Diviciacus *and ate a lying worm.*

They did and landed on Tara 6.

Then Diviciacus sent for the Madrawt porters.

The wounded one was terribly ill; his untreated wound was a festering stink. In his confinement, Mingo had cared for him with soothing words of hope that he knew were lies.

"Where do you come from, Birdman?" The other porter asked in disbelief.

"From Maponos," Mingo had replied.

The Madrawt, a native of a loveless world, declares, "Your foe stands before you; however, you offer compassion."

And Mingo shuffled close to the Madrawt, "Soon I will kill him quickly to end his suffering, that will be mercy," making sure the wounded porter could not hear.

"You may as well kill me, for they plan to torture me, for I am a Madrawt," the man replies sadly, without hope.

"Courage, remember your gods," Mingo comforts.

"I am a kitchen porter; I do not believe in gods.
REFLECTION.

All I know is that Henry has placed a bounty upon Madrawts. The pirates plan to scalp me before doing terrible things. They will hang me from a beam and beat me till my bones break, then skin me and dry what they take to make belts; they will empty my bowels, make a soup with it, and force me to drink the broth hot. "

Just like the ancient heirs to Alexander treated the Hebrews. Nothing is new; everything has been done.

So, the pirates will do to me," and the Madrawt prophesied his death *except for one detail?*

The pirates finally arrived at the Madrawt, aiming to carry out their plan, only to find Mingo choking the injured man.

And they beat Mingo, who, being a cornered beast, attacked them and killed two till someone coshed him.

Then Mingo awoke alone.

Unaware of one detail, Diviciacus, to amuse his new crew, cut out a Madrawt heart to give to Huitzilopitchli, who would then punish the porter in hell for his lack of belief.

As for the wounded Madrawt, Diviciacus found the stench of wounds so offensive after taking his scalp and throwing the lad overboard. *Verns flew and ate him, for they minded not if the food was off.*

Why a bite from a Vern can give you blood poisoning? Because their mouths are vile.

Diviciacus told his crew that they were about to become rich.

They wondered how, as all this priest did was promise wealth. The two scalps were insufficient reward.

"You have Mingo Drum Vercingetorix aboard ship, and Henry will pay a galaxies' ransom for him," Diviciacus tells them, and slowly, it dawned upon their alcohol-drug-abused minds they had only one Birdman aboard ship, **and he must be?**

Then, Dictator Cedric Henry did not believe the pirates' claim, but upon reflection, why not?

It was a Madrawt ship coming from Planet Madrawt, the last known place of Mingo Drum; this was Tara 6, Maponos, Mingo's home.

Anything was possible with **that** Mingo Drum.

"Incidentally, Madrawts remain confined within the engine room," Diviciacus tells the crew.

*

Now Mingo smiled; he was facing the open door, and there stood Cedric Henry.

"Tzu Strath once threatened you with death."
PAUSE.

The soldiers grabbed Mingo, who fought back fiercely, taking many blows. Despite the brutal treatment, Mingo, a veritable beast, clung to life. Like a wild animal refusing to give, he bit, scratched, and spat.

Even the pirates admire him for their drinking songs, called themselves the 'Last of the Free,' but now know their songs were lies.

He caught sight of his friend Divipatreus through his half-closed, puffy eyes, giving him a smile before being shoved into the back of a hover lorry.

Mingo a prisoner again? Only if he had Law.

It did not occur to him **why** his friend was standing next to Henry, except that he was about to be questioned.

"You have done well, Diviciacus," Henry tells him, disliking the wicked man.

"Thank you, but that smile, he knows who I am." Diviciacus was wrong, but fear crept in.

"I shall keep my word and offer you aid, Diviciacus, but keep yours," Henry warned, knowing the priest's idea would hurt the Madrawts.

Soon, Diviciacus would announce to the planets he was alive, secretly done away with by Ce-Ra, and call upon Madrawts loyal to Huitzilopitchli to offer Ce-Ra's heart to their god or more doom will befall.

Any contribution to the war effort was welcome.

Afterward, Henry would hang Diviciacus on cacti for Vern.

But Diviciacus had original plans; he was planning to apply for the coming vacancy of the Madrawt throne. He could see the loathing Henry had for him. The tea leaves revealed the truth: **he needed to escape.**

As he climbed aboard another hover lorry, as Henry would not have him in his staff hover car, he saw the pirate crew rounded up, and they saw him and spat. They were going to get their riches but, in another dimension, hellfire and brimstone!

As the hover lorry lifted Diviciacus heard the telltale sizzling sound of a laser Gatling gun and thought what a waste of fine beating hearts he could have offered to Huitzilopitchli and told his guards so, hoping to spread his lying worms again.

But these well-disciplined imperial troopers smiled inwardly, knowing the wicked priest's time was running out, and they expected being the lucky ones to pin him on that cactus.

And Mingo Drum Vercingetorix coughed and grunted loudly so everyone heard.

So, Ce-Ra on a far distant planet awoke out of a nightmare, for he had seen the last Madrawt soldier die on Tara 6 as Mingo Drum Vercingetorix choked him.

And there were Madrawt soldiers on Tara 6 under Reeman Black Hair who had maps in front of him showing the latest isolated pockets of hostile Bird men holding out against the Dictator

Henry's imperial forces massing for a last assault.

And Diviciacus was on the radio, denouncing Ce-Ra.

Well, Reeman Black Hair always liked Ce-Ra, who treated him fairly.

Self-reliance became essential.

Mutinies were occurring in the ranks, the Madrawt Empire

was in trouble.

Reeman Black Hair took a similar course to the Roman Empire's collapse.

He helped the fall, declared himself Emperor of Madrawt Tara, and sent peace envoys to Dictator Henry, who hung them to feed the Vern.

What could Reeman Black Hair do?

Escape?

The Dictator's fighters controlled the skies.

Many of his men deserted a risky move, considering the wilderness was their only choice.

A Madrawt's appearance was distinctive, unmistakable, and beyond question.

Hostile birdmen were scarce in the wilderness these days. So, he would flee into the wilderness with amassed wealth and take his chances. Such thoughts floated into Reeman's right temple from someplace unknown. As any alien money counted, a wealthy Madrawt was welcome in some brothel.

He was thinking of disposing of Diviciacus, whose fault all misfortunes fell upon the Madrawts, especially himself.

Then imperial shells rained down.

The demoralizing effect was horrid as the Madrawt front lines evaporated, as all sought their chances in the wilderness *as help, as the seventh cavalry was not coming.*

"Bugger this," Reeman Black Hair finding no staff manning his control room as

the radio cackle needed tuning.

So, had to carry his own bags to his private staff hover car.

"Bugger this," again, someone had taken it and gone into the wilderness **without him.**

Then the shells landed on his residence, and Reeman Black Hair fled with two suitcases of wealth only, leaving a galaxy's fortune behind.

On the way, a shrapnel splinter ripped one open, so a million imperial dollars blew away.

Frantically, he tried to catch the floating bills.

Then burning beams from the roofs fell about him and his other suitcase went poof.

No one welcomed a poor Madrawt in any brothel!

"Mummy, did you hear?" Arthur excitedly.

Boudicca stood up and looked towards the city.

Yes, she had heard the coughing grunt.

He was back.

Should she stay or keep fleeing?

"When I deliver you to the Artebrate, you will be safe," Kenala says, so she adds, "And then I will return and free my friend. Take care of Arthur."

She knew he was right.

"I want to fight," Arthur jumps excitedly.

The boy pulled Boudicca's light silk dress, so the hem parted under her body armor.

"Naughty boy."

So, it was then that Boudicca and her party looked upon an empty City of Winds; all was desolation and destruction.

Broken skeletons, household artifacts, spoiled food, and burned-out hover tanks with Cedric Henry's twin grinning black skull heralds on their turrets were ample evidence as to whom and what caused the looting and allowed hell to exist.

"We have nowhere to hide," Boudicca as she cries.

Arthur put a protective, comforting arm about her waist and then cried as well. He still was not that big, and Mingo would have cried when seeing his beloved city in ruins.

Little Drum cried as well. She had failed to find Mingo and tell him he had a daughter.

Kenala searched for clues about his people's escape route as they wept.

Then a single laser shot puffed up in front of him.

"Freeze, Birdman," the voice was human.

Out of the rubble appeared seven humans and two alien settlers and deserters.

Boudicca told Arthur to run, and she did, too.

Whoops and howls followed her.

"The boy can fly," walked into her right temple.

"Fly Arthur, fly, get daddy," she cries and, with all her strength, swings him into the air, where he stretches his wings, flaps, and hovers instead.

He wanted to fight and raked the heads about him with his small talons.

"Shoot the little bugger," one human says, and Boudicca attacks the men with her fists.

Arthur sensed someone would kill him. That mummy was doing this for him, to give him time to get help, Daddy, so he flew away hating himself for not being a full-grown beast like Daddy.

As for Boudicca, her struggle tore her dress further, revealing more of her flesh.

The men now had bad ideas.

As for Kenala, a deserter stuffed a laser into his mouth as he watched Boudicca at play, **at play?**

Someone kicked Little Drum out of the picture.

He delayed killing Kenala; a price was on their wings and scalp. Kenala could walk to a military outpost where they would kill him, saving him from carrying that greasy, stained weight.

A ditty song by drunkards does not need to be translated, Vern.

> *"A woman's flesh.*
> *For touch.*
> *More ale.*
> *We are men.*

Where is the ale?
A woman's touch.
More ale.
We are men."

CHAPTER 46   A CHRISTIAN, MUSLIM, AND JEW ROLLED IN ONE

Orange death

"I cannot do this no more; I did not join up to kill every damn living thing created by
God and I do not mean by that false devil Dispater. I am a Christian, a Muslim, and a Jew rolled in one.

I believe in God Almighty and the devil and that is whom I am supposed to be fighting.
"Not plants, bugs, or poisoned water—that's what is making the Birdman chicks sick, blind, and vomiting," Billy McNeish complains to Colonel Horatio Nelson.

Nelson reached out a hand and took young Billy's pocket bible from him.

He exclaims, "New English Bible—amazing!"

"Can you believe this? Henry makes us do this," Billy complains, his voice laced with annoyance, as a birdie woman drifts by in the now bright orange river.

It was full of deforestation chemicals that killed birds, men and fish birds ate.

"I will poison no one else, Colonel. Shoot me if you want, but I am done with that," Billy declares.

Meant it.

A swamp dragon splashed by ignoring them, blood oozed from its mouth, poisoned by them.

Carp bloated dead lay at their feet in the lapping stinky shallows.

A dead crane nearby, its body covered in poisoned flies.

The crane smelled something worse than the carp.

"Three centuries I sought the light; I found it last night." The colonel muttered to himself, and McNeish started listening once he realized no one had shot him.

"Last night I found the truth,

'Think about what you do?' I cry as I know this is murder. PAUSE.

"Tzu Strath would never order this," Nelson tells McNeish, who looks at him hopefully, "A man serves one boss, and Tzu is not here. I am not serving Henry."

Why, McNeish picked up a spanner, ready to open the cocks on the barrels of chemicals and let it spill onto the soil, then fire it.

"We will blame hostiles. Cannot be sure Henry killed them off hereabouts? Some are bound to have escaped; did not we see a band yesterday?" Nelson asks.

"Yes, sir, I did," McNeish exuberantly lied.

"Should a colonel and private manage this alone?" The colonel then directed his remaining soldiers to search the swamps for hostiles and end them.

When he came back, McNeish had created a pool of orange ooze.

"Colonel Nelson here, Charlie 19, under hostile attack. Urgent help needed," he conveyed while tossing grenades into the nearby swamp and firing shots into the air for the radioman to hear.

Then, switched off, McNeish burned the orange muck.

Both men's God genes were awake.

Two men, journeying towards the pearly gates.

Or a long military holiday.

The thick cloud of orange smoke displeased Dictator Cedric Henry.
Billowing above the swamps. He knew what it meant before he was told.

He did not believe for an instant Birdman had survived his attack on Torrs.

"Bird lovers," he snarls, "arrest Colonel Nelson!" He orders the man's imprisonment without trial, then secretly plans to feed him to a swamp dragon. *Why did the ancient Romans throw*

cowards off bridges for not fighting the enemy?

It made for better soldiers.

McNeish Ditty
"I love my budgie.
The squirrels and sun.
The wind and rain.
But not those that spoil.
Those that poison
My squirrels and budgie."

Lucas

CHAPTER 47 THE CALL OF THE BEAST

Bat Wing, Boy Defender

"Mingo sat looking out of the basement grills. He was moody. Today was Arthur's Birthday, a day he never forgot; around his neck apart from the gold torc was a beaded necklace, a bead for every son and daughter born to him now dead.

He was not a selfish man; he loved his other son Cuchullain and wondered how Cartimandua fared.

He learned to share his thoughts with each member of his family, living or dead.

Was a poor father; his children were absent.

"Curse the humans for coming to Maponos," he says before he hears the call.

Each Birdman has an individual call, you know.

Mingo Drum coughed back.

Arthur smiled. His daddy was in an ordinary cell. Escape would be easy. What had horrible Henry been thinking of?

A trap.

Now fifty miles to the west, a skim jet was hurtling, twisting, zooming, snaking this way and that as its terrified occupants tried to control it.

For Reeman Black Hair, this fun human craft designed to glide sixteen-year-olds over the dunes was a horrid machine.

He only found Henry's stormtroopers and friendly Bird men fighting the last Madrawt zealots.

Madrawts who wanted to get to Huitzilopochtli's promised paradise.

People say, "If a Madrawt would not give his heart on the altar under Diviciacus's knife, he would give it in battle."

In front of Reeman Black Hair, the City of Winds.

There is a group of men from the Stardust Corporation examining Kenala.

Those deserters got a bonus when the Imperialists realized who he was.

Mingo's buddy.

He was a good catch for the laboratories, strong and healthy.

The corporation moved into Tara 6 big time.

Buying genes from friendlies, extracting genes from prisoners and from Birdmen corpses.

The man always wanted to fly.

And poor Kenala was a fine specimen, sucking every gene from every cell and dumping his corpse on an anthill.

Word was circling amongst the birdie population as to Kenala's fate. Mingo would hear and his spirit break more.

Now the President of The Stardust Corporation, Mr. Glen Zowanski of Atlantic City, Old Earth had decided FLIGHT was fashion and was a willing ally to Cedric Henry, thus bypassing Tzu Strath who would not allow such operations again on his beloved planet he had forgotten because all he remembered these days was his young **wife.**

Although Tzu wouldnot admit it, he regarded Tara 6 as his home, just as Custer regarded the Great Plains as his.

It was something he had neglected to tell his young, pretty wife, Oona, who wanted to retire to Old Earth society and power.

Oona did not understand how power lived with its architects, not solely in Earth's title.

Earth was fashion, the ancestral roots of the emperors.

Everything else was provincial.

Oona wanted London.

She also wanted America, India, and the Great Wall of China.

Earth was full of monuments reflecting human power; it was also a burial ground for billions who died of climate change.

Tara 6 was windswept and had strange-looking birdlike creatures walking the pavements with folded-up wings, trying to imitate humans with baseball caps.

Tara 6 was the frontier; Whether Tzu knew it, Oona was going to Earth, where she would behave like an empress.

Tara 6 she could not do that as everyone knew her as Conchohbar's daughter, a mare, to be divorced and remarried for alliances; sure, people showed respect. Her loyalists punished dissenters.

Tara 6 was an imperial bed companion who made babies whose futures were questionable depending on who ruled threatening their existence!

Tara 6 was for the Birdman: Mingo languished in a tiny cell that was dank, six feet by three wide, with a toilet hole.

A definite improvement on the Madrawt stocks, Cedric Henry thought.

"Hart Woo, Hart Woo," Mingo called as he recognized her scent.

Remember, he was the beast lover of Boudicca.

Now Hart Woo came closer, looking to her right, to her left, making it obvious she was up to mischief, but the day was hot, and the twin purple suns belched their heat upon Tara 6, and the human soldiers sought shade.

The soldiers were not
Englishmen or mad dogs.

"Mingo?" she eventually answers.

He saw the human soldier with her and sank back into the cool blackness of his cell.

"He is my man, Mingo," Hart Woo says, assuring.

PAUSE AND SHUFFLING OF CHAINS.

"Help me, Hart Woo?"

Hart saw the security cameras watching her.

"My man is a major of the Old Guard of Tzu Strath; I will get a pass to visit you."

She looked at the cameras, hating them.

The security cameras were not the only ones watching. A little bird boy sat hunched behind his wings on a ledge of a tower block three stories away. *He was not Batman's son.*

But the masked space adventurer Bat Wing of Galaxy 5, a fictional descendant of Batman of Old Earth.

Arthur hid his comic reading from his mother.

Boudicca did not like Arthur reading too many comics.

They gave strange ideas like he was a superhero and diverted him from homework.

He had wings, so she endured his comics as he flew around shouting, **"Prepare for Bat Wing, the Caped Defender."**

She even bought him a Bat Wing caped defender suit for

a present. Now Arthur, in his fantasy world playing his part, knew no fear.

He was the masked defender, Bat Wing.

Then he soared off the ledge and followed Hart Woo, not knowing who they were except that they had stopped to talk to Daddy.

Mingo Drum Vercingetorix swelled his lungs, threw back his head, and called forth his grunting cough.

It left his cell.

The call was long and invaded listeners' ears with high and low notes.

A drunk Friendly staggering from a bar failed to understand the message of the cough. He gave a cough back that made him sick.

Human and alien soldiers soon demanded the call's meaning.

A Birdman friendly was still a Birdman.

He was drunk, so ignored them. They beat him severely! He needed hospitalization, but they ignored him as he lay broken in the gutter, becoming infected.

He was a beast, a bird. He heard other answering coughs and smiled.

Above nearby, a Friendly missed the lights in his hover car as he listened. Soon cars behind were honking. The Birdman driver coughed and drove. He got away because the lights were red, and humans understood what red meant.

A hostile P.O.W. stopped cutting grass on a human-front artificial lawn. The message he understood and who sent it, and he grinned and coughed back.

But the human owner came from his domed house and kicked the Birdman like a dog. He was property, and the dictator wanted them dead, anyway.

Another hostile P.O.W. stopped raking the green algae off the surface of a sewer as he read the call. He called back his own individual grunt for the winds to carry away.

Guards came and threw him in the septic pool. He was garbage living on borrowed time; they were saving the dictator the cost of a bullet.

As the sewer mincer sucked in the Birdman, he dreamed revenge.

His guard's time was up!

Another P.O.W. road sweeping stopped and called back, and the human dump truck driver ran him over just to be on the safe side.

Soon, every hostile P.O.W. was grunting and coughing, and guards did not whip, beat, mince, or squash them all.

And the wind carried the grunts of half a million condemned bird men, condemned because of their race across the City of New Alexandria.

So, the friendlies stopped drinking beers, rutting human/alien working girls in imitation of their betters and whipping their P.O.W. slaves to work harder to be human.

Everyone silenced their TVs, listening intently.

And the human/alien population stopped what they were doing. They stopped beating up drunken friends who were too drunk to speak.

They stopped watching Birdman Chum float back up the sewer mincer plug hole.

Stopped beating their gardeners.

They stopped watching speeding fleeing birdmen in hover cars.

They were unaware Vercingetorix, of Mingo Drum, would soon be free.

The entire city of New Alexandria had gone crazy because of one man's coughing grunt.

However, some recognized Bird men's rights. The Great War Lord's regime classified civilized birdies **as people.**

These were the Bird lovers of Tzu Strath.

And there were many.

Dictator Henry feared them and why encouraged mass immigration to silence them, for it was with the new settlers and his troops that he was popular.

He was the great Bird Man Fighter; he gave their lands to humans and aliens who deserved them by divine right.

Then large families, picket fences, roses, and peaceful nights would be commonplace.

Hart Woo had married a bird lover.

She refused the dictator's orders.

"I am the last of the free,
To the north, polar ice caps.
To the south the foe.
Die a free man
Then slave," on the wind from a million coughs."

Vern Lukas as told by Hart Woo

CHAPTER 48 HE THOUGHT OF TARA 6 AT LAST!

Landscape Tara 6

"Then, we will take Old Earth," the Empress Oona insists.

The Emperor of the East, Alexander Caesar Conchobhar, was hesitant. His empire boarded the Madrawt domain. He would prefer to finish them and have all their territory as his. What good sharing it with his new friends whose domains were far afield. Then he marches through the old empire of his father and takes.

The Great War Lord Tzu Strath, preferring his old title to

'Emperor,' suspected this.

Oona besots Tzu who knew she had ambitions nor betrayed him yet, but Conchobhar, family or not, suspicion remained.

Oona sat back; her stomach stretched under the light dark blue toga. She groaned and allowed her hands to touch the bulge that hid the child struggling to come into her world; *another for an assassin down the line?*

Tzu Strath smiled over his virility.

"I know about the time I went back to Tara 6 and visited Henry," Tzu avoided committing himself to an expensive war.

Oona's face grew red. Her husband had displeased her.

Conchobhar hid his mirth.

Whatever happened, he was the winner.

His genes were in the coming child.

Thoughts of a future puppet boy ruler suited self-interest. There were drugs available to make sure he stayed a boy.

"We all hear how well the dictator is doing on Tara 6," Oona says with a smile as she slipped a hand across Tzu's knee.

"Only too well, my dear."

"If you have Old Earth, what is one miserable planet far from anywhere?" She asks.

"Homesick," he replies, this was true; these meetings with Conchobhar and talk dividing known space between them had made him remember old faces and wonder about their fates.

"You think of Arthur?" She probed, showing hurt.

PAUSE **THEN VENOM**.

"You will make him king over your own child?"

Tzu Strath shook his head. He could forgive his Oona anything. She was still a child thrust into an adult vicious world.

Poor little fair Oona.... *somebody needed to tell Tzu he was the child.*

"You carry my child," he replies and strokes her distended belly. He hoped the medicines for stretch marks would clear quicker than the recommended two weeks.

He wanted his Oona's belly back the way it was quick.

"Draw up a legal document, then?" Oona challenges.

"Your daughter is too much!" Tzu grins, complaining to her father.

"No, your wife Tzu," Conchobhar reminds.

One would have thought it a happy family get together.

*

But what changed the course of events was Ce-Ra, who, desperate for a victory to show his people he was still in Huitzilopochtli's grace, launched a sneak attack with his rallied troops upon Conchohbar's borders.

Conquerors looted and conquered many planets.

Ce-Ra, Lord of Madrawts, claimed, "Huitzilopitchli smiles upon me," and thus gained a reprieve for his troubled reign.

Vern Lukas, whom you know well.

*

The Dictator Cedric Henry heard the news and smiled; the Madrawt offensive would force Conchobhar to seek help from Tzu Strath, keeping his boss away from here.

But Tzu was pushing towards Old Earth for his wife. Next year, Henry will be a major player. He was drifting up the Madrawt planet chain of supply, towards Planet Madrawt itself *and total victory.*

Why he

was the darling of the press.

Already he had moved west and taken over a whole galaxy that once belonged to the deceased Vortigern.

Henry was Tzu's Mark Anthony to Augustus Octavian.

*

Arthur sat on a tree branch huddled behind his wings, a scowl upon his face, his eyes narrowed. He was Bat Wing, the caped defender who was watching hovercraft arrive at Hart Woo's during one of Maponos' (Tara 6) sudden rainstorms.

He tracked them to a remote farmstead, then found himself clueless.

"Hart Woo, we are being watched," Hamon Ma of old says as he shuts the skimmer door.

A machine resembling the one stolen by Reeman Black Hair is comparable to the old motorcycle.

Except it has doors. Hamon Ma *knew how to drive it, unlike poor Reeman,* who had a terrifying experience with his stolen one, poor Madrawt fool!

Anyway, once inside, Hart Woo and her husband looked out from the drawn screens.

"A child?" Major Odo says.

Hamon Ma looked, "He is rocking about; he has fallen asleep and will fall off and crack his head?"

"I know that bird chick. It is Arthur."

So quickly, they formed a plan not to scare Arthur away. Hart Woo would go alone talking to herself about how she wished she could free Mingo, of course, within Arthur's hearing.

And the rain stopped.

Hart Woo came out and carried off her plan.

Arthur, hearing her, awoke with a jerk, so the caped defender Bat Wing lost his grip and fell off his branch.

THUD,

Hart Woo suppressed her urge to cuddle Arthur, or not. This was a Bird chick and dangerous.

Her past encounters with bird people remained vivid.

Frightened chicks: she knew the danger, why?

They had talons.

Even though Arthur lacked his father's beak and resembled Boudicca facially, Hart Woo was cautious.

"Uh, argh," Arthur wailed as he scrambled to his feet.

"We are Mingo's friends," Hart Woo had to repeat several times before Arthur stopped climbing the tree to get away; he forgot he could fly Boudicca's magic.

"Of course, I know, or I would not come here," he puffed.

"We are going to help him. Will you help too?" She asks, pulling a honey candy bar from a jerkin pocket.

Arthur's mouth started dribbling.

He was the Caped Defender!

Honey candy bars are one thing little bird men cannot resist. It is honey and, much better, chocolate.

Arthur came down and took.

"He is coming in," Major Odo says aloud.

By the time Arthur was inside, his mouth was a gooey mess and his fingers
needed to be wiped.

That is something the real masked-capped defender would not have done.

Anyway, Major Odo was wearing his uniform.

"He is a friend, do not be afraid," Hart Woo tells Arthur, who clings to her light flower printed skirt from behind.

He peeked around from her rump. He decided she had a nice rump; Bird chicks become fertile much earlier than human kids.

Arthur was growing up.

Major Odo was still standing there, trying as he might with grins and hellos, and offered handshakes. Arthur would not come over.

"I am Hamon Ma, a flightless Birdman, and a human; Mingo was my stepfather. We are going to free him, want to help?" Hamon poured out a large plastic cup of cool milk.

Arthur started climbing Hart Woo's skirt to his full height to drink.

There was a skirt ripping, exposing knickered moons. Arthur had to peek; his testosterone levels were high.

Major Odo offered Arthur an open biscuit box that a small hand quickly pulled
closer for examination.

Chocolate butter cookies.

Great.

They were the crumbly type.

Hart Woo itched; crumbs do that.

"Like a seat?" She asks.

The boy nodded.

He held onto her skirt.

She started losing her balance.

Somehow Arthur pulled down her skirt and ended up sitting on her lap, his milk and cookies over her body.

"We know where Mingo is," Major Odo helping Arthur off an embarrassed Hart Woo, "Do you know where Boudicca, your mummy, is? Does she need help?"

Someone winded.

The boy giggled; it was him; bird gas is lethal.

He was a naughty little boy who would take a keener interest in girls.

"Mummy needs help," then he started telling them about what he knew. In the end, he cuddled asleep against Hart Woo on a sofa; the soft warmth of her chest was motherly, safe, and cozy.

He was, after all, a chick and not the masked, caped defender Bat Wing.

Keep that from him.

Reader, she better wear rip-proof skirts as Arthur likes her moons.

Major Odo and Haman Ma loaded up a hover car with guns and explosives.

"I dislike you looking at her bosom," Odo tells Hamon.

"We are very much Bird folk," Hamon replies, meaning their prolific society.

Major Odo went silent, **imagining dreadful things.**

He could not adjust to the idea he was sharing Hart Woo with anyone else. For this reason, deep down, he hated Birdman culture and had given up trying to get Hart Woo to see she was human, not a bird.

"Everybody is doing it," was Hart Woo's defense.

But what society did elsewhere did not mean Hart Woo had to do it.

"Rest assured, when it comes time for conception, it will belong to you."

That had mollified Odo.

But the truth might be more profound; she might not really love him and was still seeking that special someone, Vercingetorix.

"If you campaign and need me, but I am absent. Do you get a sheep or whore?" Odo remembered Hart Woo asking.

He had gone silent, so she took it as an affirmation.

She vows, "Give me a disease, and I will get rid of it," stating, "What benefits one benefits all."

Little separated human and Birdman societies.

Provided we continue to love one another, correct? Listen, Daniel Odo, we were brought up in a sexually free society, so accept that way as normal, so tell me how we stop thinking like that?"

Major Daniel Odo had suspected Hart Woo might have bird genes in her. She had promised to conceive this month, and now Mingo Drum Vercingetorix, the past love of her life, was here!

Could he handle the situation, or would the worm of jealousy eat him?

Whose child would it be?

The worm was already awake.

He built a family home, not a commune.

But she had a nice chest and could not blame Hamon for staring, but he could stare somewhere else!

*

What happened to Boudicca?

Major Vernpatgus was an alien and did not like Tara 6.

Someone seconded him to Star Dust Corporation as a liaison officer. He figured life was cruel; he had two bosses, the Dictators Henry and Glen Zowanski, both ruthless.

Now they had a Birdman, and the messy business of extracting genes began.

Vernpatgus abandoned **the seven beings** to examine the

captured human female.

Seven Star Dust employees.

Boudicca's beauty struck him.

Next, what was she doing here with a Birdman? Which fledgling flew away?

She had not answered his questions.

He had never encountered her previously.

He was a new arrival, lived at the Stardust barracks and amused himself with the local beer and friendly Bird woman and other female life forms that took THEIR INVITATIONS TO TREAT outside base.

"They will be quite a while with your man friend, bird lover, are you?" It was an accusation. He was a hypocrite!

She stared at the floor, hoping to draw him to her so she could ram her clenched fist into his obtrusive codpiece.

But he read her thoughts, stood back, and drew his laser pistol. The Dictator's reign meant death for bird lovers. He had spent the last nine weeks out here, and he found the frontier stunk of sweat, stale beer, urine, and dirt.

Corpses needing burial; hostiles, in fact, bird folk, left to the Verns, rotting the place up.

People gave the settlers a decent send-off.

He also had a drinking problem and had a few under his belt, so his thoughts were greasy!

Apart from drinking and extracting genetic material from unwilling birdmen, there was nothing to do.

A woman's inclusion would improve things.

They wanted women, aliens. Human or birdie. Black, brown, red, or blonde-haired.

Stardust got them later.

This man had no moral code.

Never mind the Officer's Code.

His small unit scouted local talent.

No enemy presence existed, resulting in relaxed troops mirroring their superior officer.

A few months passed, and they had come across a Gododdin party, mostly the old women and children coming into surrender as they needed food.

His men slaughtered all; it was difficult to distinguish between hostiles and friendlies; they all looked the same.

The shallow communal burial trench was getting full and smelly as the local Vern was too well-fed to clean the land properly.

The Dictator's tyranny permeated society.

Even Major Vernpatgus had a bird woman for private use, and she had a child, Mag.

Her mother had so far diverted the major's attention away from her to herself.

The nights on Tara 6 were cold.

By becoming the major's household pet, the woman avoided a trip to the Star Dust laboratory, where they would have treated her worse before extracting all her genes, leading to cell collapse.

The problem was that bird women were pretty, nature's way of attracting the best mate for a healthy gene pool.

The problem was that everyone was jealous of Bird people who could fly naturally.

The problem was that humans/aliens needed machines to fly in.

The problem, power rested with Cedric Henry and this major.

The problem was, bird folk were easy to keep, just throw them the meal waste as they could eat anything. *It was that or starvation.*

The problem was that they performed better than a circus bear.

The problem was that the major **had slid his laser into Boudicca's mouth and was stroking her hair; his mind was full of greasy thoughts.** Similar to those deserters who handed her in.

The problem was, not enough McNeish's or Nelson's.

*

Kenala update.

Kenala lay on a table.

They did not need to; they had his genes. The did not need to remove organs.

Schools paid for them for classes.

Plastic replicas existed.

The problem was he was a Birdman that the Dictator Henry wanted removed from society.

The problem was a garbage dump behind the Star Dust base where Kenala found himself.

At least they could not steal his last private thoughts.

Then he heard the coughing grunts, swelled his chest, and grunted back and that grunt was his last.

He knew Mahbon had returned, their young god who would bring the sky down upon humans and cause tidal waves to swamp the land, washing away filthy human settlements.

Judgment day was at hand.

In his mind, Kenala witnessed a white Maponosian Eagle, larger than a Vern, transporting his spirit through the purple gates to the realm of the deceased.

*

It was well I, Vern Lukas, half man half Birdman who gave one of the answering calls to Kenala's last grunt of the free.

My upbringing as a non-Birdman prevented me from learning the various calls of tribes, nations, kings, and important individuals and friends, so I could not identify the other call.

Some I knew, such as Cartimandua's and Ena's. Kenala's I did not recognize, but I understood by the pitch it was the last breath of one of the free, understood, and answered.

And realized that Star Dust would want the Bird people's ability to hear sonically next.

What about the feathers? Why not pluck them while we were at it? No doubt? They did. Nothing new, *Māori's had feathered cloaks, fashion repeats.*

I was unaware that Dictator Henry planned a flying,

telepathic shock corps using the Birdman's sonic pitch.

The dictator had dreams to fulfill!

Tara 6 belonged to him, not Tzu Strath, luxuriating on Old Earth.

And Glen Zowanski of Stardust was backing Henry because flight gene sales were up because of a surge in supply and a price drop.

Glen, however, planned to exclude Henry from profits by breeding his own Bird Men off Tara 6, thus ensuring no friendship developed.

Already, Glen's powerful salespeople had started a rumor that ground Bird bone was a powerful sex stimulant, which it was not, but who cares? They had ostrich farms, so why not bird farms?

(During the night, Kenala would vanish as a settler did bone him and sell them.)

It created work and depended on how you saw animals. Crocodile farms were ok.
No one liked them. They ate people so they became shoes, but Bird folk could speak, and you could cuddle into a bird woman, so birdmen farms were questionable!

But Glen would have to act quickly and bribe many to stop the wildlife agencies from putting Bird Folk on the endangered list along with Dispater, the imperial god, and rhinos.

Everything about Bird was chick now.

But Henry was as bad; he had plans for pushing Glen out of the market when he learned the business ropes. His dreams were a betrayal of his friendship with Tzu Strath: he was not a good alien.

He had stolen several elite troop prototypes.

They called them volunteers, but they were actually deserters, subject to execution at their commanding officers' whim.

These volunteers gained enhanced vision and hearing.

Two developed cancer that killed them.

One went mad because he could not cope with sonic

hearing.

Two flew into pylons and frizzled.

Troops mistaking one for a hostile shot her.

His comrades survived; he had work. Find Boudicca and Arthur. *And do not bring them back alive.*

And Henry went and inspected his new troops, told them they had a passing out parade and ushered in trolleys of drink and women.

Of course, his new elite troops thanked him. They were glad they were not hanging from a telegraph pole as Henry tried extreme measures to lower the desertion rate.

It seems nobody liked Henry.

Neither was the hell Tara 6 had become.

Too many young recruits these days had conscious, bleeding hearts. They were Vern Lukas's Dime novels, raised them as bird lovers.

The white eagle carried souls through the purple, other world.

Dying Vision of a Birdie, heard and translated by Vern

"My purple Other World.
 Before me.
Peace.
 I am a big bird
There.
Collecting what owed to me.
That is it.
Ha sin.
No settlers.
Before me.
Just a bird.
Bird to take me home.
My purple, other world.
Mo shaoghal eile purpaidh." **Lucas**

CHAPTER 49 A NEW BALL GAME

New Scene New Personalities.

Diviciacus

Wookey had a big proboscis sticking out of his forehead. It was Sonar, or supposed to be. Whatever, he was proud of his colored wings and looked like a right dandy, a Burke. Yes, he was the product of genetic mutations and a poor soldier. He also had big ears and a tail, so it was no wonder

he was top secret. People stared and got frightened.

"They put me in charge of you mutants," Scout Theodosius Wookey Hole says.

He, a half-breed born on Tara 6, knew his priorities and the passing of the old world of freedom.

"They are sending us after a bird chick Henry wants dead; therefore, the chick must be important. We will find and kill her after interrogation and play.

The elite prototypes understood quick cash, and a ticket off Tara 6 was on offer.

"We must work as one to succeed," Theodosius tells them.

Mutual distrust, leading to mutual extermination, ensured a single winner.

And these were the new elite troops of the Dictator Cedric Henry. Oh well!

Theodosius needed little brains to figure out who the chick was? There was a death squad waiting to silence them, and if they escaped for the rest of their lives, Tzu Strath would seek them.

Without a degree to figure out this angle, he, and his men, who also lacked degrees, managed to figure it out!

That was the right part; the wrong part was if misfits like himself had dirt jobs to do, they were safe.

Where could they go to lie low?

These mutants were gross and outcasts!

These were not the new flight personalities wanted by human/alien high society?

These men belonged to the Dirty Platoon, A.W.O.L.S.

They obeyed orders and were taught to fear only Dictator Henry.

As for the scout Wookey Hole, as he preferred being called, he was dead meat without this fear installed in these men. All hated Wookey Hole, friendly and hostile. He was the scout that sniffed out hostiles for friendlies to butcher. Deep down, he knew some adolescent bird chick did slit his throat as the frolicking distracted him because he had butchered her twelfth cousin on some raid he could not remember.

He had killed so many hostiles, infirm and young.

Cousins, bird people, and their extended families. Good grief, how many cousins of his own had he butchered?

He allegedly sold his Bird mother, purebred, to Star Dust.
And since he only trusted himself, that was why he was watching the security camera at Mingo's cell.
Theodosius Wookey Hole felt delighted.
He saw something.

*

So it was, Hart Woo entered the dirty cell where Mingo was imprisoned.

A scented hanky to her nose.

Wookey noticed and grinned, glad he had sent the men on red-alert patrols.

Only a dame used perfume; he was no longer bored; *and what a nice rump to.*

Hart Woo swore if she did not know Bird men were intelligent creatures, she had entered the wrong cell. A wild, ferocious beast lived here, *so flee.*

The place stank like a public loo badly kept by a poor council. Mingo probably went insane, she would have!

She wished he spoke.

She had forgotten she was part bird herself and just had to call upon that uncivilized bit!

Suddenly the door closed behind her, plunging her into darkness.
Feet shuffled straw.

"Hart Woo," the voice was soft, "it is you, yes?"

Hart Woo edged towards the voice for comfort. It was Mingo.

She protested, "Tzu Strath would not permit this," he agreed. He would show mercy by killing him.

"I am Mingo, a birdman," admitting he was no longer free

and defeated.

Holding her made him remember of love gone, He no longer roamed his domain while Vern cleared the land of carrion. The herds of antelope being food for a whole ecological system, had collapsed from hunting for meat, hide, and trophy hunters.

A wilderness dotted with megalithic monuments built by his people.

And the Griffin, that Maponosian lion and other predators chased the antelope below his flight.

Almost gone, surviving here and there only.

Replaced by irrigated farms, theme parks, and hot dog sellers.

Wooden bird-men statues selling cigars stand outside the park gates.

In vantage viewing points, a caged free one with no room to move, sitting on a perch quite mad while kids threw peanuts at him to eat.

Birdmen were not apes; someone threw birdseed.?

Quickly Hart Woo stripped off cosmetic skin from her body for him to disguise himself under, but his stink, which would give him away as an unwashed beast.

With her false fingernails, she broke up and stuffed into the key locks on his manacles; chemical reactions happened as iron melted.

His freedom was secured.

His ankle locks.

Or wrist and body clamp.

But he would be free sort of?

To hobble out and attack his guards and die a free one.

Fat chance, he had.

Dictator Henry chained him!

She left him feeling she had speeded up his execution.

But Theodosius Wookey Hole knew otherwise?

He wanted Mingo free, but not free enough to escape. He was making sure Mingo got out of his cell. Wookey had killed so many he thought he was Battleship Invulnerable.

*

The guard room held someone besides Mingo. Wookey was watching from the cameras.

Mingo threw his face at one, so Wookey and the watching returned platoon behind were so startled they drew back.

Wookey fell, cracking his head.

The face of a snarling Birdman suddenly appeared up close, with saliva.

Upon seeing the face, everyone instantly recognized the individual, recalling the wanted posters.

Had his private thoughts about that face.

Each expected death.

That face belonged to a genuine birdman, unlike a fictitious trooper some surgeon had stuck wings on.

Each wished he were back in Mama's womb.

Thought about what Dispater taught, that you chose your fate line before birth, now each wished they had protested before birth about their chosen end.

Frightened, Theodosius knew Hart Woo's address; he planned to play with her, then give her to the men.

Dogs always liked titbits.

But right now, he wanted Mingo to lead him to Arthur and Boudicca. Now, she was a prize worth risking his life for.

And he would risk his men. Among them were females, and two were transgender, having been fed numerous lies.

Wookey Hole was indeed a hole of darkness.

But Bird men do not do as humans plan, especially one called Mingo Drum Vercingetorix.

He was a beast, stunk like one, thought like and killed like one.

And a lucky beast because Hart Woo told him where his sword Law was. His sword, the metal, had a spirit of its own and music that his heart heard. Hart Woo reunited them.

He was going to a wedding in a pressed suit, top hat, and gloves, but no shoes in case his talons messed them up.

He was going to his own freedom wedding, and his spirit was soaring.

Because it was daylight, Wookey Hole had to muster his men's faith in him and go after Mingo and stop the public from discovering them.

Theodosius Wookey Hole wanted Arthur and Boudicca, especially the latter, so you can guess what he did do to the discoverers.

There was this human settler woman pushing a pram.

Seeing Mingo, the woman screamed, "Hostile!"

Then only her pram remained, for she was gone.

Wookey's platoon took her with them. What sort of bird men were these? They were Star Dust's and Theodosius Wookey Hole's men; she was desert.

A man pulling down the shutters on his shop window flew through the glass plane; it was messy, but Wookey wanted him dead.

A party of tourists gaped, horrified at the hurrying Mingo.

And as Mingo passed, Wookey tossed a grenade amongst them.

Wookey Hole wanted his prize.

A policeman was drawing his laser pistol to shoot down Mingo

He gagged; a blade pierced his back.

Wookey Hole could smell his prize close.

Boudicca, I am coming to get you!

One of Wookey Hole's men approached Mingo too closely, who was sent to investigate.

Mingo had gone.

Mingo had gone nowhere; he wanted the man's weapons and, with them, shot away the locks on his ankles and wrists.

Wookey found the man as he rounded the corner. It was messy. Some sort of animal had ripped the dead man's throat open like a werewolf.

Theodosius Wookey Hole got the same fear that had crept into his platoon.

Then it happened.

A real platoon of imperial soldiers rounded the street.

And Mingo thrust himself out from behind cardboard boxes.

Wookey Hole was looking closely into the incisors of a man-eater.

Wookey Hole froze. So did most of his men. The rest fled.

Troopers across the way saw armed Bird men so opened fire.

No one had told them about the Dirty Bunch. It was the Dictator's secret, and Mingo Drum flew away and because he had to duck laser fire, he only had Wookey's right ear in his mouth.

He spat it out; it did not taste like a snake.

The ear fell in front of a hungry black rat; it was food.

Theodosius Wookey Hole ran, holding his head, cursing Mingo.

Following him, imperial troopers intent on killing him,

He was another **hostile.**

The mother of the baby in the pram told them everything.

What comes around goes around.

Be joyful readers.

After five minutes Wookey looked up from a small market square. There was Mingo Drum heading for the museum?

What was the Birdman up to?

Was it a suicide run? Freedom: Was it past the walls, within the wild?

It is also a shame that Wookey could not shoot Mingo Drum Vercingetorix out of the sky. He was busy holding where his ear should have been.

He was also drawing attention to himself; was he right in the head?

Blood covered him; onlookers watched.

Then he remembered what was in the museum, **a sword named Law.**

The dictator would strap him to a bench and drop hot coals

on his torso watching them burn, so daylight shone through for failure and pure meanness.

That sword was a symbolic rallying totem for every hostile on this planet.

Why Wookey looked about him, he saw sixteen skyscrapers under construction by Star Dust and friends that included Cedric Henry.

But Mingo's brandishing of "Law" threatens global peace.

Theodosius Wookey Hole was not all that bright. He had wings, yes? Maybe he should have thought about using them, but he was too full of doom, and his ear wound hurt awful!

As some of Wookey's men joined him, increasing numbers boosted their bravery to do silly things.

"Let us go, boys," Wookey led them towards the museum.

And the sounds of dying further behind told them those imperial troops were busy killing their friends.

Wookey looked his men up and down; they were all men; the women and transgender dirty platoon members were doing the dying back there.

Killing was about to happen here because Mingo Drum appeared from the museum. He was a savage beast because it was not just 'Law' he was waving in front of him; he was tossing a museum guard's head toward Wookey Hole and his remaining men.

"Come on lads, he is only one. Let us get him?" Wookey Hole and got no reply.

That trophy of Mingo's had rolled to his feet.

The lingering light within those dimming eyes hinted at a persistent consciousness.

Theodosius Wookey Hole was leading just himself towards that beast Mingo Drum Vercingetorix.

He remained free, determined to avoid recapture.

Poor Theodosius Wookey Hole just cannot help but feel sorry for the man.

A grunt announced Mingo's freedom; he summoned his

people.
"This is my domain,
  My lands extend beyond my sight.
  My word is law.
  I am the last of the free.
  To the north is the polar ice.
  To the south, the enemy.
  It is better to die free than a slave.

Theodosius Wookey's avian side stirred, prompting shame, a feeling inappropriate for a duel.

He should have noticed he was a lone shadow.

A deserter's ditty.

"I never signed up to die.
To make others die.
Sure, and to runt another day.
I never signed up to die.
Sure, to loot as I flee.
Alive, not like those.
Upfront.
I never signed up to die.
To run, loot, and kill,
Yes, but not to die." Vern Lukas and imaginative license.

CHAPTER 50 THE HUNT BEGINS

Henry took Boudicca's guards and caged them as they were budgies.

Colonel Horatio Nelson and young Billy McNeish, military prisoners, stood by the roadside about three miles from New Alexandria when the air...erupted at the sound of wild beasts.
Just like the film Jumanji, reader.

They looked at each other understanding and then at their four executioners
who looked afraid, hoping a circus was coming, *fat chance boys and girls?*
They were waiting for the nearby monoliths to come alive with hostiles but had seen none here during their two-year

stay, except in chains and cages.

People said hostile bird spirits roamed here seeking revenge.

Then a lone bird man appeared in the sky, coughing, and grunting to his kind that was answering.

Behind him came a lone figure on a zoomer.

Behind him was a group of FREAKS troopers with WINGS. Were they hostiles?

And behind them a darkening sky it filled with birdmen following the one up front.

It was also obvious the leading bird man had seen all, for he was heading there way.

Which meant the horde also?

"Dung," one executioner fled.

Others shot wildly at the prisoners but missed.

Nelson and McNeish refrained from running.

Then the lead bird man was upon them.

He landed'

The birdman felt deep compassion for those imprisoned by the dictator.

I wonder why?

"You are free, go," he tells them after cutting their bindings. *They might have been deserving of their fate, murderers?*

"I am Colonel Horatio Nelson," one of the newly freed.

"You are famous but still free," Mingo says before flying away.

The two men recognized him from a thousand posters and ran after him.

Mingo today was in a generous mood, today he had given away freedom.

The four executioners ahead, well, one was a goat, and he stopped and aimed his rifle at Mingo and the three sheep followed suit.

They would have lived if they had just kept running.

Now Mingo showed the true worth of aerial tactics that

inspired Tzu Strath to admire this race.

He swiftly slashed with a cutlass, leaving a trail of his floating feathers behind.

Then he shot them.

Who fell like drunkards?

Mingo flew away. He had a destination.

Nelson and McNeish reached their executioners, armed themselves and followed Mingo.

And contrary to Wookey Hole's belief, Mingo did not go straight to Hart Woo's.

She was going to meet Mingo elsewhere and was waiting.

She was there; he knew she was waiting for him.

"What about your husband?"

"We were not married legally anyway," she replies. She was still the same Woo.

"I love another," meaning Boudicca.

"Thanks to Vern Lukas, we all know," Hart Woo replies and hands Mingo a shotgun. He was a better aim.

He pointed it at the closing zoomer and fired.

"An excellent gun fires true and straight," he says, taking a bandoleer of shells from her.

Mingo's pellets were well-aimed at Theodosius Wookey Hole, or he never swerved crashing **into cacti**.

"Bloody heck," *we can only imagine what he cursed.*

This accident made Wookey Hole realize he was alone; his men were some behind swerving away. They had seen the hostiles.

Wookey saw them, *"Bloody heck,"* he has followed his men. He consistently noticed things last.

"I left a note for him," Hart Woo explains.

Mingo did not smile or show disfavor; he just allowed her onto his back. She would keep him warm tonight.

No comment.

Below the mass of hostiles, Colonel Horatio Nelson, with

young McNeish, gave the universal hitchhikers signals.

"I am Tincommius of the Artebrate," a landed burly Birdman introduced himself to them.

Had McNeish done the right thing by bringing attention to themselves? The warrior was not alone.

Tincommius had a short sword stuck in his belt; red blood was congealing
upon it.

"We have joined Mingo to fight for freedom," McNeish hotly.

Why Tincommius strode to him and looked deep into the boy's eyes.
Seeing innocence, excitement, and truth, he gave life.

In an instant, Tincommius had gotten Nelson and McNeish on the backs of big
men and they were airborne.

"We are the last of the free,
  Behind us are the polar ice caps.
In front the enemy.
Better to die free than to live as a slave," McNeish sang.

Colonel Horatio Nelson was smiling.
The boy had an innocence and likability.
Tincommius also smiled; it was great to be free.
Thousands of throats now sang the song in coughs and grunts.
Mingo traveled far, and people heard him.

It was an inhuman sound, challenging human ways.

As if nature was revolting?

Tincommius was glad he had brought the humans. The young one must be good at igniting all these beastly throats. The gods were with the man. Luck would follow. They needed lots.

Horatio Nelson and young Billy McNeish received something for free.

Glen Zowanski and Dictator Henry must pay for:
FLIGHT.

The grimness that lined the jaw of the responsible officer left Nelson's face with the thrill of rushing air zooming away under his feet.

No one needs to tell young Billy McNeish to enjoy. With a war yelp of his own making, he thought not of the danger ahead, but the grand adventure embarked upon.

Cedric Henry, the *Great Dictator*, left the front to go back to his capital.

The rioting hostiles' damage to commercial and residential establishments did not amuse.

Only the thought of thousands of dead hostiles lying in the streets cheered him, he ignored the thousands of citizens and troops they had killed.

Only good birdmen were dead ones.

Fires raged.

The air was thick with smoke and decay.

He cursed Theodosius Wookey Hole for his incompetence and for not underestimating
Mingo Drum Vercingetorix.

How could Dictator Cedric Henry blame himself?

A character flaw.

He reached Hart Woo's place and discovered the note. "Dear Daniel Odo,

I have joined Mingo to fight everything rotten.

I do not think we should live together.
past makes us strangers when you think about it.

Our time together was fun, and I found you to be a great lover.

We could get together afterward for fun.
night.

Your friend Hart Woo.

Cedric Henry handed the note to an aid, Captain Roger Peacock.

The note showed the major was innocent of freeing Mingo.

"You will arrest this Major Odo and inform him if he wants a pardon, he must
find Hart Woo a**nd hang her**. You will then kill him. Take men from the special services. The dictator was not a forgiving man. He wanted someone punished. He was giving **Hart Woo what she wanted, a swinging night**.

The dictator disapproved: the major should not have housed a bird. After a night out with the boys, it is okay to seek birdie girls. But living with one as if she was your wife. *Remember, he kept bird girls in cages like fish in a tank.*

Roger Peacock understood.

He had just been condemned to death.

Happens all the time.

*

Hart Woo was showing the way Hamon Ma and Major Odo had taken. Now Major Vernpatgus was not there when Mingo arrived. He was out on patrol with his small troop.

But the five humans (all female troopers) and two aliens who worked for the Star Dust Corporation were.

Making seven employees.

Boudicca heard Mingo's personal call to her through all that chatter, cat-cawing, and birdsong.

She rose from her sitting position.
Gathered up her soiled clothes and held them close to her to cover her nakedness.
An officer spoiled her, remember?
Allowed herself to cry. The bad actions by Vernpatgus were coming out.
She could go home now. There was no pistol in her mouth.
She did not know where home was.
Despite years of distance and conflict, Mingo remained a reliable source of support.

The thought of losing her daughter made her feel she deserved this punishment.
She felt filthy; please, Arthur, do not hug me.

Mingo was the one who made her belly swell.
Had awoken a passion in her in his presence.
Left his face upon Arthur.
He always came to her rescue.
His love for her remained.
People knew him as Mingo Drum Vercingetorix.
His grunt, added to the thousand, had frightened the Star Dust men.

The din was terrific, Bird men were celebrating, Mahbon returned, things
must get better and they celebrated.

That day, Wookey Hole set fire to Tara 6 and should not bear full responsibility for the wave of vengeance that swept through hostile and friendly hearts that one day.

Remember Wookey was a mutant, something not on display, a secret military project. *Cedric Henry had a noose and stool to be kicked away, ready for him.*

That special day went on for weeks. Refugees packed roads and flights from the wilderness, hostels were back.

No Bird man was safe now; a friendly was a bird, so shoot it dead.

And Mingo knew he could not stop the vengeance on one word, "STOP." It needed an outlet for years of second-class citizen treatment.

Before resuming, Star Dust's **seven employees**: what became of them?

Some historians called those weeks the 'Weeks of Bloody Revenge,' but the dictator wrote of them, 'Weeks of Treachery.'

Birdmen continued to raise children.
Still burned farmsteads down.

Stole your woman.
Alternatively: Birdmen either killed or enslaved you.
Unchanged: The Birdmen.
The birdmen faced unforgiveness this time.
Neither friendlies nor hostiles would exist if there were no birdmen.
Anyway:

Seven Star Dust employees hid under dissecting tables, fearing discovery.

Vern smelled the hormones released from the dead and dying bird men on the pile outside.

Now Mingo Drum Vercingetorix stood looking at the dead.

They had already pulled the living away.

He had also found his good friend Kenala!

A broom closet offered employees superior concealment.

Birdmen learned quickly of the piled birdies.

Many lonely farmsteads did be attacked for vengeance.

Tincommius stood just behind Mingo with Horatio Nelson and young Billy McNeish.

"Let me execute those responsible to clean my soul of my race's sin," Horatio asked.

Mingo turned and saw who had spoken. "What did you do wrong?" He smiles, again, "To deserve execution?"

Nelson elaborated on Mingo's report.

The young Tincommius grunted. He was right about these humans; they were Being good men, they would end up as friends with Mingo Drum Vercingetorix.

Then die as good men always do.

Mingo's warriors watched him intently as he stated, "These dissected birdmen held the secret of flight," his smile gone.
A MINUTES SILENCE.

Then one young warrior grunted, and they all went crazy. Something tore those *seven employees* to shreds, leaving only red smudgy bits.

"Listen to me,

Mingo PAUSED FOR HIS MEN TO LISTEN.
We are the last of the free.
THE HOSTILES GRUNTED AGREEMENT.
To the north are the polar ice caps.
THE HOSTILES NODDED SILENTLY.
Before us, the enemy.
THE HOSTILES SNAPPED THEIR BEAKS ON IMAGINARY ENEMY.
Better to die freemen than slaves.
THE HOSTILES GAVE A GREAT ROAR OF APPROVAL THAT RENT THE AIR.
Reach the City of Winds, then wait.

Tincommius, I know you from the Manticore Legion, shows those who are not Artebrate the hidden armories. I make you Color Stripes, Manticore Legion.

Standard Bearer.

I enlist you all as cohorts of the Legion."
THE HOSTILES ROARED THEIR PLEASURE AND AGREEMENT.

Then the slight whiff of her scent came to him, and his brain found it was hers, Boudicca's.

He saw her standing alone on the edge of the cave, high above.

The way she stood, stripped, and disheveled.
HE KNEW.

He rented the air with an anguished scream.

So even Tincommius, who was giving orders for the assembled host to follow, fell silent.

All observed the woman and realized through Mingo's soulful scream that someone had violated her.

They would kill imperialists for this.
They shared his grief.

And Boudicca, seeing him not move but hearing him scream in pain, knew Major Vernpatgus, the alien, had soiled their love.
She felt broken and cheap.
She was impure.

She knew that Vernpatgus remained inside her.
Recently, she had endured a great deal of suffering.
She threw herself off the cave ledge.
Mingo yells "No!", too late to fly to her aid.

Boudicca hit the ground with a hard thud.

Before he got to her, he knew she was dead.

And he died there, inside, his world gone, his reason to live finished.

Love does that.

Tincommius led the host quietly away to the City of Winds, leaving Mingo to grieve.

Something Boudicca did in death she had not done alive, each Birdman there swore revenge and to keep fighting as one till Maponos was their home again.

she had united them.

Major Daniel Odo was arguing with Hamon Ma over Hart Woo ten miles away.
As Arthur recovered from his ordeal,

He was leading the rescuers to save mummy.

Then the sky in front darkened with the host of freed hostiles and converte friendlies.

Major Odo stopped the hover lorry.

"We are not required," he says.

"We are," Hamon Ma disagreed.

This led to them splitting up and Hamon Ma walking on ahead alone.
Because Hamon Ma focused his attention on the dark sky ahead and a...
feeling he was going home. He had no intuition the hover lorry was.
heading straight for him.

Major Daniel Odo had not forgotten the man he hit with the lorry had slept with his Hart Woo; her sin, *born with a good-looking moon.*

*

Arthur's arrival coincided with Tincommius' forces taking flight.

They saw the lonely little figure land and Tincommius gave the order to circle.

A large dust column was visible to the south, some hundred miles away.

Cedric Henry was coming.

The Birdmen saw him and jet vapors.

They also knew who the little boy chick was?

Verica, whom the humans/aliens called Arthur.

And Arthur landed beside his daddy.

Nelson tried to hold him away.

Mingo turned and held his hands out to his son.

Nelson let the boy go.

Father and son united at last over mummy's still body.

That boy was so close to his mummy, and now she was gone. He started

screaming and hitting his daddy because he wanted mummy to stand up and hug

him, but she would not get up.

He tried lifting her arms and putting her hands on his head. They just dropped.

off.

Despite waving his hands in front of her eyes, she did not acknowledge him.

He tried calling her name, but she did not answer.

He tried hugging her, hoping she would hug back.

He knew mummy was dead.

He did not want to accept.

Then the first missile launched from an imperial jet a hundred miles away landed nearby, blowing a chunk out of a sandstone monolith.

It was time to leave.

Mingo handed his son to the waiting escort and instructed them to go to the City of Winds.

Little Arthur did not want to leave his mummy.

He was all alone.

Daddy, to him, was a name; mummy was real, with arms to hug him, lips to kiss his bruises and fingers that slid through his mop of hair.

Now she would not get up.

And so, they dragged the boy away, screaming.

And he hated his daddy for taking him away from his mummy.

Why had Boudicca thrown herself from the cliff face of the cave? Those who have endured rape can empathize with the mental anguish, feelings of filthiness, and lack of value. Vern Lukas stated that there was no counselor for her, only her tortured and disturbed mind.

Readers, truly Romeo and Juliet.

Boudicca's funeral chant translated by Vern.

"Not your time.
Yes, it is.
To my purple world.
My time.
Home.
Oh well, bye then."

CHAPTER 51 THE GREATEST GIFT

Hostile.

*"Legend says Boudicca still lives.
That she did not die.
And is still Mingo's woman.
And he is her man."*
Vern Lukas.

    The hostiles forced Tzu Strath to return to Tara 6.
    With him came the Empress Oona and said a thousand hanger-ones.'
    Seeing what he saw made him an unhappy man,.
    Confirming Oona's view that Tara 6 was not suitable for an empress because of the desolation caused by the Birdmen.

    "Boudicca is dead?" Tzu could not believe it.

Dictator Henry stood some distance from his master with a small personal escort that had not gone unnoticed either by his new emperor or his bulging wife. She knew how to deal with Henry, *swat the bug.*

Tzu was angry and listened to Henry's report that it was Mingo's doing.

Tzu's past few years unfurled, revealing mistakes.

He treated his daughter badly, and forgotten the Golden Age Prophecies of
    'The writings of Vern Lukas' as he called them.

He remained Tzu, the great warlord, viewing life as a chess game.

Henry's escort revealed deadly intentions to him.

Tara 6 was Henry's.; *fat chance. He also knew Mingo would never harm Boudicca; he loved her.*

Henry would pay!

Tzu would return with a conquering army and impale Henry on a pole.

Even then he would keep the traitor alive for further pain **for Boudicca** was
dead.

The dictator was aware of this, knowing he needed to get ready to defend himself.

The bloody Bird men were like a third element destroying his fortifications, his bases, and his empire from within. *The beastly birdmen had proven good.*

Henry's settlers depended on him for land, thus enlisting.

Tzu observed everything.

His survival depended on it.

He also wished for Arthur for he did declare the boy King of Maponos and stop the hostiles on the wing.

This chess game lacked **A** pawn.

Tzu was indeed a warlord and conqueror of planets.

And he was pleased his old enemy Mingo Drum Vercingetorix was out there,

Bleeding Henry.

Tzu's escape would trigger an immediate blockade.

Henry would be made an example to aspiring military governors.

Plenty of wild beasts to feed in the arenas.

"I admire the old empire's concept of stability?" Tzu.

SILENCE.

Henry grasped the concept of loyalty, but now it was a different era.

Planet barons seized thrones for themselves.

"The dark ages are here," Henry answers.

"The phoenix emerges from destruction to usher in a new era," Tzu.

Henry understood Arthur was coming.

Time's course remains immutable.

Before a man's birth, the idea of predestination is mentioned in the New Testament, involving demons, angels, Tom Hanks, and the Vatican.

Henry sensed a shadow passing over him; had he been more perceptive, he might have noticed the Vate.

*

In one of the most deserted places, Diviciacus discovered a Temple of Spirit.

Tara 6. At the South Pole where ice caps a hundred feet thick floated upon rough seas. *So, penguins with sense went elsewhere.*

As part of this agreement with the Dictator Henry, he still broadcast to Madrawts calling upon them to topple Ce-Ra, then their beloved shaman priest of Huitzilopitchli would return to save them from this god's vengeance.

He had built about him an extensive private hospital and had a clone growing. Insurance in case he should meet an untimely end. *So much for faith in his god.*

How is your faith in today's pet food reader?

Expert pills kept you alive and virile, but they had

previously unknown side effects. It was rumored that the very aged who had taken them suddenly **grew duplicate organs.**

If you happened to find an organ buyer, you got a bonus.

Regrettably, most sellers died from complications.

Glen Zowanski initially cautioned seniors against this pill, meant for the young to stay youthful, not for the elderly to regain youth.

But he still made sales, money was *lovely.*

And Colonel Horatio Nelson, because of his rank, knew of Diviciacus's hospital.

And why is this so important?

"She Is alive, by the gods she is alive," Horatio says feeling a weak pulse in
Boudicca's left wrist.

Vern Lukas: I witnessed this.
Cartimandua and my little Ena.

"Where can I take her?" Mingo asks meaning he needs modern medical equipment.

NO ONE ANSWERED.

"To Diviciacus," Nelson quickly explains, so removed from their faces the shock he put there.

"I will take her; I have a score to settle with Divipatreus otherwise known as Diviciacus," Mingo says.

Everyone questioned the aggression's origin.

Diviciacus,

"Let us take her to an army field hospital immediately.

I know a friend there; come with me and bring lots of your men, Mingo, lots, and my friend can stabilize her till we take her south," Horatio Nelson asked of the Birdman.

And Mingo accented and brought with him a cohort of his famed Manticore
Legion, *not just banners fluttering but weapons.*

So, it was done, and Boudicca was taken to an imperial

army field hospital and because the Birdmen outnumbered the humans, Boudicca was admitted.

The surgeons worked swiftly and, in their eyes, a lack of hope.

This was not Diviciacus's hospital.

Ethics were in effect here.

Mingo worried as a lot of gyro machines and military craft were building up on the horizon, his presence was known,

He thought of Verica (Arthur),
Thought of Cuchulain,
He thought of the Birdman nation he must rebuild,
Became fretful,
He was in a demanding situation.
He was needed; the new army lacked leadership without him.
His daughter's existence was unknown to him.
That is why I Vern Lukas offered with Cartimandua and the others to take Boudicca to Diviciacus and get specialized treatment.

"Why was I born a mortal?" Mingo asks.

"Why was I born a king?

All I want is my family.

"Out of the women I have known, she haunts my dreams," he says.

I observed Cartimandua's displeasure.

Would her jealousy allow me to keep my promise to Mingo?
He was Mingo Drum Vercingetorix.
He was the King of the Birdmen.

The struggle to live must go on.

"Life is a bitch, then you die," he says.

"At the moment I fear brain death." The human army doctor says adding, "You can take one of our ambulances for safety, and our soldiers will think there is a normal casualty inside!"

"Why do this extra for me?" Mingo asks.

"My oath mirrors that sworn millennia ago by Earth's first physicians. I have not broken it, and I do not plan to." He was referring to the Hippocratic Oath.

He was virtuous; let us emulate him. I think I had learned that much from the Birdman wars, *Vern.*

"We differ from the dictator." The doctor.

Now Mingo extended his hand in human fashion, his hand was so big, and his fingers open. The doctor hesitated, for it looked like he was holding a giant sea urchin.

But he did, and they shook.

Post-war, this physician headed Tara's medical school.

An excellent choice, a wise choice, and they even built a bronze statue of him in the Birdman quarter of New Alexandria.

If you are interested, his name was Dr. John Bates.

And as I Vern have included his name as it is about time, we built more statues of our good people.

And Mingo thanked the gods for the lax laws regulating gene research in deep space. Boudicca may be repaired.

So, we left, Mingo, promising to come south as soon as he secured a base for Boudicca's return. With a smile, he turned and headed towards the City of Winds.
front lines.

Now before we left, I hugged Ena and kissed Cartimandua, thinking I sensed coldness on her lips. It was exceedingly difficult leaving Ena. Her little hand slipped from my grasp and she waved goodbye from her mother's back repeatedly as Cartimandua looked towards the rays of the two purple suns, him and not me.

I had hoped my closeness to our daughter would have drawn Cartimandua to me and away from Mingo Drum Vercingetorix, but I was mistaken, *yes or no reader?*

I was following the footpaths of Mingo Drum, and those steps were leading to oblivion *were they not?*

A warrior never at home with his family and in his heart, the unknown graves of his children.

While journeying toward the southern polar ice caps, a warrior showed something to me.

Mingo's black obelisks where he had written that Bird men and humans should not kill each other but live in peace.

I learned its existence only that day. Of course, I knew about the others.

His familiar words, but this asking his people to live in peace was new.

Amazed, it had survived the horrors of conquest, unlike his other monoliths.

Someone had chiseled them into garden mosaics.

I promised I would write beside it:

"We warriors fight evil where it exists,
Whether we are Bird men or human aliens.
Evil is strong and wicked.
It forces us to leave our homes.
Our loved ones.
The little people who trust us.
And we bury their tiny bodies.
So, we lose hope and life itself.
But we must remember what we endure.
So, in the end, we become mighty beings.
For although evil destroyed us,
It could not destroy the goodness in our hearts.
So, we are victorious.
And defeat evil and all its kindred kind."

This explains why there is a smaller red sandstone edifice next to the black stone of Mingo's exists.

Some later historians went on to condemn Mingo for leaving the woman he loved in my care. Let me defend him, he was truly a king, a leader of his defeated
people who put on his responsibility. If he had gone with us, he

would be telling the hostiles; 'every man for himself.'

This was the Bird nation's hour of peril.
Mingo was needed.

Friendlies left their own wives and children to join his cough. The hostiles were united under his name. They would have judged him, *woman, or nation.*

Mingo Drum Vercingetorix was a living legend, he had the living to take care of.

Leading his warriors, rather than remaining with Boudicca, pained him deeply.

He yearned for her survival.

"I promise you, I will return soon," he tells me, and I believe him because of who he was.

Mingo Drum Vercingetorix.

So go to war, my friend; I shall try to make your wife well for you.

He must have felt the fates always dealt him bad cards.

Some mediums from distant planets once said our paths are predetermined.

We each have unique doors to open, some leading one way and others another. Remember, the power of choice lies within you.

Be careful.

And he chose and led his warriors.

In the City of Winds were his sons, Verica (Arthur) and Cuchulain, and he feared fate, as before, would take them.

Never to hold their small hands or gaze into their innocent, mischievous eyes.

Children explore how far to push their parents and drive them mad. Children are intelligent, more so than their adults who lord it over them.

Mingo returned to the City of Winds.

Tzu Strath Mourns.

"The beast took my daughter.
  Now she is dead.
  The beast killed her.
  Edric, what have you done?
  My princess is gone.
  Left me with a beast Grandson.
  I want my pound of flesh.
  The weighing scales are ready.
  The beast took my daughter."

Has Tzu learned anything but to quote Shakespeare's Merchant of Venice?

Lucas

CHAPTER 52 REEMAN FOLLOWS

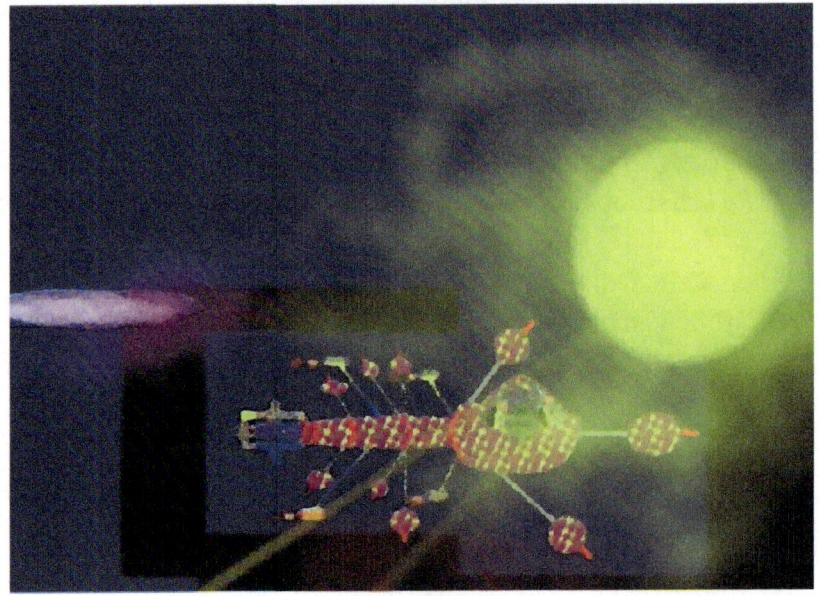

Gunship

Reeman Black Hair watched Mingo and followed, as did Wookey Hole. These two
would play important roles in the play of life.

Reeman Black Hair, the coward, was not so brave that day, more demented.

Eavesdropping was difficult, for he had to double up inside a desert flowering thorn bush on a path that led into the field hospital.

He hated the biting type of insect, but humans were coming, and he was more afraid of being discovered and ended.

A human female and male approached him holding hands and talking sweetheart.

"Divipatreus," the hated name, drifted to his ears.

Free from thorns, he found the humans disappeared around a bend.

Reeman Black Hair was now extremely angry, covered in thorn itchy pricks.

He is slightly unhinged recently.

He was **whispering** to himself as he walked, drawing out his laser pistol.

A quiet, lonely spot: the couple's destination.

Shielded by limestone walls, they lay down on their jackets to cuddle.

They giggled, talked, stroked, and fondled, leading to clothes being whipped off in a hurried frenzy of desire.

And Reeman Black Hair, the slightly insane one, watched it all.

For he was truly evil.

And fired one shot through the back of the male's skull.

No one heard her scream as she fought to free herself of her lover's *brains.*

Now Reeman Black Hair advanced, allowing the human female to free herself with energy, only to stare into the dark, blank eyes of the Madrawt.

Reeman Black Hair had always been a lazy son of a gun.

And placed the barrel of the laser pistol on her navel and asked her what he wanted to know.

She told him everything from fear and hope he would spare her.

She did not want to die.

Then he frolicked with her till way past sunset and when he was too tired, he shot her.

Then he walked away and mounted his zoomer. Headed south, determined to get equipment for the long, cold southern nights.

He was feeling more confident after his sexual encounter.

When he thirsted, he would steal drink; when he hungered, he would steal food. He repeated what he had just done when he wanted a human woman. He captured someone when he wanted to bore someone with his one-way monologue. Yes, many human/alien settlements on the way south.

And he went with delightful thoughts about Diviciacus's Approaching END.

Now Theodosius Wookey Hole needed information as well.

So, he walked into the field hospital and demanded what the Birdman Mingo wanted.

When refused, he had his mutant platoon rip the drips out of the arms of the wounded. He was asking for Henry to hunt them down; these were Henry's men.

Dr. Bates thought it would not cause any harm, so he disclosed that Mingo had been.
received treatment then headed for the City of Winds.

"His son Arthur needed stitching up also," Bates lied, *indeed a bird lover.*

"I wish I could believe you?" Wookey suspicious.

"I am a doctor, I treat the wounded. On both sides, I took an oath to remember, doctors do!" Bates went on.

Wookey Hole left it at that. He was reminded of his lack of education.

The doctor was his peer. Wookey felt he was with his headmaster when he killed him. The doctor was fortunate to be alive. Just sometimes Wookey's mind went submissive when dealing with educated peers.

At least the brat half-breed was still with Mingo.

Listen to the half-breed?

And Wookey led his mutant towards the City of Winds.

*

Two lone hostiles acting as rear-guard scouts watched the Dictator Henry's dust
swarms come roaring through the wilderness.

The two Atrebates were watching for the illusive major

Vernpatgus, who had soiled Boudicca.

A black sedan hover-car pulled into the dissolute area near where the pile of dead birdmen had been.

A heavy troop of stormtroopers poured out of a convoy of assorted transports
while overhead gunships.

Cedric Henry took no chances.

And Major Vernpatgus greeted him. The two watching Birdmen realized he was the one they were seeking.

He arrived early, soldiers in tow.

The dictator gestured toward Stardust's open door; a man in black stood there.

They did not know that Glen Zowanski was upon Maponos.

The two birdmen exchanged glances.

Mingo had told them to wait for the return of the military and learn their names. Now, their most despised was present.

The youngest Birdman unfolded his dart pipe and took careful aim.

The older Solid Rock Artebrate knew Hot Head Alclud was the best dart blower and could not miss.

The hiss of compressed gas sent the dart hurtling toward the exposed back of the dictator.

It was not a poisonous dart, a pity.

Just a dart with a six-inch needlepoint.

The dart hit his right shoulder.

Cedric knew what to do.

He got into the car.

It was assassin-proof.

Glen jumped in, also not wanting to be the next target.

Above the gunships blasted the perimeter area, extinguishing life out of dozing lizards basking in the sun, flowering plants ready to pollinate, flying insects, snakes, and small rodents like animals.

But missed two birdmen.

Below, the black hover sedan roared away to New Alexandria with the wounded dictator.

And Major Vernpatgus once again found himself alone in the wilderness.

A positive outcome of the attempted assassination was that he got extra platoons to guard the underground labs housed in the area.

Glen Zowanski had invested much capital in them.

Glen Zowanski wanted returns.

Under night's cover, two avian humanoids silently crossed the newly electrified zone fences!

They wanted names to go with faces.

The names of all the troopers who witnessed Boudicca's presence.

Mingo would track them down and get back his woman's honor.

Remember, Mingo was only half civilized, and these two were worse.

All had unreasoning beasts in them.

Mingo, halfway through a millennium, possessed ample life span.

Cloning did not come into it; you making way for the young.

But cloning machines had appeared in some Birdman cities; but not yet amongst the Artebrate. Would Mingo clone then?

Regardless, the two birdmen swiftly dealt with the first guard they encountered, an alien trooper with long antennae with eye stalks on the end and two sets of arms.

He was carrying a heavy machine gun with ease.

And together, the two birdmen carried the alien into the shadows.

"Vernpatgus is the only name he seems to know," Solid Rock spat. "He does not know how to speak our language.

SOLID ROCK TURNED THE CAPTIVE'S HEAD checking for a LANGUAGE IMPLANT.

"Nope, just our luck," then Solid Rock strangled him.

Hot Head went off in search of another guard.

He only found a long, brown tent, brightly lit. Inside, several officers getting slowly drunk; one of whom he recognized as Vernpatgus, who had greeted the hatred dictator.

Also, two scantily dressed Bird women were the subject of indecent prodding.

Now Hot Head went back to Solid Rock and dropped the machine gun.

"These were Birdmen warriors who feared nothing, not even death; well, they did the sky falling on their heads and tidal waves drowning them.

And they knew none of that would happen tonight. It never did.

They were hostile, believing in their invincibility.

Knew it needed a hundred imperial troopers to kill one birdman, and the trouble was the imperialist troopers were so many you could not count them.

Plenty to go around.

Two hundred troopers were needed to capture two birdies.

They had nothing to fear.
Nothing to lose.
If they died, they were about to die well.
They felt immortal.
They believed their enemy was about to die, though!
They were Bird men, they thought differently from us," Vern Lukas

And together they calmly walked into the long brown tent.

Vernpatgus had been holding a lighted cigar close to one breast of one of the Bird women to see how far a bird's pain threshold was; in truth, he was just a cruel drunken bum.

Then he noticed two shadows behind his victim through

the midge netting.

And his alcoholic fumed brain fought to recognize those shadows.

Then Solid Rock Artebrate threw open the tent flaps and Hot Head Alclud walked in holding the machine gun.

Vernpatgus slid to the floor and *slithered* under the tent flaps into a beer storage tent.

Very calmly, Solid Rock asked for names.

A young officer went for his absent pistol.

What he planned for the girls involved being undressed.

Solid Rock stabbed him, end of plans.

Now he received names; the young lieutenant's fate deterred others.

Young fool.

A quick sweep of Solid Rock's short sword sent the officer's head rolling inside the storage tent, Vernpatgus was met with the gaze of dying eyes.

"And the innocent die for the guilty," Vern Lukas says.

Now Vernpatgus realized he was a marked man, so felt fear creep from his bowels and the need to empty them came upon him.

"Mingo will hunt them down one by one by one until they are dead," Hot Head was saying.

Vernpatgus crawled out of his tent in a hurry and his foot caught a tent rope and pulled out the pegs, shame.

The storage tent naturally collapsed.

So, Vernpatgus got up screaming for help and lost his shoes and dragged the tent with him.

Foolishly believing help was near, the officers in the tent looked for weapons.

So, the women started butchering them before Hot Head could live up to his name.

"Let us fly," Solid Rock pulled Hot Head with him, and the women followed.

But Hot Head was amongst his most hated enemies,

human/alien troopers whom his ancestors wanted revenge.

So, landed, turned a circle, sprayed the camp with his machine gun laser bolts till his magazine was empty and slew many, a hundred.

Throwing the gun away, he turned to run to get flying.

A dark, nasty shadow appeared from behind a rock.

Vernpatgus stood there with an air-to-air shoulder missile launcher.

Someone squeezed the trigger.

Hot Head was smiling as the missile slammed into him; it took a hundred enemies to kill one bird man and Vernpatgus was one hundred and one.

"I think he saw the White Eagle that would take him to paradise," Vern Lukas says.

Anyway, Solid Rock was safe amongst the sandstone monoliths.

Despite losing his trousers while hurriedly escaping, Vernpatgus reloaded and fired in that direction.

Solid Rock smiled, the missile was off target.

Mingo will relentlessly pursue this man.

They would avenge Hot Head and Boudicca.

Vernpatgus donned fresh pants that night and went A.W.O.L. following the theft.

Hover lorry loaded with looted valuables from the laboratory safes.

People rumored Diviciacus ran a regular flight out of Tara 6 for AWOLs.
to annoy the dictator whom the shaman loathed like a woman's scorn.

> "I am Hot Head,
> The white eagle comes for me.
> I am Hot Head.
> One hundred and one.
> To kill me.

I go to the purple otherworld.
Hot Head.
Ceann teth." Like other birdmen, death chants are heard by **Vern**.

CHAPTER 53 FLIES

Vercingetorix fell on Law, did he? So his spirit went home to the peace Vate promised.

A month had gone by since I Vern Lukas had left for the South Pole; during that month many adventures happened to me on the way to evil Divipatreus that scoundrel Diviciacus.

But none of us expected what we found: a city.
We were unaware that Divipatreus and Diviciacus were the same person.
same.

Mingo had not passed this information onto us; it was

442

personal between him and that monster. Law, the famous sword that sang, would settle any scores.
Mingo's spirit.

*

Daniel Odo tried ridiculously hard to pull his superior rank over Captain Roger Peacock but failed.

Peacock's boss was the dictator.

Major Odo was no fool despite being influenced by matters of the heart.

Like Roger, he was aware that he had received a death sentence but could hope for life if one breathed.

Then, later that day, they set off on the trail of Hart Woo.

"He was a conspirator, I killed him for the dictator," Odo says showing Roger the body of Hamon Ma.

Roger began to believe in Odo's innocence.

"I will send a report," and he did so by phone.

But at the other end, the dictator tossed it into a waste bin. He did not have any respect for men who set up homes with Bird women.

The hunters departed.
Wookey Hole was after Mingo.
Roger and Odo after Hart Woo.
Major Vernpatgus after Divipatreus.
I Vern sought Diviciacus.
Mingo sought Vernpatgus.
Reeman Black Hair, Diviciacus.
The Emperor Conchobhar sought an empire of his own.
The Empress Oona the same.
The War Lord Tzu Strath, the death of the dictator.
The Dictator Cedric Henry, his own survival.

And somewhere amongst this entire scheming lot ordinary folk like Vern Lukas wanting everyday things. A secure haven for my wife and Ena to live and write.

What hope?

The spider had laid the silken strands of its web, and all it needed was the final addition,
flies to enter," Vern Lukas.

In the meantime, hostiles raided at will and Mingo raised a new phalanx of army ants and he wrote his thoughts upon a new sandstone monolith edifice.

"I dream of pitched battles and pushing the
Humans/aliens from my world.
If they want peace, they can have it on my terms.
They must learn that we must exist.
Or not at all."

And the battle came, and forces repeatedly defeated Mingo Drum Vercingetorix.

Whenever he led his warriors into the wilderness, he would scatter them till next time.

Outnumbered ten thousand to one and they still came to fight and die free.

And one day he was standing alone atop a lonely wind-swept red sandstone monolith.

"The gods have deserted me," he complains to the sky, "I cannot bring Boudicca home, I have lost everything. As soon as I take the field, my surprise attacks are successful until the hated dictator sends in jets with their neutron bombs.

Killing all in their path, beast, and man, even his own men, if he kills birds.

For every dictatorial army I destroy, I lose one of my own. The supply of Bird men warriors are running out while the dictator draws fresh men from other planets.
Indeed," and Mingo Drum thought of throwing himself upon his sword Law.

"Do not," it was the Vate.
Mingo turned and grinned.
"My ghostly friend," he says.
Vate smiled, joining Mingo looking across the wilderness.
"You are bleeding Henry, do not throw away the hopes and

dreams of your nation, victory will come soon enough," Vate said.

Now Mingo laughs, "Bleeding him?"
INCREDULOUS.

"Yes, and now Tzu Strath has landed an invading army and taken the imperial Capital, so numbering Cedric Henry's days.

Soon the Golden Age will come with the boy Arthur.
BELIEVE ME MINGO."

Now Mingo was hurt because the Vate had not used the name 'Verica.'

And Mingo thought of those he loved.

"I must see Boudicca," he says.

"That would be nice Mingo."
SILENCE.

Now Tincommius and the others will keep the standards high.
AGAIN SILENCE.

You will get your peace Mingo; Tzu Strath is of Arthur's blood. You will get your peace," the Vate repeated and vanished.

And Mingo again looked over the wilderness he loved, and a cold shiver crossed his soul.

His peace was death and hearing the wind screaming down a distant gully, "Yes he would add his call to the wind."

Time to find Boudicca in the south.

Tincommius will keep the standards high.

*

"Divipatreus,? I asked the butler who welcomed us into his palace. That is all I can remember of the shaman's priest's abode in the South Pole.

Diviciacus was not hated by everyone, and some still viewed him as the one who stood beside the imperial gods.

And therefore, wealth was no problem to him; with it, he built a hotel complex to house the growing number of faithful, **who sought him for a change of luck.**

Vern did not recognize the overweight man who had cosmetic facial remakes, so none of us saw him as that evil Diviciacus; he had fooled us.

His gaze fixed on Boudicca.

Tinkling promise of evil, but we missed that too.

He had such a gentle smile, and his hands were folded in piousness.

Yes, smiling he now had Mingo's woman whom he would violate even in the state she was in and then offer her heart to his god Huitzilopitchli.

I Vern Lukas would have killed him there and then for his wicked thoughts.

His minions then took Boudicca away and injected various vials into her.

We were amazed at the sudden rosy cheeks the result; she would definitely live?

"I swear my life to you Divipatreus as will Mingo when he sees Boudicca again,"

Foolish Vern Lukas.

And then the spider's web drew in the players around the South Pole home of evil Diviciacus.

First came the news that Emperor Ce-Ra had been taken from his throne by his loyal palace guards and thrown across the altar of Huitzilopitchli.

And he still lives for they took his heart but rigged him up to an artificial One, so he can stare at the switch that Diviciacus has to switch off.

Tzu Strath made peace with the new senate of Planet Madrawt for he wanted all his resources brought against Dictator Henry.

Henry did not know what was coming.

One must start the peace process, and then the others will join, as these three humans/aliens below understood that the final battle had commenced.

Tzu Strath.
Conchobhar.
Cedric Henry.

So, the Madrawt pilgrims arrived at Tara 6 seeking Diviciacus and the Dictator allowed the shaman priest to live for he was a potential Madrawt leader and ally against his own enemies.

And the Dictator Henry became the other fly seeking Diviciacus in the South Pole.

Behind him came the wasp Tzu Strath as the dictator's forces, sick of their cruel leader deserted to Tzu whom they remembered as a fair man, *who incidentally had*
more men and ships.

Thus, Reeman Black Hair walked through the gates of Diviciacus's home to
avenge his friend and master Ce-Ra.

And found Diviciacus in his splendid animal robes in front of a mosaic image of Huitzilopitchli behind a burning altar.

So, Reeman Black Hair joined the queue of dutiful obedient worshipers.

Inside him an insane thirst for revenge.

Scanners prevented him from bringing weapons, but he had his hands and had grown long fingernails which he had filed to points.

In front of him the butcher's knife lying across the coals in the middle of the altar.

Then it was his turn to be close to Diviciacus.

Who stood on a raised platform, something the Madrawt assassin had not noticed?
effectively putting Diviciacus out of reach.

For an instant Diviciacus and the Madrawt's eyes locked, and the shaman smiled.

"Seize him," Diviciacus shouts in a deep voice.

Reeman Black Hair leaped for the alter knife but found Diviciacus's strong hands over his own.

The temple guards hauled Reeman back to where

Diviciacus wanted him,
over the altar.

Poor Reeman found it painful to breathe with his arms pulled down behind him, so his chest was forced to open like a lobster cage.

What a big, pointed cap you have!
What a kind smile you have!
What bright white teeth do you have?
What sharpened teeth do you have?

And Reeman noticed on the ceiling a mosaic of the god Huitzilopitchli and the the knife he had tried to get hold of was descending slowly to his chest.

With terror-filled bulging eyes, he craned his neck to see.

Diviciacus was not in a hurry.

Reeman was forced to see his heart dangling in front of his eyes and thrown upon the coals where he heard it sizzle, then lost consciousness.

Diviciacus was not keeping him alive like Ce-Ra, he was a dangerous man Reeman Black Hair, a threat and Diviciacus knew how to deal with threats.

One less fly on the web.

The corpse became fertilizer for Diviciacus's religious palace had many outhouses where he grew prize tomatoes, cabbages, and other greenness.

The place was self-sufficient.

Another fly came along alone.

Mingo.

When Diviciacus was told he changed his blood-stained clothes for those of the scarlet robes of a healer.

"My good friend," *they greeted each other but their minds sent daggers.*

"I could not believe my change in good fortune when a human soldier called Colonel Nelson told me you were here and able to help Boudicca," Mingo.

"When I found out she was the famous Boudicca, how could I refuse to treat her?"

Diviciacus would use the beautiful Boudicca to draw Mingo into his sticky web and be devoured.

Evil rotten Diviciacus?

Please, readers, warn Mingo.

"Stay with your friends," Diviciacus tells Mingo who grunts satisfaction and asked to see Boudicca.

"She will not remember you," Diviciacus warned.

Boudicca's forgetfulness regarding Mingo remained unknown then, remember Diviciacus, only him, as her lover.

This evil Diviciacus?

He wanted Boudicca's beauty for himself.

Readers, why are beautiful women lonely?

In his drug-induced mind, his god had rewarded him with her,

For all time.

Or until his dreams demanded otherwise.

Then another fly arrived.

Bigger and juicier than the Madrawt variety.

Wookey Hole and his mutant platoon.

Wookey refused to disarm himself.

He wondered whether Mingo entered armed, or with Vern Lukas. **But** here the spider Diviciacus did not want to alarm these favored meals, Wookey Hole had trouble branded across his forehead.

"Like bull and pigs too you priest. I am coming in the way I am," Wookey Hole and entered the palace gates.

In no time at all armed zealot retainers of Diviciacus attacked.

"Blooming heck," Wookey says as he takes refuge in a greenhouse with half his men, the other half dead or being dragged to an altar.

Diviciacus viewed them through a camera placed in a flower; he was smiling.

They found garlic to eat.

And Mingo, hearing battle, sought Diviciacus.

Who reassured Mingo that everything was under control. Bandits at the door and his guards had dealt with them.

Bullets Diviciacus hated, especially in his direction, so blamed Mingo for drawing all the scum to him.

Why Mingo took care of the greenhouse issue.

The casualties amongst his guards were high, and all knew of the prowess of Mingo Drum Vercingetorix whom a part of him hoped would get killed.

He withheld from Mingo: sleeping gas filled the greenhouse.

The humor of watching Wookey Hole and his men survive on garlic was wearing thin?

Only Huitzilopitchli knew who else was coming to the South Pole.

The dictator himself?

Mingo needed sacrificed now.

Not tomorrow.

Now Diviciacus hated to bring his amusing game to an end.

He had a sense of humor.

Yes, he did.

*

"On the orders of the dictator himself let us in," Captain Roger Peacock demands as he saw smoke billowing from the greenhouse.

"I do not like this," Major Odo adds.

Peacock looked at him with an obvious answer.

Diviciacus himself attended to their needs.

"What dictator? Diviciacus," they did not know Tzu Strath had landed.

And Diviciacus took magnificent pleasure in telling them.

"Now what can I do for you?" The evil man's sense of humor was coming back.

"We ask permission to wait here and see events out," Peacock asks HUMBLY.

He did not like the odds; armed zealots surrounded them.

That is why they allowed themselves to be disarmed.

Diviciacus had decided to use them in his GREAT GAME.

He offered them life; attack the Bird men from behind, and their weapons would be returned.

Diviciacus watched the three-way battle from his screen; he was highly amused and had placed bets on Mingo because there was none like him.

That is when the dictator arrived.

This time Diviciacus found himself playing the role of the humble willing servant of his master.

Cedric Henry had brought a small army with him.

Diviciacus saw his GREAT GAME ENDING.

"There is your enemy, Mingo King of the Bird people. See how I aided you, my dictator?" Diviciacus bowing.

The dictator recognized the bow's theatrical nature.

He was not amused.

Even as Cedric Henry addressed Mingo ordering him to surrender, Tzu Strath also arrived at Diviciacus's spider's web.

"We are the last of the free.
 To the north are the polar ice caps.
 To the south our enemy.
 Better to die free men than a slave," Mingo Drum Vercingetorix, King of the Bird people replied.

So, the battle begins.

Diviciacus was pleased, "Mingo, a man like him, could have altered my path," and these were his exact words as testified by witnesses.

*

"Birdman, I, too, am a bird like you. Your speech has touched our hearts," Wookey Hole in the note he passed to Mingo.

Mingo read on.

He was not illiterate.

'We wish to join you for the dictator has death awaiting us. We want a chance to die as free men.

Theodosius Wookey Hole.'

"What do you think Vern?" Mingo asks.

"When Wookey Hole uses the forename he hates, he is serious," I Vern Lukas tells Mingo.

"So be it," Mingo said and coughed loudly.

And there stood Wookey Hole.

I can only presume that Wookey Hole was impressed by what he saw. Mingo was not your usual under-starved friend.

He was Mingo Drum Vercingetorix, the Birdman King.

"I am all yours," Wookey Hole tells him, and Mingo turns to face the new enemy roars his grunting war cry, and flies at the foe.

The defection of Wookey Hole brought much-needed reserves to Mingo.

Time to live and die.

Then the fighting stopped.

Amidst the commotion, the actual battle went unnoticed between Cedric Henry and Tzu Strath.

"Quiet, yes?" Wookey Hole says peering through a gap in the shattered toughened glass of the greenhouse and at once ice crystals formed around his face from the chill air rushing in.

Toxic hot gas escaped; that is the explanation. little detail! Blew back towards its sender.

And so, Mingo grunted.

That was not rudeness; it is simply being Birdman.

"Mingo," the voice I swear made the king's face white.

That voice echoed life's journey concluded.

"The Vate said I would find peace," Mingo says aloud.

"Am I glad I changed sides, that is Tzu Strath himself,"

Wookey Hole laughs. He did return a hero, not a villain.

I saw Birdman's face; sadness and defeat were evident.

Tzu's voice had killed him.

The Vate promised peace, a different peace than Wookey Hole envisioned of?

THE PEACE OF THE COFFIN.

Mingo might obtain one.

"Tzu Strath," Mingo grunts back.

"Surrender now Mingo," Tzu orders.

Wookey Hole stopped smiling, usually when he told some wanted person to do that he shot them as they walked out with their hands up.

Dead or alive, the reward remained unchanged. It was unnecessary to feed him, accompany her to the toilet, and keep an eye on them to prevent escape; it would be preferable for them to be deceased.

"Guess we are going to die, are we?" Wookey asks.

"Guess so," Vern replies.

Mingo grunted.

"All I want is Mingo, the rest can go free," Tzu Strath shouted.

Wookey Hole opened his mouth and closed it again.

"This is not your fight; you can go if you want?" Mingo tells him.

Now Wookey Hole looked deep into that Birdman's eagle eyes.

Do not forget Wookey Hole was half-breed, Wookey was not looking into a chicken's gaze before slaughter. His gaze was fixed on the eyes of a n eagle's who knew the hunter had it snared, so would fly out, golden wings spread in all nature's glory and get killed.

"I cannot speak for lads, but I am staying," **and I guess Wookey Hole entered the Halls of Iowa Jima and the Marines would have been proud.**
John Wayne as well.

His prototype platoon remnants were not human

anymore; they had wings, the first prototypes of Glen Zowanski's dream of Flight.

They opted for the winged. They had found family; they did not feel they belonged anywhere else.

"Vern, you have to keep living. Arthur and the rest require someone like you to portray us as heroes truthfully.

Forever in bardic songs," Mingo told me.

Why me? I am always the one fleeing. As if he read my mind, "Someone must tell the story for the people back home, Tzu Strath fears your pen."

PREGNANT PAUSE.

"It takes a brave man to walk away and leave his friends," he adds.

He was offering me a way out to live.

He was being selfish.

Vate's promised peace was his and his alone.

I wanted some of that peace.

"Go and take care of the living," he orders.

I held out my hand.

He grunted.

That was it, a grunt.

Damn him, we had come a long way together and he grunts.

Damn all Bird men and I left him angry and crying.

The warrior Vern Lukas was human even if he had wings.

And reached Tzu Strath, behind him stood *the dictator manacled.*

I locked eyes with Tzu Strath, and he carefully examined me from head to toe.

He shook his head, "Bird lover," he spat, guess I was for the chain gang?

Then the Vate appeared.

I do not think anyone else saw him.

"You are worth your weight in gold because you can write the truth," he says to me.

Then Tzu smiled and said, "I will make Arthur King of Tara 6, of humans, aliens, and what Bird men are still living. This should please you Vern, now write how
merciful I was to this planet."

I smiled back and nodded but inside I was
Angry,
Shamed,
Joyed that Arthur was to be king.
Tzu filled me with hatred.
Loathing was closer.
And for myself.
So, I did not trust myself to speak.

Vern Lukas was silent for once.

"If you know where Arthur is, bring him to my capital. HE WAS NO LONGER
SMILING.

Go, Vern Lukas, go," he ordered, and if I failed, a firing squad was waiting for me.
I stopped passing the hated dictator Henry and looked into his dark eyes.

Then spat into his right eye.

That made him move and he leered back, and I saw him hate all I stood for, Birdman, so spat into his left eye this time.

So, I walked away still with my weapons, and he was in chains.

I intended to locate my wife and child.

My Bird folk.

At the entrance to the corridors that linked the greenhouses to the kitchens I stopped looking back.

"I have made Arthur King of Tara 6 Mingo. Do you hear me?" Tzu Strath was shouting.

A grunt was a reply.

Tara does not need you.

Understand Mingo?

Finished," Tzu Strath was loud.

I knew then that Mingo was about to die, and my heart

saddened.
Pain ripped across my heart.
By the gods, I would miss that Birdman.
I met Boudicca who was walking aimlessly.
Something was wrong.
Zombie like she stared at me.
So sought our good Diviciacus?
And found him in front of his altar.
"Welcome friend," he says.
"I am not a friend monster?" I answers back and then he argued how could anyone who had shown kindness to Boudicca and Mingo be regarded as such?
Shadowy figures seized pinning me against the altar.
Diviciacus flashed a knife.
He cut my chest to inflict pain.
Plucked feathers and threw them onto the altar coals.
Obviously playing with his food.
He screamed.
But instead, he grabbed one of his minions holding me and used him as a shield so a probe spear sunk into the misfortunate man and exploded.
Diviciacus ran toppling bronze incense burners. One of which hit my head, dazing me.
I remember a scream and warm blood saturating my hair.
That is all.
At times, as a writer, I am an extremely poor observer. I learned later that it was an escaped Mingo who went in search of Boudicca who had saved me. He wanted to.
1, escape with her.
2, Tell her he loved her before he died.
But I do remember soldiers pulling me to my feet.
Where dead minions clustered.
Mingo Drum Vercingetorix, I salute you, Birdman King.
So, followed and together with Tzu Strath and the dictator we saw Diviciacus standing on the tower's stonework, gazing out over the icy sea below.

The air was rent with a roar as Mingo threw himself at Diviciacus and together fell entwined.

Tzu Strath immediately commanded his men to attack the tower's base while Mingo and...

Diviciacus hurtled towards it.

I saw blood, much, and before Diviciacus let go of his grasp of Mingo, Mingo managed to slow his fall with his wings.

In time to land softly.

Then he took something from Diviciacus.

He held up to the sky a heart.

"This is my domain,
 My roar is my law,
 Over my lands,
 Justice has been done."

Witnessing Tzu Strath shake his head, I realized the lines were not welcomed.

The beast Mingo Drum Vercingetorix in his new world order.

"Mercy is next to godliness," I say quickly.

Tzu denied the existence of gods, so ordering my removal.

Tzu did not want any witnesses.

Thus, it is reported to me:

"By your own sword, Law, take your worthless life.
The future of Arthur demands it.
He is the king of peace.
Or are you a king of war?
Chose Mingo Drum Vercingetorix."

There was silence as men of all races tried to hear Mingo's reply. Their ears competed with the howling arctic wind and the crashing freezing surf at Mingo's feet.

THEN SILENCE.

I tell you not a seabird chattered,

Not a sea mammal barked.

Not a motor was turned on.

And then the winds quietened, and the sea calmed.
The gods Tzu doubted were here.

The Planet Maponos waited for the return of Mahbon the young god reborn to be given back to the cycle of life.
 Mahbon, the young god of the Bird nation, was sacrificed for the sake of the seasons To be plentiful again; the children grow strong and be mighty warriors.
"Fall upon your sword, or I will give the order to kill you BEAST," says Tzu Strath.

And he broke the silence.
I saw Mingo from where I stood, and he grunted,
"I am and was the last.
of the free born."
I have nowhere else to run and fight.
Better to die a free man than a slave," thus he confirmed Tzu Strath's belief that Mingo would never change his warrior habits and live in peace with the human
settlers.

"Blooming savage," Tzu muttered and wanted the savage dead; already he blamed Mingo for Boudicca's death, and even upon learning she was alive, he still harbored resentment as taking her here instead of to him for help made Tzu hate Birdie more.
 Additionally, there was a negative reason - Mingo posed a challenge to the rule of Arthur, a boy king whom Tzu hoped to control was still a bird chick.
A bird with wings? There could be only one power behind the Birdman Throne, Tzu.
AND I SAW MINGO FALL UPON HIS SWORD LAW and into the sea that became wrath and foaming.
 The waves carried his body under the ice caps.
And swear I saw Vate standing where Mingo had fallen on Law.

Later it was reported that the sword Law lies in an ice flow and the ice refused to yield it to any of Tzu Strath's engineers trying to free it.

It awaits the rightful king; another legend is born to keep the War Lord Tzu awake
>   at nights.

> *"I am the last of the free."*
> >   ***Vern is a witness.***

> >   ***Did Mingo use his loop the loop to avoid Law?***
> >   ***So much bad weather?***

CHAPTER 54 LIES OR TRUTHS?

Tzu Strath took Boudicca home, and true to his word he proclaimed Arthur King of Tara

6.

The boy King Arthur Verica

A boy of nine?

Let assassins start queuing?

This effectively ended the hostilities immediately.

And Birdmen can vote.

Awesome stuff and created welfare agencies for the friendlies, and hostiles surrendering.

Yet some hostiles remained aloof.

Mingo's death was not believed.

"Mingo Drum Vercingetorix flies the monolith winds.

See there he is, see his huge wingspan.

He is here.

Our El Cid Mahbon?

We read his laws.

We know where the edifices are.

We are his free people.

He is still our leader,"

As heard from hostiles."

Vern Lukas.

And Tzu Strath heard, so had nightmares. No matter what his Empress Oona did or give him his daughter Siobhan to cuddle.

"He is alive, I know it," he replies with distant eyes, "Mingo won, He might add, "I tried to kill a legend but created a myth."

"My sins caught me up,"

"My actions proved the existence of gods; I played God, thus completing the cycle of life, and now I pay the price."

"I hate you, Mingo. Do you hear me," Mingo made him sick.

What the heck of it was? The dictator was spared and allowed to command armies against the remaining Madrawts.

The powerful do not execute the powerful, it sets precedents.

Guess Dictator Cedric Henry was the real winner of the game?

"Major Vernpatgus here?" The question was asked by the half-breed Wookey Hole who had survived.

The place was a seedy bar in New Alexandria. For all the Bird hater Vernpatgus was, it did not stop him from having a female chick on his lap stroking his hair for him to buy a drink.

Major Vernpatgus had gone downhill, sort of? It had started when Solid Rock Artebrate had escaped with his I.D. Not even the news of Mingo's death raised his spirits.

He was skeptical.

Vernpatgus recognized the half-breed.

Beside him stood Solid Rock Artebrate.

The major knew his time had come. He went for the pistol he kept loaded

SAFETY OFF in his open quick quick-draw holster.

Except it was gone.

He threw the bird chick off his lap.

Stood swearing, with disbelief, and shock on his face.

"Looking for this?" The chick asked.

Every Bird folk knew what he did to Boudicca.

No one liked Vernpatgus; in fact, they hated him.

Not even his own kind liked him.

He was out of favor with his top brass.

Wookey Hole shot him dead.

Do you hate him, reader?

*

I stood with Cartimandua, the Gododdin Queen, at the Temple of Skulls summit, with Ena, our little daughter, and Cuchulain.

They were beautiful children.

"Can I really rest Mingo now?" Cartimandua asks.

I knew what she meant; could she put her love for the great warrior king to rest and live again? **"I do not know. Did any see his body?"**

"I will love you as no woman can love a man, Vern Lukas," she tells me, and she

swung herself into me and kissed me.

"Mummy," a very jealous Ena protested.

"Mummy loves you, Ena," her mummy replies.

She never added love to Vern.

*

Boudicca was regent, and no one believed Mingo dead.

The hostiles accepted Arthur's good wise rule.

Boudicca did miss Mingo, but the ruling came naturally. It helped her hide the pain of the death of a loved one. Time heals a soul so violently torn. The pain becomes less sharp, that is it.

Also, what Diviciacus did to her mind helped her forget Mingo.

So, she suffered two pains of grieving.

Eventually, she healed and saw Mingo in Arthur. She took on lovers to forget but still loved someone else; *yes, readers, you know she did.*

Major Odo worried about Hamon Ma.

Was he not a friend of the mysterious visitor called Vate?

A ghostly apparition called out his name, "Daniel, look whom I have brought to visit," and there stood Hamon Ma smiling for he knew that what goes around comes around.

And obsessed with these thoughts Major Daniel Odo was

crossing a road so never noticed the tank.

What he did to Hamon Ma, Karma did to him!

What goes around comes around.

And Glen Zowanski of Stardust kept smiling all the way to the bank.

THE END?

NO NOT THE END.

Doctor Bates, hearing of Boudicca's fate, came to her aid and stayed several years till she was Boudicca **again**.

Memories, "Where is my winged barbarian?" She shouts from high verandahs, so thewinds carry her voice to Mingo.

"Where are you father?" Verica knew Mingo would keep him as king over a united bird people.

And reports filtered back from outlying lands, where imperial law, and indeed the law of Verica was lax, as was the same law, Mingo Drum Vercingetorix was seen flying.

To eat and sit on a high stone cairn and meditate.

Casting his shadow.

"I am coming one day Boudicca," he did cough, and several thousand miles away Boudicca on that verandah felt her spirit jolt for she heard the whisper, "I am coming one day Boudicca,"

When free time allowed, Boudicca would answer, "Where is my winged barbarian?"

And Mingo high on his stone cairn heard her, smiled, and coughed:

"This is my domain,

My roar is my law,

Over my lands."

Many humans/aliens heard, stood, shivered, elated, and wondered why Mingo was not back.

Some called him 'COWARD,' but all agrees to call him

"BEAST."

They had forgotten: HE WAS THE BIRDMAN, A LAW TO HIMSELF.

And I thought, "Justice has been done," Tzu Strath as he was one of them who shivered but I understood Vercingetorix, Mingo Drum, was no coward, only patient.

For legends, were ripe. **He would return.**

"Damn you Mingo," Tzu, who missed the old times.

Vern Lucas.

THE END? **NO?**

Hot Head Alclud's dart left a scar on Henry's right shoulder so he could brag of a war wound.

Cartimundua shaved her head as a sign the old ways were shaved away. New growth would be peace. **Also to mourn Mingo.**

Boudicca tells Tzu. **"When he comes back, I am going with him,"**

"Past my dead body," Tzu threatens.

"If be," Boudicca.

"I am your father," Tzu says.

"Make me laugh," Boudicca says and does. Then adds,

"Where is my daughter?"

"Bird lover," her father's reply.

*

Let us remember sayings to help us in our daily lives.

"I have nowhere else to run and fight.
Better die free than enslaved."

'Do not sign your life away in legal agreements, drink, or drugs.' Lucas.

'Mingo, Mingo, Mingo Drum.

Mingo man of steel.

Mingo, Mingo, Mingo Drum.'

A strong spirit world yours.

Behind us is the polar ice,

In front of us enemies.

We are the last of the free,

We fight and die for liberty?"

'Fight against temptations,' Arthur.
"Times have changed,

Birdmen are past.

We want our sons and daughters to live.

Reservations we have been given.

Corn, we plant.

We cannot fight anymore.

We are beaten.

Go away, Mingo, and leave our sons be."

'Listen not to your inner self,' Cartimandua.

"I am the last of the free.

A Birdman.

An Artebrate.

I will die with a spear in my hands.

And my sword Law in my enemy.

I am free, born and die free.

I fly where I want.

Hunt where I will.

The land is my friend,

  So, bury me where I fall."

  'Good advice not to join street gangs,' Lucas says.

"They threw away their top hats,

  Greatcoats and tacky boots.

  Brushed out their feathers.

  To be civilized.

  And took to the air free painted war paint."

"I hate you Mingo Drum Vercingetorix," Tzu Strath.

And the hate was not his alone.

Hate is an eater of the soul. Vern.

"What use a king if he cannot keep his son?

A king's worth: What is a king without his queen?

Where are my subjects?

Where are my laws?

Where are my enemies?

My subjects are slaves,

My laws were broken,

My enemies eat at my table,

The food from my people."

'Good thoughts for our rulers,'
Arthur.

END.

Printed in Great Britain
by Amazon